A CREED FOR THE THIRD MILLENNIUM

Books by Colleen McCullough

Tim

The Thorn Birds

An Indecent Obsession

Cooking with Colleen McCullough and Jean Easthope

A Creed for the Third Millennium

Colleen McCullough

A Creed for the Third Millennium

1817

HARPER & ROW, PUBLISHERS, New York
Cambridge, Philadelphia, San Francisco, London
Mexico City, São Paulo, Singapore, Sydney

F I C
Mᶜ C

FIRST EDITION 6|85 B+T 10.96

Designer: Sidney Feinberg

Library of Congress Cataloging in Publication Data

McCullough, Colleen, date.

  A creed for the third millennium.

  I. Title.

PR9619.3.M32C7   1985   823   84-48609

ISBN 0-06-015301-6

85 86 87 88 89 10 9 8 7 6 5 4 3 2 1

Fooa myse tintola, myse in e eye, myse fish—en fooa ucklun!

Prepared for J. R. Johnson in appreciation of a job well done

I

The wind was particularly bitter, even for January in Holloman, Connecticut. When Dr. Joshua Christian strode round the corner from Cedar Street onto Elm Street it hit him full in the face, a stream of arctic air with fangs and talons of ice chewing and clawing at the little sections of facial skin he had to expose to see where he was going. Oh, he knew where he was going; he just wished it wasn't necessary to see his way.

So different from the old days, when Elm Street had been the main drag of the black ghetto; parrot colors and proud people wearing them, laughter everywhere, lots of children spilling out of doorways on skate boards and roller skates. . . . Such beautiful children, glossy and full of fun, and always so many because the street was the best place of all to play, the street was where it all was at.

Maybe one day Washington and the state capitals would find the money to do something about the northern inner cities, but right now there were much higher priorities than deciding what exactly to do with a hundred thousand streets of empty three-family houses in a thousand northern towns and cities. So in the meantime the grey-weathered plywood nailed across windows and doors rotted, and the grey paint peeled, and the grey tiles flapped off the roofs, and the stoops crumbled, and the grey sidings gaped. Thank God for the wind! It broke the silence. It screamed in the wires overhead, it moaned through gaps narrow and stagnant, it sobbed a little in the back of its mighty throat drawing breath to wail again, it chattered as it swept frozen leaves and empty cans into heaps, it thundered against a hollow iron tank in the vacant lot next to the long-closed Abie's Liquor Store and Bar on the corner of Maple.

Dr. Joshua Christian was a Holloman man: born, bred, educated, shaped. He could not conceive of living anywhere else, had never dreamed of living anywhere else. He loved the place, Holloman. Loved it! Untenanted, unwanted, unlovely, economically unfeasible—no matter. He loved this town still. Holloman was home. And in its ineffable way it had molded this whatever-it-was he had become, for he had dwelled in it through the last phases of its dying, and now he wandered alone amid its desiccated remains.

In the grey afternoon light everything was grey. Grey the rows of empty houses, grey the streets, grey the bark of leafless trees, grey the sky. *I have worked upon the world and it shall be grey.* The color of no-color. The epitome of grief. The form of loneliness. The quintessence of desolation. *Oh, Joshua! Wear not the color of grey, even in your mind!*

Better. Better. He was moving farther up Elm now, and now there was an occasional occupied house. A tenanted dwelling possessed a certain subtle lack of dilapidation; other than that, both deserted and lived-in houses looked the same. Both were boarded over every window opening, front doors were boarded over too, and no chink of light showed anywhere. But the porch and stoop of an occupied house would be swept, the weeds would be kept down, the siding super-thick aluminum and therefore fresh-looking.

Dr. Christian's pair of three-family houses was on Oak just around the corner from Elm and just beyond the big junction of Elm with Route 78; about two miles from the main downtown Holloman post office, to which he had walked on this grey afternoon to post his mail and see if there were any letters in his box. The mailman came not any more.

Approaching numbers 1045 and 1047 Oak Street from the other side of that well-named thoroughfare, with its eighty-year-old trees poking their knobby toes out of the sidewalk, Dr. Christian paused automatically to check his residences out. Fine. No light. To see light from outside meant there was air getting in. Cold unwelcome air. The normal opening and closing of the back door and the opening of a useless hot air vent that led to a furnaceless basement was quite sufficient exchange of that essential but freezing commodity.

His two houses were grey, like nearly all the rest, and had been built, like nearly all the rest, back around the turn of the twentieth century to accommodate three separate sets of tenants. However, his two houses were joined at their waists on the second floor by a bridge passageway, and had been renovated to serve a different purpose than the original three-family one. Number 1045 housed his practice, number 1047 his entire family.

Satisfied nothing was amiss, he crossed the road, not bothering to look either way; there were no cars in Holloman and no bus route down Oak, so three feet of obdurately frozen snow humped itself unevenly all over the open space of the street, thrown there when the sidewalks were cleared.

Ingress to 1045 and 1047 from the outside was around the back, so he walked beneath the connecting passageway and turned left at the end of 1047; he had no patients booked and did not want to tempt fate by entering 1045.

The small deck which used to occupy the landing at the top of the back steps had long been closed in, its solid core door opening outward over the steps. A key in the lock, and then he was inside the makeshift cubicle which added a much-needed second area of insulation against the inclement world. Another key, another door, which led him into the original outer vestibule; here he hung up his fur-edged bonnet, his scarf and his outermost coat, and stacked his boots on the rack. After donning slippers, he opened the third door, not locked this time. He was inside his home at last.

The kitchen. Mama was at the stove, where else? Given all the premises of her nature and her choice of occupation, she ought by rights to have been a little dumpy woman in her middle sixties, wrinkled of face and thick of ankle—he laughed aloud at the ridiculousness of it, and she turned around, smiling, holding out her arms to him in generous welcome.

"What's so funny, Joshua?"

"I was just playing a game."

Because she was the mother of several psychologists, familiarity with the breed often made her seem more intelligent and

3

better educated than she actually was; as now, when instead of asking, "A game?" or "What game?," she asked, "Which game?"

He sat down on the corner of her work table and swung one foot, fishing in the bowl of fruit she always kept there until he found a sweet sound apple.

"I was imagining," he said between crunches, "that your appearance matched the rest of you." He grinned at her, half closing his eyes in a mock assessment. "You know—old and plain and marked forever with the stigmata of years of toil!"

She took this in the spirit intended, and laughed. Her face creased up deliciously, dimples popping out in either smooth silky cheek just where the pink bloom over the high bones faded quite sharply into palest cream. Never sullied by cosmetic, her red lips parted to show perfect teeth, and the great blue eyes, myopically misty, shone with liquid health between their long dark lashes. Not a thread of silver marred her glorious hair, gold as ripe wheat, thick, wavy, glossy, long, worn simply in a knot on her neck.

And he caught his breath, astonished—oh, perpetually astonished—that his mother—*his* mother!—was still the most beautiful woman he had ever seen in all his life. She was utterly unconscious of it, or so, fondly, he thought; no, Mama didn't have a vain bone in her body. And though he was thirty-two, she was still four months short of her forty-eighth birthday. She had been a child bride; they said she had loved his much older father to distraction, and had deliberately got herself pregnant in order to overcome his scruples against marrying such a beautiful young girl. Comforting, to think that his father could not resist her blandishments either!

Joshua Christian remembered his father only vaguely, for he had perished when Joshua was barely four years old, and Joshua was never sure at that whether he actually did remember, or whether he saw his father in the mirror of his mother's many stories. He was the image of his father—poor man, then! What on earth had he owned to make Mama love him so much? Very tall and very thin, sallow-skinned, black-haired, black-eyed, with a face that caved in below its cheekbones and a big narrow eagle's beak of a nose. . . .

He came to with a start, realizing that his mother was watching him out of eyes brimming with love; the simplest, purest

4

love. So pure he never felt it as a burden, even, but could accept all of it without fear or guilt.

"Where is everyone?" he asked, going to stand beside the stove so she could talk to him more comfortably.

"Not come in from the clinic yet."

"You really ought to pass a few of the domestic chores to the girls, Mama."

"I don't need to," she said firmly; this was an ever-recurring topic. "The girls belong in 1045."

"The house is too big to run alone."

"It's children make it hard to run a house, Joshua, and there are no children in this house." Her voice was faintly sad, but carefully devoid of reproach. Then she made a visible effort to cheer up, and said brightly, "I've no need to dust, which must be the only advantage of a modern winter. Dust just can't get in!"

"I'm proud of your positive thinking, Mama."

"A fine example I'd be to your patients if I complained! One day James and Andrew will each have his child, and I'll be in my element again, because the mothers will go right on being needed in 1045. After all, I'm the one with the *real* mother experience! I belong to the last lucky generation, I was free to have as many children as I wanted, and I wanted—oh, dozens! I got four in four years and if your father hadn't passed on I would have gotten more. I'm blessed, Joshua, and I never forget it."

He couldn't bring himself to say what he burned to say, of course: oh, Mama, how selfish you were! *Four!* Double yourself and Father at a time when most of the rest of the world had gone down not to duplicating its parents but to halving its parents, and a large part of it was asking itself louder and louder why we in America should continue to have it all? Now your four children must pay for your blind and insular thoughtlessness. That is the real burden we carry. Not the cold. Not the lack of privacy and comfort when we travel. Not even the strict regimentation so far from any true American heart. The children. Or rather, the no children.

The intercom screeched.

Dr. Christian's mother beat him to it, listened a moment, then put the receiver down with a word of thanks. "James says if you're free he'd like you to come over. Mrs. Fane is there, and she's brought another of the Pat-Pats with her."

5

Undoubtedly he should see James before encountering Mrs. Patti Fane and her other Pat-Pat, so Dr. Christian elected to go up one floor and cross via the bridge to 1045, thus avoiding the waiting room.

Sure enough, James was hovering at the 1045 end of the passageway.

"Don't tell me she didn't cope, I won't believe it," said Dr. Christian, turning to walk with his brother toward the front of the middle story, where his office was located.

"She coped magnificently," said James.

"Then what's the problem?"

"I'll bring her up. She can tell you better herself."

By the time James showed Mrs. Patti Fane in, Dr. Christian had settled himself not behind the enormous desk straddling one whole corner of the room, but on a lumpy, friendly couch.

"What happened?" asked Dr. Christian without preamble.

"It was a disaster," said Mrs. Fane, seating herself on the far end of the couch.

"How?"

"Well, it started off okay. The girls were all glad to see me after my four-month absence, and very taken with my tapestry work, Doctor! Milly Thring—I must have told you how dumb she is—couldn't get over the fact that I'm earning money doing work for antique restorers."

"Were you the source of the disaster?"

"Oh, no! So long as I was talking everything went fine, even when I told them the cause of my breakdown was the letter I had from the Second Child Bureau notifying me I hadn't been lucky in the lottery."

Though he watched her closely, he could detect no real distress emanating from her as she spoke of this most bitter disappointment. Good. *Good!*

"Did you mention coming to me for treatment?"

"I sure did! Of course the minute that news came out, Sylvia Stringman had to put in her two cents' worth! You are a charlatan because Matt Stringman the world's greatest shrink *says* you're a charlatan, I must be in love with you because otherwise I'd see straight through you—honestly, Doctor, I don't know which of them is the bigger pain in the ass, Sylvia or her husband!"

Dr. Christian suppressed his smile, continuing to watch his patient minutely. Today had been her first real trial of strength,

6

for today had seen the first Pat-Pat convention Patti Fane had felt well enough to attend since her breakdown.

She was the elected elder of the Pat-Pat tribe, if a group of seven women all much the same age could be so described. Seven women, all christened Patricia, who had been fast friends ever since the day when fate had thrown them into the same freshman classroom at Holloman Senior High. The resulting confusion had been so great that only the first of them in age, Patti Fane—or Patti Drew, as she had been then—had been allowed to retain a Patrician diminutive. And though all seven Pat-Pats were very different in nature and appearance and ethnic background, that catastrophe of nomenclature had welded them into a gestalt nothing since had managed to dissolve. They had all gone to Swarthmore, then they had all married highly placed faculty or executives of Chubb University. As the years went by they continued to meet once a month, taking turns to provide the venue; so powerful still was the bond of affection that their husbands and children had been drafted into the Pat-Pat ranks as auxiliary troops, and bore with resignation Pat-Pat solidarity.

Patti Fane (whom he catalogued in his mind as Pat-Pat One) had come to Dr. Joshua Christian as a patient some three months before, in the grip of a severe depression brought on by the drawing of a blue loser's ball in the Second Child Bureau lottery, a rejection made all the more difficult because she was in her thirty-fourth year of life and therefore subsequently would be crossed off the SCB books as the potential mother of a second child. Luckily, once he penetrated the outer defenses of her depression Dr. Christian found a warm and sensible woman, amenable to reason and easy to channel into more positive thought patterns. As indeed was the case with the majority of his patients, for their woes were not imaginary; they were all too real. And real woes responded to reason allied with spiritual strengthening.

"Boy, did I open a nasty can of worms when I told them why I'd had a breakdown!" said Mrs. Patti Fane. "Can you tell me why women are so secretive about applying to the SCB for permission to have a second child? Dr. Christian, every single one of us Pat-Pats had been applying every single year! But did any of us ever admit it openly? No! And why hasn't one of us at least managed to draw a red ball? I find that amazing!"

"Not really," he said gently. "The odds in the SCB lottery are ten thousand to one, and there are only seven of you all told."

7

"We're all comfortably off, we've qualified on the means test and the medical since we married and had our first children, and that adds up to a lot of years."

"Even so, the odds are stacked against you, Patti."

"Until today," she said, a little grimly. "Funny, I thought Marg Kelly looked colossally pleased with herself when she came in, but of course everyone was chiefly interested to find out what had happened to me and then how I was, and they kept on marveling over my state of mind, this new content and acceptance—" She broke off, smiling at Dr. Christian with genuine, affectionate gratitude. "If I hadn't overheard those two women in Friendly's talking about you, Doctor, I don't know what I might have done to myself."

"Margaret Kelly?" he prompted.

"She'd drawn a red ball."

He understood and could have told her everything that followed, but he merely nodded, encouraging his patient to tell her story in her own way.

"My God! You've never seen women change so fast! One moment we were all sitting around drinking coffee and having the same kind of conversation we've been having for years and years, the next moment Cynthia Cavallieri—we met at her house today—Cynthia looked across at Marg and asked her why she was looking like the cat that got the cream, and Marg said she'd just had a letter from the SCB informing her she could go ahead with a second child. Then she reached into her pocketbook and brought out this stack of papers—every page looked as if it was notarized and stamped with some big official seal—I guess the SCB has to be super careful about forged permissions, or something."

Patti Fane stopped, her eyes straying back to that scene in Cynthia Cavallieri's living room; she shivered, shrugged it off. "They all went so *still*. The room was cold anyway, of course, but I swear the temperature dropped way below zero in a split second. And then Daphne Chornik jumped up out of her chair. I've never seen her move so fast! One minute she was sitting, the next she was standing over poor Marg Kelly and she had snatched the SCB papers from Marg's hands, and—and—I've never seen or heard anything like it from *Daphne!* I mean, Daphne's always been a bit of a joke among us Pat-Pats, with her churchgoing and the way she's always preaching kind deeds and actions—we've

8

always had to be careful what we say when Daphne's around. She stood there and she tore the SCB papers to ribbons, all the while accusing Nathan Kelly of pulling strings with the SCB in Washington because he's the President of Chubb and had an ancestor on the *Mayflower*. Then she said she ought to have been the one to get an SCB approval because she'd bring up a second child to fear and love God just the way she'd brought Stacy up, where all Marg and Nathan would do was teach a child not to believe in God. And she said the way we lived was wicked and profane, that it was in defiance of the laws of God, that our country had no right to sign the Delhi Treaty and she didn't understand how God could have permitted His spiritual leaders to be the prime movers behind the Delhi Treaty. And she began to spit out the worst foul language—I never dreamed Daphne even knew the words! Some of the things she called poor old Gus Rome, and Pope Benedict, and the Reverend Leavon Knox Black!"

"Interesting," said Dr. Christian, feeling Patti Fane wanted some response from him at this point.

"Then Candy Fellowes jumped up, and she started in on Daphne—who did Daphne think she was, what right had Daphne to criticize Gus Rome, who just happened to be the greatest President of all time—then she started shouting about how much she despised Bible-thumping Sunday hymn singers because they were all such hypocrites, wore holes in their knees praying then went out to do everybody down to make a buck or climb one rung higher on the social ladder—*wow!* I thought Daphne and Candy were going to tear each other's eyes out!"

"And did they?"

Patti Fane preened visibly. "No! *I* stopped it! Me, Doctor! Can you imagine that? I shoved Candy and Daphne back into their chairs and I took the floor! I told them they were all behaving like kids and I was ashamed to call myself a Pat-Pat. That's about when it all came out that all of us were applying every year to the SCB. So I asked them what was the big disgrace about applying, and what for crying out loud was the big disgrace about being turned down? I asked them what right they had to take out their frustrations on poor Marg? Or on Augustus Rome or the religious leaders, for that matter? I told them to get it out of their minds once and for all that *anyone* can pull strings with the SCB, and I reminded them that even Julia Reece herself had never managed to get a second child permission. Why, I said, couldn't we just be happy for Marg? Then I told Marg not to cry, and I asked her if I could be the godmother."

Her concluding words were spoken triumphantly; she sat looking as if the degree of her pleasure in herself surprised her, and perhaps her strength in the crisis as well.

"You've done wonderfully, Patti. In fact, so well that I don't think you need to see me any more." Dr. Christian sounded very sure, and very proud.

He's so much more than other people, thought Patti Fane; I couldn't even begin to explain to the other Pat-Pats today what this man has done for me. Every time I tried to tell them, it came out all wrong. Ineffectual. He *cares!* And maybe that's something you have to experience in person. You can't see it, you can't repeat it, you can't spread it out for people's third-hand inspection. They have to discover it for themselves. And why oh why do shrinks like Matt Stringman feel it's so wrong of a psychologist to encourage his patients to lean on God? Do they think they're God? Or is it that they don't like Dr. Christian's ideas about God?

"I brought Marg Kelly with me," she said out loud.

"Why?"

"I think she needs to talk, really talk. Not with good old Nathan, bless his heart, but with someone on the outside of her problem. Today was a terrific shock to her. I don't think she had any idea what the consequences of having a second child are. I mean, she really seemed to think we'd all be over the moon with joy for her!"

"Then, Patti, she must be living with her head buried."

"She is! That's the trouble. She is the wife of the President of Chubb! She lives in a huge house, she has servants, they're allowed a car full-time and she had dinner at the White House last week and Gracie Mansion the week before. Her only contacts with the outside world are through the Pat-Pats, and we're—not in her economic league, maybe, but a hell of a lot better off than most of the rest of the world. So I thought if Marg could talk to you, it might help her."

He leaned forward. "Patti, can you give me an honest answer to a hurtful question?"

The seriousness of his tone cut through her elation. "I'll try."

"If Marg Kelly were to ask you whether or not you thought she should actually go ahead and conceive this permitted second child, how would you answer her?"

10

It was a hurtful question. But the days when she had sat in her room staring at the wall twenty-four hours at a stretch scheming to find a surefire way to kill herself were behind her now, and what was more, those days could never come again. "I would tell her to go ahead and conceive."

"Why?"

"She's a good mother to Homer, and in her world there's enough insulation to prevent much spite."

"Okay. What if it were Daphne Chornik rather than Marg?"

Patti frowned. "I don't know. I thought I knew Daphne like a book, yet today was a revelation. So—I just can't give you an answer."

He nodded. "And what if the lucky person had been you? How do you think you might decide now, after going through your breakdown and seeing the reaction of the Pat-Pats today?"

"Do you know, I think I might advise myself to tear up the SCB papers? I'm not so badly off. I've got a good husband, and a son who's doing real well in school. And—I don't honestly know if I could take the grief. There are a lot of Daphne Chorniks out there."

He sighed. "Take me to Margaret."

"But she's already here!"

"No, I mean come down to the waiting room with me and do the introductions. She doesn't know me, she knows you. So she can't trust me, where she does trust you. Be her bridge to knowing and trusting me."

It was a very short bridge, however. Patti Fane's hand in his, he walked into the waiting room and went straight across to the pale, pretty woman drooping in a corner chair.

"Marg, honey, this is Dr. Christian," said Patti.

He said nothing, just held out his hands to Marg Kelly. Without volition she put hers into them, then seemed astonished to find this physical union was an accomplished fact.

"My dear, you don't need to talk to anyone," he said, smiling at her. "Go home and have your child."

She got up, smiling back at him, and clasping his hands quite hard for a moment. "I will," she said.

"Good!" And he released her.

The next moment he was gone.

Patti Fane and Marg Kelly let themselves out the back door of 1045 and began the two-block walk to where Elm Street inter-

11

sected with Route 78, and the buses and trolley cars tootled along. However, they just missed the North Holloman bus, and reconciled themselves to a five minutes' wait; in winter one rarely waited longer.

"What an extraordinary man!" said Marg Kelly as they sheltered in the lee of a ten-foot-high wall of frozen snow.

"Did you feel it? Did you really feel it?"

"Like an electric shock."

Dr. Christian beat his team into 1047, and was back standing by the stove talking to Mama again when his three siblings walked into the kitchen, two of them accompanied by their wives.

Mary, his nearest, and his only sister. A spinster still at thirty-one years of age. So very like Mama to look at, and yet—not beautiful at all. She's out of whack, thought Dr. Christian. She has always been out of whack. Maybe having a genuinely beautiful mother does that to a girl? Look at Mama and then look at Mary, and it's like gazing at Mama's reflection in a subtly warped mirror. A sour sharp enclosed girl, Mary. Always had been, probably always would be too. And yet with his patients (she acted as the clinic secretary) she was wonderfully kind and gentle, nothing was too much trouble.

James was properly the middle child, since Mary was the only girl, and therefore had the distinction of her sex to free her from this handicap. He too looked like Mama, but in Mary's way, blurred and indistinct and neutral. His wife Miriam was a strapping zestful girl stuffed with energy and brisk, cheery pragmatism; the group's occupational therapist, she was a tower of strength in the clinic and a happy match for James, all considered.

Andrew was the beauty, fitting in the youngest. Mama in a masculine mold, fair as an angel and hard as a rock. Why then was he so self-effacing? His wife Martha, the clinic psychological testing technician, was seven years younger than he, and such a mouse that Mouse was her nickname. Colored like a mouse, sweetly pretty like a mouse, timid like a mouse, twitchy like a mouse. Sometimes in one of his more whimsical moods Joshua Christian would imagine himself not a cat but a gigantic pair of hands, poised to deliver the clap that would stun the girl dead on the spot.

"Lamb shanks, Mama? How absolutely super!" Miriam was

12

English, very upper-crust in speech and manner. She rather awed the Christians, for not only was she accredited the best occupational therapist in the world, she was also a very gifted linguist. Her most oft-repeated jest was to the effect that she spoke not only French, German, Italian, Spanish, Russian and Greek, but American as well, and so much did the Christians love and esteem her that they never had the heart to tell her how thin that particular joke had worn.

Mama had done it all, of course. Mama had tailor-made this remarkably efficient and self-sufficient little group to complement him, her eldest and her most beloved. Whatever he might have chosen to do for his life's work, he knew Mama would have driven James and Andrew and Mary to espouse it as well, so that they might help him. The measure of her success in brainwashing her younger children to this end could best be seen in James's and Andrew's choice of wives; they had both married women superlatively qualified to join the family business and family group. The clinic had lacked an occupational therapist, therefore James married one. The clinic had needed a psychological testing technician, so Andrew married one. By nature both women were genuinely content to take a back seat to Mama and content that their husbands took a back seat to Joshua. And Mary his sister had never once fought against her rather menial office destiny, even after Joshua had gone to her many years ago and offered to fight the battle with Mama on her behalf.

Had any symptoms of discontent ever shown themselves, Dr. Christian would have ridden roughshod over Mama for the sake of these people he always felt more as his children than his siblings; much though he loved and admired Mama, he knew her shortcomings well enough to recognize that she was not wise, not farsighted. But his family had defeated him without a battle; neither friction nor faction had ever marred the unmistakably joyous satisfaction the Christians got out of their work and each other. So, bewildered but grateful, Joshua Christian had accepted the position Mama cut out of his eminently suitable cloth, of family head and family-business head.

They sat down to eat in the dining room, Mama at the foot of the elliptical lacquer table and therefore closest to the kitchen door, Joshua at the head of the table gazing at her, Mary and James and Miriam down one side, and Andrew and Martha down

13

the other. Mama had long ago issued the dictum that no shop might be talked until the coffee and cognac were served after the meal itself was concluded, a rule they all respected scrupulously; but it did tend to leave large chunks of silence hovering while the food was consumed, for everyone save Mama worked next door in the clinic and saw little of any environment beyond 1045 and 1047 Oak Street. Positivity was the keynote of their code, which meant that for most of the time any discussion of world or national or state or urban affairs was impossible, too depressing unless the day had seen some happy milestone reached on the long road back to World Human Population Energy Equilibrium, always referred to as WHOOPEE.

They all ate well, for the food was as good on the tongue as it was on the eyes; Mama was a culinary artist, and had reared her small flock to appreciate what finer things of life were still readily available. Her hardest battle in this respect had been Joshua, who had always shown a distressing tendency to indifference about his own bodily needs, let alone comforts and indulgences. Not that he was masochistic, or even monastic; he was just not terribly interested.

Coffee and cognac were dispensed in the living room, a big apartment which communicated with the dining room behind it through a wide and graceful archway. And it was here, sitting in a three-quarter circle about a round palest-pink lacquer coffee table, that the full effect of the first floor of 1047 Oak Street could truly be appreciated.

The walls were satin-white, and of the window apertures there was no sign beyond the thinnest of dark lines bordering the sheets of wallboard cunningly inserted over the windows like covers into manholes; the architraves had been entirely removed, reminders of what lay sightless between them for half of each year. The floor was tiled in white plasticeramic, and this was covered in the sitting areas by white synthetic replicas of sheepskin rugs; everyone agreed that real skins would have been much nicer, but with all the water that got spilled each Sunday, real sheepskins would have been too liable to rot. Upholstered in palest pinks and greens, the sofas and chairs reflected the same colors in the lacquer tables.

And everywhere there were plants, tubs and pots and baskets of lushly healthy plants, mostly green, but red and pink too, and purple. They stood on white pedestals of differing heights, trail-

14

ing down in foaming cascades, sticking stiffly up like bayonets, branching delicately sideways and all around. And every leaf, frond, blade, bract and tendril shimmered in the brilliant white light diffused through a milky plexiglass ceiling. Ferns, palms, bromeliads, proteas, orchids, shrubs, vines, cacti, creepers, bulbs and corms and tubers and rhizomes, bonsaied trees. In the spring much of the growth burst into flower, long spikes of cymbidium orchids arching between spindles of hyacinth and clusters of daffodils, twenty different sorts of begonia massed with blooms, cyclamens and gloxinias and African violets; a mimosa in a tub smothered its entire eight feet of branching height in tiny powdery golden balls; and the house was redolent with the perfume of orange blossom, Sweet Alice, stephanotis, jasmine and gardenia. In the summer the hibiscus began to flower and continued through the fall into early winter, joined by a copper-pink bougainvillaea that rioted across a trellis on the living room's front wall. Only in the depths of winter were the flowering things quiescent, but then they continued glossy and green amid the more colorful leaves of the nonflowering plants that seemed to feel they had no need of further glory.

The air was always sweet. Dr. Christian's plants were half of a symbiotic respiratory relationship, the human beings its other half; carbon dioxide fed the plants, oxygen the human beings, and each inhaled what the other exhaled. This bottom floor was always many degrees warmer than the bedroom floors higher up, for the plants produced heat, as did the ostensibly cool fluorescent lighting that was never turned off. To this floor had gone almost all their precious ration of electricity, and literally all their minute allowance of gas for heating, hoarded for the stretches when it was so cold only radiant energy could keep the plants alive. On this floor the family lived all of its waking leisure hours; the two upper floors were used for actual slumber, nothing else.

Each Sunday the entire Christian clan devoted its day to the plants, watering and feeding, washing and pruning out dead growth, anointing wounds and eliminating pests. They all enjoyed this change of pace enormously, not inclined to call it a chore when the rewards were there all around them. On Sundays too the hardier plants which had spent a week in the clinic next door were carried back to the bottom floor of 1047, and other plants were carried to the clinic for temporary duty.

15

This day had constituted the most distasteful day of Dr. Joshua Christian's month; it was the day when all the forms had to be filled out and mailed to Holloman and Hartford and Washington to satisfy the bureaucratic appetite for paper, paper, ever more paper; the day all the bills had to be paid and the books brought up to date. Normally he didn't visit the clinic on what he called his Day of Atonement, but the Pat-Pat crisis had come deliciously late in it, and now he wanted to see how the others felt about the events which had occurred in Pat-Pat Five's living room.

Mama gave him his coffee, James his brandy balloon; food was something Dr. Christian could take or leave, even Mama's food, but there was no doubt, he thought, eyes closed to savor the fumes of Bisquit Napoleon, that the combination of truly excellent coffee and cognac warmed a man from belly button clear through to backbone. The best prelude to bed in these times, which was probably why consumption of strong spirits after meals had gone up in recent years, where pre-dinner drinking had declined.

Their great-grandfather and their grandfather on the paternal side had both been wholesalers in French wines and brandies, and drinkers of them too, so in those times imposing cellars had been laid down. Of course with the passing of the years the wines had long perished, especially after it became impossible to keep bottles at the cool constant temperature they needed; a cellar that was too cold had just as deleterious effect as a cupboard that was too hot. But the brandies had survived, and though the glaciers were creeping down across Canada and Russia and Scandinavia and Siberia at a heart-chilling rate, France in most years still managed to produce cognac and armagnac, so the Christian stocks were kept replenished. The family did not drink very much wine these days; cognac was better value.

"Our Patti Pat-Pat did very well today," he said.

"Bloody well!" said Miriam proudly.

"I discharged her from the clinic."

"Good! Did she tell you she and her husband were going to apply for relocation? Apparently Texas A & M has been after Bob Fane for a long while, but he's hung on at Chubb for the usual reasons—rats deserting sinking ships, fear of the unknown, once a Chubber always a Chubber, Yankee mistrust of any part of the country other than New England—and Patti's horror of being the first Pat-Pat to leave Holloman and thus break up the group." This came from Andrew, spoken in measured tones which sat oddly on his youth and beauty.

"The Pat-Pats fascinate me," said James. "It's rare outside of blood ties for an association of women to take precedence even over marriages. Thank God one of them has finally managed to stand outside herself successfully enough to see the group for what it is. And permanent relocation is the perfect way to break free. I'm surprised a husband or two hasn't thought of relocation as a way out of the Pat-Pat dilemma long since."

"Relocation is a very big step," said Mary heavily. "I don't blame anyone for hesitating. And these are all Chubbers, tenured and entrenched at that."

Dr. Christian refused to be sidetracked, so he ignored James and Mary, homing in on Andrew's news. "No, Drew, she didn't tell me they'd applied for relocation. Good for her! It's high time she put the needs and welfare of her family ahead of the Pat-Pats. Did she admit she'd been afraid of being the one to break up the Pat-Pats?"

"Yes. Honestly and openly. But she'll be all right now. I'm glad Margaret Kelly's news about her second-child approval stripped off a few masks. What Patti saw gave her the courage to make up her mind—and made her see that the Pat-Pat league should have dissolved naturally when they all left college, if not high school."

"They were only trying to hang on to their youth," said Mary. "It's not much fun these days to be an adult."

"I *do* like Patti Fane!" said Martha, contributing an unexpected mite.

Dr. Christian leaned forward, smiling into the wide grey eyes he compelled to meet his; since early childhood he had been able to marshal his will, bend it upon an unsuspecting person, and literally force that person to meet his gaze. "Oh, my Mouse! Don't you like all our patients?" he asked reproachfully.

Pinned helplessly and hopelessly by his eyes, she blushed painfully. "Oh, yes! Of course!" she gasped.

"Stop teasing the Mouse, Josh!" snapped Mary, always ready to spring to Martha's defense.

"Fancy none of those artificial sisters admitting to any of the others that she'd been applying to the SCB each year," mused

17

James. "Just goes to show how furtively women approach the whole problem of the SCB."

"Well, James, between the odds against winning and the means test, the SCB is guilt personified."

Dr. Christian would have expounded upon this theme, and not for the first time, but Mama got in too quickly, hungry for a display of real fireworks. Aside from listening to this nightly shop, Mama's contact with the clinic consisted of the tours of the bottom floor of 1047 Dr. Christian felt all their new patients should experience, wanting them to see what could be done with an unheated, naturally lightless, largely airless house through the long months of winter.

"The SCB is vile!" cried Mama now, summoning tears. "What do those heartless wretches of men in Washington know about the needs of women?"

"Mama, Mama, why do you persist in saying such things?" asked Dr. Christian, irritated. "Why *shouldn't* they know, for pity's sake? For that matter, how do you know they're men? And why, even if they are men, should any man feel the sorrow of enforced barrenness less than a woman? Do I have a clinic full of women patients? Do I? Mama, next door is fifty-fifty, women *and* men! And railing against fate is not the answer. The Second Child Bureau was a sop they threw us in return for our peacefully signing the Delhi Treaty, and in my opinion the SCB has turned out the worst feature of that whole miserable, humiliating decade! You should remember the time a great deal better than I do, Mama, you were a grown woman where I was a child."

"Augustus Rome sold us out," she said, teeth clenched.

"Oh, Mama! We sold ourselves out! Listen to one of your generation talk, and you'd swear it fell on us like a bolt out of the blue. It did not! We sowed the seeds of Gus Rome and the Delhi Treaty way back in the past. Ninety years ago, when our population stood at a hundred and fifty million, we were at the apex of our power—and our pride. We had everything. And what did we do? We threw our money around like it was going out of style, and the world hated us for it. We held up our know-how as the ultimate, and the world hated us for it. We offered the peoples of the world a way of life they had neither the means nor the talent to imitate, and the world hated us for it. We fought foreign wars in the names of justice and freedom, and the world hated us for it, not least the peoples we fought for—and I'm not thereby say-

18

ing the wars we fought were always altruistic, but a great many of our little folk believed they were. And even as we went on deluding ourselves with outmoded thinking—martial *and* altruistic!—at one and the same time we were busy making orthodox war an impossibility, plague a thing of the past, religion a laughingstock, and people into digital ciphers."

He was away, and the sofa was too confining, so he got to his feet in the ungainly yet oddly graceful series of unwindings his abnormally long bones demanded, and he paced a room never designed for pacing, in and out of leaves that shuddered in the breeze of his fevered progress, rattling pots, sending pedestals a-quaking, while his family sat in utter thrall, pinned on the thunder of his voice and the lightning of his eyes; his sister stunned by fear of him and shame of herself, his sisters-in-law consumed with admiration, his brothers incapable of resenting him, and his mother—ah! his mother screaming away inside her quiet face with a gargantuan triumph. For when his passions cohabited with his intellect and he began to speak, he worked a magic on his listeners that galvanized them. Even in this most intimate of circles, composed solely of the people who had been hearing him in full spate for years on years, still he had the power to transfix.

"I don't remember the dawn of the third millennium, because I was literally born in it. But what did it bring? There were those who sang hymns and prepared to die in the blaze of the Second Coming, there were those who sang anthems and prepared to live in the blaze of technological mastery of the universe. But what *did* it bring? Pain. Impotence. Anticlimax. *Reality!* A reality harder and crueler and more unendurable than any reality in the history of our planet since the Black Death. We were cooling down in a hurry. God knows why! No one else seems to. The best explanation the best men can offer is a mini ice age. Oh, they talk of currents and atmospheric layers, continental plates and reversing magnetic poles, solar force fields and tilting axes, but it's all pure speculation. However—however! They assure us that in a few more decades or maybe centuries they'll have enough data to tell us exactly why, and in the meantime, God at least knows. We are assured it's not going to last too long, a matter of a mere millennium or two—the most infinitesimal mote in the eye of time! But the reality we face is quite long enough to outlast us and our posterity for many generations to come. The land mass

19

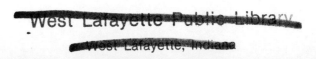

we can use fruitfully to live on is shrinking rapidly, most of our available water is on its way to imprisonment in the polar ice cap, and the population of the world is still far too large. That's what the dawn of the third millennium brought us! And no matter how we might try, we can't get around it."

He shrugged and stopped for perhaps ten seconds, a pause exquisitely but quite instinctively gauged to be exactly the right length for maximum effect; and when he continued, his voice had dropped both in volume and tone, drawing his audience along with his change in mood.

"Not that we Americans were very worried. We were the most advanced nation on earth, we knew we could cope. We didn't think we'd even need to pull in our belts more than a couple of notches. But what we forgot was the rest of the world. And the rest of the world ganged up on us! One in, all in. Permit the United States of America to grow and multiply while the other major powers brought in population reduction programs they *had* to bring in? No way! One-child families for every single country in the world for a minimum of four generations and then a two-child maximum in perpetuity, that was the agreement. Well, we stood out against it utterly alone. And when the chips were down, we discovered we didn't have enough of anything to take on the rest of the world united against us. We couldn't have fought a war that big even at our peak, and let's face it, we were not at our peak. We had wasted so terribly much of what we once had to waste, most of all the spirit and the strength of our people. We'd fried our brains on dope and our hearts on loveless copulation and our souls on trash.

"When the borders of the Eurocommune met the borders of the Arabicommune—and try as we did, there was nothing we could do to prevent that—we had nowhere left to go except the treaty table at Delhi."

His voice had dwindled to whispering sadness; the pyrotechnics were over. Or they would have been over had Mama been content to let them die; she, who knew with unerring exactitude where the goad pricked worst, wanted more fireworks.

"I will *never* believe we had to sign or perish!" she cried. "Old Gus Rome sold us out for a Nobel Peace Prize."

"Mama, you are typical of your whole generation! Why will you not see that on your generation fell the blow to pride, the loss of face, the humiliation? It's done! It's done, done, done, done!

But it's my generation that has to pick up the pieces, get things going again, lie low and guard everything America was and will be again! You suffered the injury to pride. I *have* no pride! So do I care whether Gus Rome was right or wrong in committing us to the Delhi Treaty rather than to a war we couldn't win? No! I don't!"

His brain—it was going to burst, come spewing out of the sutures of his skull and the orifices of his head. . . . Slow down, slow down, Joshua Christian! He took his fiery face between his cold hands and held it, rocking it between them until the tiny cords under the skin of his temples dwindled away. And then he dropped his hands back to his sides and resumed his pacing, but more slowly now, his dark eyes flashing in the grottoes of their sockets.

Suddenly he stopped and turned to look at his family, still sitting rapt.

"Why do I keep thinking it has to be me?" he asked them.

No one replied, least of all he himself. This was a new question he had only begun to ask in recent weeks, and the other Christians were not yet sure what he meant by it. However, each night that went by saw him less concerned with the abstract, and more concentrated upon the personal.

"How can it be me?" he asked. "I am here in Holloman, and is Holloman the center of the human universe? No! It's just one of a thousand old industrial assholes pathetically farting their way into a mass grave, waiting for the bulldozers of some future time to push them down and plant forests. They tell us we have a few centuries to go yet before the glaciers bulldoze the trees down. Time enough for forests. But once—ah, once Holloman made shirts as well as scholars, it made typewriters and guns, scalpels and piano wire. It fueled learning, it clothed bodies, it propagated words, it mowed men down, it cut out cancers and it made music possible. Holloman was a distillation of where Man had arrived at the dawn of the third millennium. And that's why maybe it's fitting that a man from Holloman could be chosen."

No one knew what to answer, but three of them tried.

"We're with you, Josh," said James softly.

"Every inch of the way," said Andrew.

"And may God have mercy on us," said Mary.

"Sometimes," said Miriam slowly, teeth chattering as she divested herself of her layers of clothing and climbed into her Dr. Denton's, "I think he cannot possibly be human."

21

"Oh, Mirry, you've known him for so many years, and still you can say that?" asked James, already in the bed with his feet hogging the hot-water bottle. "Joshua is the most human person I've ever known."

"In an inhuman way," she insisted, then added quietly, "He's getting worse. There's been a change this winter. Now he's coming straight out and asking how can it be him?"

"He's not getting worse, he's getting better," James said drowsily. "Mama says he's coming into his full strength."

"I don't know which one of them frightens me more, Joshua or Mama, so I'm going to echo Mary's comment. May God have mercy on us, Jimmy-boy! Oh, oh, where are you? Put your arms right around me, I'm so *cold!*"

Martha the Mouse scurried into the kitchen, terrified that she might find Mama still reigning there; every night she waited patiently until she thought Mama must surely have lain down her scepter and gone regally upstairs, then she would make her foray kitchenward to prepare the hot chocolate Andrew liked to drink once he was tucked up in bed.

At first she thought the big black shadow on the white wall was Mama, and her heart galloped, took a flying jump and missed, pittered away faintly.

But the shadow was Mary's, its author standing at the stove watching a saucepan of milk.

"No need to go, little one," said Mary, tender-toned. "Keep me company and I'll make your chocolate for you."

"Oh, no! Don't trouble—I'll do it, honestly!"

"How can it be trouble when I'm making some for myself anyway? And why don't you send Drew down for a change? Do him good to wait on you. You spoil him as much as Mama used to, Mouse."

"No! No! It—he—I volunteered, honestly!"

"Oh, honey, why are you always so scared?" Mary smiled into the surging contents of the saucepan, added powdered chocolate, stirred well, turned the gas off, and demonstrated that she had anticipated Martha's advent by pouring not one but three full mugs of hot drink. "You're such a nice little thing," she said, putting two of the mugs on a small tray. "Too nice for us. Far too nice for Drew. And our Joshua will end up making mincemeat out of you."

The meek little face lit at mention of the magical name. "Oh, Mary, isn't he *wonderful?*"

The moment the Mouse uttered her ecstatic superlative, all the animation died out of Mary. "Yes, indeed, he is certainly that," she said tiredly.

Her reaction was not lost on Martha, whose face dimmed. "I've often wondered—" But she lost courage, couldn't finish.

"Wondered what?"

"Don't you *like* Joshua?"

And Mary went stiff, trembled. "I hate him!" she said.

Mama was excited. Somehow this winter Joshua had been different. More alive, more enthusiastic, more sure of himself, more—mystical? Maturity. It had to be maturity. He was thirty-two now, just about the age when a man or woman tied and neatly spliced the final cords that bound together brain with hands as one integral unit. He was very like his father, a late bloomer. Oh, Joe, why did you have to die? You were finally coming into your own, you were going to make it after all. And yet, isn't it typical of you that you didn't have the sense to find a Holiday Inn before death found you?

Only that wouldn't happen to Joshua. For one thing, he was more than his father. He was her as well. In that lay his greatest advantage. And she was still young enough to be of help to him. Years and years of work left in these arms yet. A ton of spirit left, too.

Every night she dealt as efficiently with her bed as she did with the house. First the hot-water bottle, filled to the last gasp of steam with *boiling* water, the hell with what they said about leaky caps; she screwed hers down and then tightened it by sticking a spoon handle through the loop in its top and levering it an extra half-turn. Next she wrapped it in a thick towel, two layers of terry between the scalding rubber and her skin, and fixed the fabric securely around it with diaper pins. And after that she put the bottle right near the top of the bed, just where her shoulders would rest, placed her pillow over it, and pulled the covers over the pillow. Five minutes by the clock, and down would go the bottle by its own width but leaving the pillow behind, down would go the bottle five minutes at a time all the way from where her shoulders would rest to where her feet came. At which moment in time she took off cardigan, sweater, skirt, petticoat (she detested trousers and only wore them outdoors), undervest, long woolly drawers, thick pantyhose and bra, sliding like an eel—nothing middle-aged about the movement, either—into the fleecy nightgown she wore in defiance of the cold. She would not wear Dr. Denton's. Dreadful things they were, like long johns with feet; though she would not admit it even to herself, she was beginning to suffer from urgency of micturition in the very cold weather, and not for anything would she have permitted herself to soil a garment while fumbling with its trapdoor.

The last task was to lever the top bedclothes back just far enough to insert herself beneath them and simultaneously to turn upward the warmed underside of her pillow. Then into the bed like a flash, and warm warm warm warm *warm*. The greatest luxury of the day, contact of herself with an actual radiator of tangible heat. She would lie, mindless in bliss, and let the warmth soak through her skin and flesh into her bones, as ecstatic as a child with its first ice cream. And then, with her warmed feet encased in knitted bootees, she would ease the hot-water bottle slowly up the bed until she could reach to drag it, beautiful warm radiant thing, up across her chest, where it remained cradled within her arms for the rest of the night. In the morning she used it, still faintly tepid, to wash her hands and face.

Yes. He was growing into his strength at last. He was a great man, this senior son. From the moment she had known he was conceived she had also known that no matter how many other children came out of her body, he was the *one*. And so she had geared her whole life, and the lives of her other children, to a single purpose—assisting her firstborn to fulfill his destiny.

After Joe died it had been hideously hard—oh, not so much from the money point of view, because Joe's people had money and she came into his share of it, but from the fact that she was not by nature cut out to be father as well as mother. Still, it had been done, the paternal aspect of her troubles largely solved when she thrust the role of father onto Joshua almost immediately. And undoubtedly that had helped Joshua develop by obliging him from early childhood to assume the role of man rather than boy. Not ever one to shirk responsibility, her first-born. Not one to complain, either.

And in the big front room of the second floor (he shared this floor with his mother and sister, leaving the top floor to be divided between his married brothers), Dr. Joshua Christian prepared for bed. His mother always put a hot-water bottle in the middle of it, but the moment he climbed in he always shoved it down indifferently to his feet and lay without feeling the cold, even on the thirty-below nights when on waking he found his hair frozen to the fabric of his pillow. He did wear his Dr. Denton's, and a pair of hand-knitted socks, but no nightcap ever invented remained on his head, and his sleep pattern was so restless his mother had been obliged to deal with his down bedclothes by sewing them up into a kind of sleeping bag, much narrower and more confining than the German down cocoons the rest of the family—and the rest of America—used.

Someone had to tell them, all those bewildered people wandering out there afraid and crying in this craven new world. If you cannot grow babies, grow potted plants in the winter and vegetables in the summer, find work for your hands and plenty of challenge for your brains. And if the God of your church no longer seems to bear any relationship to your plight and your way of seeing the universe, have the courage to strike out to find your own God. Don't waste your years in grief! Don't curse a central government that has no choice, only remember that the choice was forced upon it. Only remember that you can keep yourself and America alive if you give the children of the future an ethic and a dream tailored to suit *them*. Don't wish for what might have been, for what your mother and grandmother had in plenty and your great-grandmother in excess. One is infinitely better and greater than none! One is a hundred percent more than zero. One is beauty. One is love. One perfect one is worth a hundred genetically warped ones. One is one is one is one is one is . . .

II

There had been a faint powdering of snow, but nothing slippery
enough to slow the buses down, and the temperature hovered
just sufficiently above freezing to take the fear out of walking.

Dr. Judith Carriol sat about halfway down the cold and stuffy
bus, her furs wrapped about her tightly. Inside them she was too
warm, but they were a barricade against the man pressing himself
hard along her thigh. Her stop was approaching; she reached a
gloved hand up to pull the bell cord, then rose to give the man
battle in earnest. Sure enough, he was not about to let her climb
across him unmolested, his hand was groping under her sable
hem while his eyes stared straight and innocent ahead. The bus
was slowing down. Her foot encountered his, and she brought the
full force of her thin high heel down on the base of his toes. He
had guts, give him that. He didn't scream, only jerked his foot
away and withdrew himself from all contact with her. From the
aisle she turned to quiz him derisively with brows and eyes, then
sidled between the seats to the front of the bus as it came to a
final squealing halt.

Oh, for a car! Insulation against the likes of the smarting predator back there in the bus alone. When a man boarded a bus
empty save for one woman, and sat himself down next to that
woman, she knew exactly what she was in for; an uncomfortable

26

ride, to say the least. And it was no use appealing to the driver for help, he never wanted to know.

Half expecting the man to make a last-minute leap off the bus, she stood militantly on the sidewalk at the stop without moving until the lumbering vehicle pulled away, unpleating its accordion middle with a groan. His eyes were glaring at her through the grubby window; she raised her hand to him in a mocking salute. Safe.

The Department of the Environment sprawled across the entire acreage of its very big block. Dr. Carriol's bus dropped her on North Capitol Street near H Street, but the entrance she used was on K Street, which meant she had to walk right up North Capitol Street, past the main entrance, and turn the far corner into K Street.

A small crowd had gathered about the main entrance and was too involved with whatever lay at its middle to spare her a glance as she strode by, tall and fashionable and elegant though she was. Her sideways glance was cursory, her mind scarcely recording the fact that Security was dealing with another suicide. The grandstand brigade all came to Environment's environment to state their cases in the most forceful way they knew how, convinced within the darkness of the tiny corners into which they had boxed themselves that it was all Environment's fault, and therefore Environment ought to see with its own eyes to what agonized abyss they had come. Dr. Carriol felt no urge to check whether this one was throat or wrists, poison or drugs, bullet or something more novel. It was her job—given to her by the President himself—to remove the reason why people needed to come to this squat vast white marble building in order to put paid to existence.

Instead of a uniformed battery of attendants manning a battery of telephones, her entrance door had a combination lock triggered by voice, and the phrase varied day by day to a code gleefully chosen by that arch joker in high places, Harold Magnus himself. Secretary for the Environment. Surely, she thought sourly, the man could find better things to do. But then she was prejudiced against him. Like all permanent career public servants with real seniority, she dismissed the titular head of her department as an incubus around the Departmental neck. A political appointee, he came with a new President, was never a career public servant himself, and went through a predictable sequence from new broom to worn-down stubble—*if* he lasted in the job. Well, Harold Magnus had lasted, and lasted for the usual reason; he possessed the good sense to let his career people get on with their jobs, and on the whole was secure enough within himself not to be causelessly obstructive.

"Down to a sunless sea," she said into the speaker buried in the outside wall.

The door clicked and swung open. Crap. Useless shit. No one in the world could have duplicated her voice well enough to fool the electronics analyzing it, so why have a changing password? She disliked the sensation it gave her of being a powerless puppet hopping up and down at Harold Magnus's slightest whim; but that of course was why he insisted upon doing it.

The Department of the Environment was an amalgamation of several smaller agencies like Energy that dated back to the preceding century's second half. It was the brainchild of that most remarkable of all chief executives, Augustus Rome, who had dealt with the people and both Houses so deftly they had empowered him to serve four consecutive terms as President of the United States of America. Thus he had guided the country through its most troublous of all times, between Britain's entering the Eurocommune, the series of bloodless popularly acclaimed leftist coups which brought the entire Arab world under the Communist umbrella, the signing of the Delhi Treaty, and the massive internal adjustments which came out of that action. There were those who said he had sold them out, there were those who said only his ability to give ground had preserved and cemented the United States of America's sphere of influence in the much-closer-to-home western hemisphere; certainly the entire western hemisphere from pole clear to pole had swung markedly toward the U.S.A. in the last twenty years, though cynics said that was simply because there was no alternative.

The present Department of the Environment had been built in 2012, replacing the scattered suites of offices it used to occupy all over town; it was the physically biggest of all the federal departments, and it alone among them was housed in a comfortable state of energy conservation. The waste warmth from its computer-filled basement fueled an air-conditioning unit that was the envy of State, Justice, Defense and the rest, trying to achieve the same end result in structures never designed for the purpose. Environment was white, to obtain maximum illumination from its lighting; low-ceilinged, to save on space and heat; acoustically perfect, to reduce noise neurosis; and utterly soulless, to reassure its inhabitants that it was after all an institution.

Section Four occupied the whole top floor along K Street, and incorporated the offices of the Secretary himself. To reach it Dr. Carriol walked easily up seven flights of chill stairs, down many corridors, and through yet another voice-triggered door.

"Down to a sunless sea."

And open sesame. As usual Section Four was in full swing when she arrived; Dr. Carriol preferred to work at night, so she rarely appeared before lunch. Those she encountered were respectful but not familiar in their greetings. As was meet. She was not only extremely senior in Environment, she was also the head of Section Four, and Section Four was the Environment think tank. Therefore Dr. Judith Carriol was an enormously powerful woman.

Her private secretary was a man who had to endure the most ludicrous misnomer in the whole Department. John Wayne. Five feet two, eighty pounds, astigmatic myopia and a mild Klinefelter's syndrome that had prevented his attaining full sexual maturity, so that he sported no beard and spoke in a childish falsetto. The days when his name had been a hideous burden to him were long behind him now; he had long ceased to rail against the fate which had decided that the original owner of his name should outlast almost all his movie contemporaries to become something of a modern cult figure.

He lived for his work and he was a fantastic secretary, though of course he rarely did any basic secretarial work; he had his own secretaries for that.

He followed Dr. Carriol into her office and stood quietly while she divested herself of the cuddly masses of sable bought at the time of her last promotion and just before she ceased to buy clothes in order to buy a house. Below the furs she was wearing a plain black dress unrelieved by jewelry or other ornamentation, and she looked stunning. Not pretty. Not beautiful. Not attractive in the usual connotation of that word. She exuded sophistication, calm elegance, a touch-me-not quality too daunting to permit of her name's being on the list of Departmental lovelies. A touch-me-not quality that meant her occasional dates were invariably with men who were extremely successful, extremely worldly and extremely sure of themselves. She wore her faintly wavy black

29

hair like Wallis Warfield Simpson, parted in the middle and drawn softly into a chignon on the nape of her neck. Her eyes were large, heavy-lidded and an unusual muddy green, her mouth was wide, pink, well sculpted, and her skin was densely pallid, too opaque to show the veins beneath and without any bloom of color anywhere. This interesting paleness against the black hair, brows and lashes endowed her with an alluring distinction she was well aware of, and used. The spatulate fingers of her very long slender white hands were slender also, the nails kept short and unvarnished, and they moved like a spider's legs; but her body, long in the trunk and neither hippy nor busty, moved with a sinuous strength and unexpected celerity that had given her the Departmental nickname of The Snake. Or so people explained defensively when taxed with reasons why.

"Today's the day, John."

"Yes, ma'am."

"Still at the arranged time?"

"Yes, ma'am. Four, in the executive conference room."

"Good! I wouldn't have put it past him to change it at the last minute so he could override me and be there."

"He won't do that, ma'am. This is too important, and *his* boss is watching things rather carefully."

She sat down behind her desk, swung the swivel chair sideways and unzipped her black kid boots. The plain but equally high-heeled black kid pumps which replaced them were laid ready neatly side by side in the roomy bottom drawer of her desk; Dr. Carriol was obsessively tidy and formidably efficient.

"Coffee?"

"Mmmm! What a terribly good idea! Anything new I ought to know before the meeting?"

"I don't think so. Mr. Magnus is anxious to speak to you first, but that's as predicted. You must be very glad the preliminary phase of Operation Search is finally over."

"Profoundly glad! Not that it hasn't been interesting. Five years of it! When did you join me from State, John?"

"It would be . . . eighteen months ago."

"We might have taken less time setting it up if I'd had you from the beginning. Finding you was like tripping over the Welcome Stranger nugget in the middle of the usual State Department minefield."

He went slightly pink, dipped his head awkwardly, and slid round the door as fast as he could.

Dr. Carriol picked up the receiver of a green telephone to one side of the beige multi-lined console on her desk. "This is Dr. Carriol. The Secretary, please, Mrs. Taverner."

The connection was made quickly, without protest, and in scarcely more time than it took to engage the scramble button.

"Dr. Carriol, Mr. Magnus."

"I want to come!" He sounded plaintive, petulant even.

"Mr. Secretary, my investigative teams and their chiefs are still very much under the impression that Operation Search has been a purely theoretical exercise. I want them to remain under that impression, at least until they can't help but see the results we thrust under their noses, and we're some months off that. If you turn up in person today, they're going to smell a great big rat." Her breath caught as she made the Freudian slip. Fool, Judith, *fool!* No one was quicker at words than Harold Magnus.

But his mind was too busy dwelling on his exclusion to notice. "You're just afraid I might upset your carefully stacked apple cart before you can point out the best apple to me. Because you think I'm going to pick the wrong apple."

"Nonsense!"

"Tchah! Let's hope phase two will go faster than phase one, anyway. I'd like to be sitting in this chair to see the final result."

"Sifting the haystack always takes a lot longer than arranging the apple cart, Mr. Magnus."

He muffled a giggle. "Keep me informed."

"Of course, Mr. Secretary," she said blandly, and hung up, smiling.

But when John Wayne came in with her coffee she was sitting looking at the green telephone pensively, and chewing her lip.

At four o'clock that afternoon Dr. Judith Carriol entered the Section Four executive conference room, with her private secretary in grave attendance. He would take the minutes in old-fashioned shorthand, a decision he and Dr. Carriol had taken long before if a meeting was classified top secret. A tape recorder was too vulnerable; even if someone managed to lay hands on his shorthand notes and could read shorthand, that person would also have to contend with the fact that it was modified markedly by his

31

handwriting. From his minutes he would do the typescript himself onto an old-fashioned typewriter minus any kind of memory device and not susceptible to a listening microphone, as was the modern voicewriter. Then he would shred his dictation and his rough draft before personally copying and collating the final draft for distribution in files marked TOP SECRET.

It was a small gathering. Including John Wayne, only five people attended. They were seated two down either side of the long, ovoid table, with Dr. Carriol in the chair at one end. And she got down to business at once, the fingers of her left hand spread poised to strike across the uppermost of a bundle of files in front of her.

"Dr. Abraham, Dr. Hemingway, Dr. Chasen. Are you ready?"

Each nodded seriously.

"Then let's begin with Dr. Abraham. If you please, Sam?"

He needed glasses to read, so he put them on, only the slight tremor in his fingers betraying his high degree of excitement. He adored Dr. Carriol, was intensely grateful for the chance to participate in an exercise of this scope, and did not look forward to the day when he must return to more mundane activities.

"My caseload numbered 33,368 when I began, and I have followed the prescribed regimen in whittling them down to my final three choices. My chief researcher selected the same three persons absolutely independently of me. I shall concentrate on each candidate equally in my presentation, but I will discuss them in my order of preference." He cleared his throat and opened the top file of the three which lay on the table at his right hand.

There was a rustle as the other four people in the room also opened a file and perused its contents while Dr. Abraham spoke.

"My number-one choice is Maestro Benjamin Steinfeld. He is a fourth-generation American of Polish Jewish stock on both sides. Aged thirty-eight. Married, one child, a boy now aged fourteen, in school, straight A's. His marital and parental statuses rate ten on the ten-scale. A previous marriage contracted when in his nineteenth year ended in a divorce two years later, the divorce action being brought by his then wife. A graduate of the Juilliard School of Music, he is currently the director of the Winter Festival in Tucson, Arizona, and he is single-handedly responsible for the series of concerts and allied musical activities which CBS has televised nationwide for the past three years to an ever-increasing audience. On Sundays, as you probably know, he hosts a televi-

32

sion forum on CBS devoted to airing current problems, but presented with such tact and restraint that he does not exacerbate people's pain or stir up people's emotions. It is the highest-rated program in the United States. I am sure you must all have watched it at some time or another, especially given our task in hand, so I do not intend to go into detail about Maestro Steinfeld's personality or ability to speak or possible charisma."

Dr. Carriol had been following this summary from the top file in the stack in front of her; frowning, she held an eight-by-ten matte color photograph of a man's face to the light, studying it as mercilessly as if she had never seen it before, though it was, as Dr. Abraham said, a very familiar face indeed. She noted its striking bone structure, the firm well-cut lips, the large dark shining eyes and the unruly quiff of light-brown hair that fell across the high wide forehead. It was a conductor's face, true enough; why did they always seem to have masses of floppy hair?

"Objections?" she asked, looking toward Dr. Chasen and Dr. Hemingway.

"The previous marriage, Sam. Did you investigate the reason why Maestro Steinfeld's first wife severed her alliance with him?" asked Dr. Hemingway, her intelligent little dog's face looking as if she was enjoying every moment of this long-awaited reporting session.

Dr. Abraham looked shocked. "Naturally! There was no enmity involved, nor does the matter reflect badly on the Maestro in any way. His first wife discovered in herself a preference for her own sex. She told Maestro Steinfeld about her feelings, he understood completely, and as a matter of fact he was her staunchest support during a rather troubled first few years in lesbian relationships. He asked for a divorce so he could remarry, but he permitted her to initiate proceedings because at the time she was in a very ticklish work situation."

"Thank you, Dr. Abraham. Any other objections? No? All right, then, please give us your second choice," said Dr. Carriol, clipping the photograph back inside the front cover of Maestro Steinfeld's file, closing it, and laying it neatly to one side before opening the next file.

"Shirley Grossman Schneider. An eighth-generation American of mixed Jewish blood, but mostly German Jewish. Aged thirty-seven. She is married, one child, a boy now aged six, in school, classified very bright. On the scales of ten, she scored perfect as wife and mother. An astronaut still on the active NASA payroll, she was head of the Phoebus series of space missions which built the pilot solar generator in earth orbit. Author of the best-selling book *Taming the Sun,* and currently NASA's chief spokesman to the American people. She is president of Scientific Women for America. In her college years at MIT she was a much-publicized feminist who was responsible for feminist adoption of the word 'man' as generic in any situation where either sex or both sexes are involved. You may remember her still famous quote of the time: 'When I chair a meeting I am not going to be palmed off as a chairperson, I intend to be the goddam chair*man!*' Her public speaking is superlative, eloquent and witty and emotionally moving. And, unusual in such an outspoken and militant feminist, her popularity is as high among men as it is among women. The lady is loaded with charm as well as personality."

A strongly beautiful face, thought Dr. Carriol, with a jaw that confirmed the astronaut's extraordinary record of physical and psychical gutsiness. But the widely opened grey eyes were the eyes of a genuine thinker.

"Objections?"

No one had any.

"Your number-three choice, Dr. Abraham?"

"Percival Taylor Smith. American right back to 1683 on his father's side and 1671 on his mother's, of White Anglo-Saxon Protestant background. Aged forty-two. He is married, one child, a girl now aged sixteen, in school, straight A's. Maritally I rated him ten, and parentally ten also. He is the head of the Community Social Adjustment Bureau in Palestrina, Texas, one of the biggest Band B relocation towns in the whole country, centered on Corpus Christi. His achievement record is without parallel. Not only does Palestrina have a suicide rate of zero, but its psychiatric services report no patients suffering from environment- or relocation-based neurosis. His personality may be labeled as winning, his public speaking is first class, he is the most dedicated worker my caseload uncovered, and his attitude to our current problems in America is magnificent."

Dr. Carriol looked at the photograph of Percival Taylor Smith carefully. A frank, open, smiling and careworn face, caught off-guard in the act of speaking; freckles across the cheeks and nose, endearingly lopsided ears, reddish hair, blue eyes, laughter lines

34

and worry lines making a most pleasing pattern around mouth and eyes.

"Objections?"

"Palestrina is a Band B town, which means its relocatees are permanent fixtures. I suggest that Mr. Smith's task has been correspondingly easier than in a Band C town," said Dr. Hemingway.

"Well taken, Dr. Hemingway. Dr. Abraham?"

"Valid. I acknowledge this. But I would point out two facts. One, that even so, Palestrina's record is without peer. And two, that a man of Mr. Smith's caliber would nut out some kind of approach that would work in any situation."

"Agreed," said Dr. Carriol. "Thank you very much, Sam. I can see no reason why we should not proceed to Dr. Hemingway, but before we do, does anyone else have a general objection to Dr. Abraham's choices?"

Dr. Hemingway leaned forward; Dr. Abraham leaned back just as far, frowning. The puggy little lady's persistence was beginning to wear him down.

"I note that your first and second selections were both Jewish. You yourself are Jewish. Your chief researcher is Jewish. Was there any bias in your decision?"

Dr. Abraham swallowed, pulled his lips back from his teeth, and drew his breath in with a gentle hiss that indicated he was not going to lose his temper no matter what Dr. Hemingway came out with. "I can see where you might think you had a valid point," he said. "I will answer you by asking Dr. Carriol if there was any Semitic bias in her selection of the heads of her three investigative teams for the purpose of this exercise. I am a Jew. So is Dr. Chasen. Two to one, Millie!"

Dr. Carriol laughed, so did Dr. Hemingway.

"Say no more, Sam. And thank you. Now it's your turn in the hot seat, Millie." Dr. Carriol put the first three files to one side, and pulled the next pile of three to where she could conveniently study them.

"Okay!" said the little pug-dog lady, not at all put out by Dr. Abraham's counter; she was a scientist of the questioning kind in everything, was all. "My team and I elected to use the alternative selection process, namely that every member of the team voted, rather than just me and my chief researcher. Our three final can-

35

didates were unanimous choices, in the order in which I will present them."

Dr. Hemingway opened a file. "First choice is a woman, Catherine Walking Horse. Father, a full-blood Sioux. Mother, a sixth-generation American of Irish Catholic background. Aged twenty-seven. Single, no children, no previous marriage, but strongly heterosexual in her relationships of an intimate nature. You've undoubtedly heard of her and heard her, she is a very well-known singer of Indian and other folk songs. A most engaging and happy person, with the most positive attitude to life in our times that we encountered in our thirty-three-thousand-plus sample. She's an extremely intelligent woman. Her doctoral thesis in ethology from Princeton is being published this fall by the Atticus Press as a major contribution to the field. She is of course a brilliant public speaker, and has a most magnetic personality." Dr. Hemingway paused, then added, "She's a bit of a witch—by that I mean she has a spellbinding quality—she *draws* people to her. Quite amazing."

This photograph showed a young, hawklike dark face, its mouth half smiling, its eyes staring eagerly into what Dr. Carriol mentally classified as a "vision."

"Objections?" asked Dr. Carriol.

"At twenty-seven she is too young," said Dr. Abraham emphatically. "She should not even have been included in your caseload."

"I concur," said Dr. Hemingway, on her mettle to appear no less accommodating to criticism than Dr. Abraham had been. "But the fact remains that the computer did throw her name up, and after running several checks we assumed that meant her other qualifications negated her age in the computer's judgment. Also, she has emerged as our clear-cut number-one choice. I would respectfully submit that her age not militate against her."

"Agreed," said Dr. Carriol. "However, there is something in her gaze I find disquieting. When it comes to personal investigation, I want a lot of digging to make sure Dr. Walking Horse is neither on drugs nor possessed of mental instability." Her hands laid the file down, opened the next file. "Your second pick, Dr. Hemingway?"

"Mark Hastings. An eighth-generation American, at least. Black. Aged thirty-four. Married, one child, a boy now aged nine, in school, a straight-A student and a promising athlete. Dr. Hastings scores ten maritally and parentally. Quarterback of the Band B Longhorns, and still holding his own magnificently against the youngsters coming up. Rated the greatest QB in the history of American football. A summa cum laude graduate in philosophy from Wesleyan, with a doctorate from Harvard. He is an indefatigable worker among the youth of all the relocation towns in Texas and New Mexico, founded and supervises the running of the youth clubs that bear his team's name, is a first-class public speaker, a highly personable man, and is chairman of the President's youth council."

He looks such a brute, thought Dr. Carriol; how very misleading faces can be. And indeed the face was an almost classic example of dumb brute strength, with its flattened nose, dented jawline, stitched-up brows. What punishment he must have taken on the football field! But the eyes always gave away the soul, and the eyes said the soul was profound, beautiful, humble, possibly poetic.

"Objections?" she asked.

Silence.

"Your last choice, Dr. Hemingway?"

"Is Walter Charnowski. A sixth-generation American of Polish extraction. Aged forty-three. He's married, has one child, a girl now aged twenty and a sophomore at Brown, an A-plus-plus-plus student in basic sciences. My group and I agreed unanimously that he was a ten maritally and parentally. Of course, as you all know, he won the Nobel Prize for Physics in 2026, for his work on generation of power from the sun in space. He is currently the scientific director of Project Phoebus. But the main reason we chose him among our final three subjects is that he is the founder and perpetual president of Scientists for Humanity, the first—and only—association of scientists which has managed to cross barriers of race, creed, nationality and ideology and achieved a truly international, actively contributing membership. He has charisma, I think. He's a much better than average public speaker in eight languages, and he has a warm and charming personality."

Dark yellow-blond hair, yellowish eyes, fine tanned skin, a broad face with the beginning of a network of lines which would only add additional charm and fascination to it. Though she had never met him personally, Dr. Carriol had always privately thought him one of the sexiest men in public life.

"Objections?"

Dr. Abraham was dying to object. "Am I or am I not correct, Millie, in remembering that Professor Charnowski was one of the formulators as well as signatories of the Catholics for Free Life petition which attempted in—2019?—to persuade Pope Innocent to reverse Pope Benedict's ruling on contraception and population control?"

Dr. Carriol glanced from Dr. Hemingway to Dr. Abraham and back again, but said nothing.

"Yes, Sam, you are quite correct," said Dr. Hemingway. "I was not aware, however, that we were supposed to detail the *negative* aspects of our candidates in this short verbal report! If you look in your copy of his file you will find all the relevant information there. Nothing in Professor Charnowski's conduct since 2019 indicates that he has not accepted Pope Innocent's response in a spirit of genuine reconciliation."

"It's a black mark against him that would have led *me* to eliminate him, especially considering the religious implications," said Dr. Abraham.

"My job, Sam," said Dr. Hemingway, with a look in her little black eyes that said she was going to punish him for inferring that she was ever less than completely on top of that job, "was to wade through the better than thirty-three thousand cases the computer assigned to me and my group of six investigators, and select by one of two alternative methods the three most suitable persons among those better than thirty-three thousand people, given certain parameters as guidelines."

She leaned back in her chair, closed her eyes, and with elaborate care proceeded to tick the points off on her fingers as she made them. "To enumerate! One, that the chosen person be at least a fourth-generation American on both sides. Two, aged between thirty and forty-five years. Three, of either sex. Four, if married be rated ten as a spouse, if a parent be rated ten as a parent, each on a scale of ten designed by Dr. Carriol, and if single to be as Caesar's wife whether homo- or heterosexual. Five, that the chosen person's career be a public or community-oriented one. Six, that the said career be uniformly beneficial to the community as a whole or in particular, that self-interest be minimal. Seven, that the personality be extremely stable and attractive. Eight, that he or she be a superlative public speaker. Nine, that, if possible, charisma be present. And ten—the only negative point you might say, Sam, old buddy—that the chosen person not have a formal religious occupation."

She opened her eyes and stared straight at Dr. Abraham. "Given this protocol, I would say I have done my job."

"You have all done your jobs," said Dr. Carriol before Dr. Abraham could reply. "It is not," she went on, fingering the file under her hands with spidery purpose, "a competition we are engaged upon, even if it is only an exercise designed to check the efficiency of our data resources, computers, methodology and personnel. Five years ago, when you were assigned this task, as well as the money and the computers and the personnel to carry it out, you may privately have thought it was a helluva long time and a helluva lot of Environment money to tie up on nothing more than a drill. But I do not think any of you were more than three months into it before you began to realize how essential a drill it was. Section Four has emerged from phase one of Operation Search with the best data-collection protocols, the best computer programs, and the best statistical and humanity investigative teams in the whole of the federal bureaucracy."

"Granted," said Dr. Abraham, feeling, he didn't know why, as if his knuckles were being rapped.

"Good! Now, are we finished with Dr. Hemingway? Has anyone any general objections to her candidates?"

Silence.

"All right. Thank you, Millie. And thank you for that admirable précis of the criteria for Operation Search."

Dr. Hemingway winced, but thought better of saying what she wanted to say.

"Dr. Chasen, would you give us your candidates, please?" asked Dr. Carriol smoothly.

Wounded feelings were forgotten immediately; as Dr. Moshe Chasen gathered his little heap of files together, a certain expectancy began to charge the atmosphere in the conference room. Dr. Chasen was a bull of a man, big and stubborn and given to strong opinions; he was also a formidable data analyst whom Dr. Carriol had stolen from Health, Education and Welfare some ten years before, and like his colleagues Abraham and Hemingway, he loved working for Judith Carriol.

That he had remained silent throughout the presentation of the first six candidates was perhaps surprising, but Drs. Abraham and Hemingway now thought they knew why. The anticipated name had not cropped up among those six people, therefore it must come from Dr. Chasen, and naturally it would come as his first choice. To a large extent it robbed his, the last presentation, of much of its thunder; and Dr. Moshe Chasen was not a man who liked seeing his thunder stolen. Thus the atmosphere of expectancy was not bated-breath in nature; rather, it was anticlimactic. Yet—Moshe Chasen did not look or act like a cheated man as he shifted his bulk in his chair and opened his first file.

"I chose the first alternative when it came to a method of selection," he said, his voice as deep and growly as his face. "Not so democratic, Millie, but in my view a lot more effective. My chief researcher and I reserved the decision making for ourselves, and of course our choices were mutual."

"Of course," said Dr. Carriol, slightly minatory.

He glanced down the table at his boss quickly, then dipped his head. "Our first choice—and by a very large margin of preference—is Dr. Joshua Christian. A seventh-generation American of mixed Nordic, Celtic, Armenian and Russian blood. Aged thirty-two years. Single, no children, and never married. Voluntarily vasectomized at age twenty. We have not been able, given the information available to the computer—and that is very considerable for every citizen of this country—to discover what if any is Dr. Christian's sexual preference. However, he lives within a stable family unit consisting of his mother (his father is dead), two brothers, one sister, and two sisters-in-law. He is the undisputed head of the family, what I would call a born father figure. He graduated summa cum laude in basic sciences from Chubb and went on to do a doctorate in philosophy, subject psychology, also from Chubb. He runs a private clinic in Holloman, Connecticut, and specializes in the treatment of what he calls millennial neurosis. His cure record is really phenomenal, and he has what for want of a better word I must call a cult following. This may be because his therapy encourages his patients to find solace in God, though not necessarily in any formal religion. His personality is disturbingly intense, and he speaks very well indeed to any size of audience. But my main reason for picking this man as a definite first—I venture to say, only—choice is his astonishing charisma. You said you wanted it. Well, he's got it."

This speech was greeted with stunned silence. Dr. Moshe Chasen had produced the wrong name.

Dr. Carriol sat looking at Dr. Chasen so intently that he put his chin up and refused to switch his gaze away from her eyes.

"I shall voice my own objection first," she said at last, in a level, unemotional tone. "I have never heard of the term 'millennial neurosis.' And I have never heard of Dr. Joshua Christian." Outside of her position as head of Section Four in the Department of the Environment, Dr. Judith Carriol was one of the country's leading psychologists.

"Valid, ma'am. Dr. Christian has never published or given a single paper after his doctoral thesis, which—I've read it, of course, and had it read by experts in his field—almost completely consisted of a mass of experimental data presented as graphs, tables and the like, with the shortest, baldest written text I have ever seen. But the work—on mu feedback in anxiety neurosis—was so brilliant and original it has become the standard reference and the jumping-off spot for all investigation in this field."

"All right, outside my expertise area, but I ought to have heard of him, and I haven't," said Dr. Carriol.

"That doesn't surprise me. He seems to have no ambition to be famous, he just seems to want to conduct his little clinic in Holloman. Among his peers he is either an object of contempt or an object of amusement, and yet the man does very good work."

"Why doesn't he write?" asked Dr. Hemingway.

"Apparently he suffers from writer's block."

"To the degree that he can't even produce a *paper?* In this day and age, with all the modern tools available to a nonwriter?" Dr. Hemingway sounded incredulous.

"Yes."

"Then he's very seriously flawed," said Dr. Abraham.

"Where does it say in the parameters Millie so succinctly itemized that a man has to be perfect outside of his marriage and his children? Are you inferring brain damage, Sam?"

"Well, it's a possibility," said Dr. Abraham defensively.

"Oh, come on! Don't be so goddam precious!"

"Gentlemen, gentlemen!" said Dr. Carriol sharply. She plucked the photograph out of the file she had opened but not even glanced into, so attentively had she listened while Dr. Chasen described his bombshell first choice. And she studied the picture now as if it could offer her some clue as to why Moshe Chasen had preferred this man to the man he should have preferred. Yes, it was an attractive face. Half starved looking, though. Not a bit handsome, with that scimitar of a nose—the Armenian showing, maybe? Dark, very brilliant and arresting eyes. And the face had an ascetic austerity every face so far had lacked. Yes, an intriguing face. But . . . She shrugged.

"And who is your second choice, Dr. Chasen?" she asked.

Dr. Chasen grinned wickedly. "I can hear you all asking yourselves, Which made the booboo, my computer or me? Relax! There's nothing wrong with my computer. It put him in my sample. Senator David Sims Hillier VII. What more can I say? Need I say more?"

The moment Dr. Chasen uttered the name, there was a huge collective sigh. The golden boy! There he was in an eight-by-ten color print under Dr. Carriol's eyes; the most liked, the most admired, the most respected man in America. David Sims Hillier VII, U.S. Senator. At thirty-one too young to be President, but bound to be President before he turned forty. Six feet four inches in height, therefore not afflicted by the Napoleon complex. Beautifully built, therefore not afflicted by the Atlas complex. Fair hair, wavy and likely to remain enviably thick into old age. Deep, brilliant blue eyes. Classically regular features, yet not at all pretty. Even in the photograph one could see how masterfully the chin would jut in real life. The curves of the mouth were firm, disciplined, unsensuous, and the eyes looked strong, intelligent, resolved, wise. He was all those; nor was he selfish, cruel, shallow, impractical, or indifferent to the plight of those born into less affluent circumstances than he himself had been.

Dr. Carriol put the picture away. "Objections?"

"Did you dig deep, Moshe?" asked Dr. Hemingway.

"Yes, indeed I did. Into everything. And if he has feet of clay, I can't find a trace of the substance." Dr. Chasen nodded seriously. "He's—*perfect!*"

"Then why," demanded Dr. Abraham, voice cracking to a squeak, "did you pick an obscure half-mad-looking psychologist from a backwater like Holloman, Connecticut, ahead of the best man in America?"

This question Dr. Chasen considered with obvious respect. Instead of galloping in with a glib pat answer, he frowned and took his time and was honest about his own ignorance. Most unusual behavior from Moshe Chasen when dealing with the skepticism of his colleagues. "I cannot explain why," he said. "I just know in my bones that Dr. Joshua Christian is the *only* man who

42

fits the criteria of the commission we were given, at least in my sample of possible candidates. I still think it! Very vividly do I remember Judith sitting five years ago right where she's sitting now and giving us this job, and I remember how she kept hammering away about charisma. That, she said, was what was going to make this exercise the most important exercise of its kind ever undertaken. Because we were going to use the most modern tools and methods to try to pinpoint an intangible. If we could do it, she said, we would make statistical analytical history. And prove a point, and put Environment so far ahead even of Justice and Treasury that we'd be the undisputed kings of data processing. So when I nutted out my programs for the computer, I skewed them toward factors indicating charisma."

He ran his fingers through his hair in exasperation, sensing that he wasn't home yet. "I mean, what *is* charisma?" he asked rhetorically. "Originally it was a word used only to describe the God-given power of saints and holy men to capture and mold the spirits of those they encountered. Then during the last half of the last century it got so bowdlerized it was used to categorize the impact of pop stars, playboys and politicians. Now we should all know Judith pretty well. We knew her well even before Operation Search began! And knowing her, I figured that what she meant by charisma was something a lot closer to the old definition than the current one. Judith doesn't deal in superficialities."

He had captured them at last, even Dr. Carriol, who had sat up much straighter in her chair and was staring at him as if she had never really seen him before.

"Most of the time, especially since the advent of mass media, *how* a person speaks and acts out his ideas is as important as the content of his ideas. God help the person who writes a genuinely significant book and then lays an egg on the Marlene Feldman Hour, because that's where thinking America gets its impressions of Joe Blow the significant writer! How many times has one Presidential candidate aced the opposition on a televised debate simply because he can project himself and his ideas better than the opposition? And how do you think old Gus Rome managed to keep the country on his side and overpower both Houses? Televised fireside chats to the nation is how! He'd sit there and look straight into the camera without blinking those big clear fascinating eyes, pouring his mind and his spirit across the gap between the White House and Main Street Anywhere so effectively that everyone who watched him and heard what he said was convinced the man spoke from his heart to that one listening person alone. He was a strong, indomitable and utterly sincere man, with the ability to project what he was! And he knew the ideas and the words that act as keys to unlock emotions."

He grimaced, looking as if suddenly he was repelled to nausea by what he was thinking, then he visibly got himself under command, and said, "Have you ever heard any of Hitler's speeches, or seen him in old film clips haranguing a crowd? Ridiculous! He comes across as a posturing, screaming, infantile little man. There were plenty of Germans who used the same tactics Hitler did, appealed to the same frustrated national feelings, put up the same hapless and innocent scapegoats, but those other Germans didn't have what Hitler had—the ability to *inspire*, to bury good sense and intellect under a landslide of emotion. He was evil personified, but he had charisma. Or take his arch enemy, Winston Churchill. The bulk of Churchill's most telling speeches were either pinched straight out of the works of other people, or paraphrased. Little of what he actually said was original, and often to us he comes across as unbelievably sentimental, real cornpone hokum stuff. But the man had the most magnificent way with him, and like Hitler he was there at the time the people could be reached and influenced by what he said, *and* how he said it. He inspired! Charisma. Neither Hitler nor Churchill was sexy or handsome or, I understand, particularly charming. Unless they needed to be charming, when, I understand, they could charm the birds right out of the trees. St. Francis of Assisi had charisma, and he could literally charm the birds right out of the trees. Now he had the real McCoy. But so did Hitler, and Churchill, and Augustus Rome. Okay. Let's move on a bit, take a look at Iggy-Piggy the pop star and Raoul Delice the playboy. Do they have charisma? No! They're both sexy, they're both colossally charming, they're both objects of adulation. Yet when the winds of time blow them away, no one will even remember their names. They do not have genuine charisma. They don't have what it takes to lead a nation to its finest hour, or to the nadir of its history. And Senator David Sims Hillier VII? The computer says he doesn't have charisma of the kind I'm sure our Judith is looking for. My chief researcher agreed with the computer. And I agree with both of them. Where right from the first early pass of the entire sample through the first of the early programs, Dr. Joshua Christian's name kept popping to the top. No matter what we did, his name was a cork we couldn't keep under. That simple."

Dr. Carriol nodded. "Thank you, Moshe." She smiled. "I know it's a bit of an anticlimax after all this, but you'd better get on and give us your choice for third place."

Dr. Chasen came down from where he had been dwelling, and opened the last file. "Dominic d'Este. An eighth-generation American. One-quarter black blood from a full black grandparent. Aged thirty-six. Married, two children, SCB second child approval number DX–42–6–084, the older child a girl aged eleven, in school, straight A's, the younger a boy aged seven, in school, classified extremely bright. He made a perfect ten on the Carriol scales for marriage and parenthood." This with an ironic nod toward the head of the table.

Dr. Carriol acknowledged it, and went back to studying the handsome face in the photograph between her hands. A superlatively handsome face. The black blood didn't really show except in the eyes, which were night dark and of that curious, wonderful liquidity peculiar to people of black origins.

"Dominic d'Este was an astronaut on the Phoebus series, specialty solar engineering, but he is now Mayor of Detroit. He devotes all his time and energy to preserving his city as a spring-summer-fall center of trolley car and omnibus building and other metal engineering. When contracts are advertised in Washington regarding Phoebus or relocation or any major project calling for either massive or precision metal engineering, he's right there lobbying like crazy for Detroit. He received the Pulitzer Prize for his book entitled *Even the Sun Dies in Winter*, and he serves on the President's council for urban preservation. He also hosts the ABC television talk show 'Northern City,' very strong indeed on the Sunday ratings. Finally, he is accounted the finest public speaker in the country after Senator Hillier."

"Objections?" asked Dr. Carriol.

"Just—*too* good-looking," growled Dr. Hemingway.

Everyone grinned.

"I agree, I agree!" cried Dr. Chasen, extending his hands in self-exculpation.

"You haven't mentioned a fact I happen to know because I know Dominic personally, Moshe," said Dr. Abraham, an ex-NASA data analyst. "Mayor d'Este is a serving elder of his church."

45

"I am aware of it," said Dr. Chasen. "However, after several further looks, we decided—the computer, my chief researcher and I—that the degree of Mayor d'Este's religious commitment and involvement was not sufficient to disqualify him from our sample." Dr. Chasen grunted. "Or disqualify him from final selection, for that matter."

Dr. Carriol put the last file on top of all the others and pushed them to one side; in the space she cleared by so doing she laid her hands, one folded lightly over the other, the fingers of both writhing gently.

"I would like to thank you most sincerely, and congratulate you on a very long and very demanding job done very, very well. I trust that all of you have returned your entire samples to the Federal Human Data Bank and removed all trace of your programs from the computers?"

They nodded, Dr. Abraham, Dr. Hemingway and Dr. Chasen.

"Of course you will retain your programs for future use, but filed in such a way that their true meaning is unintelligible to anyone outside this room. Have any of you any paperwork or tapes or other evidence of Operation Search left undestroyed?"

They shook their heads.

"Good! I will take charge of all copies of the files here this afternoon. Before we go any further, maybe John will find some refreshments?"

She smiled at her secretary, whose pencil had not paused since the meeting started; he laid down his notebook and rose immediately.

Dr. Hemingway excused herself to visit the adjacent toilet facilities, while the other three sat rather limply, not speaking. But by the time John Wayne had wheeled in his cart bearing coffee and tea, cakes and sandwiches, wine and beer, and dispensed it with his usual efficiency unimpaired by the marathon stint of shorthand notation, Dr. Hemingway was back and the other three had regained their vitality.

"I could kick myself for not working out a program more skewed toward charisma," said Dr. Hemingway as she nibbled on a smoked salmon sandwich.

"I think Moshe read far too much into the original commission," said Dr. Abraham.

All three looked to Dr. Carriol, who merely wiggled her eyebrows, and that helped elucidate nothing.

"It was good fun," said Dr. Chasen, and sighed. "I hope phase two is as much fun, Judith?" A fishing statement, but again Dr. Carriol vouchsafed no reply.

Finally she waved the cart away, and waited until John Wayne had disposed of it and resumed his seat and his pencil before getting back to business.

"I am aware that you're rather in the dark as to exactly what phase two of Operation Search entails," she said. "Until today I haven't wanted you to know, because I thought you should be devoting all your energies to phase one, and I didn't want any of you shortcutting because subconsciously you were relying on phase two to get you out of any possible dilemma." She paused, and looked straight at Dr. Chasen. "Before I discuss phase two, I had better say that I am removing Dr. Chasen from Operation Search entirely as of today. You're going to a fresh project, Moshe. *Not* because I consider your contribution to Operation Search unsatisfactory! Quite the contrary." Her official stiffness relaxed a little. "You did very well, Moshe. I confess you have amazed me."

"Don't tell me our work didn't measure up!" gasped Dr. Hemingway, face screwed into anguished wrinkles.

"Don't panic, Millie, it measured up fine. I believe the overall outcome is not altered by Moshe's prejudicial tack with the data. Don't forget that phase one provided for the unexpected by offering three candidates from each team. I had thought it would be phase two that would refine these nine possibles to the point where intangibles could be dealt with properly. I was thinking of phase one's computer work more as a tool to remove any human error from what I considered truly computer-assessable data. So I admit I am fascinated that one of you did manage to devise a program capable of assessing a massive sample with respect to an intangible. But it is possible that phase two will reverse Moshe's findings. Which does not detract in the least from the brilliance of Moshe's approach to phase one. It will merely show Moshe where he went wrong, and next time he won't go wrong. Don't lose sight of the fact that there are nine candidates entering phase two, six of whom did not belong to Moshe's lot. Moshe skewed to favor one of his ten parameters, the intangible one. But there's

47

every chance that in so doing, he tampered with the data in such a way that the other nine parameters did not receive sufficient emphasis."

"*No!*" barked Dr. Chasen.

Dr. Carriol smiled. "Okay, okay! But phase two will go ahead as originally planned, if only because we are dealing with nine people, not just Moshe's three."

"Would it help any to run our six through Moshe's programs?" asked Dr. Abraham.

"We could, yes. But I'd rather not. That is leaving too much to chance and Moshe, no offense."

"I take it phase two is human investigation?" asked Dr. Hemingway.

"Correct. No one has yet managed to define what I call gut instinct, but I guess it's some kind of ostensibly illogical human reaction to other human beings in human situations. So I've always been of the opinion that in this particular exercise, where human emotion is of paramount importance, there should be a period of time in which we can personally observe or interview or test a small, select number of possibles. Today is February first. I will call today the last day of phase one, and tomorrow the first day of phase two. We have three months. May first must see phase two of Operation Search completed."

Creep creep went her hands across the table, an unconscious mannerism that always had an uncomfortable effect on those who watched. As if, independent of her mind, her hands could sniff after prey, and weave webs of entrapment, and *see*.

"As of tomorrow," she went on, "your teams are disbanded. Only we in this room will have any knowledge of phase two, so you will give out to your teams that Operation Search has achieved what it set out to achieve without a phase two. And during the next three months you, Sam, you, Millie, and I myself in lieu of Moshe, will undertake personal investigation of the nine candidates. Three each. Sam will take on Millie's three, Millie will take on Sam's three, and I will take on Moshe's three. So— that's Dr. Walking Horse, Dr. Hastings and Professor Charnowski for Sam. And for Millie we have Maestro Steinfeld, Dr. Schneider and Mr. Smith. I inherit Dr. Christian, Senator Hillier and Mayor d'Este. You are experienced field investigators, so I need not enlarge upon the protocol governing phase two. Tomorrow John will allow you to look at the files of your three candidates, but you will not be permitted to remove those files from my office, nor to take notes. Phase two is going to have to chug along on memory, though of course you can ask to see the files at any time."

She grew stern. "I must remind you that the top secret classification of Operation Search is even more in effect during phase two than phase one. If any of these people tumble to the fact that he or she is under investigation, we are in for a roasting, because most of these people are important people in their own right, and some have real clout in this town. You will proceed with the utmost caution. Is that understood?"

"We're not fools, Judith!" yapped Dr. Hemingway, stung.

"I know that, Millie. But I'd rather make myself unpopular now for uttering words of warning than regretful later that I didn't."

Dr. Abraham was frowning. "Judith, this disbanding of our teams is very abrupt! What am I going to tell my staff tomorrow beyond the fact that they're out of a job overnight? They're all sharp enough to have guessed about phase two, and I'm afraid it never occurred to me, for one, that I would be stripped of my team. So I haven't prepared my staff for this shock, and shock it's going to be."

Dr. Carriol raised her brows. "Out of a job is putting it a bit too strongly, Sam. They are all graded Environment data people and will remain so. Actually they'll be going to Moshe to assist him on his new project. If they want to. Otherwise they will be given the opportunity to transfer to some other Environment project. Okay?"

He shrugged. "Okay by me. But I'd appreciate a written directive from you about it."

This did not please her, but her answer was as smoothly civil as always. "Since written directives are Section Four policy, Sam, that surely goes without saying."

Dr. Abraham saw the shadow of a sword suddenly materialize above his head, and hastened to make amends. "Thanks, Judith. I'm sorry if I've offended you. It's a shock, that's all. When you work with people for five solid years, you're a poor boss if you don't grow protective of their interests."

"Provided you also retain a measure of detachment, Sam, I quite agree. I take it some of your people won't want to work with Moshe?"

"No, no, it's not that!" He looked depressed. "As a matter of fact, I think all of them will be delighted."

"Then what are you worried about?"

"Nothing." He sighed, moved his hands helplessly, hunched his body over. "Nothing at all."

Dr. Carriol looked at him with cold speculation, but all she said was, "Good!" Then she rose to her feet. "I thank you again, everyone. May I also wish you well? Moshe, report to me tomorrow morning, okay? I've got something very special lined up for you, and believe me, it's going to take everything you've got and everything your augmented team is capable of giving you."

Dr. Chasen had not said one word because he knew the chief of Section Four better than poor old bumbling Sam did. Judith was a great chief in some respects, but it was wise not to get on the wrong side of her. Her brain was so dominant that sometimes her heart was quite frozen by the winds blowing off it. He was bitterly disappointed at being removed from Operation Search; nor could any new project, no matter how alluring, remove the desolation any scientist worth his oats must feel at being removed from his work untimely. However, to argue would get him nowhere, and he was sensitive enough to know that.

But the faint sourness of rebuff and injury lingered in the conference room atmosphere, so the three investigators trickled out sooner than would otherwise have been the case, leaving Dr. Carriol and John Wayne in sole possession of the field.

Dr. Carriol looked at her watch. "Mr. Magnus will still be in his office, no doubt, so I'd better go see him." She sighed, glancing at the thick block of used pages in her secretary's notebook. "Poor John! Can you start transcribing right away?"

"No trouble," he said, and began to gather up all the file copies from the places where the Operation Search chiefs had sat.

The Secretary for the Environment's offices were down the same hall as the executive conference room, which he too used when necessity demanded.

The big anteroom which served as a reception and waiting area was deserted, for it was well after five; from its sides it opened through discreetly closed doors into the typing pools, the photocopying rooms, ancillary offices, and conveniences which the Secretary commanded entirely for his own work. The door ahead of the two glass entrance doors led into the spacious office of the Secretary's private secretary, who was still there when Dr. Judith Carriol strolled in. Mrs. Helena Taverner's extramural life was the object of considerable Departmental curiosity, since she seemed to spend all her time dancing devoted and largely thankless attendance upon Harold Magnus; some said she was divorced, others that she was widowed, yet others that Mr. Taverner had never existed at all.

"Why, hello, Dr. Carriol. Nice to see you. Go right in, he's been hoping you'd come. Shall I send in coffee?"

"Please, Mrs. Taverner."

Harold Magnus sat behind his gigantic walnut desk, which was his own personal property, his big leather chair swung away from the entrance door to face the window. Through this he could watch, when he so chose, the small amount of traffic that proceeded up and down K Street. Since darkness had fallen and there was no rain to coat the road with a little gloss from reflected lights, it was a dimmer version of his own office and himself that he was watching so intently. But as the door closed he rotated a full circle and a half and ended facing Dr. Judith Carriol.

"How did it go?" he demanded.

"In a minute, after Mrs. Taverner brings coffee."

His brows mated. "Dammit, woman, I am far too eager to find out how things went to bother with food or drink!"

"So you say now. But two minutes into it, when I won't want to stop, you'll decide you're going to die without some form of sustenance," she said, not in the indulgent tones of a female in mild defiance of entrenched power, but matter-of-factly. For the true situation was the reverse; hers was the entrenched power, his the grace and favor of political caprice. She sat down in a wide chair which stood in front of his desk and to one side of its middle.

"You know, when I first met you, I made a great mistake about you," he said suddenly, as was his habit darting off down what seemed an irrelevant sidetrack.

Dr. Carriol was not fooled; this man's irrelevancies were usually calculated. "What mistake was that, Mr. Magnus?" she asked.

"I wondered whose bed had got you where you were."

She looked amused. "What an old-fashioned attitude!"

"Garbage!" he said vigorously. "Times may change, but you know and I know that there will always be a certain amount of bed hopping when women maneuver for power."

"*Certain* women," she said.

"Exactly! And I thought you were that kind of woman."

"Why?"

"You looked the part. Oh, there are plenty of very attractive women who don't use the bed to climb higher, but I've never thought of you as attractive. I think of you as glamorous. And in my experience—which is considerable!—glamour usually goes hand in hand with the oblique approach."

"But of course you've changed your mind about me."

"Of course! After one short conversation with you, in fact."

She settled into her chair more comfortably. "Why tell me this now?"

He looked derisive, but didn't answer.

"I see. To keep me in my place."

"Perhaps."

"It isn't necessary. I know my place."

"Good!"

Mrs. Taverner came in bearing coffee and a pair of fine decanters, one containing cognac, the other extremely rare unblended Scotch whisky. "Sun's way over the yardarm, Mr. Magnus."

"Thanks, Helena." But he poured himself coffee only, and nodded toward the tray. "Help yourself, Dr. Carriol."

He was a fat man, grossly so without giving an impression of grossness; the sort of adiposity that said power rather than self-indulgence, though he indulged himself mightily. His lips were thick, nicely balancing his prawnlike eyebrows, and his sandy thatch of hair showed no sign of thinning or greying despite his sixty-plus years. He had the tiny, delicate hands and feet which so often went with his type of physique, so that the hands resembled starfish and the feet fallen-down sections in his trouser bottoms. His voice, as rich and full and round as his paunch, was a melodious instrument he knew how to play with the aplomb of a master, and did. Before Tibor Reece had appointed him to this most important of all the Executive portfolios, he had been a famous legal advocate specializing in cases with a bearing on the environment, and he had argued as persuasively on behalf of those who sought to destroy it as he had on behalf of its champions. This fact had made him an unpopular choice in many circles, but President Reece had routed the opposition by observing with characteristic detachment that surely Harold Magnus's hopping from one side of the fence to the other had given him an unparalleled opportunity to taste the grass in both yards. His job as Secretary for the Environment was to ensure that the policies of his superior in the White House were faithfully carried out by the Department, and because he did largely confine his activities to this end, he was suffered with fairly good grace by the permanent chiefs of the Department. Indeed, had he not dabbled in things like secret passwords, they would probably have apostrophized him as the best Secretary in Environment's short history. He had been in the job for the seven years which had elapsed since Tibor Reece had been elected President of the United States of America, and by now it was generally felt throughout the Washington establishment that he would remain in Environment as long as Tibor Reece remained in the White House. Since the Constitutional amendment of Augustus Rome's time had never been repealed, and the election coming up in November held out no hope for the opposition, that meant at least another five years of Harold Magnus.

The Secretary studied Dr. Judith Carriol, who also chose to drink nothing stronger than coffee, without affection. He could esteem her, and he did, but he could not like her. An ineffectual mother followed by an ineffectual wife had not inspired him with a high opinion of women, so he had never bothered to pursue his acquaintance with the sex further, preferring to direct his marked sensual proclivities toward food and drink. That this choice had seriously undermined his health was something he flatly refused to admit, either to his doctor or to himself.

Judith Carriol. Indisputably the *éminence grise* of Environment. By the time she had come to him five years earlier with her plan called Operation Search worked out to the last predictable detail and all its reasons for being meticulously tabulated, he already knew enough of her to want to steer a wide berth around her whenever he could. She set his teeth on edge; to be so brilliant, so cold, so awesomely efficient and so freed from emotional fog just didn't agree with his conception of Woman. His may have been an outdated attitude, it may have been an erroneous one; but all that Judith Carriol was, that he knew her to be, sat so ill upon such a glamorous, feminine-looking woman that she threw him into disorder. Afraid of her was putting it too strongly. Wary of her was nearer the mark. Or so he told himself.

53

When she had first presented Operation Search to him, his reaction had been mixed and cautious. But no administration had ever been as conscious of the mood of the people as Tibor Reece's. Nor had any President ever been faced with such profound consequences of national humiliation and demoralization, even Tibor Reece's predecessor in office, Augustus Rome. For old Gus Rome had held the people together by the sheer force of his personality, and in that respect his successor in office was not so fortunate.

Harold Magnus, playing safe, had taken Dr. Judith Carriol and her schema for Operation Search to the President, and the President, while not wildly enthusiastic (he did not have an enthusiastic nature), had seen enough potential to direct them to go ahead immediately.

Dr. Carriol was perfectly aware of how Harold Magnus felt about her, for he was not a man able to conceal his instinctive reactions to people. It suited her to work for a man of this type; she didn't have to waste time and energy flattering and fluttering him into assent. Actually they understood each other very well, for they were both ring-wise fighters who had learned to spar for points.

"Hillier, of course," he said.

"Yes. And eight others."

"It *has* to be Hillier!"

She looked at him very directly. "Mr. Secretary, if Senator Hillier was a foregone conclusion, we had no need to spend so much time and money mounting an Operation Search! Hillier's was the name that sprang to mind in the beginning, but he was too young then. However, Operation Search was not mounted merely to buy the Senator time! It was mounted to make as sure as human fallibility can that we pick the one and only man for the job. It is the most important job this country—or possibly any country—has offered a man in God knows how long. I can't even think of an equivalent."

"Hillier," he said, obdurate.

"Mr. Magnus, if I had had *my* way we would have excluded political men and women even from our first sample! I do not consider a politician suitable for this job."

They would never agree about Hillier, so he abandoned the argument. "What about phase two?" he asked.

"It goes forward at once. I've given Dr. Hemingway Dr. Abraham's candidates to investigate, and vice versa. I am investigating Dr. Chasen's three people myself."

The Secretary sat up straight. "What's happened to your blue-eyed boy Chasen?"

"Nothing. He did brilliantly. To use him on phase two would be a waste of the man. Besides which, he's not a good personal investigator, where the other two are. So I'm giving him the job of revamping our relocation methodology."

"Shit! That ought to keep him busy!"

"Yes, it ought. I've turned over Abraham's and Hemingway's teams to him as well as allowing him to keep his own staff. There's no point in having trained twelve people to really complex work and then putting them back into chickenshit computer routines like analyzing the amount of money we're having to spend dropping feed by helicopter to starving deer in the national parks. The relocation mess is big enough for Moshe to use eighteen assistants, probably until they and he are due for retirement."

"Pessimist!"

"*Realist,* sir."

"So phase two involves only you and Hemingway and Sam Abraham."

"The less people involved, the better. With John Wayne holding the Washington fort, we certainly won't need the U.S. Cavalry," she said, and grinned.

"What shall I report to the President, then?"

"Oh, that we're moving from phase one to phase two right on schedule, and that phase one went very much according to expectation."

"Oh, come on! I'll have to tell him a bit more than that, Dr. Carriol!"

She sighed. "All right, then tell him Hillier rose to the final nine, as predicted. That of the nine selected for phase two investigation, seven are men and two are women. One candidate has two children, SCB second-child approval, of course. Only two are unmarried, one man and one woman. Three of the nine are directly concerned with NASA and with Phoebus in particular, which just goes to show how important our space program has become, and how prominent its personnel have become. Tell him too that no candidate met with hard-line opposition from anyone present this afternoon."

"Any genuine household names besides Hillier?"

"Oh, I would classify seven as household names, including the two women. Two of the men are not nationally well known."

"Who didn't get to the top of the pyramid?"

"Impossible to tell, really, as I deliberately refrained from personally checking the hundred thousand names in the final sample. There must, I imagine, have been many who didn't even make it that far. As to who fell by the wayside between one hundred thousand and nine, I don't know that, either. If I did, Mr. Secretary, I would be defeating the whole purpose of Operation Search."

He nodded, swung round rudely to face the window. "I thank you, Dr. Carriol. Keep me informed," he said to the big sheet of triple-layered glass insulating him from the cold hard world outside on K Street.

She didn't go home at once. Section Four was deserted until she entered her own offices, where John Wayne looked up from his desk as she passed. Good John! If you want your boy to be a tower of strength to those around him, name him John. What's in a name? Dr. Carriol believed in names, only from personal experience. She had never known a Pam who wasn't a sexpot or a John who wasn't a tower of strength or a Mary who wasn't down to earth. Joshua Christian.

In the small safe built into the lower regions of her desk all the files were already tucked away, filling it to the last millimeter of its capacity. She brought them out and strewed them around the desk in front of her, frowning as she debated how many of the nine candidates' file copies she should retain, how many destroy. John Wayne walked in just as her hands crept over Joshua Christian.

"Sit down, John. What did you think?"

Section Four's chief recreation was rubbernecking to see exactly what was the nature of the boss's relationship with her odd-looking secretary, its chief amusement ribald and mostly physically impossible speculations about them; but when Section Four was not present to see Dr. Carriol with her secretary, he changed, became much less a neuter without becoming more a man. Only he and she knew that with the single exception of herself, he possessed the highest security rating in the entire Department; they both rated far higher than Harold Magnus.

"I think it went very well," he said. "A few surprises, one really unexpected. Do you want the minutes?"

"Done already?"

"In very rough draft only."

"Thanks, but no thanks. I remember enough to suit my purpose for the moment. Plenty to mull over." She sighed, put her fingertips against her closed eyes, then suddenly dropped her hands and looked at John Wayne piercingly; this was one of her favorite tricks, and a very effective one. It didn't work on John Wayne, nor had she intended it to. Sheer habit was all.

"Old Moshe Chasen really trumped the other two, didn't he? I knew that man was worth stealing from HEW!"

"A brilliant man," John agreed. "You're going to put him to work on relocation, of course."

"Of course."

"And have a look at his three candidates yourself."

"There's no way I'd let anyone else!" She gave a huge involuntary yawn and smothered it behind her hand, her eyes watering. "Oh, Lord, I'm flagging! Do you mind getting me some coffee? I don't want to take any of this stuff out of my office, so I'm going to stay for a while."

"Does that mean you'd like me to order you a dinner of some kind?"

"Too much trouble for you. If there's a sandwich left from the conference cart, that'll do."

"Who are you going to tackle first, ma'am?" Even when they were alone he never addressed her by her given name, and she never asked him to. It kept the status quo nicely.

She opened her eyes wide and contorted those expressive brows. "Why, who else than Senator David Sims Hillier VII? He's right here in Washington." She shivered, a new thought occurring. "Brr! Do you realize I'm going to have to go to Connecticut and Michigan for the other two? In *winter!*"

John Wayne smiled wryly; he had nice teeth, but this was not the kind of smile that showed them. "The new Alaska."

"Oh, not quite!" Then she shrugged. "Well, not yet."

In the end she stayed in her office until after the sun had risen. By then she knew the entire contents of every file, could place names and faces with even the most unimportant scraps of history, and hypothesize about possible strengths and weaknesses. Two of the candidates she had mentally discarded already, sure that when the big moment came they would not be worth mentioning to Tibor Reece.

Of course Dr. Joshua Christian was not one of the two candidates thrown onto that internal refuse heap; after reading the thick wad of notes and reports on him, she was intrigued. The man had coined some very quotable quotes, and his name for the increasing depression and lack of hope which had begun to creep across the country thirty years before she found most satisfyingly apt. Millennial neurosis.

He was going to be difficult to investigate, though. Already she had tabulated the points his dossier revealed as negative; he was a maverick in his field rather than well accepted and respected by his peers, he was not always very consistent in his attitudes, his operation was so small-scale it suggested he thought on a small scale, and there was a distinct possibility that he was riddled with Oedipal guilts. Dr. Carriol did not think highly of the internal resources of men in their thirties who still lived with Mother and to all intents and purposes had never embarked upon a sexual encounter with man or woman. Like the rest of the world, she found self-imposed celibacy a great deal harder to understand than any alternative sexual state, including the basest perversions; and this in spite of the fact that she was herself a frigid woman. The strength to resist one's primal urges was far more suspect than the weakness of succumbing to them or avoiding them. For he didn't have the eyes of a cold or an unfeeling man. . . .

No use just fronting up to his clinic out of the blue; after studying his file she thought him bound to view her with alarm and mistrust. Nor could she breathe the word "Washington" to him; his opinion of the federal capital and its bureaucracy was not exactly hostile, but it was wary. Unlikely too that she could wangle an invitation from him to visit by going through one of her many contacts in the Chubb psychology echelons. No, whatever approach she finally selected would have to seem so natural that he would find it—and her—unimpeachable.

Time to go home. Time to run the gauntlet of the main entrance and its daily suicides on the way to catch the bloody bus. It wouldn't be forever, she told herself. One of these days she would be numbered among the very few people anywhere in the country privileged enough to command a car for going to and from work. In the case of the general population, cars were permissible for vacation purposes only, a maximum of four weeks annually. Sensible and farsighted, turning vacation time into a precious interlude eagerly welcomed and mournfully farewelled. No government in the history of the United States of America had been so dedicated to sensibility and farsightedness as the one currently in office. But no government in the history of the United States of America had been so depressing, either. Hence the need for an Operation Search.

Georgetown was home, and home was charming. Since this part of the country was not yet consistently excruciatingly cold in winter, Dr. Carriol had decided to forgo the additional degrees of warmth boarding up the windows of her little red-brick house would have given her, preferring to look out all year round onto the delightful tree-lined street and the lovely old houses along its far side.

All her spare money and her prospects had been mortgaged two years earlier to purchase the house, and she was still groping through difficult financial woods. Oh, *pray* this major gamble of her professional career paid dividends to her as well as to the country! If Harold Magnus had his way, she would receive very little of the credit, but (and luck had nothing to do with it) she had managed the conduct of Operation Search in such a manner that he would find it very difficult to steal all her thunder.

There was no man in her life apart from the occasional date she accepted more to be seen to be dating than from any genuine desire to court an intimate relationship. She cared nothing for the sex act, so obliged indifferently whenever it was demanded of her without attaching one iota of importance to it, neither resenting nor thinking better of a man who did demand it. Washington was an easy city to become a mistress in, a hard city to find a husband in. However, a husband would not have suited her at all; he would have taken up too much of time and energy she needed to apply to her work. And a lover was basically a nuisance. Children she had taken care of when she turned twenty-five by undergoing hysterectomy. These were not times to pin your hopes and spiritual fires on domestic bliss anyway, but she was the kind of woman who genuinely adored her work and could not imagine any close relationship with a man rivaling it in her affections.

It was cold, so she changed into a glove-tight pure cotton velour track suit, put on thick socks of wool and a pair of knitted woolen bootees, and warmed her hands over the gas flame as she made herself a snack of stew and boiled potato, the stew out of a can and the potato fresh. Eating would warm her up. And then, even though the sun had risen several hours before, she could go to bed fueled for sleep.

III

When the fog came down at the end of January some aspects of life stopped and some started. Out of its all-pervading furtiveness it bred furtiveness. Things dripped hollowly. Footsteps came and went muffled, directionless, threatening. Two people could pass within a yard of each other and not know they had even passed. Some sighed and some died, each a kind of giving up the ghost. An infinite weariness, that fog, as if the very air itself gave up the ghost and sank in upon its own skin and in so doing condensed enough to make itself visible at last. So much sighed in it, so much died in it.

Among those who died in it was Harry Bartholomew, of a gunshot wound in the chest. He was cold, poor Harry, he was always cold. Perhaps he felt the cold more than others, or perhaps he was essentially weaker. Certainly if he had had his way he would have been heading for the Carolinas or Texas or anywhere in the warm south for the winter, but his wife wouldn't leave her mother, and her mother wouldn't leave Connecticut. Yankees did not venture south of the Mason-Dixon line for any reason short of a civil war, said the old lady. So each winter Harry and his wife stayed on in Connecticut, though Harry's job finished on November 30 and didn't start again until April Fool's Day. And the cantankerous ungrateful old lady gobbled up every bit of what precious little warmth the Bartholomews had. Harry's wife saw to that, and Harry went along because it was the old lady who had the money.

The result was that Harry became a criminal of the worst kind. *He burned wood.* His house was relatively isolated in the middle of its square six-acre block, so on windy nights he could get away with it fairly easily. Oh, what a difference that gloriously glowing mass of ignited carbon made!

Their stove dated back to the latter decades of the last century, when everyone had begun burning wood in the carefree days before local and state and federal authorities had clamped down hard. For the trees were going far too fast, and the cold damp air clotted around the huge increase in carbon particles to form genuine pea-soup fogs. The fogs kept getting worse. And worse. More and more people burned wood, more and more power was generated from coal.

At first the smokeless zones were urban and suburban only. Harry lived in the countryside of middle Connecticut, where the hills are gentle and rolling and the forests used to be extensive. Then wood as combustible fuel was completely outlawed; wood must be saved for paper and construction. And coal was to be conserved for generation of power, production of gas, manufacture of synthetic materials. Most precious of all, petroleum consumption was cut back to the barest minimum. The Smokeless Zones became a single Smokeless Zone affecting every county in the country, north and south.

People still burned wood clandestinely, but less and less as time went on; there were plenty of tree-loving environmentalists to form local vigilante groups, and caught offenders were punished drastically by the levying of huge fines, plus removal of privileges or concessions or both. But even knowing all this, still Harry Bartholomew went on burning wood, terrified, panic-stricken, haunted, incapable of kicking the habit.

The fogs no longer came down all winter long, as they used to during the final ten years before the burning of wood and coal in homes and apartments was completely outlawed, but they still came down whenever atmospheric conditions were right; the powerhouses, factories and institutions contributed more than sufficient carbon from their coal burning to the air when fog conditions were at optimum. And when the fogs did come down, they were a godsend to people like Harry Bartholomew. He had developed a method of stealing wood, and it worked.

62

A string line ran between Harry's house and the eastern boundary of his property, a low stone wall that cut him off from his eastern neighbor, Eddie Marcus. Eddie's property was a lot bigger than Harry's, something over sixteen acres, and it was solid trees because Eddie didn't farm. In the days before wood burning became so difficult and culpable, Eddie had lost many trees, but gradually his position as the local vigilante leader (Eddie was a militant Green Earther, as was his father before him) and the size of his threats made tree thieves look elsewhere. Until the night Harry ran his string line to Eddie's boundary wall and hid the big spool to which it was still attached in a cavity well camouflaged by leaves, as was the played-out length of string.

There the spool lay until a fog came. And when it did, Harry followed the string from his house to the stone wall, stepped over it, and played out more string. In the interest of speed he had elected to use a chain saw rather than an axe or a manual saw, relying on the deadening effect of the fog itself, the long distance between his boundary and Eddie's house, the fact that of course Eddie's house was well boarded up, and, in the event he was heard, his ability to make a quick getaway by following his string line. The chain saw he equipped with extra mufflers and while he used it wound it in blankets as well; a good mechanic, he had squirreled a little arsenal of spare parts away, and painstakingly repaired the damage all this swaddling did to the chain saw's overheated motor.

For five years he got away with stealing his neighbor's trees. Of course Eddie discovered the remains of Harry's depredations, but blamed them upon a man who lived behind him, with whom a feud had been going on for over twenty years. Congratulating himself upon his cleverness, Harry watched the hotted-up feud with glee, and cocksurely went on stealing Eddie Marcus's trees.

At the end of January in the year 2032 the fog came down with most satisfying thickness, coinciding with a thaw that had become almost unheard of in the midst of winter, a thaw that held promise of a rare early spring—and plenty more fogs, thought a very happy Harry Bartholomew.

He had stretched his string in a new direction, and followed the knots he had tied in it, confidently counting distance, over the wall, into the thick of Eddie's trees. But Harry's system failed at last. He ended up too close to Eddie Marcus's house, and the sound of his chain saw penetrated behind Eddie's sealed windows.

Grabbing the old Smith & Wesson carbine from above his mantel, Eddie plunged out into the fog. At his trial he protested that he had only meant to frighten the culprit. He called out a warning to the invisible tree thief to stand where he was or be shot, heard what he thought was a slight movement going off to his left, aimed the gun to his right, and pulled the trigger. Harry died immediately.

The case aroused a lot of mixed feelings in the state, and received a lot of publicity nationwide. The two trial lawyers were brilliant, and old foes. The judge was famous for his wit. The jury was composed of diehard Connecticut Yankees who refused to go south for the winter. And the public benches were packed with people to whom this case meant much, people who remained in Connecticut all year round, and suffered the cold dumbly, and didn't quite understand all the reasons why the government was so adamantly against wood burning, and now felt an unaccustomed stirring of old, buried emotions.

"I'm going to Hartford to sit in on the Marcus trial," Dr. Christian announced to his family after dinner one evening at the end of February.

James nodded, understanding at once. "Oh, half your luck! It will be fascinating."

"Joshua, it's too cold and too far from home!" cried Mama, who never liked to see him leave 1047 Oak Street, Holloman, while winter stalked outside; the memory of Joe's fate terrified her.

"Nonsense!" said Dr. Christian, uncomfortably aware of the reasons for Mama's distress, but knowing that he was going to Hartford no matter what. "I must go, Mama. It's cold, yes, but we've already had one massive thaw, and all the signs say this is going to be a short winter for once. So I doubt I'm going to run into a blizzard."

"Hartford is always at least ten degrees colder than Holloman," she said stubbornly.

He sighed. "I must go, Mama! Feelings are running very high, there hasn't been a situation in a long time so likely to air buried resentments about our current anguishes. A murder trial is highly charged to begin with, and this one in particular is connected to all the emotions right at the roots of millennial neurosis."

"I'd like to come with you," said James wistfully.

"Why don't you?"

"Not at this time of year. One is all the clinic can spare, and we've had a vacation more recently than you, Josh. No, you go, and tell us all about it when you come back."

"Are you going to try to talk to Marcus?" asked Andrew.

"I sure am! If they'll let me, and he's willing. He probably will be, because I imagine he's clutching at every straw that comes his way right now."

"Oh!" said Miriam. "You think he'll be convicted."

"Well, he has to be. It's really a question of what kind of sentence, isn't it? A matter of degree."

"Do you think he meant to kill, Josh?" she asked.

"Until and if I see him, I'd rather not hazard a guess. I know everyone thinks he did, since he assumed it was the other guy he was pointing the gun at. That's the trouble with loudmouths. But when the chips are down—I don't know. I'm not at all sure a man of Marcus's type would intend to kill unless he was physically surrounded by plenty of moral support in the shape of his fellow vigilantes. When he went out into that fog to see who was cutting down his trees, he was very angry, yes, but he was also very alone, and fog is the kind of substance that damps emotion right down very quickly. I don't know, Mirry."

Mary heaved a huge sigh and looked grumpy. "Then if you won't take James, I had better come with you," she said ungraciously.

Dr. Christian shook his head emphatically. "No. I'm going on my own."

She subsided, looking even more grumpy; and it never occurred to any member of her family that she was dying to go—*anywhere!* That her private thoughts and dreams were filled with visions of herself traveling, traveling, shriven by distance of the pain of unrequited love, shriven by distance of the tyranny of this suffocating, dedicated family. Yet if she had looked eager, bounced up and down a bit, clapped her hands in joy at the prospect of going somewhere, Joshua would undoubtedly have taken her. So what did that mean? That she didn't really want to go? No! No. It meant that they were stupid, unperceptive, so unconcerned with the welfare of Mary Christian that they couldn't be bothered levering up the edge of the façade to see what lay beneath. So the hell with them. Why should she help them? And yet—oh, to be free! Free of love, free of this hideous Cyclopseyed family. . . .

A daily bus covered the forty miles between Holloman and Hartford, a grueling journey because of the frequency with which the bus left the main highway to pick up and set down passengers. No between-town roads other than proper highways were ploughed in winter, just as the only in-town roads kept clear were bus routes.

Had the Marcus trial been scheduled a week earlier, the journey would have been a great deal easier. But the thaw had come and gone, the snow was piling up again, and the temperature had dropped below zero Fahrenheit. By the time the bus got to Middletown it was snowing hard, and it continued to snow all the rest of the way, making the journey longer and even more miserable.

His credentials had obtained him a room at a motel only a short walk from the courthouse; like all public hostelries the motel was allowed to heat its premises to a full sixty degrees Fahrenheit between 6 A.M. and 10 P.M., and to burn a gas imitation of a log fire in its residents-only dining room. When he came in to eat on that first night he was surprised to find the room almost full, until he realized that like himself the other guests were in town to follow the Marcus trial. Journalists mostly, he supposed; he recognized Maestro Benjamin Steinfeld eating alone at a corner table, and Mayor Dominic d'Este of Detroit at another table in the company of a dark-haired, white-skinned woman whose face looked vaguely familiar. As he passed he bent a puzzled stare at her over his shoulder; to his surprise, she responded with a small polite smile and bow of cool yet ready acknowledgment. Not a famous television face, then. He must indeed have met her somewhere, but where?

The hostess was tired, poor thing, he could feel it in the bruised molecules of air around her. So he sat down at the table just behind Mayor d'Este and his companion, and took the menu the hostess handed him with a specially sweet smile of thanks. And she received the smile, as people seemed to, he didn't know why, as if he had handed her a cup of some life-giving elixir. What a magical thing a smile is! he thought. So why then if one tried to preach the smile as bona fide therapy did it come out

66

sounding trite and shallow and banal, like a particularly bad greeting card?

The menu was far from intolerable, a fairly wide range of old-style Yankee or East Coast dishes from three kinds of clam chowder to pot roast to scrapple to Indian pudding. Oddly enough (considering the quality of Mama's cooking), he was always more interested in food when away from home, especially when, as now, the trip was not connected with the ordeal of a professional conference. He ordered the New England clam chowder, a London broil and Russian dressing on his salad, and deferred a decision on dessert until later, all this done with the same sweet smile for the waitress he had given earlier to the tired hostess.

Maestro Steinfeld got up to leave the dining room, nodding regally to this and that acquaintance, and pausing for a word or two with his television colleague from Detroit. The woman with Mayor d'Este was introduced to him, Maestro Steinfeld bowing to kiss her hand; this movement flopped his hair forward and thus allowed him as he straightened to throw his head back dramatically, settling his disheveled coiffure into place again as if it had been designed for just this contingency.

Dr. Christian watched out of the corner of his eye, amused. Then the first of his food came, so he bent his attention upon the big bowl of steaming milky chowder and discovered that its bottom was laudably full of minced clams and diced potatoes.

When the time came he declined dessert, for the meal had been almost too plentiful, fresh, and excellently cooked.

"Just coffee and a double cognac, thank you." He nodded toward all the occupied tables. "Quite crowded tonight."

"The Marcus trial," explained the waitress, mentally agreeing with the hostess's whispered aside to her that she was serving by far the most attractive man in the room. Oh, Maestro Steinfeld was gorgeous in a standoffish way, and Mayor d'Este was so handsome he looked a bit as if he was made of wax, but Dr. Christian was really *nice;* his smile said he found you genuinely interesting and likable, without giving you the slightest suggestion of a man on the make.

"They had to call me in to help," the waitress went on, and then added, in case this sounded as if she was not a professional waitress, "I don't work Tuesdays as a rule."

An up-country girl from somewhere like the "land of Goshen,"

Dr. Christian decided; unsophisticated and down to earth. "I didn't realize the Marcus trial was such a big issue," he said.

"It's going to be in all the papers," she said solemnly. "That poor man! All he wanted was a bit of wood."

"It's against the law," said Dr. Christian, his manner reassuringly free from disapproval.

"The law don't have a heart, mister."

"Yes, that's absolutely true." He looked at her left hand. "I see you're married. But you work."

"Gotta pay the bills, mister, they don't pay themselves."

"Have you had your child yet?" He asked because mostly when a woman had her child she gave up work.

"Nuh-uh. Johnny—he's my husband—says we gotta wait until we get a permanent relocation in the south."

"Very sensible! When do you expect to go?"

She sighed. "I dunno, mister. Johnny's gotta find a job there first, and it's gotta be some place where there's room. We've got our application in. Now—I guess we just wait."

"What does Johnny do?"

"He's a plumber with the Hartford city plant physical."

Dr. Christian threw back his head and laughed. "Then he'll find work somewhere warmer, never fear! Even the machines which replace men don't like dealing with drains."

She looked brighter, chirpier; it would be days before she stopped telling her family and friends about the real nice man she waited on in the motel dining room.

The coffee was good and the cognac a VSOP Rémy Martin, and the waitress was attentive about replenishing both cup and glass. Warmly replete, Dr. Christian found himself wishing for a cigar, a sure sign that he had found a rare degree of pleasure in dining. But smoking indoors was anathema, and outdoors tonight was no summer evening. So he contented himself with admitting to himself that it did him good to get away from the confines of home and clinic occasionally. A pity he found so little enjoyable in professional conferences; but no man could enjoy an environment rife with ridicule and contempt, all directed at himself. Whereas a murder trial—it fitted the bill very nicely.

He got to his feet a little regretfully, having added a generous tip to the bottom of his check, and wended his way slowly out of the room without remembering to look in the direction of the dark-haired woman he obviously ought to know from somewhere.

Behind him, lingering in the company of Mayor d'Este, Dr. Judith Carriol thought about the conversation she had shamelessly eavesdropped upon between Dr. Christian and his waitress. Most interesting! He had spoken to the girl so very kindly. An ordinary enough passage of civilities, but he had endowed it with real meaning, and the waitress had visibly blossomed. Charisma. Was that what it was? Was that what Moshe Chasen thought it was?

She frowned, but inwardly only; Dominic d'Este was in the midst of a monologue about the relocation program, the thrust of his argument a vigorous defense of continued federal funding of winters-only relocation. All he required her to do was nod occasional encouragement, so Dr. Carriol's mind was free to stray where it wanted. Charisma. This candidate most definitely did *not* have charisma. Warm and charming and personable though he was, he also had a tendency to be downright boring once he climbed aboard his hobbyhorse. As now. However, be thankful for small mercies, she told herself wryly; at least he wasn't one of those people who made sure their audience listened properly!

Senator Hillier was over and done with, an easy subject for one in her Washington position to get to meet without a meeting seeming odd. He had impressed her, but she had fully expected to be impressed. A most dynamic, intelligent, caring man. Brought up from silver spoon infancy in the old American tradition of public service without personal gain. And yet, and yet— Dr. Carriol had come away from a most enjoyable afternoon spent in his company with a profound conviction that Senator David Sims Hillier VII was deeply in love with power. Patently he neither needed nor craved the money power could bring any more than he did the status power could bring. No, he wanted power for power's sake only, and that to Dr. Carriol's way of thinking was infinitely more dangerous. Also, she agreed with Dr. Moshe Chasen; Hillier quite lacked charisma. The man had to *work* to capture those who swung into his sphere, you could see the cogs and wheels and gears churning nonstop behind his eyes. Charisma was definitely an effortless phenomenon.

By coming to Hartford she was killing her other two birds with the same stone, though the Mayor was not actually the reason she had come to Hartford. Dr. Joshua Christian had proven as difficult to get close to as she had felt he would be after reading his file for the first time. It was John Wayne who thought of putting private detectives on his tail. Brilliant! Not ten minutes after Dr. Christian had made his bus booking and his motel booking, Dr. Carriol was in the process of getting herself from Washington to Hartford.

And, hey presto, Mayor d'Este as well! Of course he would attend the Marcus trial; Hartford was a northern city, and his television program "Northern City" would be able to use the footage shot in Hartford for several different purposes throughout the season besides for airing the Marcus dilemma. So today she had devoted to the Mayor, scraping acquaintance through their mutual friend Dr. Samuel Abraham. Dominic d'Este knew enough of her to want to get her on-side, thinking she might come in handy during his perpetual struggles in Washington to secure work for Detroit. Thus Dr. Carriol had not found it hard to prolong her initial overture into an afternoon watching him direct his television crew, and then dinner à *deux*.

Good. The Mayor was finished with, undoubtedly. From now until May first she could concentrate entirely upon Dr. Joshua Christian, who in her mind was steadily acquiring the status of heir apparent to the outcome of Operation Search.

The following morning Dr. Christian came early to the courthouse, with Dr. Carriol a discreet distance behind him all the way from the motel. She waited until he had chosen a seat three rows from the back and in the middle, then she strolled into the same row, but remained on the aisle. She was careful not to glance in his direction. As people entered the row she merely moved up each time a little closer to her quarry. He had struck up a conversation with two women in the row in front of him, and from the way he was talking it was obvious they were the widow and mother-in-law of the murder victim. Only when the court rose to commence the session did he cease talking to Mrs. Bartholomew and Mrs. Nettlefold and direct his attention toward the podium; by which time Dr. Carriol was sitting right next to him.

It was a small courtroom with good acoustics because it was old and liberally bedizened with plaster excrescences, hanging lights, niches and differently textured surfaces; therefore it was a pity that the morning's proceedings were so dull. Such a room was made for vocal fireworks. The jury had been picked and sworn in the previous day without real opposition from the Defense, and now there seemed to be a mass of inconsequential

70

technicalities to get out of the way; finally the Prosecution rose to commence a long preamble presented not by the Prosecutor himself, but by an underling. Everyone dozed in the relative warmth except Dr. Christian, who gazed everywhere save toward the woman alongside him, eagerly drinking in every facet of this new experience.

When the luncheon recess arrived in due course, Dr. Carriol turned to face Dr. Christian quite naturally, as if assuming he was going to move out of the row in the direction away from her, and she intended to leave the same way. Her start of surprise was well done. She emitted the sort of noise loosely called an inarticulate exclamation, and looked searchingly into his face with the same expression she had used on the previous evening.

"Dr.—Christian?"

He nodded. "That's me."

"You don't remember? But why should you, indeed!" she said, the second part of her speech following too hard on the heels of the first to permit him to begin edging away.

He stood looking down at her politely, his attention caught by her eyes; they reminded him of the pond in West Holloman Park, murky amber water overlying thick green weed. Fascinating eyes which might harbor anything from crocodiles to drowned ruins.

He smiled back at her very warily, understanding that he was in the presence of a peer. "I have seen you somewhere," he said slowly.

"Baton Rouge, two years ago," she said.

His face cleared. "Of course! You gave a paper, didn't you? Dr.—Dr.—Carriol?"

"That's right."

"It was a good paper, I remember. The social problems peculiar to Band C towns. In fact, I thought you had a really excellent grasp of the logistics, but not much deep insight into either the spiritual problems or the answers."

His frankness took her aback; she blinked heavy white eyelids but was too good at concealing her thoughts to show more. No wonder his colleagues didn't like him! And could anyone so blunt possibly have charisma?

"I'm not alone in lacking deep insight," she said evenly. "Is it a quality you possess?"

"I think so," he said, not in the tones of an overweening conceit, but quite matter-of-factly.

71

"Then how about having lunch with me, Dr. Christian, and filling me in on what's wrong with the Band C towns?"

He had lunch with her, and he filled her in.

"The Band C situation is only one aspect of what I call millennial neurosis, but it's perhaps the most severe one. More severe certainly than the Band D situation, where people admittedly have to face the trek back north each spring too, but have their love of the land and their land-based occupations to sustain them. I know I'm not telling you anything you don't already know when I say that the Band C relocatees are industrial transplants from the poorer parts of the big northern and midwestern cities, and truly I'm not trying to patronize you. But have you considered the poverty of their *inner* resources? For one thing, they're not spiritually linked to the changing seasons the way the Band D people are, nor do they have the national togetherness of the Canadian Band E relocatees. And there are only so many ball games and hockey games and mardi gras they can attend during those idle months in winter quarters. They're not permitted a car for longer than a month out of the four they spend in the south all told. Bread and circuses didn't work all that well for the Romans, so why should they work any better now? Our urban proletariat is far better educated and more sophisticated than any other in the history of the world, including the present time. It needs direction. It needs a purpose. It needs to feel—*wanted!* Yet what it feels is utterly unwanted. The Band C people are poor, yes, but the bulk of them are not egalitarian at heart, they're genuine American elitists. In many ways they took the worst blows to pride and honor when we signed the Delhi Treaty. They've certainly taken the worst blows to comfort and convenience! Oh, sure, their winter quarters are undoubtedly more luxurious and better planned than their homes in the north and midwest, but I think they feel as if they've simply been bought off."

"So what's missing?" she asked.

"God," he said simply.

"God," she echoed.

"Consider their circumstances," he said, leaning forward eagerly. "In the last hundred years these are the people whose exposure to God has kept on shrinking. Fewer and fewer religious vocations, more and more churches closing—they lost the very real contact with God they had always enjoyed. All the major religions of the western world went through massive internal upheavals during the last century, designed by the various church higher-ups to make the churches more appealing to the masses. But the result was exactly the opposite. Church attendance went on falling, so did vocations. Only in smaller or more affluent communities were there any gains that may have lasted. Now they blame education of the masses, they blame increased prosperity of the masses, they blame television, they blame slackened morals—you name it, they blame it. There's a bit of truth in it all. But the chief blame lies within the churches themselves, for failing to be flexible, for changing outwardly while refusing to change inwardly, or for changing too late. Many people had gained an awareness of their own intrinsic goodness, and maybe that came out of education, out of a broadening world. People didn't want to hear any more how evil they were, nor were their lives so grindingly poor that the prospect of living in paradise in the next life was all that kept them going in this one. They had more, they wanted more, they felt entitled to more. In *this* life! Yet everyone betrayed them. Their churches, by not even trying to understand what they needed. Their governments, by curtailing their liberties, curbing their spending power, and subjecting them to all the nightmares of nuclear war threats. That, incidentally, is where you'll find if you dig the only upsurges in church attendance— when the possibility of nuclear war increased. But people shouldn't have to turn to God out of fear! They should turn to God as naturally as a child turns to its mother."

He sighed. "Well, the Delhi Treaty was a great leveler. Because in the end it was the very planet we live on that betrayed them most. The threat of nuclear war disappeared, so too did really irresponsible government. I think what happened between 2004 and the present time is so novel in many respects that no one has understood it well enough to deal with it positively. A great many of the nightmare situations which have dogged Man since the beginning of the race have actually diminished to relative unimportance—the prospect of mass annihilation, territorial usurpation, even starvation. People are looking at *living*, not dying! But the living is so strange. And they've lost God. The third-millennial world is a totally new kind of world. By its very nature it can't be hedonistic for anyone, yet it can't be nihilistic either! And we're doing the same old thing with the people— applying yesterday's concepts to tomorrow's realities, imposing

73

yesterday's facts on tomorrow's unrealities. Hanging on to the past, Dr. Carriol!"

"This isn't Band C you're talking about, Dr. Christian," she said. "It's everyone."

"Band C *is* everyone."

"You're not a psychologist, you're a philosopher."

"They're both just tags. Why do we have to tag anything, even God? Millennial neurosis is the result of the fact that the tags don't fit the goods any more. People don't know where they're going, or why they have to go. They're just wandering in a spiritual desert without the Godly star to guide them."

Her gut was crawling, shivering horrific tides of joy washed higher and higher up the shores of her mind. A new sensation for Judith Carriol, physical as well as intellectual. That was what he did to his audience. But how? Not the ideas themselves, interesting though they were. A something in the man. A power. A huge—oh, what was the word? *Was* there a word? It was his eyes, and his voice, and the way he moved his hands, and the tension in his sinews, and—and . . . When he talked, you *believed* him! He *made* you believe him! You looked into his face and into his eyes and you heard what he said, and you believed him. As if he had command of the universe. Or could have had, had he wanted.

"Let's get back to the Band C situation," she said, keeping her voice cool and level. Oh, what an effort that was! "You said you had some answers, and I'd like to hear them. I'm very much involved in relocation."

"Well, first off, relocation has to be reorganized."

She laughed. "People have been saying that for years."

"And rightly so. The problem stems from the fact that there was a big—I might almost say a mass—movement of people out of the northern and midwestern cities long before official relocation was even thought of. It started back about 1970, when the cost of winter heating began to drive industries south to places like the Carolinas and Georgia. Take my town, Holloman. Holloman isn't a victim of increased glaciation and the Delhi Treaty and relocation! Except for Chubb, Holloman was already dead by the turn of the third millennium. Every one of its factories had moved south. Downtown Holloman was boarded up ten years before I was born, and I was born at the end of the year 2000. The first people to go were the ghetto people, the blacks and Puerto

74

Ricans. Then followed the working-class whites and the middle-class whites—Americans of Italian, Polish, Irish and Jewish extraction. The bulk of the elderly disappeared to Florida, the WASPier elderly to Arizona. The young—including many with Ph.D.s who couldn't even find jobs as cashiers in supermarkets—followed the work. And the sun was where it all was at. One of my patients is an old man from East Holloman. I call him a patient, but I suppose these days he's more an institution with us than an actual patient. I can never bear to discharge people from the clinic if they continue to need us even after they're cured. This old man is just lonely, and we fill a gap in his life there's nothing else there to fill. Now his family had lived and worked in Holloman for five generations. He was one of five children born around the 1950s. By 1985 the father was dead, the mother had gone to live in Florida, his brother was in Georgia, one of his sisters was living in California, a second sister was married to a South African and living there, and the third sister was in Australia. That, he assures me, was typical of his neighborhood all through the last quarter of the twentieth century, and I believe him."

"I don't quite follow what this has to do with the plight of the Band C relocatees," she said, smiling to take the sting out of her words.

"What I'm trying to say," he said patiently, "is that for the Band C people, official relocation did not come like a bolt out of the blue. They had already been relocating themselves for years. The difference is that when relocation became a function of the government, they lost the option of choosing where they would go. Had those decades of voluntary relocation not gone before, I doubt they would have submitted. But glaciation and the Delhi Treaty were simply frosting on a cake they'd already been chewing so long they didn't notice the taste any more."

"But it isn't that we *want* to offer them no option," she protested. "It's just too big! Later on—"

"No, you mistake me. I'm not accusing Washington or anyone else of heartlessness, and I do understand very well the size of the task. The way relocation was planned was well-meaning enough, and all approaches to the problem were hypothetical. But splitting up the permanent and the winter-only people into different communities was the wrong thing to do. I understand why it was done—it's hard to trek back north in April if your neighbor's settled permanently in your and his new southern town. But the crux of the problem with the Band C people is their homelessness. What is home? Where is home? Is home the place where they rest between November and April? Or is home the place where they work between April and November? I can tell you what I think. I think the northern and midwestern cities already too cold to support industries without massive shoring up should be closed down altogether. Detroit, Buffalo, Chicago, Boston, the rest. I think with the possible exception of the Band D rural folk, all relocation towns should be made over into year-round centers where people can settle properly, live *and* work. I also think there should be a complete shakeup, full integration of Band C people with everyone else, on the same new streets in the same new towns. The old stratifications aren't necessary and shouldn't be perpetuated—nor should we be creating new ones. Everyone from highest to lowest suffers the SCB and lack of winter fuel and lack of private transport. Almost everyone has enough in common with everyone else these days to make it possible for everyone to get along together."

She smiled. "A bit garbled at the end, but I get it."

He didn't smile; she found herself wondering if indeed he had much sense of humor, and concluded he probably didn't.

"It isn't enough any more to live with self at the sole center of the personal universe. If it ever was," he said, half to himself. "Spiritually the Communists are very much better off than we, because they've got the State to worship. We love America passionately, but we don't worship it. Our people must find God again. They must learn to live again with God *and* self at the center of their personal universes. Only not the same old Judaic God distorted by yet another recutting. He's been demolished and put together again by so many men—Paul, Augustine, Luther, Knox, Smith, Wesley—and on and on. And He was a graft in the first place, between the God of the Jews and the Roman pantheon. He's a human concept. Yet God is not human! God is God, is ever and always simply God. I tell my patients, *believe*. I tell them, if they cannot believe in any existing concept of God, then they must find their own concept. But they *must* believe! For if they don't, they will never be whole."

Dr. Carriol caught her breath, visited by an enlightenment so clear and defined she saw a whole world unfolding; not a visita-

76

tion from God, any God, but a visitation from her own intellect. Without knowing it, he was telling her how and what to do.

"Oh, bravo!" she cried. Unimpelled by her conscious brain, her hand went out to rest on his. "I would dearly like to see you get your chance to prove your contentions, Joshua Christian!"

He blinked, taken aback at this fervid response after so much cool listening (he was not, he realized, used to cool listening). Then he stared down at the white slender sinister arachnoid fingers curled around his own; he removed them gingerly with his other hand. "Thank you," he said, rather lamely.

The mood was over. He had pulled down the shades and switched off the light, even to himself.

She rose to her feet. "Time to go back, I think."

That night in her room Dr. Carriol paced the floor, oblivious to the chill; the heating had been cut back severely at ten o'clock. All good guests were supposed to be abed and snuggled down by then, and if they were not, they had perforce to suffer the consequences.

Damn fool thing she did, touching him! From the moment he felt her hand he had shied away from her as if from acid. This was not a man to appeal to through his hormones. But still, if he could provoke a Judith Carriol into putting out her hand in the first place—what a man!

And somewhere between the midnight moon and the rising of the sun all misgiving vanished. Dr. Joshua Christian, unknown, untried, was the man. What a man. *The* man! If he could affect her that way, he could affect millions. No doubt about it. And finally she understood how tortuous were the ramifications branching out from the central conception behind Operation Search. Maybe all along her subconscious had divined what the overall pattern must be, but the layers of thought that had risen higher than that part of her she called her living consciousness had never sniffed down the alleyways and corridors she saw stretching away now. Yes. He was the man.

From here on in it was merely a question of logistics, getting the man to his millions. Something was working in his mind already, he was warm wax that only needed shaping.

However, a major overhaul of the relocation system was not the answer. *He* was the answer, complete in himself. In him they would find all their answers. In him they would find healing for their pain. And she was going to give him to them. She. No one else.

Somehow the woman had spoiled the whole of the rest of his day, thought Dr. Christian, lying in his bed between layers of down. It was not easy any more, controlling the tides that flowed sucking in and out of his mind and tossed the frail ship of his soul up and down and around as if he the person he the being he the living house no longer possessed true validity compared with that awful force working within him. All wondering and afraid, he debated the nature of that force, whether its origins were internal or external, whether he had generated it, or it had generated him, unknowing and uncaring, to fuel him and use him and toss him aside when his purpose was fulfilled.

He had to search. Through this long winter he had thought and thought and thought. That his time was running out, that he had something to do. But *what?* He didn't know. A mission? He didn't know! Yet he was aware that he would not be able to resist himself much longer. Resist himself doing *what?* He didn't know! He just didn't know what he had to do or how he had to do it.

And what was the significance of the woman? Such a very unusual woman, Judith Carriol. Mysterious. Her eyes were like lustrous but opaque pearls, layer upon ultrathin layer that a man would have to keep peeling off forever to come at the kernel of truth in their centers. Still and lissome, elegant and remote. Leonardo da Vinci would have used her instead of La Gioconda to produce his most memorable painting. Though indeed she was a painting. A self-portrait. The question he should be asking himself was, How cunning was her hand as artist? She had been wearing violet, a color exactly opposite to the color of her eyes, a color that shaded her thick white white skin with exquisite opalescent subtlety, and made her hair seem blue-black.

When she had touched his hand with her hand, he had undergone a presentiment. Not a thrill of the flesh; more the opposite, a thrill of the unflesh. And in the throes of the moment he knew she possessed meaning for him. So he became instantly hideously afraid, and recoiled from her. Now he lay without sleeping, thinking of all the things he least wanted to remember. He had his niche, he was happy and content in it. But why had she come *this* winter, the winter of his discontent, and made his vague restlessness more lonely and acute? Why had she come now? Patterns. Of course there was God. How else could a single thread make so much sense out of so much randomness?

She was not young. Forty, at least. He was good at delving beneath a well-preserved exterior to guess at real age. It would have been better had she been young. Youth was easier to spurn, youth was insecure and could be brought to blame itself without questioning why it was spurned. She was psychically perceptive, she was a knowing one. Not one to be turned away without a valid and intelligent reason. He didn't know why he should feel so incredibly strongly that he must succeed in turning her away, that he must go back to Holloman and the predictable tenor of his days. Could a man read his future in a woman's face? Could a future be so great, so awful?

Mama. I want my mother! I want my family! Why did I refuse to let James come with me? Even Mary would be better than this isolation. Why did I congratulate myself on slipping their delicate loving and serving leash?

And as the night wore on his eyes grew sloppier, their lids more willing to be flaccid. O sleep, great healer, take this pain from me! Give me peace! And sleep did. The last conscious vestige of thought he remembered when he was awake again was a steadfast resolution. That he would not let her steal his soul. That somehow, no matter what, he would remain his own man.

They both slept in, so neither of them went to the trial of Eddie Marcus the following morning. And they met quite accidentally at the street corner beyond the motel, he coming back from a walk, she starting out.

They stopped to look at one another, her eyes eager and bright and young, his eyes apprehensive and tired and old.

Then he turned and began to pace alongside her.

"Part of you," she said, her breath spreading as white as the snowy world, "is very happy in Holloman."

His heart lurched as his mind recognized the beginning of the fulfillment of a presentiment. "*All* of me is very happy in Holloman, Dr. Carriol."

"After listening to you through lunch yesterday, there's no way I can believe that. There's at least one part of you which cares too much about the whole world to be happy living and working in Holloman."

"No! I have no wish to be anywhere else or do anything else!" he cried loudly.

She nodded. In violet she had been enigmatic; this fine, agonizingly cold morning she was triumphant in scarlet. "That is undoubtedly true. Just the same, I want you to come to Washington with me. Today."

"Washington?"

"I work in Washington, Joshua. The Department of the Environment. I am the head of Section Four, but I suppose that news doesn't tell you a thing."

"No, it doesn't."

"Section Four is the Environment think tank."

"Then you have a very responsible position," he said, not knowing what else to say.

"Yes, indeed I do. I care about my job, Dr. Christian." She seemed unaware that a moment before she had called him Joshua. "I care enough to risk a rebuff, enough even to persist in the face of a rebuff. Because you are trying to rebuff me, aren't you?"

"Yes."

"I know you're a loner. I know what a brilliant little clinic you have in Holloman. I know you're completely dedicated to the individual approach. And I am not trying to wean you away from your chosen life and work, believe me. I'm certainly not about to offer you a job in Washington, if that's what's worrying you."

Her voice was beautiful, deep and lazy and tranquil; it washed over those who heard it like a fall of silk, and it could if it wanted mitigate the effect of the words it uttered. As it did now. Listening to it, Dr. Christian began to relax, to think of his fears if not as baseless at least as too morbid. She wasn't trying to persuade him to leave Holloman for good!

"I want you to come with me to Washington to meet one of my very dear colleagues. Moshe Chasen. You won't know the name, because he's not in our field. Moshe is a purely statistical analyst working in Section Four. On relocation. Since lunch yesterday I have done nothing but think about what you were saying, and I am very concerned that you and Moshe should meet before he gets into stride. You see, I have just given him the task of completely reorganizing relocation, and he's groping for the right direction to head. Come with me today! If he could talk to you, it would be a godsend for him."

He sighed. "I have too much work in Holloman."

"Nothing that can't wait a week, or you wouldn't have come to Hartford to sit in on a trial," she countered.

"A week?"

"Just a week."

"All right, Dr. Carriol, you can have your week. But not one minute longer."

"Oh, thank you! My name is Judith, if I didn't tell you that already. Please call me Judith! Because I intend to call you Joshua."

They turned back toward the motel. "I'll have to go home first," he said, thinking that might shake her.

But she had no intention of letting him shake her. "All right, I may as well come with you," she said, linking her arm through his cozily. "We can catch the night train from Holloman straight through to Washington. It isn't even out of our way."

"I'm not booked on the train."

She laughed. "No problem! I have priority status."

Dr. Christian had no choice save to give in.

They caught the noon bus from Hartford to Holloman with ten seconds to spare, Dr. Carriol sitting carefully hugging her glow of victory within her, Dr. Christian sitting silently wondering what he had let himself in for.

He didn't like being away from the clinic, though there was really no reason why he couldn't absent himself more often than he did; and she was inarguably right when she contended that he could spare the time to come to Washington if he could spare the same space of time to sit in a court. How to explain to her that the Eddie Marcus trial had been in the nature of a small vacation? And that a trip to the federal capital complete with serious conferences would be anything but a vacation? She was pushy, not the sort to take no for an answer once she had made up her mind to get a yes. He detested the feeling that he had been and was still being manipulated by her, yet on the surface he had no grounds for calling her conduct manipulatory. However, gut instincts were feelings he respected deeply; and his gut instinct about this trip to Washington was to get out of it at all costs.

She elected to walk the mile from the Holloman bus depot to 1047 Oak Street, declining to let him carry her suitcase.

"I travel light," she said, "on purpose, so I don't have to stand around looking weak and helpless, waiting for a nice man to rescue me. Such a waste of time!"

Outside his twin dwellings he lost his courage, a typical bachelor son unable to face his mother's inevitable curiosity. So he took Dr. Carriol into 1045 instead, put both their suitcases down in the back stairwell, and ushered her soberly through the inner door. What had originally been the kitchen of the bottom apartment was now a reception and waiting room. Empty. Thank God! They tiptoed through it into the hall.

Just as they approached his office, Andrew came out of it and stood stock-still, astonished.

"Back so soon? What happened?" But his eyes were on the woman behind his brother, too smartly clad in her scarlet to be a Holloman woman. She smacked of a big prosperous city.

"Judith, this is my youngest brother, Andrew. Drew, I'd like you to meet Dr. Judith Carriol. We were at the Marcus trial together, but Dr. Carriol thinks it's more important that I go to Washington than kibitz in Hartford. It seems she's got a week's work for me to do."

"Dr. Carriol! What a pleasure!" said Andrew. A startlingly handsome young man who looked not a scrap like his brother, he stepped up to her with hand extended. "Of course I know who you are, I've read your papers. James! James!" he called.

And then there were flurries of greetings, all that family she had read about in Dr. Christian's dossier and mentally catalogued as X or Y or Z. Much as she had expected. Yet she had greatly underestimated the quality of the relationship between Joshua Christian and the rest of them. They—*reverenced* him. He voiced a wish, and they were at once galvanized. He moved his hand, and they sprang to attention. How then had he managed to escape the taint of egocentricity? He *had* escaped it! But after a while she decided he simply didn't notice. To him, his family's behavior was absolutely normal. It was the way his world worked, had always worked. So he didn't attribute it to any personal power or authority; he just assumed he was filling the role his mother must have assigned him upon his father's death. His mother. Dr. Carriol was dying to meet his mother, about whom the file was quite informative.

She did meet his mother, but only after several hours had elapsed with patients and discussions and a general tour of 1045, from its waiting room at the bottom back to the occupational therapy rooms which filled the entire top floor. What a coup to have collared Miriam Carruthers! So this was where she vanished when she suddenly gave up her massive teaching job at Columbia!

The clinic was, Dr. Carriol decided, the neatest and most self-sufficient setup of its kind she had ever seen. You couldn't beat a family business when the members of that family loved working together and regarded one member as undisputed leader. And after watching Dr. Christian deal with a new patient, she could appreciate better the disclosures in his file about a cult following. He had no professional mannerisms, because what most others in his line of work had to be taught, he knew by instinct. And his patients sensed that. They also drew enormous spiritual strength from him. No wonder the old patients she talked to had never really lost their closeness to him, or their sense of belonging to an inner sanctum. The difference between a superlative clinical psychologist and the rest of the breed lay in a combination of personality and insight into the workings of minds other than his own. Dr. Christian knew how people ticked, he felt the depth of people's pain, and he loved people far more than he loved himself. Or his family. Poor family. He gave and he gave, but obviously always to strangers.

Given the world to deal with, she thought as she walked with him across the bridge from 1045 to 1047, he would bend the world. Only he must never suspect the world was given to him; he must always think he found it for himself.

Mama gushed and cloyed and simpered out of pure quietly frenzied nervousness; Mary had warned her of Dr. Carriol's advent hours earlier, and with considerable enjoyment—and a little embroidering of the truth. So Mama, tickled pink that her son had finally brought home the woman of his choice, and a fitting one at that, brilliant, sophisticated, in his own field—Mama gushed and cloyed and simpered. No fool, Dr. Carriol guessed why his mother was so flustered; during a lull which occurred just after Mama had persuaded them to remain long enough to eat dinner, Dr. Carriol found her eyes resting on Mary. Joshua Christian's only sister was standing well back from the group, and she was watching her mother's antics with dour—contempt? shame? Fair of face was Mary, but dark of soul; not evilly dark, not even maliciously dark, just dark because probably no one had ever kindled her light. In any family there always had to be one member less remarkable, less noticed than the rest; in the Christian family, that member was Mary.

His dossier had said nothing about the rest of the family's spectacular frost-fair good looks. Dr. Carriol made a mental note to circularize all the members of Section Four's investigative staff with a tart reminder that files were about human beings and therefore interesting comments on human physical characteristics were not only permissible, but mandatory. However, a large photograph of Joshua's father in a pale-green, gold-speckled Murano glass frame on a lacquer side table in the living room set Dr. Carriol's unspoken doubts to rest. He was the image of his father. The offspring had all thrown purely to one or the other parent, an interesting fact in itself.

How very beautiful his houses were! The bottom floor of 1047 especially was like walking into a Rousseau painting of jungle; it had the same unreal symmetry and magnified perfection of leaf, no spot of brown or curled edge or bare dead limb. If lions and tigers had appeared, and the place suggested they well might, they were sure to have a round-eyed Rousseau moonishness about them, not devoid of fang and claw, yet innocents in Eden. How could one remain sick of soul in this so beautiful environment? The future unrolled before her eyes in one staggering revelation after another, all named Joshua Christian. A way of living, an ideal of living, a place of living . . .

And Mama. Astonishing! The very last kind of mother she had expected was a silly one. Yet Mama was a silly woman. Oh, strong as an ox. Powerful. Not unintelligent in everything. Not weak-willed. But it was as if a part of her had never grown up satisfactorily—which would fit with her history of an extremely early marriage, of course, though not with her almost equally early widowhood. Dr. Carriol began to grasp the nature of Joshua Christian's upbringing, and understood better now why he was such a tremendous patriarch in spite of his relative youth. So much of what Mama had done was instinctual; not for one moment did Dr. Carriol believe Mama capable of cold-bloodedly fashioning her son in his present mold. She achieved what she wanted simply by wanting it single-mindedly, blindly, primitively. A rare accomplishment. And only possible because the unformed human clay she had produced out of her body happened by chance and genetics to be perfect for her purpose. That little boy of four had actually owned shoulders broad enough to take on the burden of fatherhood and chieftainship. No wonder his younger siblings reverenced him, and his mother shamelessly adored him. No wonder too that he had buried his sexual urges so deeply they would probably never plague him between cradle and grave. For the first time in her life Dr. Carriol experienced a surge of simple and very painful pity; poor little boy of four!

And finally, a fresh bag packed for Dr. Christian, they got themselves away on the night train for Washington. Dr. Carriol's brandishing of her certificate of priority had got them a private compartment, a luxury that rather opened Dr. Christian's eyes as to his traveling companion's real importance in the Department of the Environment. It was one thing to hear a job description from the mouth of the job's owner, quite another to experience these side effects. The porter brought them coffee and sandwiches without being asked, and for the first time in his life Dr. Christian found himself actually enjoying the sensations of travel.

But mostly he was conscious of a huge tired sadness that hung over his shoulders and draped itself down him like a clinging grey veil. Why should he feel that his coming to Washington with this woman was going to change his life out of all recognition? It was just a trip to see some data man, instill in the data man a bit of appreciation for the fact that the statistics he played around with on his computers were not abstractions but actual living people, souls and bodies, feelings, individual identities. By this time next week he would be back in Holloman going about his usual business. Yet he couldn't bring himself to believe that. There was something in the woman who sat alongside him (why had she chosen to sit alongside him instead of opposite him, surely a more normal choice for any woman on friendly but not intimate terms with her companion?) that she was not going to admit to, but that he felt. An excitement. A terrible drive. All to do with him. Yet they were not emotions generated out of sexual attraction or even sexual difference. Oh, Judith Carriol and Joshua Christian were extremely aware of each other as woman and man, but neither was the kind to fracture a delicate mental balance by yielding to grosser sensations. Neither of them lived for fleshly gratification, which was not to say they were indifferent to it or unattracted by it. She had long recognized the toll it took, weighed up how much she had of expendable energy, and brought the scales

85

crashing down on the side of intellect, of work. He could not have borne the spiritual weight.

The train slowed to an amble and voluntarily engulfed itself in the stygian warren of tunnels below Manhattan; only then did Dr. Christian find voice.

"I remember reading a short story once, about a train in these New York City tunnels that slipped through a little hole in the space-time continuum and was doomed for all eternity to travel in the darkness, rushing down one tunnel and up another, on and on and on. . . . I can believe that story, sitting here."

"Yes, so can I." Her voice sounded bled of vitality.

"Take us. If we were doomed never to emerge into the light again, what would we do, you and I, sentenced to sit here together for all eternity? What would we find to talk about? Would you finally have to be utterly honest with me? Or would there still be virtue in concealment?"

She stirred, sighed. "I don't know." Her head came round to let her eyes look at him, but he was so gaunt and pallid in the single wavering dim overhead light that she turned her head away again. Then, comfortably looking at the vacant seat opposite once more, she smiled. "It might be rather nice. Certainly I can't think of anyone I'd rather spend eternity with, and I don't mean that in a vulgar way."

"Vulgar!" He inspected the word closely, struck by it. "Now why did you choose that adjective?"

She ignored the question. "Well, if we wished hard enough, we might be able to force the train through that little hole in space-time. I've always suspected that the true seat of infinity is right inside the human cranium. No boundaries, if only we knew where we built our own, and could knock them down." Thank God she didn't have to look at him! Not only because she would have found his gaze unsettling, but because she wasn't sure how much he would read in her own. She lifted her chin, but continued to stare straight ahead. "You could do it, Joshua. You could help people find the walls they build inside their heads and show them how to knock the walls down."

"I do that already," he said.

"Poh! With a handful! What about the whole world?"

He went stiff. "I know nothing of the world outside Holloman. Nor do I want to know." And he withdrew.

So they sat silently and watched the darkness go by in unending sameness. An eternity of darkness. Was eternity dark, or was darkness eternal? His sadness insisted upon lingering like a musky perfume, and when at last the train drew into the gloomy dirty corridors of Penn Station he blinked in the miserable paucity of light as if it were a million candlepower all concentrated just on him, and he the cynosure of a million prying prurient eyes.

From Penn Station through the countless stops and starts and clickety-clacks they both slept uneasily, heads back against opposite corners of the long seat, feet propped up on the seat opposite, and only woke when the train drew groaning into Washington with the porter adding tympani by banging on the door.

This was Dr. Carriol's home territory, so she led the way out of the marble mausoleum of Union Station to the correct bus stop, with Dr. Christian stumbling dazedly behind.

"The Department of the Environment isn't far from here," she said, waving her hand in a direction he didn't know was roughly north, "but we'd better go home first and freshen up."

Miracle of miracles, the Georgetown bus had actually timed itself to connect with the train, on account of the fact that the train was an hour late.

The time was mid-morning and the month was barely March, but the day was relatively warm as well as sunny; they were predicting an early spring for the country this year. No sign of pregnant cherry trees yet, alas; everything bloomed later and later. O skies, breathe life into the trees! Dr. Carriol begged silently, sick to death of winter. Only let me live to see another froth of blossom! Am I too a victim of this millennial neurosis he talks about? Or am I simply his victim?

Her house looked and smelled fresh, for she had left one window at the front open a crack, and one window at the back too, and yet another down the sheltered side passage.

"The house isn't finished inside yet," she apologized, leading the way into the front hall and gesturing to him to keep his bag in his hand. "I ran out of money. But I fear you'll deem my decorating very dull after your houses."

"No, it's lovely," he said sincerely, approving in this warmer climate of the lightly graceful Queen Anne furniture, the brocaded chairs and sofas, the carpet that looked like shadow-dappled sunlight.

Up the honey-colored wooden staircase, down a honey-colored wood-paneled hall to a honey-colored wooden door. On its other side lay a bedroom, unfurnished save for a wide bed protruding from its far wall.

"Can you be comfortable here?" she asked doubtfully. "I don't have many guests, so the guest bedroom is about last on my priority list. Maybe it would be better to put you in a hotel—at Environment's expense, of course."

"I'll be fine here," he said, putting down his bag.

She indicated a door. "There's a bathroom attached."

"Thank you."

"You look beat. Would you like a nap?"

"No, just a shower and a change of clothes."

"Oh, good! I figured we'd go on over to Environment and have lunch there, then I'll introduce you to Moshe Chasen. You can spend the afternoon with him, then we'll go straight on somewhere for dinner." She smiled ruefully. "I'm no cook, I'm afraid."

And she shut the door and left him to himself.

IV

$D_{r.}$ Christian's mother and brothers were vigorously in favor of his relationship with Dr. Judith Carriol, his sisters-in-law and his sister just as vigorously against it.

Ever since Dr. Christian had gone without warning to Washington the feud had waxed and waned, and it reached new heights of passion on the following Sunday, when the family congregated early in the morning on the ground floor of 1047 to begin the day's attendance on the plants.

Armed with leaf feeder, baskets and small secateurs, the women were deputed to spray-feed, pick and prune, while the men uncoiled the various lengths of polyethylene tubing which led to water, and carried various sizes of steps. Every plant was watered by feel, which meant a hand had to be pressed against its soil to ascertain how damp it was before any water might be delivered. Long familiarity had bred a concentrated efficiency into the whole routine, for almost every plant was known with the intimacy of a close relative; how much water it drank, what pests it was likely to develop, which way its fronds or branches were likely to grow. Normally the only squabble was about leaf gloss, of which Dr. Christian disapproved strongly but his mother always hankered after.

"Perfection can be improved!" she would announce, and he would answer imperturbably, "No, Mama. It plugs up the stomates."

This day, when his absence might have won her a chance to apply leaf gloss and show him by how much perfection could be improved upon, she was too busy defending her most beloved child to think of leaf gloss.

"I tell you, it's the beginning of the end," said Mary in the voice of doom. "He won't think of us, he never does."

"Nonsense!" said Mama, carefully tugging at a half-dead leaf on a philodendron to see if it would come away without being forcibly yanked off.

"He will never be here because he and that Carriol viper are going to establish a grand practice in Washington. We will be relegated to the status of a branch office," Mary insisted. *Pfffft pfffft* went the feeder spray over the leaves of a Kentia palm.

"I don't believe you, Mary," said James, climbing a tall ladder to deal with a Boston fern in a basket. "What has Joshua ever done to make you think so poorly of him? When has he ever not thought of us?"

"All the time," muttered Mary defiantly.

"That's as unfair as it's unkind. All he's done is go off to Washington for a few days to see some Environment data analyst," said James from the top of his ladder.

"Analyst schmanalyst!" snorted Miriam, who could produce plenty of Americanisms when she so chose. "That was just an excuse the Carriol woman used to get Josh away from us so she could work on him. Honestly, sometimes Joshua is so *dense!* And so are you, Jimmy!"

Andrew had gone outside to fetch white-coated cup hooks and a battery-powered drill, but he returned in time to hear this exchange. "Jimmy, give me a hand with this Black Prince, will you? It needs another hook and tie," he said, setting up a ladder. "If you ask me, you women are just plain jealous of poor Josh's lady friend. All these years he's plodded on and never looked at anybody. Now he's found himself a girl. Well, I for one think that's great!"

"You won't when *she* takes over," said the Mouse gloomily, on hands and knees after erring plantlets of Sweet Alice that had seeded among a shallow tub of cacti.

"Takes over?" gasped Mama, too outraged to continue nipping seed pods off a huge chain-of-hearts before they burst and dewed the floor with fluff. "Garbage!"

"Bright red clothes at her age," sneered Miriam, whose hands were trembling so much she spilled as much soil as she managed to press around a needy begonia.

"She's a man-eater," said Mary. "And she'll ruin him, you just wait and see."

Mama climbed off her low set of steps and moved it to a pot of maidenhair all of two feet in diameter. "Joshua needs a wife, and the only kind of wife for him is one who can take a positive part in his work. Judith Carriol is perfect in every way."

"But she's old enough to be his *mother!*" squeaked the Mouse, indignation overpowering diffidence.

"For God's sake, you women, lay off!" cried Andrew, goaded. "Josh is plenty old enough to make his own plans, his own decisions, and his own mistakes if necessary!"

"Come on now, what harm can Dr. Carriol really do?" James asked, trying to make peace. "It's high time Josh let his hair down, you know. He never has, and that's a fact ought to be worrying all you possessive females a lot more than his going off with Dr. Carriol."

"*Why* has Joshua never had an affair?" asked the Mouse, burying her head deep into a clump of cymbidiums, appalled at her own daring in asking what she had long burned to know, but aware that today's unusual familial friction made today the only chance she might ever get to ask her burning question without throwing the family spotlight on herself for asking.

"Well, Mouse, it isn't that he's not human," said James slowly. "He's not a prude either, as I'm sure you know. But he's a tremendously private person, and on this subject he's never been forthcoming. So—your guess is probably as good as mine."

I love him, said the Mouse, but not out loud. I do love him, I do, I do, so much. . . . I married his brother, and then I found out it was him I loved.

"I am determined he'll marry Judith Carriol!" said Mama.

"Over my dead body he will!" snarled Miriam.

"Oh, Mama, I'm surprised at you," said Mary derisively. "I know you don't think things out before you make up your mind, but—do you really want to dig your own grave? If Joshua marries a woman like Judith Carriol, you'll be made totally redundant."

"I don't care," said Mama bravely. "Joshua's happiness is all that matters."

"You are so right!" said Mary.

"Shut *up!*" yelled Andrew suddenly. "Not another word about Josh and his own private business!"

The rest of Sunday's plant duty was done in silence.

Dr. Christian and Dr. Chasen had indeed taken to each other, much as Dr. Carriol had predicted.

Their first meeting had given rise to curious doubts in Dr. Christian, or maybe for doubts read qualms. Or inchoate fears. He didn't know how to catalogue what he felt. Dr. Carriol had brought him into the part of the Department of the Environment known as Section Four, and down yet more corridors to Dr. Moshe Chasen's big, paper-littered office.

"Moshe, Moshe!" she had called out, bursting in on him unannounced. "Moshe, I've brought someone to see you! I met him in Hartford and I heard more sense from him in a few minutes about relocation than I've heard from the whole of Environment in years. So I persuaded him to come to Washington and talk to us. This is Dr. Joshua Christian. Joshua, I'd like you to meet Moshe Chasen, who is just starting out on the gargantuan task of revamping Environment's relocation program."

But Dr. Christian could have sworn that somehow Dr. Chasen no sooner set eyes on him than a peculiar kind of recognition took place, not the vague seen-you-somewhere-before reaction Dr. Carriol had produced for him in the Hartford motel dining room, but something more profound by far. The only way Dr. Christian could satisfactorily type it in his own mind was by classifying it as similar to the kind of reaction a man would have when accidentally introduced to the person he knows to be his wife's lover. Yet the reaction in Dr. Chasen passed so quickly that Dr. Christian could not even be sure it had actually existed. By the time Dr. Carriol had reached the end of her short speech, Dr. Chasen was on his feet, was smiling with polite but sincere warmth, and was extending his hand in impersonal welcome.

Indeed Dr. Chasen had recovered from his stupefaction very quickly, because his job—nay, his whole career!—was on the line. A typical Carriol action, to waltz in gaily trailing a man's fate behind her, with never an allowance for human weakness. Or the decent thing. He wished he didn't respect her so much, and that for him, respect predisposed liking. He supposed too that if he looked at her action in another way, her unheralded advent was actually a compliment to his own ability to dissemble.

Ever since she had pulled him off Operation Search he had

been smarting, not fooled by her sweet words and promises. Oh, Moshe darling, you're too good to waste on phase two, I need you to streamline and update and reorganize the whole relocation program! As if something that big and omnipresent couldn't have waited a few more weeks. No scientist worth his oats likes being pulled off a project he has worked on before its conclusion, no matter how enticing the new project dangled as bait or consolation prize. And though by nature she was a born paper person and did that best, she was still surely enough of a scientist to appreciate what an amputation job she had done on him. For five weeks he had scarcely summoned the necessary enthusiasm, freshness and detachment something as huge and meaty as relocation deserved. He just sat trying to force himself into the right mood while images of what was happening on phase two of Operation Search knocked frantically at every entrance to his brain. And while he fought himself, he fought equally hard to understand the enigma of Judith Carriol.

Then he nearly blew it. He nearly let his face show what it meant to him to have Dr. Joshua Christian walk through his door—not a file, not one of over 33,000 units, but the flesh and blood *man*. His face he knew he had managed, yes, but he wasn't as sure of his eyes, and sometimes he would catch Dr. Christian looking at him in a way which said that this very sensitive and acute fellow had noticed something, but luckily didn't understand what, because he didn't own so much self-importance.

That had been Thursday. In transports of gratitude he had realized how great and how subtle indeed was his reward for his work on phase one of Operation Search. He was to witness the unfolding of phase two, yes, but more than that; he was being told by his chief that he had pulled the rabbit out of the hat, that Operation Search was not after all a mere drill, that it was possessed of a phase three, and that he was to be permitted to stand by in full knowledge of—of *what*, in God's name?

Thus between Thursday and Sunday of that week, Dr. Chasen accomplished more fruitful work on the conundrum of relocation than he had since commencing five weeks earlier. For one thing, he understood now that he had his chief's wholehearted approbation; and for another, by his side, talking, worrying, dissecting, criticizing, was Dr. Joshua Christian. The winner and new champion. But champion of *what*?

The two men really had taken to each other. So the time and the days between Thursday and Sunday passed in an interested, happy collaboration that brought sufficient novelty and freshness to each man to make the other's presence a joy. However, while Dr. Joshua Christian merely went on liking Dr. Moshe Chasen, Dr. Moshe Chasen passed from being intrigued to being fascinated to loving to loving deeply.

"I don't know why," he told Dr. Judith Carriol during one of their infrequent chances to speak together without the third member of the trio.

"Nonsense!" she said crisply. "Simple hedging, Moshe. Of course you know. Kindly elucidate."

He leaned forward across her desk. "Judith, have you ever loved anyone?" he asked.

Her face didn't change. "Of course I have!"

"You wouldn't just say that, would you? Because I don't think you're telling me the truth."

"I only lie when it's necessary, Moshe," she said without discomfort at admitting it, "and it is not necessary for me to lie to you in this present situation. I do not need to protect myself from you, because you can do me no harm. I do not need to conceal my motives from you, because you can't affect the outcome of my motives even if you guess them. And you're hedging, my friend, but you're not going to deflect me. Kindly elucidate."

He sighed, an exasperated sound rather than a defeated one. "I'm trying, already, I'm trying! Look, you wanted a particular man. The man. A man who could draw people to him without even trying, but a man who would not be a threat to our nation or our way of life. Charisma, right? Like I told you five weeks ago, he's got it! So how do I know why I love him? He *makes* you love him! Don't *you* love him?"

Her face and eyes remained calm. "No."

"Oh, come on, Judith! That's a lie!"

"No, it is not. *I* love—the possibility of him. Not him in himself."

"God Jesus, you are a hard woman."

"Still more hedging, Moshe. Why do you love him?"

"There are any number of reasons. He's given me the biggest boost of my career, how's that for a start? You don't fool me, I know you've picked him. I don't know what for, but you've picked him. How could I not love the man who has brought me that satisfaction, given that he was picked in the first place because he can make people love him? How could I not love a man who sees so clearly? How could I not love a man who loves so

94

much himself? How could I not love a man who is so *good*? I don't mean good at his work, I don't mean good at being a man. I mean just *good!* I never met anyone good before! I always thought if I did, I'd be bored out of my mind, or I'd hate his guts. But how can you hate a truly good man?"

"You could if you were an evil one."

"Well, he makes me feel evil often enough," said Dr. Chasen with reminiscent emotion. "I start talking about the trend I see in this or that group of statistics, and he just sits there, and he smiles, and he shakes his head, and he says, 'Oh, Moshe, Moshe, they're people you're talking about!' And I feel—well, maybe evil's the wrong word. I feel—ashamed. Yes, that's it. Ashamed."

She frowned, suddenly out of patience with him, she did not care to ask herself why. "Mmmmm!" she said. And got rid of Dr. Chasen as quickly as she could. Then she sat at her desk and thought.

On Monday morning Dr. Carriol suggested they not go straight from Georgetown to her place of work on the bus; instead, she suggested a walk through the Potomac parks and gardens on their way Environmentward. Her excuse was that it was a beautiful day, which indeed it was, warm, cloudless of sky, sweet and still of air.

"I hope you don't think I've wasted your time in bringing you to see Moshe," she said as they wandered through West Potomac Park.

He answered without hesitation. "No. I quite see why you wanted us to meet, and I appreciate—no, I applaud—your reasons for talking me into coming. Moshe is a truly remarkable scientist. He's brilliant and original. But like all his kind, he's more in love with bits than bodies. As a man he's not nearly so brilliant or original."

"Were you able to change his way of thinking?"

"A little. But the moment I go back to Holloman his memory of me will begin to fade, and he'll end up reverting completely to type."

"I didn't expect you to be a defeatist."

"There's a big difference between realism and defeatism. The answer, Judith, is not to change the Moshe Chasens. The answer is to change the people who comprise his information."

"How would you do that, Joshua?"

"How would I do that?" He stopped on a grassy slope that slid away above him and below him, steep in its tilt; she noticed that he did not stand awkwardly, though most would have needed to be awkward in order to retain balance. Maybe that was because he was awkward in repose, all arms and legs, but give the arms and legs something difficult to do and they were gracefully at home doing it.

"Yes, how would you do that?" she repeated.

One moment he was standing easily, the next moment he had collapsed amid a tangle of long bones, and had to sort them out until he was sitting comfortably on the slope with his arms about his knees.

"I would—I would tell them that the worst of the shock is over. That the time for self-abnegation is past. I would tell them to pull their pride out of the mud and their feelings out of the freezer. I'd tell them to accept their lot and get moving to live with it. So we're cold in winter and we're going to get a lot colder. So along with every other country in the northern hemisphere at least we're having to deal with mass migration away from the pole. So we're saddled with the one-child family. Well, we've got to stop harking back to the good old days and bemoaning our fate and passively resisting the inevitable. We've got to stop yearning for yesterday, because yesterday is gone and it can never come again.

"I would tell them to get started on tomorrow, Judith! I would tell them only they themselves can throw off this millennial neurosis, by thinking positively and living positively. They have to realize that today we must suffer, because more passed away with the old millennium than just a milestone passed. Today we must suffer, and nostalgia is the common enemy. I would tell them that the tomorrow of our children's children's children can be more beautiful and more worthwhile than any age since the dawn of Man—*if* we start to make it so now. I would tell them that the one thing they cannot do is produce their pitifully few children in the old mood of indulgence and relaxation. Our children and their children and every generation thereafter must be *strong*. They must be reared to obtain their pride out of their own accomplishments and their own hard work; they must not be reared to rest on their parents' laurels. And I would tell every American of every generation, including my own, not to give away too freely what they have worked so hard to win. Because it will not earn them the gratitude and friendship they imagine it must, even from their own children."

96

"Well and good. You're advocating work, self-help, and a positive attitude toward the future," she said thoughtfully. "So far not very original."

"Of course it's not!" he snapped, nettled. "Common sense never is original! And what's so desirable about originality, anyway? Sometimes it's the oldest and hoariest commonplaces that people see least clearly, because everyone who ought to be guiding the people is trying so desperately hard to be original! Common sense is common sense is common sense, men have owned it since men were!"

"Granted. Bear with me, Joshua, I'm not playing Devil's advocate for kicks. Go on, what else would you tell them?"

His voice dropped to rumbling, purring warmth. "I would tell them they are loved. No one seems to tell them they are loved any more. That's a large part of the trouble. Modern administrations are efficient, caring, dedicated. But they dismiss love the way an insecure and weak man will neglect to tell his wife or his mistress that he loves her because, he will say defensively, surely she ought to know that without being told. But oh, Judith, we *all* need to be told we are loved! To be told you are loved lights up the day! So, I would tell them they are loved. I would tell them they are not evil, they are not festering with sin, they are not beneath contempt, they are not simple nuisance value. I would tell them that they already have every resource they need in order to save themselves and make a better world."

"Concentrate on this world rather than the next?"

"Yes. I would try to make them see that God put them here for a purpose, and that that purpose is to make something of the world He put them in, not channel their thoughts into an existence they can only enter by leaving this world, by dying. Too many people are so busy earning salvation in the next life that they only end by screwing this one up."

"You're drifting from the point," she said, mostly to needle him; she wanted to see how well he coped with extreme and niggling skepticism.

"I'm groping, I'm groping, I'm groping!" he said between his teeth, pounding his fists on his knees three times in time to his words. Then he sucked in a huge breath, which seemed to calm him, and when he spoke his voice was stern. "Judith, when people turn to me for help, they look at me with a plea for help in their eyes, and that's so easy! Where you are looking at me the way you'd look at a specimen under a microscope, and I don't

97

even know why the hell I sit here putting up with it! You're not interested in my views about God or Man, you're only interested in—what exactly *are* you interested in? What kind of things do interest you? Why do I interest you, because apparently I do, and I shouldn't! You seem to know so goddam much about me, and I know nothing about you! You're a—a—a mystery!"

"I'm interested in setting the world to rights," she said coolly. "Maybe not the whole world. Just our part of it, America."

"I can believe that, but it answers nothing."

"There will be time later to worry about me. Right now it's what you are that's important."

"*Why?*"

"I'll tell you in a minute, if you'll tell me more about you and what you are and what you think."

He gave a Bronx cheer, loud and derisive. "Well, if you insist on tagging me, call me a meliorist."

It hurt to admit he had used a word she didn't know, but her curiosity was too great for her to salve her dignity by letting the word go by now and looking it up later. "A meliorist?" she asked.

"One who believes the world can be made an infinitely better place through the efforts of Man rather than through the intercession of God."

"And you believe that."

"Of course."

"Yet you also believe in God?"

"Oh, I'm sure there's God," he said very seriously.

"I notice that you never preface God with the indefinite article. Never 'a' God. Simply—God."

"God is *not* indefinite, Judith. God just is."

"Oh, fuck all this, I'm getting nowhere!" she said violently, and leaped to her feet so that she could look down into his face, her own face pointed and wide-browed because she had tilted its chin down.

He laughed up at her joyously. "Oh, fantastic! I've found a chink in your armor at last!"

"No you have not!" She was angry. "I don't have any armor! Do you want to hear a riddle?"

"A riddle about what?"

"If you can answer it, Joshua Christian, you will know everything there is to know about Judith Carriol."

"This I've got to hear. Hit me!"

> "Bright is the ring of words
>   When the right man rings them,
> Fair the fall of songs
>   When the singer sings them.
> Still they are carolled and said—
>   On wings they are carried—
> After the singer is dead
>   And the maker buried."

He looked blank, said nothing.

"Stumped?"

"You're just getting back at me for using a word you didn't know," he said, only half joking.

"Not at all. Can't you solve it?"

"I'm no Oedipus. It's pretty, but unintelligible."

"All right then, I'll be less abstruse. But not about me. About you. Why I'm so interested in you."

He grew immediately attentive and serious. "This I've got to hear. Shoot."

"You're a man of ideas, Joshua Christian. Important and I venture to say imperishable ideas. I'm not a person of that kind myself. Oh, I do have ideas, but mostly about how to implement and channel other people's original thought. I want you to write a book."

That surprised him. He got to his feet and stood not beside her but lower on the slope, so that they saw eye to eye. "I can't, Judith."

"There are ghosts," she said, turning away and commencing to walk carefully down the slope.

He followed. "*Ghosts?*" He interpreted the word in its supernatural sense, so far from her train of thought was he.

"Oh, Joshua! Not specters! People who write books for other people."

"A ghoulish word for a ghoulish occupation."

"You have a great deal to offer people, and you should be offering it to more than the small amount of people you can see in clinic. So, since you feel you can't write, why not a ghost?"

"I do have a lot to offer people, I know that. But only in the flesh."

"Nonsense! Think of it this way. At the moment the only people you can help are a small number in Holloman. I agree, you did exactly the right thing in not making your clinic larger and your patient intake so big you'd never be able to keep track of them all yourself. Your kind of treatment program is intensely personal, and it depends on you rather than on any training you could give to other therapists. I exclude your family, because they're a special case, they're really offshoots of you. But a book—not a textbook for the experts, just a simple book for the people out there who desperately need to hear the message you *want* to disseminate—such a book would be a godsend! You can put yourself into it in a way you can't in any other form except personally, and we have already admitted the limitations of that approach. A book can reach literally millions of people. With a book you could have a profound effect on millennial neurosis throughout the country. And maybe the world when it's ready to hear. You say they need desperately to be told they're loved, and that no one is telling them? Well, you tell them! In your book! Joshua, a book is the only answer!"

"A fine idea, I'll give you that, but impossible! I wouldn't even know how to begin."

"I can show you how to begin," she said persuasively. "For that matter, I can even show you how to end. Oh, I don't mean I would write the book for you! But I can find you a publisher, and a publisher will find exactly the right person to collaborate with you on a book."

He chewed his lip, torn between eagerness and fear. A chance at last. And what a chance! How many people might he reach through a book? But if it didn't work, would he only succeed in making matters worse? Wasn't it better to continue to help the little number he did help in Holloman than to interfere with the lives and welfare of many thousands of people he would never even know by name? A book could reach people, yes, and it was personal provided he made sure it said what he wanted to say, yes. But it wasn't like seeing people in a clinic situation.

"I don't think I want that kind of responsibility," he said soberly.

"You do, you know! You love responsibility, you thrive on it. Be honest with yourself, Joshua! What really turns you off the whole idea is that you're not sure it will truly be your book, because you'll need help in physically writing it. That's understandable, because you're as much a doer as you are a thinker. Look, the reason I want this book from you is because your ideas are so worthwhile. And you've got the guts to carry a spiritual message. That's rare these days, and I agree with you, I think people need spiritual help more than any other kind. I don't blame you for being scared," she said, her eyes and her face earnest as she turned them up to search his. "But you *must* produce that book, Joshua! It is the beginning of the way to reach the people."

Such a beautiful world! He gazed around it, trying to give himself new, innocent eyes. This was the world he had tried and would try his hardest to help preserve, to see it at some distant date in the future once again the paradise of loveliness and comfort it should be and probably used to be before Man overran it. Man could learn! Man must learn! And underneath his fear and doubt he knew that he, Joshua Christian, had a very real and very significant contribution to make. He had always known that. When they wrote of men like Napoleon and Caesar they referred to it as a "sense of destiny." He had that sense, too. But he didn't want to think of himself as a Napoleon or a Caesar! He didn't want to feel chosen and special and privileged. He didn't want to think that he could be mistaken enough to interpret his own ability as better than anybody else's. Fatal, to start manipulating the lives of others in the belief that your own role as a chosen one qualified you to do so—nay, demanded that you do so! And yet and yet and yet . . . What if this opportunity being offered to him now was the right opportunity, the golden knocking one-and-only opportunity that if ignored would never come again? What if he turned this chance down and as a result his country went down into ashes? When maybe—just *maybe*—he could have helped significantly to save it.

Did he dare think of his future in those terms? But had he not already thought of such a mission, time and time again in his dreams and of late in his waking hours as well? Oh yes he had, but only, he told himself, now frantic for excuses, as a child dreams of chocolate factories and no school and a self-exercising self-feeding puppy. Not as a reality! Not out of a sense of his own exclusiveness, except deep inside where surely every man and every woman ever born also thought of himself and herself as uniquely exclusive and precious.

What if he did turn this opportunity down and his country did perish because its people wandered alone and unguided too long? When maybe—just maybe—he might have made the contribution that saved it and them? Or maybe he was meant to serve as a precursor for some other man, a stronger and better man than he, but for whom he was necessary to pave the way. . . . After all, he thought, chewing his lip and staring out at dogs and birds gamboling in the sunny park, could any contribution he possibly had to make screw the world up worse than it already was? Could anything he was capable of doing possibly make so much difference? Wasn't thinking it might merely another form of exclusivity? Oh, could could could could could might might might maybe maybe maybe maybe . . . *If!*

Was she sent to ask it of him? Who sent her? *God?* No, it was no part of God's policy to intervene personally, even by proxy. Did the Devil send her? But he was not so sure the Devil existed as he was sure God did. It seemed to him that the invention of a Devil was more necessary to the psyche of Man than the invention of God. God was. God is. God will be. But the Devil was a whipping boy. Evil existed, but as a pure spirit; it had no form, no hoofs or tail or horns or human mind. Ah, but that was God! God had no form, no arms or legs or genitalia or human mind. Yet God's pure spirit was knowing, cognizant, organized. Where Evil was just a force.

Was she any more than she purported to be, a senior federal public servant of the United States of America? Benign. Malign. Question mark. That was the real trouble. Life was one unpredictable, incomprehensible question mark. You grabbed it at the top, and you slid down it; you grabbed it at the bottom, and you could get no higher.

"All right then, I'll try," he said tensely, hands bunched into fists, trembling.

She didn't make the mistake of going into rhapsodies, she just nodded briskly and said, "Good!" Then she started walking faster, back in the direction of Georgetown. "Come on, my friend, if we get moving now we'll make the New York train this afternoon."

"New York?" he asked stupidly, not yet recovered from the shock of his answer.

"Of course New York! That's where Atticus Press is."

"Well yes, but—"

"Yes but nothing! I want to get going on this now! I can spare the time from my work this week, but next week, who knows?" She turned to grin at him so bewitchingly he couldn't not grin back. And he felt better immediately, letting the reins slide entirely to her who knew so much about everything he didn't know, like books and publishers. She was a person who knew how to pull strings, and that was an art he had never mastered, never would. Besides, it was enough for the moment to have made the decision. Let her carry him until he got his breath back. How-

102

ever, it did not occur to him that the last thing in the world she wanted for some time to come was for him to get his breath back.

"We have to see Elliott MacKenzie right away," she said, walking even faster.

"Who's he?"

"The publisher at Atticus. Luckily he happens to be a very old and dear friend of mine. His wife and I went to Princeton together."

The Atticus Press owned the seventy-floor building in which it occupied the bottom twenty floors, and had split off an annex of the main foyer which served as entrance to the publishing house only. When Dr. Christian and Dr. Carriol walked into that private vestibule the next morning, they were greeted like visiting royalty. There was a beautifully dressed woman executive waiting for them; she escorted them immediately to the one elevator Atticus, being more than ten stories and less than twenty-one, was allowed to operate, and she put a special key into its controls that permitted them an uninterrupted ride all the way to the seventeenth floor.

Elliott MacKenzie was waiting outside the elevator, a hand already warmly extended to Dr. Christian; he had a kiss for Dr. Carriol's cheek. And then they were settled in his book-lined office with coffee, the woman executive introduced as Lucy Greco. Polished-looking people, MacKenzie and Greco, he tall and trim and elegant and sandily handsome and supercharged, she an attractive little middle-aged bundle of quivering energy.

"I must say when Judith broached the idea of your book to me I was very excited," drawled Elliott MacKenzie with the faintly nasal tone and rigid jaws which denoted one whose pedigree and social circle were impeccable.

When broached . . . very excited . . . Dr. Christian went numb, his belly lurching about like a child on roller skates for the first time.

"Lucy is going to act as your editor," Elliott MacKenzie went on. "She's had an enormous amount of experience working with nonwriters who have something to say we can't afford not to read. It will be her job to get your book on paper, and she's the best in the business."

Dr. Christian looked immensely relieved. "Thank God for that! A coauthor," he said.

But MacKenzie frowned with the regal displeasure of a man

103

who not only sat in the publisher's chair but also owned the publishing house. "Of course not! *You* are the sole author, Dr. Christian. They will be your ideas and your words. Lucy is simply going to act as your Boswell."

Dr. Christian got stubborn. "Boswell," he said, "was a biographer. Dr. Johnson did his own writing, and no one was better."

"An amanuensis then," said Elliott MacKenzie smoothly, not betraying the fact that he had disliked being caught.

"But that's not fair," said Dr. Christian.

Mrs. Greco entered the fray. "Of course it's fair, Dr. Christian. You must learn to think of me as a midwife. My task is to pull the most beautiful healthy book baby out of you as quickly and painlessly as possible. The name of the midwife isn't among the birth data registered with the First Child Bureau! Nothing I am going to do for you entitles me to the prominence of coauthorship, I assure you."

"Then you don't stand a chance of succeeding," said Dr. Christian, suddenly enormously depressed.

He felt pushed, accelerated beyond comfortable self-speed, and in his confusion it did not occur to him that all these people seemed to know a great deal more about the difficulty he had with the written word than he remembered telling either Dr. Carriol or Dr. Chasen. Later on he would think of this point, but she would not be there to tax about it, and things would happen with such frightening, exhilarating rapidity that, a minor point, it would fail again to reach the surface of a mind suddenly too concerned with its own mortality to be concerned with anything else.

Elliott MacKenzie was sensitive to nuances, and he was extremely good at his job. "Dr. Christian, you are not a born writer," he said gently and firmly. "Now we all accept that, and believe it or not, this same situation occurs quite a lot in any publishing house, especially with the nonfiction list. A man or woman has something important to say, ideas that must be promulgated, but the man or woman may not have time to write, or may not have the talent to write. In such cases the book is merely a vehicle, built by professionals to carry the ideas you and you alone engineer. If you were a born writer, you wouldn't be sitting here without a finished manuscript, since you've not published before. A finished manuscript takes time. It takes a special talent. There's absolutely no point in debating the relative merits of doing your own writing versus having someone else do it. From what Dr. Carriol has told me, you have a contribution to make to this world that must be made as soon as possible. All we intend to do is ensure that your contribution becomes a reality. And it's an exciting process for us, believe me! At the end of it there will be a book, a *good* book! And the book is what matters."

"I don't know!" cried Dr. Christian wretchedly.

"Well, I do," said Elliott MacKenzie very firmly, and glanced quickly sideways toward his cohort.

Lucy Greco got up at once. "How about coming down to my office, Dr. Christian? We'll be working on our own, so why not get started on some kind of protocol?"

He rose without a word and followed her.

"Are you sure you know what you're doing?" asked Elliott MacKenzie of Dr. Judith Carriol when they were alone.

"Indeed I do!"

"Well, I must say I can't see why you're so excited. And I don't think he wants to write a book at all. I admit he's an impressive-looking guy, a bit Lincolnesque, but he doesn't exactly overflow with personality."

"He's doing a tortoise act, *brrrrp!* into his shell. He feels threatened and manipulated—with every justification! I would have liked a lot more time to work on him, get him used to the idea and let his natural enthusiasm surface again of its own accord, but I have very cogent and valid reasons why this project has to be far enough along to be in working manuscript at the end of the next six weeks."

"It's a tall order, and an expensive one. Not to mention the anguish of prodding your reluctant tortoise to produce."

"Leave him to me and Lucy Greco. As for the book—huh! You should worry, with the Department of the Environment underwriting you! It is not every day, my dear Elliott, that you strike a deal you can't lose on."

"Okay, okay!" He looked at his watch. "I have an appointment upstairs," he said. "Your protégé is likely to be with Lucy for quite a while, given your hurry. Have you got something else to do while you wait?"

"He is all I have to do," she said simply. "Don't you worry about me, I'll just sit here and browse among your wonderful collection of books."

But it was a long time before Dr. Carriol got up and went across to the stuffed shelves. She stared out the gigantic window first, a window made of three separate thicknesses of plate glass, each layer insulated from its neighbor by three-quarters of an inch of air space. They had tried boarding up the New York skyscrapers, but it hadn't worked. The suicide rate just zoomed, so did the acute depression rate. In the end they pulled out all the existing windows, bricked some up, and replaced others with the kind in Elliott MacKenzie's office.

The groundhog had said spring was going to be early this year, and New York had taken notice. Oh, the trees were still bare, they would be until at least the middle of May no matter what sort of weather prevailed, but the air was quite warm and the sun shone and the crystalline explosion of buildings everywhere outside glittered. A cloud floated by, but Dr. Carriol couldn't actually see it; she saw its reflection high up in the golden mirror of an adjoining skyscraper.

Be of good cheer, Joshua Christian! she said silently to the blockish panorama; it will all come together and it will be *splendid*. I know I've rushed you where you're not even sure you want to go, but it's all for the best and noblest reasons, reasons that wouldn't shame you if you knew them. What I'm pushing you to do won't harm you, you'll love it once you get used to it, I promise. You've got so much potential for good, but you'll never get off your ass unless someone pushes you. So here I am! You'll end in thanking me. Not that I'm looking for gratitude. I'm just doing my job, and I do my job better than anyone. For millennia men have been saying that women can never compete because women permit their emotions to intrude upon their work. It's not true. I'm here to prove it. And I am going to prove it. Maybe no one will ever notice that I did. But *I* will know I did, and that's what counts.

Seven weeks left. It could be done. It must be done! Because on May first she was going to have evidence above and beyond mere personal conviction that Dr. Joshua Christian was the man they were looking for. The book must be a reality by then. So must sheaves of reports, backed up by video and audio tapes of the man in action. By the time she went to see the President she had to have an open-and-closed case in favor of Dr. Joshua Christian. The President was not the man to fall for a snow job. And Harold Magnus would be fighting to the last ditch for Senator Hillier.

She moved her chair closer to Elliott MacKenzie's desk and picked up his private-line telephone.

The number she dialed was thirty-three digits long, but she

didn't need to consult either paper or the buttons on the machine as she punched it quicker than most people could have punched a much shorter number.

"Dr. Carriol. Where is Mr. Wayne?"

The telephone said he wasn't in.

"Find him," said Judith Carriol coldly.

She waited patiently, eyes glazed, cataloguing all the sources of evidence she was going to need.

"John? I'm not on a scramble phone, but this line is not through the Atticus switchboard. Would you check the computer and make sure it's not tapped? The number is 555–6273. Government wouldn't be interested, but I suppose there could be some form of industrial espionage, even in an eighteenth-century business like book publishing. Ring me back."

She waited five minutes for the phone to ring again.

"All clear," said John Wayne.

"Good. Now listen. I need some video cameras and lots of microphones installed immediately. 1047 and 1045 Oak Street, Holloman, Connecticut. The offices and home of Dr. Joshua Christian. Everywhere. I don't want one square inch of either building unmonitored, and I want twenty-four-hour surveillance. The equipment will have to go in today and be out by this coming Saturday evening, because on Sundays the Christians climb all over the place watering plants and could spot a camera. Okay? I also need a complete list of Dr. Christian's patients, no longer current as well as current. All of them are to be interviewed on audio tape without realizing they're being interviewed, of course. You will do the same with his family and his friends. His enemies too. The interviewing can take longer than the video monitoring of house and clinic, but it has to be done in time to have the tapes edited and ready to present on May first. Understood?"

She could feel his excitement. "Yes, Dr. Carriol." He ventured an unprofessional question which he had not found the courage to ask during the days Dr. Joshua Christian had just spent in Washington. "He's it?"

"He's it, John! But I am going to have a fight on my hands and I don't intend to lose. I can't afford to lose. Because he's *it!*"

Oh yes he was. The decision she had made that night in Hartford seemed more and more right as the days went on. Of the nine candidates, he was the only one who possessed what this job was going to need. Therefore it was up to her to get him the chance to do the job only he could do. The task called for a man

107

without any kind of political or career axe to grind, a man who didn't care about himself, had no image.

Operation Search was her baby. She had dreamed it up and she alone fully understood what it searched for. Since meeting Dr. Christian that knowledge had expanded and coalesced at one and the same time, a sure indication that he was the man. Five years earlier they could simply have earmarked Senator Hillier for the job and begun to groom him then. But she hadn't even wanted him included in the 100,000 names her investigators and their teams and their computers had sifted through. Tibor Reece had come down on Harold Magnus's side then, but she had been conserving her strength for five years, and she refused to consider the possibility that Harold Magnus could win the next time around. Five years earlier had been a preliminary skirmish she could afford to let Harold Magnus win, so she hadn't made the mistake of letting it assume the proportions of a battle royal. He may have thought that meant she didn't have a battle royal in her; if so, he was going to learn differently very soon.

Somewhere she had always known there was a man—odd that she, so feminist in her soul, had never honestly believed there was a woman—for whom the task was *meant*. Fated. A natural, inevitable destiny. But gone were the days when a man could walk out of the desert or the wilderness and found a way of life. This was the third millennium, so choked with people that the very best might remain buried through no fault or lack of effort of their own, and so sophisticated in its dealings with the few who did stand out from the masses that it could if it so chose remove those few, or if it so chose raise them even higher. Maybe the third millennium was just as bumbling in its way as the two earlier ones, but it had perfected the art of keeping tabs on its faceless millions, and its brand of cynicism was securely rooted in facts, figures, trends, exponentials. It had replaced ethics with synthetics, philosophy with psychology, and gold with paper. Only she for one did not believe that the gargantuan rivers of eerie silent ice creeping down from the Arctic Circle were a visitation designed to obliterate the race of Man; poles apart though they were in nature, she, like Dr. Joshua Christian, believed that Man had the power within himself to overcome all obstacles in his way.

But wasn't it extraordinary that in the long run only the stubborn personality and tangential intelligence of one man had unearthed Dr. Joshua Christian? Had his name been allocated to

Dr. Abraham's or Dr. Hemingway's caseloads, he would probably have fallen by the wayside. Instead, his name had gone to Moshe Chasen. On such tiny coincidences so much always rested, no matter how careful a method was devised, how foolproof it appeared. When all was said and done, still it came down to people. Their vagaries, their individualities, their genetic uniquenesses. Fitting. One of Joshua's "patterns" he talked of.

She put her chin on her hands and sat forward, wondering how many other nameless Joshua Christians had not emerged to the top of Dr. Abraham's and Dr. Hemingway's caseloads. Was Joshua the best man for the job? Or was someone better still buried in the fastness of the Federal Human Data Bank? Well, that was something they would not know unless they took over 66,000 names and subjected them to Moshe Chasen's programs. If in truth the 100,000 names originally culled were the right ones in the light of Moshe Chasen's approach. Well, too late to wonder. Joshua Christian had emerged. And, perforce, Joshua Christian was therefore the man.

After three hours spent with Mrs. Lucy Greco, Dr. Christian felt a lot better about his book. The professional in him fully appreciated the way she handled him, and oddly enough that gave him more confidence in the whole project. His numbness had dissipated within minutes. By the end of the first half hour in her office he was talking freely, quickly, sometimes passionately. She was such a help! If he lacked anything, it was logical progression; he was aware himself of the failing, especially since meeting Judith and Moshe, ruthless critics. Lucy Greco possessed the ability to think logically in full measure. Not only that. They clicked. He found her a perfect audience, for she sat like the open mouth of a baby bird, ready to swallow everything he threw her way, and yet her occasional questions were so well directed she actually assisted him to plump out his ideas in areas where he knew he hadn't yet eliminated woolly thinking.

"You should have been a psychologist," he said to her as they walked back to Elliott MacKenzie's office.

"But I am," she said.

He laughed. "I might have known!"

"Dr. Christian," she said, so earnestly that her steps slowed, then halted, and he therefore stopped, "this is the most important book I've ever had the good fortune to be associated with. Please believe me! I mean it. I have never meant anything more in all my life."

"But I don't have the answers," he said helplessly.

"Oh yes you do! There are some lucky people who can exist without a spiritual prop, even some who are so alone they haven't a fellow human being to use as a prop. But most people do need shoring up. I've heard enough from you in the last hours to know where we're going, and where I'm going to push you too. You've been afraid, I think."

"Yes. Very many times."

"Don't be," she said, walking on.

"I'm only a man," he said, "and it's a poor kind of man who isn't afraid. Fear can be as much an indication of sense or sensitivity as it is of inadequacy. A man without any fear in him is a machine."

"Or Nietzsche's superman?"

He smiled. "I can assure you that you are not dealing with a superman!"

They entered Elliott MacKenzie's office.

He was back long since, sitting with Dr. Carriol, and he looked up curiously, interested to see how Lucy Greco was taking her new assignment.

Her cheeks were pink, her eyes shone, she looked as if she had just spent time in the arms of a lover. And Dr. Joshua Christian had come alive. Oh, bravo, Judith Carriol! Mentally he pushed the first print run way up. Lucy Greco was that publishing house phenomenon, a born writer with absolutely nothing of her own to say. So give her a client-subject who did have something to say, and she could sing in prose. Already she was in that state where the words were roiling inside her. There was going to be a BOOK.

"I'm off to Holloman today with Joshua," she said, too excited to sit down.

"Good!" Dr. Carriol rose to her feet. She held out her hand to Elliott MacKenzie. "Thank you, my friend."

Outside the Atticus building Lucy Greco left them to go home and pack a bag, arranging to meet them at Grand Central in three hours.

Which left Dr. Carriol and Dr. Christian alone at last.

"Come on. We may as well check out of our hotel and then go

on down to Grand Central. We can sit in the coffee shop until Lucy arrives," she said.

He sighed with relief. "Thank God! I don't know why, but I thought you wouldn't come back to Holloman with me."

Her brows leaped upward. "You were right, I'm not. After I put you on the Holloman local I'm off to Penn Station and Washington. No, don't be disappointed, Joshua! I have my own work to do, and now you've got Lucy you don't need me. She's the expert."

A cold shiver ran all the way down his long back. "I wish I could believe that! This is your idea. I'm not even sure I want to do this book, even with Lucy helping me."

She hadn't stopped walking, and she didn't stop after he said that. "Look, Joshua, I am going to tell you something straight from the shoulder, okay? You are a man with a mission. And you are more aware of that than I am or anyone else. All this vacillation is no more than surface deep. I understand it. You've not had time to get it all straight in your mind, and I admit I've pushed you unmercifully. In the bit over a week since I've met you, it's all happened, and it's all happened because I've pushed you. Quite frankly, you need a push! If you were a man of religion you would have had years of preparation for this moment. If you were an evangelist you would already have jumped in the water, boots and all. And the future is a mystery, I know. For you especially, so thick and impenetrable you don't see tomorrow clearly, let alone next week or next year. But you'll get there! And without my holding your hand."

Man of religion? Evangelist? "My God!" he cried. "Is that how you think of it, Judith? As a *religious* mission?"

"Yes. I would have to say, yes. But not in the old sense."

Gnawing shadows. Greyness. "Judith, I'm only a man! I'm not equipped!"

Why on earth did he have to bring up things like this on a New York City street, where the atmosphere and the physical act they were performing in walking made subtlety and delicacy quite impossible? And how could she find the right thing to say when for her, too, events had moved too fast? She had envisioned a progress (at least inside Joshua's mind) rather in the mood of a glacier, an even grind from A to B. Not this avalanche! Or maybe without realizing it she had assumed she would be working with a man like Senator Hillier. A straightforward pragmatist with whom

111

one could plan, who would see where he was being pushed and gladly give himself a kick along as well. Where working with a man like Joshua Christian—and he was certainly one of a kind!—was turning out to be more like walking a tightrope above the Valley of Death.

"Forget I said it. I don't know why I said it. Just get your book out, Joshua. That's really all that matters."

She was right, of course. Or so he concluded somewhere around Bridgeport on the start-stop-start-stop journey home, with the train crawling along when it did move. Lucy Greco had the good sense to sit alongside him quietly and not intrude her presence, sensing that something had happened to unsettle him in the three hours she had been absent.

He was not a fool. He was not so turned in upon himself that he was blind to the behavior of others, either. And a few tiny incidents like Moshe Chasen's eyes when they met, and Elliott MacKenzie's and Lucy Greco's extraordinary awareness of the extent of his writer's block, and Judith Carriol's remarks about the nature of what she wanted him to produce—these minuscule events somehow added up to bulk as large as a mountain. Only it was a massif he couldn't see, for it was somewhere in the opacity of his tomorrows. However, nothing he sensed did he feel as malign. Be honest with yourself, Joshua Christian! Nothing you sense do you feel to be at odds with what you yearn to do, which is simply to help people.

He didn't trust Judith Carriol. He wasn't even sure he liked her. Yet from the very beginning she had been the catalyst he had desperately needed to set him afire. That awful force within him had responded to her like a beast of great power to a well-known guiding hand. And he was tugged along helplessly in its wake, as much its victim as he was Judith Carriol's.

Do what you have to do. And let tomorrow take care of itself. You cannot see what it holds.

The book, the book. The chance. So much to say! What was most important to say? How could he possibly fit it all inside the covers of one little book? He would have to be selective, then. Simple in his expression, but not mindlessly simple. The important thing was to explain to its readers *why* they felt the way they did, so useless, so dreary, so old, so futile. He thought he was beginning to get a glimmer of why Judith Carriol had used the words "religious" and "evangelist." Because what his book was

112

going to offer was a little mystical. Yes, that was what she had meant! Much ado about nothing he couldn't handle.

Once people gained spiritual strength they had a basis upon which to build something more positive out of the lives they had no choice but to live save in the prescribed manner. Not a single hint of rebellion, iconoclasm, nostalgia, terror, destructiveness. They didn't need that kind of firing, not with the future they faced—the dwindling water, the hideous cold, the shrinking land, the anti-American outside world. He had to bring them to see and believe in a future they would never live to experience. He had to give them hope. And faith. And most of all, love.

Yes! With the intelligent and capable Lucy Greco to aid him, to shape what he wanted to say into something people would want to read, he could do it. He could! And what else mattered besides that? Did he matter? No. Did Judith Carriol matter? No. And he came to realize that what he loved in Judith Carriol was her ability to put herself aside. The twin ability to his own.

When Dr. Christian walked into her kitchen with yet another sophisticated woman in tow, Mama froze to the spot and stood with her spoon dripping sauce all over the floor, mouth agape.

He leaned over to kiss her cheek. "Mama, this is Mrs. Lucy Greco. She'll be staying with us for a few weeks, so would you mind taking the mothballs out of the spare room and finding another hot-water bottle?"

"Staying?"

"That's right. She's my editor. I've been commissioned to write a book for the Atticus Press and we've got a deadline, you see. It's all right, she's a psychologist herself, so she's better equipped than most outsiders to understand our crazy household. Where are the others?"

"Not come across yet. When they heard you were coming, they decided to wait for you rather than eat at the usual time." Mama recollected the guest, still standing smiling politely and blankly. "Oh, Mrs. Greco, I am sorry! Joshua, watch the pots. I'll take Mrs. Greco up to her room. And don't worry, my dear, the bit about mothballs is just a fine example of Joshua's humor. I do *not* have moths, and I have *never* needed mothballs to keep a room fresh!"

Joshua did as he was told and watched the pots. It had perhaps been a little unkind of him not to apprise his family of Mrs. Greco's presence, especially since he had called to let them know

113

he was coming home. But occasionally they did need a jolt, and this was a delicious one, particularly for Mama. When she rushed back into the kitchen so quickly that it was obvious she had barely stayed long enough settling Lucy Greco to observe the decencies, he grinned.

"Mama! I'll bet you didn't even show Mrs. Greco where the bathroom was."

"She's over the age of consent, she'll find it. Now what's going on, Joshua? All these years and you've never displayed any interest in women, now all of a sudden you bring two home inside of a week!"

"Judith is a colleague I've just finished some work for, and Mrs. Greco is exactly what I said she was, my editor."

"You're not taking the mickey out of me?"

"No, Mama."

"Wellll . . ." She packed the word with meaning.

"You might be dizzy, Mama, but do you know something else?" he asked, moving away from the stove to pick up a cloth, and smiling at her as he did so.

"No, what?" she asked, smiling back.

"You're a really nice person." And he bent to wipe the sauce off the floor before Mama, a fast mover, slipped in it.

She took advantage of this softening immediately. "Are you sure you're not just the teeniest bit interested in Dr. Carriol? She'd be so perfect for you, Joshua!"

"Oh, Mama! Once and for all, *no!* Now don't you want to hear about my book?"

"Of course I do, but save it until after dinner, then you won't have to repeat it. I've got some news the rest already know about, so I'll tell you before they come across."

"What news?"

She opened the oven, peered inside, shut it, and unbent. "We had a national emergency this afternoon about two o'clock."

He stared. "A national emergency?"

"Yes. They evacuated the whole of West Holloman, not such a feat considering it's March and most of the houses are empty— but hard enough with the streets five feet deep in frozen snow— it would have been worse if we hadn't had that thaw—"

He interrupted her with an awful frown. "Mama, describe the emergency, not the obvious!"

"Ohhh!" She gritted her teeth in frustration, then couldn't resist going on with her story posthaste. "*As* I was saying, they evacuated the whole of West Holloman. Just came banging on our doors and hustled us out to buses and whisked us off down to the railroad station—you know, the old part that's deserted except for bums and no one knows what to do with? They fed us soup and showed us a first-release movie and then let us go home again about five. So I wasn't put out at all that dinner's late. You rang about a minute after we got in."

"How odd!"

"Apparently they thought they'd unearthed a contaminated dump of radioactive waste next door to the old gun factory. You know, where they've started the district clearance scheme? Anyway, some workman's Geiger counter went off like a siren, and the next thing we had the National Guard and the Army—full-bird colonels running round a dime a dozen! It was really fun, actually. I saw people I haven't seen in years."

His worry that the family had been duped for some unknown but nefarious purpose died. "Well, we always did wonder what used to go on in that research building of theirs, why they needed walls four feet thick and a twenty-four-hour security patrol. Now I guess we know, huh?"

"They told us they'd removed the stuff to safety somewhere else, and said it was safe to come home again."

"Let's hope we don't get it back in next year's fish," he said dryly.

"They don't do that any more, dear," she said soothingly. "They take it to the dark side of the moon."

"That's what they tell us, you mean."

"Anyway, a nice Army colonel told me there was a chance we'd have to be evacuated again, because they have to sift through the whole site now to make sure it's clean, and it might take them a few days."

The door opened and in trooped the rest of the family, full of pleasure to see the prodigal returned.

"Only he's not alone," said Mama mysteriously. "He came with his lady friend."

Mary and Miriam and the Mouse tried to look enthusiastic, the men looked genuinely so.

"How long is Dr. Carriol staying?" asked Mary sourly.

"Oh, it isn't Dr. Carriol," said Mama, purring. "This one's not a doctor, she's a missus, and her name's Lucy Greco. Isn't that pretty? She's very pretty too."

His siblings and his in-laws stared at him, stupefied.

Dr. Christian burst out laughing. "If I'd only known how much fun it was to bring strange women home with me, I'd have started years ago!" he said, wiping his eyes. "You mutts!"

"Come on now, out of the kitchen," said Mama, shooing. "Since I'm going to serve dinner in exactly five minutes, it would be nice if you set the table for me."

"Who is she?" asked Miriam, putting down forks.

"After dinner," said Dr. Christian, and refused to say any more. The moment Lucy Greco walked in he introduced her all round, then said to her, "Mum's the word until later."

Later was the living room, over coffee and cognac. He told his family about the book. Their reactions were much as expected; identically curious and joyous and totally supportive of him.

"I think it's a wonderful idea, Josh," said James warmly, speaking for everyone.

"Well, I have to thank Dr. Carriol for it, really. It was her idea."

Discovering the identity of the true author of the project made the three young women a little wary, but after examining it from all angles, they had to admit it still sounded like a great idea.

"I've always thought you should write a book," said Mary, "but I never thought you'd manage to overcome your inhibitions when you still couldn't unblock yourself after we gave you the new IBM voicewriter last Christmas."

"Believe me, I thought the same. I guess this is the only way possible for me—to have someone else do the actual writing," he said, smiling.

"So you're an editor?" asked Andrew, looking both charming and spectacularly beautiful.

She responded to the question and the man. "That's right. But I'm a specialist editor. I really do participate in the writing of the book, where most editors are withheld from a book's early stages. With the fiction writer, for instance, editors are chiefly useful in late draft, as critics. They can't tell the fiction writer what to do or how to do it, they just spot the weaknesses and inconsistencies in the plot and characters and so forth. Now I don't do any fiction at all. I specialize in collaborating on the writing of books with people who have something *significant* to say, but don't have the gift of putting on paper what they want to say."

"You make it sound as if fiction writers don't have anything significant to say," said James, who adored fiction.

116

Mrs. Greco shrugged. "It largely depends on your point of view, and never the twain shall meet. Ask a fiction editor and you'll be told the only books that survive the test of time are fiction. Personally I'm not a fiction fan. It's as simple as that, really."

"There's room for both," said Dr. Christian.

The discussion went on, lively and interested; and from a dozen vantage points around the room a battery of video cameras silently went on recording every word said and every face saying it. When the plants were tended on Sunday those glaucous lenses would be gone, for the people who had installed them during a most convenient emergency evacuation exercise would institute another such crisis on Saturday evening.

Had the room not been so full of plants a faint smell of fresh paint might have been detected, but the leaves were as efficient at absorbing smells as they were at absorbing surplus carbon dioxide. It was the new-type videotape that encoded what it saw and heard in every one-second epoch into such a minute segment of tape that, given the number of channels across its width, it would not be exhausted for a full two weeks, a much longer time than was needed in this present situation. Even the power feeding the cameras had been tapped from the mains outside the Christian residences, to make sure no trace remained of this four-day surveillance.

After Dr. Christian left Washington so abruptly, Dr. Moshe Chasen found it as difficult to concentrate on relocation as he had before Dr. Christian had appeared in Washington. When he came into his office on Monday he was aware his new colleague must soon go, but he had fully expected to see that long thin body draped around a table, had looked forward to letting his eyes rest on that dark fallen-in face. But no Dr. Christian. In the end he had telephoned John Wayne looking for Dr. Carriol, and then was told of the unexpected departure.

"Please don't attempt to contact Dr. Christian," John Wayne said in the voice which indicated the instructions were not his, but his chief's.

"I *need* him!" cried Dr. Chasen.

"I'm sorry, sir, I really can't help you."

And that was the end of that, until Dr. Judith Carriol walked into his office on Wednesday afternoon.

"Dammit, Judith, couldn't you at least have given me an opportunity to say goodbye to the man?" he roared.

Her brows rose. "I'm sorry, Moshe, I didn't think," she said coolly.

"Bullshit! You never stop thinking."

"Missing him, Moshe?"

"Yes."

"I'm afraid you'll have to get along without him."

He took off his reading glasses and stared at her fixedly. "Judith, just what *is* Operation Search?" he asked.

"A search for one man."

"To do what?"

"Time will have to tell you that. I can't. Sorry."

"Can't, or won't?"

"A bit of both."

"Judith, leave him alone!" It was a cry from the heart.

"What on earth do you mean?"

"You're the worst kind of meddler. You use other people to attain your ends."

"There's nothing unique about that, we all do it."

"Not like you," he said grimly. "You are a special breed. Maybe it's the times have bred you, I don't know. Or maybe your kind has always been with us, but the times have given you unlimited opportunities to rise high enough to do real harm."

"Claptrap!" she said disdainfully, and walked from the office, closing the door behind her gently to indicate that he was whistling into the wind.

Dr. Chasen sat for a moment chewing the earpiece of his glasses, then sighed and picked up a sheaf of computer readouts. But he couldn't see what they said because he hadn't put his glasses on again. He couldn't put them on. His eyes were too full of tears.

V

For six weeks Dr. Judith Carriol had no contact of any kind with Dr. Joshua Christian, but the middle three of those six weeks saw her watching the man in almost every smallest detail on hour after hour after hour of videotape. And when she wasn't watching him or his family or both, she was listening to his patients, his ex-patients, the relatives of his patients and his ex-patients, his friends, even his enemies, talk about him on audiotape. It was highly significant, she felt, that nothing she discovered lessened her enthusiasm for him.

Even after Dr. Moshe Chasen had taxed her so directly with the consequences of her actions, it did not occur to her that in serving her own purpose she might not be serving Joshua's; she saw the two as one and the same, indivisible, and sanctified her prying secret work as evidence of the purest, most selfless devotion. Had Joshua Christian himself known what she was doing and had he taxed her with it rather than Moshe Chasen, still she would have been able to look deep into his eyes and assure him clear through to her core that what she did was for his benefit, and enormous benefit at that. She was not consciously evil; had she been, Dr. Christian would have sensed it at once. Nor was she quite heartless. Perhaps the worst thing that could be said of her was that she lacked ethics, that she was not honorable. But then nothing in her life had been conducive to the inculcation of ethics, of honor.

Her childhood had been a middle-of-the-road case of hardship, poverty and emotional deprivation; had her situation been slightly worse, the state would have removed her to a kinder environment; had it been slightly better, she might have managed to preserve a little of the softness that is surely born into every human baby. Ten years older than Dr. Joshua Christian, and molded by far crueler circumstances, she was the third-last of thirteen children born into a Pittsburgh family just about the time the steel industry had gone into total and permanent depression. Her name then had been not Carriol, but Carroll. Looking back on those years from the pinnacle of her adult accomplishments, she decided that the plethora of children her parents had spawned (she could think of no other suitable verb to describe the process as carried on in the Carroll household) was far more the result of laziness and alcoholism than the lip-service Catholicism they professed; certainly the home atmosphere was more redolent of cheap whiskey than piety. But Judith survived, the only one of those thirteen children who did, though none of them actually died. Not then, at any rate. And she survived because she refused to consider anyone's plight save her own. At twelve she had begun to find part-time work and she continued to work all through her high school years; she kept herself clean, virtuous and healthy, and because she could spur her body to work as hard as her mind, she kept whatever work she found for as long as she wanted to keep it. To her family's pleas for handouts she turned a resolutely deaf ear, and they soon learned that not even physical torture could wring from her the secret place where she hid her money. In the end they left her to her own devices, despising her, tormenting her, but fearing her too. When she achieved a near-perfect score on her SAT's and was offered a full scholarship to Harvard, Chubb, Princeton—a half dozen Ivy League schools—she told her family she had accepted to Harvard and went to Princeton instead. The first thing she did was change her name. And from that day forward she had made it her business never to discover what had happened to the rest of her family back in Pittsburgh.

The Delhi Treaty had preceded her graduation summa cum laude, but not by so much that its upheavals were old hat. She had taken a double major in psychology and sociology and she

120

walked over the intense competition into a slot in the brand new Department of the Environment, a slot complete with doctoral opportunities. She also became an indefatigable worker for Augustus Rome and the new programs he set the nation; no one feared and detested large families more than Dr. Judith Carriol. While President Rome talked incessantly to his people of the utter necessity of falling into line with the rest of the world concerning the one-child family, she studied its implementation. She went abroad, to China, pioneer in the art since 1978, to India, achieving the same end from the opposite and bloodier pole, to Malaysia, Japan, Russia, the Arabicommune and the Eurocommune, and many other places. She even went to Australia and New Zealand, who had also signed the Delhi Treaty on condition they (like Canada and the U.S.A.) would be left severely alone in every other way from military invasion to passive immigration. She followed the teams of Chinese around a dozen nations, watching and listening as they taught, demonstrated, advised.

The Environment think tank had been her home from her first day in the Department, and she was in the forefront of the massive efforts the Department marshaled to overcome one-child-family opposition and noncooperation. Of course they had followed the Chinese pattern of appealing to good sense, patriotism and the pocket, rather than the Indian method of enforced sterilization. That the program worked was undoubtedly due to all the other enormous blows the country had received and still reeled from; that it worked was due also to the personal efforts of President Rome, who luckily was a natural one-child parent; and that it worked finally and continually was definitely due to the unassailable fact that an ice age was coming rapidly, and nothing could be postponed until a more favorable day.

So her enormously successful career had not helped her overcome the emotional desert in which her soul wandered, for it had reinforced her conviction that she was indeed superior in intelligence and courage to the vast bulk of her fellow men and women. Thus she could never be convinced that what she thought and did might contain serious flaws. And she was quite incapable of taking into consideration such picayune factors as the stirrings in a heart, the vapors stealing in a mind, the erosion in a backbone. She was of course a purely reasoning thinker, and reason was her god; whatever might come to endanger reason was anathema.

Which placed her in a precarious position when dealing with a person as instinctual, illogical and mystical as Dr. Joshua Christian. She didn't know it, except in that corner of her mind where she was wont to inveigh against what she saw as his sheer cussedness. How could he not see his own perfection for her purpose? And when he did see it, as see it eventually he must, how could he not be moved to thank her, to like her, even to love her?

Thus this molder of men, this purrer in the shadows, this grey eminence, sat hour after hour day after day looking at Dr. Joshua Christian in the most sacred moments of his most sacred privacy, and felt no qualm of conscience, nor questioned the right she had to do so. She knew he picked his nose, she knew he did not masturbate, she knew he sang and giggled and pulled comical faces while he sat to produce his morning motion of the bowels (she even knew he had no tendency to constipation), she knew he talked to himself (sometimes with fantastic passion!) whenever he was alone, she knew he had difficulty in getting to sleep and no trouble at all in getting up, she knew he most genuinely loved his mother, his brothers, his sister and his sisters-in-law; she even knew, alas, that the sister-in-law he called Mouse was deeply and despairingly in love with him, and that his sister loathed him. And her knowledge did not stop with him; it extended through his entire family in the selfsame intimate, distressing way.

At the end of the sixth week, John Wayne at her elbow as always, Dr. Judith Carriol finished compiling all her evidence, including a rough draft of *God in Cursing: A New Approach to Millennial Neurosis,* by Joshua Christian, Ph.D. (Chubb).

Separately she called in Dr. Samuel Abraham and Dr. Millicent Hemingway and obtained from each a report about the candidates each had vetted to finality. Then she thanked them and put them to work on the special aspects of relocation Dr. Moshe Chasen had cut off from the main flow of his own research as better handled independently. At that time it did not occur either to Dr. Abraham or to Dr. Hemingway that Operation Search had a finite purpose.

She notified Harold Magnus that she was ready, and Harold Magnus notified President Tibor Reece.

The meeting the three held was at the White House, the President's security force feeling that two members of Environment, even if one was its head, were less likely when traveling to attract the attention of the lunatic fringe than the President of the United States of America. Dr. Carriol didn't like the venue, feeling that she would rather put her trust in a security she knew than rely on men and women she didn't know and therefore couldn't trust. She suspected Harold Magnus was of a similar frame of mind. Who was to say how many microphones and spy holes they had wired and bored into the White House's conference rooms, and for what purposes, and even who "they" were? Her own activities in the matter of Dr. Joshua Christian were undertaken for the most unimpeachable of reasons, but she was sure she could not say the same for some of the surveillance freaks who frequented the corridors of State, Justice and Defense.

However, superficially this was just another rather drab meeting between the President and two of his departmental heads, chickenshit stuff the President would undoubtedly have preferred to hand over to someone else, except that every so often he had to make a personal gesture. Therefore just pray the guard dogs in State and the bloodhounds in Justice and the mastiffs in Defense were lying peacefully sleeping beside their own fires, immune to the scent of that modern butt of all national rancor, Environment.

She was not afraid. She was not even nervous. It suited her to have to do all the talking, for she knew her audience extremely well. Harold Magnus might claim that Operation Search was his baby, but she knew it was her baby, and she was not prepared to yield up control of it to anyone, least of all to her bosses. They didn't know it yet, but they were not going to make the decision. Her applecart was exquisitely stacked; no matter which piece of fruit they picked up to inspect, it would have Dr. Joshua Christian's name on it. She had every advantage, of course. She knew exactly what was on the agenda where they did not. She could plan a method of attack where they could not.

As a matter of course they would be expecting to see only one serious contender for the job, namely Senator David Sims Hillier VII. Magnus wanted Hillier passionately, but of Reece she was not so certain. Where Reece was concerned Dr. Carriol had two things on her side. One, the glaring fact that this job carried fantastic power in its train; if it went to a U.S. senator with executive aspirations it might end in direct danger to the present tenant of the White House. The second fact was interesting because of its sheer randomness; there was a fortuitous physical resemblance between Tibor Reece and Joshua Christian, both too tall, both too thin, both very dark in coloring, both cadaverous of face. Of course, genetically they came from not dissimilar stock; Dr. Christian was Russian, Armenian and Nordo-Celt, President Reece was Hungarian, Russian, Jewish and Celt.

Naturally Harold Magnus was aware of Tibor Reece's strong reservations about Senator Hillier, and so would have his own attack well planned. But Tibor Reece was aware of Harold Magnus's awareness, and in his turn would undoubtedly also have evolved a plan of attack. If she could make her presentation a direct hit upon Tibor Reece, she knew he would pick Dr. Christian over Senator Hillier; what she had to accomplish was to make the President see that in choosing Dr. Christian he would not be putting his own interests ahead of the country's, which he would never do. With complete faith in Tibor Reece as the rightful next President, Augustus Rome had chosen him for the slate during his last term in office, and when it came to divining what was in a politician's heart as well as in his head, old Gus Rome had been a past master. Therefore doubt not Tibor Reece's integrity.

The President welcomed Secretary Magnus and Dr. Judith Carriol very warmly, and showed how much importance he attached to the outcome of Operation Search by informing them that he had not put a time limit on the duration of this meeting. So Dr. Carriol had perforce to wait, tongue darting and long fingers creeping, while Tibor Reece and Harold Magnus said the usual litany of wives, children, friends, enemies and problems. In an age bracket where the siring of progeny had been left entirely to the discretion of the individual, Harold Magnus possessed two sons and two daughters; but Tibor Reece, in his late forties, had not married until his middle thirties and therefore possessed only one child, a girl who was mentally retarded. His wife had tried with might and main to secure a second child, bombarding the Second Child Bureau with applications so frequently, publicly and frantically that she became a nuisance and an embarrassment. Luck had nothing to do with the fact that she never had got lucky; her husband had seen Harold Magnus on the quiet and deliberately arranged her ill luck. Julia Reece was therefore the only case in the history of the SCB where in fact strings actually had been pulled. Julia Reece was offered up as a sacrifice for the good of the country. For had she drawn a winning red ball in the lottery, no one from highest to lowest would ever have believed strings

124

were not pulled; Tibor Reece knew he did not dare take the chance. But he had paid for it. Julia hadn't exactly gone mad; she merely became mad for men, which was an even greater embarrassment to her husband than her unabated dinning at the SCB door.

Naturally the litany carefully skirted sensitive topics, and ritually wound itself to a conclusion. The President buzzed and the coffee tray was promptly removed. Dr. Carriol could get down to business at last.

They were sitting in the Oval Office, which this occupant of the White House adored. Dr. Carriol had asked for and got a single videotape player with a remote-control panel she could hold in her hand. Thus she was able to orchestrate her visual presentation without a technician's help. There was an audio player on a side table which she hoped she would not have to use, feeling that the mere sound of words after watching faces utter them could not decisively influence the outcome. However, it was better to be fully prepared.

First she went briefly through the salient facts about seven of the nine final candidates, passing a photograph of each smoothly to the President as she talked, not pausing to check whether he passed them in turn to Harold Magnus. Mr. Magnus was quite capable of looking after himself.

"And now," she said, "we come to the dark horse. Dr. Moshe Chasen inherited Senator Hillier as a unit in his caseload. But Senator Hillier was *not* his prime choice. There was one person who outscored Senator Hillier in every important category. In view of this surprise development, I undertook to vet Dr. Chasen's three candidates myself, and I too came to the conclusion that the dark horse won hands down, even over Senator Hillier."

She flicked the remote-control panel in her hand, and the screen of a very large video monitor set into the wall opposite the President's desk came to life.

"This is Dr. Joshua Christian, a psychologist practicing privately in the town of Holloman, Connecticut."

There he was on the screen, a tall, gracefully ungainly man pacing back and forth between a jungle of plants in a very beautiful, peaceful room. The volume from the high fidelity, stereophonic speakers grew from a murmur until the sound of Dr.

Christian's voice, deep and clear and compelling, filled the Oval Office.

"Mama, you are so lucky. Today I found a truly valid reason for my book. A man came to me for help. But I wasn't really able to help him—at least as a psychologist—because what he was suffering from has no answer. His child died last week. Yes. *His only child!* Of course they could have got permission from the First Child Bureau to replace this boy, but his wife is hysterectomized, and that's a strike they can't overcome no matter how, no matter what. He was still capable of seeking help, his wife is not."

Dr. Christian stopped, turned to face toward a different direction, was obviously subjected to some amateurish editing on the videotape, then reappeared in the lens of another camera. "Aren't you lucky, Mama? You've got four children. Yes, I understand the loss of a child is something no parent ever really recovers from, but the only thing in life which can cushion such a loss is the presence of other children. That man was in the midst of the classic nightmare situation of the one-child family. The death of the child. He stood there with the tears running down his face begging me for help—not help for himself so much as help for his wife. As if he had been told I *could* help. I couldn't help! No one can help. But how could I turn him away? I told him he must find God. Not to help, only to understand. He said he didn't believe in God. That no God could exist and let a child die. Especially, he said, not his child. Because that's what it boils down to, Mama. God is personal, God relates to self."

There was a brief cut to the lovely face and tear-bright eyes of a young-middle-aged woman ("His mother," sotto voce from Dr. Carriol), then the picture returned to Dr. Christian.

"I asked him if he had any religious persuasion at any time, and he said no, that his family had abandoned religion when nuclear weapons began to stockpile three generations ago. But he had done some reading. He could tell me the names of the innumerable wars that have been fought in God's name with His bishops in the vanguard—he even told me Allah's wars and Jehovah's wars! He threw the Chosen People myths in my face, he reeled off the various religions still extant which teach that only *their* adherents can be saved. Saved from what? he asked. He despised God, he said—an interesting contradiction, isn't it? Then he told me I was not his first port of call on this desperate voyage for help. He had gone first to his wife's minister of religion, from whom he had never bothered to conceal his contempt for God. And the minister took great pleasure in telling him his child had been taken from him as a punishment! I ask you, how could a fellow man appealed to by one in such pain have repaid the compliment by such an answer? The old vengeful God, alive and still dwelling in our midst. How far have we come? I ask myself. That is the answer a man might have been given three thousand years ago, when there was a great deal more excuse for human ignorance! You would think that by this day and age Man must surely have come closer to understanding God than the behavior of that so-called Christian minister would indicate, wouldn't you? To attribute such mean, petty, spiteful vengefulness to a Being as far from where we stand now as we are from our arboreal ancestors—I tell you, I despair! Not of God, but of Man!"

The anguished twisted face was abruptly removed by a split second of darkness, then replaced by a face fair and beautiful as the mother's, but male ("His brother Andrew," sotto voce from Dr. Carriol). "Forget that, Josh," said Andrew. "What did you do to help?"

The picture returned to Dr. Christian. "I sat down with the poor wretch, and I talked. I talked and I talked and I talked. Trying to help him find the truth in understanding, and a God he could accept."

Another picture change, another and different male face, like Andrew but less striking ("His brother James," sotto voce from Dr. Carriol). "Did you get anywhere?" James asked.

Back to Dr. Christian. "A little. But I had nothing to send home with him except the memory of my words, and memory is treacherous. I'm going to see his wife in their home tomorrow, but again I can't stay with her twenty-four hours a day, and anyway, neither of them is really in need of my professional services. They just want a strong and understanding heart beside them constantly through the first and darkest days. And in such situations, my book would be of more help than I in person, because my book won't leave them. It will be there in the middle of the night, when the pain is worst and the loneliness most appalling. I'm not trying to say my book has all the answers, but at least it is written for people who must live through *these* days. It's utterly relevant, and I know it can help because I know how many people I've managed to help by being there in the flesh." He laughed, a broken, almost sobbing sound. "You know, a book is a little like the loaves and fishes—it can feed the multitude."

Dr. Carriol stopped the videotape player and gave a manuscript copy of Dr. Christian's book to the President, then got up to give a second copy to Harold Magnus.

"The Atticus Press is publishing this in the fall, with a full publicity tour by the author—radio, television, newspapers, magazines, personal lectures and appearances. It's too early yet to have any readers' reports on the manuscript, this is a rough draft and maybe not very fair to the author, but it's well worth reading nonetheless."

Harold Magnus was leaning forward incredulously, furious to discover that he was going to have opposition where he had most trusted for support—hadn't he made his message strong enough to her as they drove over? "Dr. Carriol, are you trying to say that this man—this Dr. Joshua Christian—is your choice for the job?"

"Oh, yes," she said calmly, smiling.

"But it's ridiculous! The man's an unknown!"

"So," she said deliberately, "were Jesus Christ and Mohammed. So it took a few centuries to get the Christian and the Muslim balls rolling. But in this day and age we have more facilities to make an unknown man known than ever in the history of the world. If the winner of Operation Search is not already famous, we can make him famous literally overnight, and you know it."

The President had gone very still, and hooded his large dark eyes. "Dr. Carriol, five years ago I gave you and your people the job of finding me one person—man or woman did not matter so long as he or she was the right person—*one person* capable of teaching a sick nation how to heal itself. A person with his finger on the pulse of the common people, capable of firing their imaginations as no religious figure seems capable of doing any more. Now you yourself are talking religion!"

"Yes, Mr. President."

"What the hell is going on?" roared Harold Magnus. "No one said anything about religion!"

Dr. Carriol rounded on him. "Oh, come on, sir! Surely you must have realized by now that the only way to cure this country's ills is to give the people not a moral boost, but a spiritual one! The man we're looking for has to be possessed of a truly unique ability to influence the mood of the people, and when you talk that kind of influence, you're talking about spirituality, religious thought, God, whatever! We need an *American* approach to it, a *contemporary* approach to it, a code for living in this time devised for the people of the United States of America by a man they can call their own! A man who understands and appeals to *them,* not the Irish or the Germans or the Jews or any other group who came here, however long ago! If our asses weren't dragging on the ground, we wouldn't be here now looking at the results of one of the biggest and most expensive investigations ever mounted! But our asses *are* dragging on the ground!"

Tibor Reece watched, his thoughts not deflected from the main business of the day, yet fascinated even so to discover what kind of people Judith Carriol and Harold Magnus really were. A man might have considerable congress with another man, and think he knew him well enough thereby, but nothing could beat a gloves-off altercation for showing up true colors. The little lady was a terrier; Harold Magnus was mostly bark.

"Look at this," commanded Dr. Carriol, abandoning the fray just when it was getting interesting. She pressed a button on her hand-held console, and the dull grey face of the video monitor blossomed into an image of Dr. Christian, sitting at a desk this time. His face was drawn and tight, and the eyes suffered.

"I don't know why I feel like this, Lucy, and I know I shouldn't even be saying it, but somehow I have always had a feeling that I have something more to do than sit here and see my poor patients. I fight it, mind you! It's too inside my own person, too self-oriented to be of good intent. Or so I keep trying to tell myself. But I *know* I have a mission! Something to do, Lucy! Something to do out there among the millions who don't even know I exist. I want to take them into my arms and love them! Show them *someone* cares! Someone—anyone—even me."

Dr. Carriol flicked the Off button, and the video monitor died completely.

"That man," said Harold Magnus, jabbing his finger toward the expired monitor, "is either a revolutionary or a maniac!"

"No, Mr. Secretary," contradicted Dr. Carriol. "He is not by any stretching of the definition a revolutionary. At heart he himself is a very law-abiding man indeed, and his ethos is constructive rather than destructive. He doesn't hate. He loves! He doesn't burn. He bleeds! Nor is he a maniac. His thought processes manifest logic and method, and he is in firm touch with

129

reality. I agree he may be a potential depressive, but if he's given the kind of work he obviously feels driven to do, he'll thrive."

"He comes across very powerfully on screen," said the President thoughtfully.

"His is the genuine brand of charisma, Mr. President. It's actually because of the charisma that Dr. Chasen and his team preferred him over Senator Hillier, and after my own personal contacts with Dr. Christian, I am just as convinced that he's the only runner in the field. I could go on showing you clips of him talking all day, but I'm not going to. The two clips I have already shown you are relevant to Operation Search and its whole reason for being. The best backup I can offer is his book. You must read it."

"I take it you yourself have absolutely no doubts about Dr. Christian's suitability?" asked the President, studying her closely.

"None, sir. He is the *only* man with the characteristics necessary to see the job done the way it must be done."

"Hillier, Hillier!" growled Harold Magnus.

"What about the Senator?" asked Tibor Reece, not of his Secretary for the Environment, but of Dr. Judith Carriol.

Dr. Carriol put the remote-control panel down on the table to one side of where she was sitting, and leaned forward, her hands clasped on her knees. In this pose, but with her head lifted so she could stare straight at Tibor Reece, she spoke. "Mr. President, Mr. Secretary, I am going to be absolutely honest with you. I can't offer you positive proof to back up my contentions, because my contentions are deduced from certain largely semiotic behavior patterns only someone with my training and experience could properly assess. It is my firm opinion that Senator Hillier *cannot* be considered for this job for one reason above and beyond any charisma he may or may not have. Recently I spent an afternoon with him, very pleasantly, very easily. And I came away utterly convinced that the good Senator is in love with power for the sake of power. We dare not give this job to a power freak! That simple."

"Interesting," said the President, whose face betrayed nothing of what he thought.

"Also, the Senator doesn't have that slight streak of compulsive I-am-chosen about him, where Dr. Christian does. You heard Dr. Christian for yourselves. I think the I-am-chosen is essential. We agreed that we couldn't put a religious in this role because of two factors. The first, that a brand of religion prejudices all those who don't share that particular brand against the religious. The second, that we are in the midst of a terminal failure of existing religions to grasp and hold the feelings and the minds of the people. Yet the right man for this job *must* have a religious aura about him! In the old days, before cars, planes, computers, education for the masses, freedom from real pestilence, inside bathrooms and all the other trappings of our age, only a religious could have done this job. It is neither my place nor my inclination to comment upon our times in respect of religion, gentlemen. I know you're both churchgoing men, and I know there are still a few churchgoing people out there. But every single year they fall away in millions! The mild rise in church attendance that occurred during the last quarter of the last century was due apparently to the hawkish nuclear weapon policies of the men in office at the time, because with the removal of that threat, down went church attendance again. And down. And down. The latest statistics show that only one in every thousand persons will admit to a religious persuasion of any kind, and only one in every fifty thousand regularly goes to church. I'm not saying that whoever does this job has to bring the people back to God, but I do think there has to be a strong element of that in him. Dr. Joshua Christian possesses the godly element, the slight streak of I-am-chosen, the charisma, and a great deal of down-to-earth common sense as well. He's not all up in the heavenly clouds, as you'll find out soon enough when you read his book. It's stuffed with the practicalities of life as well as the metaphysics: how to make a boarded-up house beautiful, how to live with the cold, how to make the most of relocation, how to deal with boards, bureaus, committees, councils and the like, how to fill the vacuum of huge chunks of leisure, how to treasure yet not spoil a single child—great stuff! In the book you'll also discover how much love there is in Dr. Christian for all the people of the world, but particularly for the people of his own country. He is first, last and always an American."

"Important," said Harold Magnus, listening but still chewing over what Dr. Carriol had said about Senator Hillier. Clever, clever woman, Carriol! That had been exactly the right thing to say to an existing President about the fundamental nature of a potential rival.

"We agreed five years ago that we have to do more for our

131

people than we are, yet we have to find a way of doing it that isn't going to cost us untold millions we just don't have. We're too committed to Project Phoebus to split off money it can't spare. So why not offer the people someone they can believe in, not as a god, not as a political axe grinding away, but simply as a good, kind, wise man? A man who *loves* them! They have lost so much of what they once had to love, from plenty of children to comfortable permanent homes to long summers and short winters. Gone! Yet is this the Sodom and Gomorrah retribution for generations of sin, as so many churchmen would have the people believe? That kind of explanation doesn't go down any more. Most people are not convinced they're wicked and won't be convinced they're wicked. They live largely decent lives, and they've come to expect credit for that. They don't want to believe that they must pay for generations of sin simply because they happen to be around at the beginning of the new millennium. They don't want to believe in a God Who they are told has sent an ice age to *punish* them! Organized churches are *human* institutions, and the best evidence for that is the fact that each and every one of them claims to be the only true church, the only God-guided church. But the people for whom they exist these days are skeptical, and if they accept a church at all, it tends to be on their terms rather than the church's."

"I take it, Dr. Carriol, that you are not a churchgoer," said the President dryly.

She stopped at once, her heart accelerating as she did a lightning calculation as to whether she had said too much, too little, or simply the wrong thing. Then she drew a deep breath. "No, Mr. President, I am not a churchgoer," she said.

"Fair enough," was all he answered.

She read that as a signal to change course, and did so.

"I guess what I'm trying to say is that no one seems to tell the people they are loved any more, even the churches. And a government can care, but by definition it can't love," she said. "Mr. President, give them a man who isn't out for personal power, or aggrandizement, or financial gain!" She unclasped her hands, and straightened. "That's all, I guess."

Tibor Reece sighed. "Thank you, Dr. Carriol. I am going to go through the seven candidates you have offered me by name, and I want you to give me your opinion about that man or woman in a very few words. I now understand Operation Search a lot better than I did, and I'm happy to admit it. But can I ask you one thing?"

She smiled at him gratefully. "Of course, sir."

"Did you always understand the purpose of Operation Search so well?"

She chewed her answer over before she spoke it. "I think so, Mr. President. But since meeting Dr. Christian, I maybe see the overall pattern better."

He stared at her. "Yes." Then he put on his reading glasses and picked up the seven files. "Maestro Benjamin Steinfeld?"

"He's been the darling of the musical intelligentsia too long for the good of his ego, sir."

"Dr. Schneider?"

"I really think she's too tied to NASA and Project Phoebus to cut the cord."

"Dr. Hastings?"

"I doubt whether we could divorce his image sufficiently from the football field, sir, which is a pity, because the man himself is worth a lot more than football."

"Professor Charnowski?"

"In some ways he's a very liberal person, but I think he's still too committed to the old form of Roman Catholicism to be able to give the way our man must."

"Dr. Christian?"

"For my money, he's the only one, Mr. President."

"Senator Hillier?"

"A power freak."

"And Mayor d'Este?"

"He's a good man, a most unselfish man. But his attitude is just too parochial."

"Thank you, Dr. Carriol." The President turned to his Secretary for the Environment. "Harold, have you any comment other than that you favor Senator Hillier?"

"Only that I don't like the way religion has crept into the picture, Mr. President. It's a hot potato, none hotter. We may be biting off more than we can chew."

"Thank you." The President nodded to both of them, a signal that the meeting was over. "I'll get back to you with my decision in a week or so."

Outside the White House Dr. Carriol discovered the extent of the Secretary's ire. He had always known she did not favor Senator Hillier, but he had not expected her to be so vigorously out-spoken to the President, and of course he had no idea that a Dr. Joshua Christian was going to upset his applecart. He and Dr. Carriol had traveled over from Environment in the Secretary's big, comfortable Cadillac, during which short journey he had thoroughly briefed Dr. Carriol on procedure.

Now he demonstrated the extent of his ire by climbing into the car and waving his driver to shut the door in Dr. Carriol's face. She stood on the sidewalk and watched the vehicle purr away down to Pennsylvania Avenue, turn the corner eastward, disappear. Oh, well! Easy come, easy go. It was back to Environment on foot, then.

The President's decision came through only four days later, and its overture was a command that the Secretary for the Environment and Dr. Judith Carriol should present themselves at the White House to see Mr. Reece at two in the afternoon precisely.

This time Dr. Carriol walked over as well, for no message came down from the Secretary inviting her to share his car, and she was not about to go cap in hand, asking. Luckily it was warm and sunny; how lovely to see an early spring! But how depressing to consider May an early spring in this part of the country. Cherry blossom time was just over, but the dogwoods were still two weeks off flowering; however, the grass was smothered by daffodils, and enough small trees were in bloom to make the walk a joy.

She arrived at the White House at the same moment as her chief, so they entered together, not speaking. She had smiled at him very cheerfully as he got out of his car, but his only response was a grumph. Interesting. He obviously thought he was going to lose. Of course he knew Tibor Reece far better than she did; until last week her only meeting with the President had been on that momentous day early in February of 2027, when he had been in office for three years and was looking forward to being reelected in November of 2028. Five years!

His predecessor had not been wrong in putting his immense personal clout behind Tibor Reece as his successor in the White House. Given the times, he was a sensible and stable choice. A caring man and an ethical one. But he was no Augustus Rome, for he was too reserved and austere to be the kind of President who inspired love in his people. Lincolnesque was the adjective usually applied to him by a mostly favorable press, and he clearly liked the comparison, felt at home with it, though in actual fact there was little resemblance either in personality or in policy. Not surprising. The Americas each man headed were not merely poles apart, but moons apart. For between Lincoln and Reece a whole ethos had perished: an ideal and dream and way of life and bright incandescent hope.

The President was on the phone when they were ushered in, looked up to gesture them to chairs, but went on talking. A compliment to her, certainly, if not to Harold Magnus. He was talking about the Russians. Nothing earth-shaking. The earth didn't shake much internationally since the Delhi Treaty. It was too busy coping with internal troubles to have the time, the energy (literally and metaphorically) or the money to fight expensive, useless wars.

The telephone conversation was about wheat. Only three nations in the world still exported significant quantities of grain: the United States of America, Argentina and Australia. People might come and go in the heartlands, but wheat went on forever. Canada's growing season had shortened too much, but the United States still managed to produce big crops, and the hybrid boys worked incessantly to develop strains able to survive colder springs and summers. The real crunch had become the length of time the ground remained unfrozen, but in future years it was likely to become the amount of rain. At the moment rainfall was sufficient, but it had been over twenty years since there had been an annual precipitation higher than the old average; mostly it was at least slightly lower than the old average, so the average in its turn was dropping. The two southern hemisphere nations were in better case, but how long that would last, no one was prepared to hazard a guess.

The President finished his conversation and bent his attention upon Environment.

"You know, Harold, yours is the most important agency in the country," said Tibor Reece. "I won't say you've got *all* the problems, but you've got the biggest and the most. Relocation, regulation of the birthrate, and conservation of our dwindling resources. You receive a full half of the federal budget money. And maybe because you don't deal with hawkish matters, you're no real trouble to a President." He grinned. "I don't lose much sleep over

135

Environment, anyway! In fact, you're very dedicated people, you believe in yourselves, and you run a tight ship. You've got the best computer setup in the world bar none, and you've come up with some brilliant ideas. So, I've done a lot of thinking about Operation Search. Mostly whether it's really necessary to implement its findings."

Dr. Carriol's heart sank; Harold Magnus's rose. Neither said a word; they just sat looking at the President.

"The trouble with any senior executive is that he tends to be cut off from the mainstream of popular thought and feeling by the demands—and the size!—of his job. It's like trying to make a Manhattanite born and bred understand the life cycle and mentality of people on the land. Or like trying to make a rich man born and bred understand what actual poverty is really about. Minds are admirable things. But sometimes I wish feelings were more admired, less derided. If there is any reason above all others why I still love and respect Augustus Rome, it's because that man *never* lost sight of the common people. He wasn't a demagogue, he didn't need to be. He was simply one of them."

Harold Magnus was nodding his head vigorously at these last remarks; Dr. Carriol concealed a smile, knowing full well what his genuine opinion of old Gus Rome was. You bloated old toady!

"However, during the last four days I found myself in the position of a shameless eavesdropper. I wandered into the kitchens on any excuse, I walked into rooms while they were being cleaned, I yarned with gardeners and secretaries and maids. Yet in the end it was my own wife who gave me the most help." He drew his lips back from his teeth and let his breath hiss between them, a tortured act perhaps, but not a contemptuous one. "I am not going to discuss my relationship with my wife. But—she's an unhappy woman, due to the times we live in. I had a talk with her, just about things like what she thinks about when she's alone, how she deals with the reality of our daughter when I'm not there to see them together, what kind of life she wants when we have to move out of here. . . ."

He paused, carefully controlling his face. It had been a painful interview for both of them, the more so because they did not communicate much in the normal course of their days. Her behavior was scandalous, yet he had never tried to reproach her for it, confining his activities to keeping her doings out of the press and keeping a tight security clamp on her. How could he reproach her when he had personally ensured she would never have a second child? Their rare quarrels were about her indifference to her daughter, moving into her teens without sufficient intelligence to know she was the antithesis of what a President's daughter ought to be. Tibor Reece loved his daughter dearly, but the amount of time he could give her was minuscule compared with the amount of time she needed, and her mother was no help.

"Anyway, I won't keep you in suspense any longer," he said to Harold Magnus and Dr. Judith Carriol. "I decided that we must implement Operation Search, and that Dr. Carriol's ideas about the nature of the man who gets the job are right. So Operation Search will move into its third phase, and I have to agree again with Dr. Carriol that there is really only one likely candidate. Dr. Joshua Christian."

Of course Harold Magnus couldn't protest, but his lips went thin and pursed, which gave to his round several-chinned face a different character, ruthless and egocentric, but also peevish and spoiled. Dr. Carriol kept her face impassive.

"Naturally," Tibor Reece went on, "the logistics are Environment's responsibility, and I am not going to inquire into them. But I will require frequent reports on progress, and I hope I'll soon see the results for myself. I've not yet approved a budget for phase three, but tentatively you can assume you've got all the money you're likely to need. There is just one further thing I would like to know now." He looked at Dr. Carriol. "Dr. Carriol, how do you intend to deal with Dr. Christian? I mean, is he to know about Operation Search? Have you given this area any thought?"

She nodded. "Yes, Mr. President, I have. Had you chosen Senator Hillier, for example, I would have said you *must* tell the man. But I am absolutely against Dr. Christian's being allowed to gain any idea of government involvement or manipulation. He's a natural for the job, therefore he does not need any boost from us in terms of his morale or his devotion to duty. It is not necessary to appeal to his patriotism, either. In fact, it is my considered opinion that were Dr. Christian to learn about Operation Search, we would immediately lose him and all the prospective benefits."

Tibor Reece smiled. "I agree with you."

"Mr. President, I think we are pinning a hell of a lot of faith—*blind* faith!—on a man we may not be able to control!" said

137

Harold Magnus, biting off his words to give them an additional emphasis they didn't actually need, his feelings showed so strongly. "We are now talking about the area responsible for my very grave doubts about Dr. Joshua Christian. It never occurred to me that we would pick a man who couldn't be told what and why—and how." He shuddered, revolted to the depths of his being. "I mean, we are going to have to *trust* the man!"

"We have no choice," said the President.

"Mr. Magnus, trust will only have to go so far," said Dr. Carriol calmly. "Dr. Christian will always be under constant supervision. I myself have established a position of some intimacy with him, and I intend to remain at the very center of his life. That means you will have to trust *me*, but I can assure you that if at any time I feel Dr. Christian is jeopardizing our project, I will deal with him before any harm is done. You have my word."

This was news to both of them. Tibor Reece smiled, Harold Magnus relaxed. Of course they both assumed she meant she was having an affair with Dr. Christian. Let them think it; it would comfort them.

"I might have known," said the Secretary.

"Is there anything further you need from me personally, Dr. Carriol?" the President asked.

She frowned, considering. "I don't think at this stage anyway that phase three is going to be expensive. A matter of some thousands of dollars is all."

"That's a break!" chuckled the President.

Dr. Carriol smiled briefly, went on. "The nice thing about choosing Dr. Christian is that he's largely self-fueling. Elliott MacKenzie of the Atticus Press says that Dr. Christian's book is going to sell millions, and Elliott is no fool. So Environment's original offer to him to underwrite any losses he might incur through Dr. Christian will not have to be implemented. Dr. Christian himself will become a very rich man into the bargain. No, the kind of assistance I am going to need from you, Mr. President, is different. I want travel approvals, priority to obtain the most comfortable accommodations, cars, planes, helicopters and the like." She stared at Harold Magnus blandly. "I will need funds for myself, since I intend to be with Dr. Christian throughout his publicity tour."

"Whatever you want you shall have," said Tibor Reece.

"I can't agree with your choice, Mr. President," said Harold

Magnus, "but I admit I'm a lot happier now I know Dr. Carriol is going to be with him."

"Why, thank you, sir!" said Dr. Carriol.

Now that he thought he knew the nature of her relationship with Dr. Christian, Tibor Reece was curious about Judith Carriol as a woman. "Dr. Carriol, do you mind if I ask you a rather personal question?"

"Not at all, sir."

"Does Dr. Joshua Christian *mean* anything to you? As a man? As a person?"

"Of course!"

"So what if it should come to a choice between the man and the welfare of the project he's engaged upon? How would you decide? What would you feel?"

"I'd be most unhappy. But I will do whatever I have to do to safeguard the project, no matter what I feel about the man."

"That's a very hard thing to say."

"Yes. But I have spent over five years of my life working toward this one objective. It's not a petty objective. Nor am I built to throw my work out the window for the sake of my private feelings. I'm sorry if that makes me sound inhuman, but it's a fact nonetheless."

"Would you be happier if you could throw your work out the window?"

"I am not unhappy, sir," she said firmly.

"I see." The President laid his big, well-shaped hand across the bulky packet of videotape, files and manuscript atop his desk. "Operation Search is passé. We need a new name for it."

"I have one, Mr. President," said Judith Carriol, so quickly she could not have coined it on the spot.

"Ah! You're ahead of us! All right then, what?"

She sucked in her breath, exultant. "Operation Messiah."

"Portentous," said Tibor Reece, only half liking it.

"It has never been anything else," she said.

VI

Dr. Joshua Christian hardly missed Dr. Judith Carriol, or indeed hardly even thought of her; he was too busy writing his book and keeping up a normal patient schedule at the same time. The book inspired him, ravished him. It was miraculous. Beautiful fluid exquisitely apt words joined together to form beautiful fluid exquisitely apt sentences that sounded like him and rang with the same clarion as his voice. Miraculous!

Mama and James and Andrew and Mary and Miriam and Martha gave him their wholehearted and unflagging support, spared him every conceivable task they could, asked no questions, were patient with his sudden outbreaks of absent-mindedness, reorganized the entire 1047 house to suit him and his indomitable amanuensis, cooked and laundered and horticultured for him, involved his patients in the general conspiracy ("He's writing a book, you know, think of what that will mean to all the people who need him but he hasn't got the time to see!"). They never complained or criticized or even expected him to notice their efforts on his behalf, let alone appreciate those efforts. So when he did notice and he did express his appreciation, they glowed and loved him anew. That is, all save Mary, who worked as hard for him as anyone and got her meed of thanks, but would have preferred no thanks.

Many of the hours and hours he spent talking to Lucy Greco

were wasted, he knew that; hours when his thoughts were undisciplined or he spoke of himself when he himself was not at issue. But the wasted hours provided grist for the hours that were not wasted, when he could manage to marshal his enthusiasm and his theories into a pattern Lucy Greco could follow. And then, while he saw patients or went off to ruminate some particularly knotty concept into smooth mental paste, she sat in the room in 1047 Oak Street given to her for an office, and she performed those verbal miracles that so ravished him when he read them. The big IBM voicewriter he had never used she used now, and never, she felt, to better advantage.

Once when he came in he looked curiously at the label on the side of the machine, and sighed.

"What?" she asked, at a loss.

"Made in Scarlatti, South Carolina," he said, very sadly. "Once, you know, Holloman made a good proportion of this country's personal printing machines—every kind from plain old typewriter to—well, not this make of voicewriter, but several others. The factory is still here. I walk through it sometimes. It's easy to get in, they've given up any pretense at a security guard or even a caretaker. What for? Who wants to steal dies and mandrels and presses you can't adapt to any other purpose? So the factory is just full of emptiness and rusting plant, there's filth on the floor and ice hanging from the rafters."

"Maybe you ought to pay a visit to Scarlatti," said Lucy, still at a loss. "There are at least half a dozen big personal printing machine companies set up there. And I'm sure everything is new and bright, with better staff facilities and a much nicer working environment."

"I never doubted that!" he said, affronted.

Lucy sighed. "Josh, honey, sometimes you do make my life hard! Here I am helping you to write a book about positivity, and what am I getting?" she asked, shutting her eyes to round up her thoughts better and exclude his person from them. "A good proportion of the talking you do to me is taken up by an utterly negative longing for a world you keep telling your readers is gone and can never come back again. Think of the hours you waste! And what a meretricious activity it is! When you go on the road to publicize your book, you can't let yourself get all nostalgic, you know. You've set yourself the task of telling the people they can't afford nostalgia! And if they can't afford it, neither can you, Josh.

141

That's a fact you've got to face up to. It's not do-as-I-say, it has to be do-as-I-do. Otherwise it will all blow up in your face."

Punctured. Pricked. Deflated. Zapped. "Oh, God! You are so right!" he cried, and collapsed in a tangle of arms and legs, a broken doll. Then he began to laugh, and he leaped from the chair, capering around the room running his hands through his stiff black hair until it looked as if the raging winds of his mind were erupting through his scalp. "You are so right! *So right!* Oh, woman, I have needed you and I have needed Judith Carriol so badly! I have needed your new minds and souls to listen to me prate instead of all those sweet slavish devoted bigots next door! How can I get my thoughts into order when they sit listening to me with such an I-love-Joshua-he-can-do-no-wrong attitude that they never give me constructive criticism? Thank you, thank you, thank you!"

He came to a halt, standing pressing his hands together over the groin he never thought of. "I want to say—oh, how beautiful rich emotions are if you can learn not to wallow in them, and how natural grief is, and what a great friend time can be, and that nothing that ever happens—*ever* happens!—is without purpose. That the new can founder on the old, and that courage and strength can be just as lovable as weakness." He stopped, glared at her. "Why can't I write all that down?" he demanded, exasperated. "I can speak words to an audience—any audience!—as if my tongue was made of silver and my voice was made of gold and my soul had wings. Yet let me stare at a sheet of blank paper or a tape recorder or one of these fantastic voicewriters and the words all rush off somewhere to hide and no matter how hard I try, I cannot roust them out."

"Well, either it's a psychological block or a physiological one," she said, more to calm him down than out of interest.

"Both," he said instantly. "Somewhere there's a little cerebral relay that's shorted out—a thrombosis or a plaque or a knot of scar tissue—and sitting right on top of it is the awful festering cesspool of my subconscious."

Lucy couldn't help but laugh. "Oh, Josh, you're such a gentle good man that I don't believe your subconscious can be any different!"

"The best kept and tightest run ship still accumulates bilge, and the most immaculate house still needs its drains, so why shouldn't human minds have to obey the same law?"

"I think that's bordering on sophistry," she said.

He grinned. "Well, the Mouse put me through her full gamut of tests, and I do have a genuine dysgraphia, if that's any consolation."

"You can also be mighty slippery," said Lucy Greco.

Elliott MacKenzie read the rough draft before passing the only copy to Dr. Judith Carriol; he had promised her not to keep a word of the manuscript anywhere within his publishing house. But he hated digesting that sort of magic and then being obliged to give it up without keeping so much as one copy. Oh, Lucy had a copy in Holloman, but that too was not available to him. What if this precious book got lost? What if Environment decided there was something subversive about it and withheld it from publication? They owned all the rights on Dr. Christian's behalf, Judith Carriol had seen to that.

Lucy Greco found time somewhere to keep in touch, and she was imbued with a kind of enthusiasm he had never seen in her before. In fact, she was behaving like a young nun in the grip of divine possession; she obviously felt herself a privileged vessel filled with Joshua Christian's essence, and found genuine ecstasy in spilling it upon the sheet after sheet of paper her voicewriter spat out.

Elliott MacKenzie thrust a cautious toe into the sea of her opinion and asked her if Dr. Christian was capable of articulating his thoughts in front of cameras and microphones, since his writer's block extended to voice-triggered machines.

"He'll knock 'em in the aisles," was Lucy's reply. "So long as there's a human face and a pair of human eyes he can look into, he'll be fantastic."

So if Environment decided to quash the Christian book, what would Atticus do?

Two weeks after he had couriered the manuscript to her office in Washington, Dr. Carriol rang him.

"It's go, Elliott," she said. "All stops out. The sooner the better. When can Lucy have a final draft ready?"

"Another month, she thinks. The trouble is he keeps producing more stuff she can't bear to leave out, and yet there's a definite reader's cutoff point for any book of this kind, so we have to keep it trimmed down to a maximum 256 pages in print. Oh, we can produce a follow-up volume next year, but that means addi-

143

tional time in editing while we look at the whole final draft and pick out what must go in the first book and what can wait until the second."

"How much extra time?"

"At the very outside, we could have it in the bookstores by the end of September."

"We would rather it was the end of October, provided it takes off immediately."

"With this one, no sweat," he said, and meant it.

"A million copies in hardback and at least five million in paperback?"

That was too much to grasp, even for Elliott MacKenzie. "Hey hey hey, wait a minute! With a book this hot, paperback not until a year after hardcover publication, Judith. There is no way I'd see it go soft a day sooner."

"Hard and soft editions out together," she said.

"No. Sorry, but no."

"Sorry, but yes, Elliott. You won't lose."

"My dear girl, it would take an executive order from the President of the United States to make me change my mind, and even then I'd fight!"

"You'll have the executive order by tomorrow at the latest, if that's your attitude. Only don't bother, Elliott, please. You can't win."

He pressed both hands against his eyes, unwilling to believe her. And yet—he had to believe her, because she was not the kind of person who bluffed. Just what in hell *was* this Joshua Christian thing?

"Come on, Elliott, you're talking the biggest book in the history of publishing, right? So how can you lose? Why get greedy, huh? I put the book in your way, and I can take it out of your way just as easily. You don't hold Joshua Christian to contract, Environment does." She sounded as if she was enjoying herself, but she also sounded as if she meant every word she said.

He gave in. "All right." Pause. "Damn you!"

"Good boy! You can start leaking scuttlebutt about the book as of yesterday, but until I give you the word, I want no copies disseminated to anyone. If you need extra security staff, I'll provide them for you gratis. Because I mean it, Elliott. No leaking the book itself. No black market in advance copies, bound galleys or manuscript. I don't care if you have to threaten to shoot your people, so long as the book stays under wraps until I say it can be displayed."

"Okay."

"Fine. Now I want the paperback rights sold at auction, and I want the press tipped off about the auction beforehand."

Where had she learned so much? He drew a breath. "I will do a deal with you, Judith. I will guarantee you advance publicity that will measure up to your wildest dreams. But no auction. Goddam it, I'm a *publisher!* And my instincts tell me this book is going to be a perennial best-seller. So I want to keep the paperback rights within the group. No auction! It goes to Scroll, our own paperback house."

"I insist on an auction," she said.

"Look, Judith, I thought you wanted no intimation of any kind that Environment is involved in this? Well, let me tell you something. If I do as you ask, the whole publishing industry is going to smell a rat, and so will the New York newspapers. Because I'm well known for my sharpness, and to do as you ask is dumb."

The phone was silent. Then, "All right, you win. You can keep the paperback rights within the Atticus group provided publication coincides with the hardcover edition."

"You've got a deal."

"Okay. Now I want a protocol from your publicity department as soon as possible. Not what they plan to do to launch Dr. Christian's book. What I want from them is their dream of heaven when it comes to publicity for a book like Dr. Christian's. The TV talk shows they'd give their eyeteeth to get him on, the radio shows, the magazines, the Sunday supplements, all that stuff. By the way, what do you think of his title? Is it good, or would your marketing people rather it was changed?"

"No. It's a good title. I like the deity angle and I like the hint of divine wrath. Intriguing in this world that still hankers after God but can't admit it."

"Mr. Reece would like to know where the title comes from. Did Lucy dream it up, or did he? Is it original?"

"No, it's not original. He and Lucy found it when they were doing the usual title hunting through Bartlett's. The lines were written by Elizabeth Barrett Browning. 'Get leave to work . . . for God, in cursing, gives us better gifts than men in benediction.' It says it all, I think." He paused. "You did say Mr. Reece? Tibor Reece, spelled as in President?"

"That's right. Mr. Reece is taking a very personal interest in Dr. Christian and his book—but that, I hope I don't need to add, is a piece of news for your ears only."

The shocks were too thick and fast. "Has *he* read it?"

"Yes. He's most impressed."

"Judith, just what is going on?"

"A little altruism for a change, Elliott. Believe it or not, the government of this country cares about the people of this country. And we feel, Mr. Reece and Mr. Magnus and I, that Dr. Joshua Christian, the man and his ideas and his book, can have a more positive effect on the national morale than anything in the last fifty years at least." Her voice changed. "You've read it. Don't you agree?"

"Wholeheartedly."

When he went home he told his wife all about it, so secure in her discretion that it never occurred to him for one moment not to tell her. Sally didn't gossip, didn't even like to hear gossip. For more years than he cared to remember she had shared his interests and his world without being involved in it other than through the bonds of matrimony. Their only child was safely in college at Dartmouth and as bookish as his parents, but with his father's strong business streak in him also to ensure that Atticus would go on being a family concern. There had been a MacKenzie at the helm of Atticus since Elliott's great-great-grandfather founded the house, and the house had gone from strength to strength, put a large amount of high-quality reading matter on the bookshelves of America, and enabled the MacKenzies to live in a very much better way than they had back in the Highlands of Scotland. But now the one-child family threatened all that. Oh, for the freedom to sire more than one child! If anything happened to Alastair— No! He refused even to think of that; instead he thought of what would happen should his son sire an unsatisfactory child. Still, he comforted himself—for he was a sensible man—he knew of other dynastic families who had sired a dozen children without managing to produce a satisfactory heir. It was all in the luck of the genes.

So he went home and told his wife all about it.

"I'm champing at the bit! Where is it? I've got to read it at once!" Sally cried.

"I don't have a copy," he confessed.

"Good God! It's very strange, Elliott. Do you fully understand what's going on? I mean, here's the President of the United States taking an interest."

"The only thing I understand fully," he said, "is the business end of it. And I can assure you that Atticus has got itself the biggest book in the history of publishing."

"Including the Bible?" she asked dryly.

He considered that, laughed, shrugged, and gave her a brave reply. "Who knows?"

Things were really going terrifically well, Dr. Judith Carriol congratulated herself as she stepped from the little subsonic helicopter that had brought her from Washington to Holloman in less than an hour, scuttlehuffing its way across the empty sky as if pursued by the Furies. Ah, this was the life! Holloman's one and only governmental car was waiting for her on the tarmac of the disused airport, amid tall weeds and windswept heaps of anonymous detritus, with a uniformed man complete to cap standing to assist her into its back seat. Not that she had any illusions about her importance. The moment Operation Messiah was over, it would be back to buses and hoofing it. Still, she could relish this opportunity to bask in the kind of importance normally reserved only for elected officials of the highest caliber, and she kept telling herself in every quiet moment during her stuffed days that she must never become so accustomed to luxury that the return to normality would prove unendurable. A leaf out of Joshua Christian's book. Enjoy, but when it's finished, don't look back. Onward and upward into tomorrow.

Strange. She hadn't seen him for two months, but at the last moment, standing on the sidewalk exactly between 1047 and 1045 Oak Street, she could not bring herself to go through the back door into 1045, where at this hour she knew he would be busy in his clinic. Instead, she buzzed to be admitted to 1047.

Mama's embrace was natural and warm; she might have been welcoming a daughter. "Oh, Judith! It's been too long." Mama held her away to gaze at her with what seemed genuine love in the soft depths of her eyes. "A car! I saw you pull up. I was out in the yard with the wash—isn't it lovely to be able to hang out the wash in the sun again instead of in the basement?"

Pain. Oh no, I don't want to feel pain! I mustn't feel pain! For what you are about to receive I cannot be held responsible.

Mama, Mama, how will you cope with the realization of all your dreams and ambitions for him? How big is the soul inside your gorgeous shell? Why do you welcome me as if I am his prospective wife, and the wife of your choosing? Where I am going to send him there will be no time or energy for a wife, and where I am sending myself there can be no husband.

"I wasn't sure if I'd be disturbing him if I went into 1045, so I thought it would be better to come here." She followed Mama through the innermost back door and into the kitchen. "How is he?" she asked, and sat down as Mama began to prepare coffee.

"He's well, Judith. Very well. But glad to see the end of Lucy, I think. Doing that book took so much out of him! He wouldn't stop pulling his weight in the clinic while he was writing it, that was the trouble. She was very good, mind you. Lucy Greco, I mean. Very nice. Very good. But he needed you very much. I kept hoping you'd come! It's time he wasn't alone."

"Mama, this is ridiculous! You've only met me once, you know nothing about me! So to treat me as if I am the center of Joshua's emotional life is—is incongruous! I'm *not* Joshua's fiancée! He is not in love with me, and I am not in love with him. And don't, please don't set your heart on a marriage between us, because it's not going to happen."

"Silly girl," said Mama fondly. She put cups down on the table, her best Lenox service, and leaned to check how the coffee was coming on. "Get your breath back. And don't be so negative! Have your coffee with me and then you can go into the living room to wait for him. I'll buzz him to come over as soon as he's free."

Interesting as well as exasperating. The Mamas of this world were disappearing, she was among the youngest of them at forty-eight, or was it still forty-seven? A dying breed, women who could afford to exude maternalism because they had a houseful of children. They had used up the staggering amounts of excess energy Nature had given them for just that purpose. It was all right for the ones like herself who could pluck a satisfactory substitute out of their own internal resources, but so many women couldn't. Or wouldn't. Well, Joshua Christian, you will certainly be able to help all the couldn'ts, but the wouldn'ts? I do not think anyone can help a wouldn't.

Windows had magically appeared among the greenery, neat unframed rectangular glass panes that let the sun stream in to dance with a billion golden motes down solid shafts of light. The plants were absolutely rejoicing, burst into a dazzle of flower, waxy spike and velvety tumble and silky mass. Pink and cream and yellow and blue and lilac and peach. Very little white. How clever of the Christians to avoid white blossoms in a white room. This was a wonderland that must surely have thrilled them every time they remembered to look, to really *look*. Only how often was that?

They are beautiful people. It takes beautiful people to make beauty in their surroundings when it is so much easier to put up with dreariness.

When his mother buzzed and gave him the news that Dr. Judith Carriol was waiting in the living room to see him, Dr. Christian found himself mildly surprised. So much had happened since he last saw her that he had largely lost sight of the fact she had been the prime mover. Oh—yes—Judith Carriol. Judith Carriol? A vague memory of violet and scarlet, of someone exhilarating to talk to, of a timeless friend and an eternal enemy . . .

Between then and now he had planted and tended and harvested and winnowed a vast field of thought, and at the moment he was gazing across the stubble wondering and wondering what must be planted next. He tingled with possibilities divorced from any fellow man or woman, he groped after the odd sensations which had plagued him so all through the winter, daring to dream that maybe after all he did have a destiny wider and bigger than this clinic in Holloman.

Why should I be so sad? he asked himself, turning at the end of the passageway that joined his two houses not toward the back stairs and Mama's kitchen, but toward the front stairs to the living room. There was nothing between us. Nothing at all beyond an intellectual stimulation and compatibility. I just knew she had significance for me, and I was afraid of her, that is true. But there was nothing else. There could be nothing else, given who and what we are. To dally unfruitfully in the arms of a lover, no matter how beloved, is a solipsistic alternative both of us discarded many years ago. She is not now intruding into my present trailing bits of the past around her like a bridal veil. Why therefore am I so afraid to see her face? Why do I not want to remember her?

But it wasn't hard after all to meet her eyes and assimilate the face which encapsulated them. Her smile was very warm and glad to see him, yes, yet it laid no claim to his spirit and it embraced him only as a dear kind friend.

"I can only stay an hour or so," she said, settling back into her chair. "I wanted to see how you were, how you feel about the book—I've read it, incidentally, and I think it's magnificent. I want to know too what you plan to do when it's published, if you've thought about that."

He looked bewildered. "Do? Published?"

"First things first. The book. Are *you* happy with it?"

"Oh, yes. Yes, of course I am. And I'm so grateful to you for steering me to Atticus, Judith. The woman they gave me was— was—" He moved his shoulders helplessly. "I don't honestly know how to explain it. But she worked with me like the bit of me that's always been missing. And together we wrote exactly the book I've always wanted to write." He laughed a little ruefully. "That is, if I had ever seriously entertained the idea. I didn't. Did I? It's hard to remember that far back. So much has happened." He frowned uneasily and moved in his chair. "It's one thing to work to achieve an end, Judith, but somehow this book is more like a gift from outside. As if my subconscious had expressed a wish, and genie Judith appeared from nowhere to grant it in full."

What a mixture the man was! Dangerously perceptive at times, at other times simple and innocent to the point of naivety. Astonishing, that with the light switched off he was the epitome of an absent-minded and particularly woolly professor, the sort you pinned a note to bearing his name and address and telephone number in case he G. K. Chestertoned off into the blue and didn't come back. But when the light was switched on, a demigod appeared, vibrant and steely-minded and electrifying. My dearest Joshua, she thought, you do not know it and I pray you never find out, but I am going to work the arc lights of your very soul!

"Have they told you yet what they expect from you when the book is actually published?" she asked.

Again he looked puzzled. "When it's published? I do seem to remember Lucy's saying something, but what would they expect of me? I've done my share already."

"Oh, I think they're going to want considerably more from you than just the act of producing the book," she said crisply. "It is a very important book, therefore you will become a very important person. And you'll be asked to do a publicity tour, make personal appearances—television, radio, luncheons and lectures, stuff like that. I'm afraid you'll also be asked to grant interviews to a lot of papers and magazines too."

He looked eager. "But that's marvelous! Even though the book is me—and you've no idea how glad I am to be able to say that!—still I would much rather *talk* about my ideas."

"That's just great, Joshua. Because I happen to agree with you, the best transmitter is definitely you in the flesh. So I want you to regard the publicity tour they'll ask you to make as the ideal opportunity to reach many more people than ever you could hope to see in your clinic." She paused, a delicate and peculiarly pregnant break in speech; in a patient he would have recognized it as the preface to a thought the patient wished to implant in him so that the tissue of lies which inevitably followed would sound utterly sincere. But what she said didn't live up to that pause, for she merely said, "I have always regarded the book as a secondary objective, a reason to offer the media you in the flesh."

"Have you? I thought you wanted the book above all."

"No. The book is a subsidiary of the man."

He left the statement unremarked. "Well, I'm sure Lucy did mention a publicity tour, but I can't remember when or how. I'm sorry, Judith. I think I must be very tired. Not keeping track of things. It's been hard these last few weeks, writing with Lucy and treating patients on my usual schedule. I'm a bit short on sleep."

"You've got the whole summer to rest up in," she said brightly. "Atticus will gear itself to publish in the fall, just before mass exodus begins and just as mass depression sets in. That's the logical moment to release this book. The people will be ready for it. Ripe."

"Yes . . . Mmmm . . . Thanks for the words of wisdom, Judith, I like to be filled in. And it sounds as if I'd better rest up all summer."

Clearly he was torn; avid to make personal contact with vast numbers of the populace, yet apprehensive about the vehicle he would be riding and the antics of his chauffeur, Judith Carriol. God, but it was going to be hard dealing with him! Out of touch with so much of the outside world because he didn't watch television and he didn't listen to the radio and he only read the *New York Times* and the *Washington Post* and good or professional books. Yet at one and the same time, he was more aware of what ailed the populace than any of the possible sources of information he might have pursued.

151

Under her eyelids she watched him closely. There was something new and odd about him, and it gnawed at the roots of her certainty. A fragility? A fading? Was his self eroding? Garbage! she assured herself. Imagination. Quite a logical combination of her own insecurity and his strenuous spring of writing and working. He was not a frail man, he was a sensitive one. He did not lack strength, he lacked egocentric toughness. And above all he was a man capable of rising to the occasion when he felt he was needed, capable under those circumstances of giving everything he had and more besides.

In the end she stayed to dinner, aware (and mildly amused by it) that the younger women of Joshua Christian's household did not regard her so suspiciously this evening as they had on the day she had first met them. Whatever Mary and Martha and Miriam had sensed in her and her relationship with their beloved brother apparently was no longer felt to be a threat. What had they sensed? What had everyone sensed that she had not? Or he had not, for that matter? How odd, when their contacts with each other had in actual fact been devoid of personal complications. Dr. Carriol left for her helicopter and Washington with the conundrum unanswered.

"So Judith finished filling in the picture for me of what is going to happen after the book is released," Dr. Christian said to his family that night in the living room.

"Well, I presume you'll be asked to do some kind of publicity tour?" asked Andrew, who had made it his business to become better informed about the mechanics of publishing since his brother's venture into literature. He had also taken to watching a few television programs and switching on the radio in his office when he had no patients and no really concentrated work to do.

"Yes. Which pleases me in one way and is likely to be an embarrassment in others. I've given all of you so much extra work to do this spring, and now it seems I'll have to take more time off in the fall."

"No sweat," said Andrew, smiling.

Mama was very happy. Dearest Joshua was back in the bosom of his family after a two-month mental absence. How nice to see him sitting placidly sipping his cognac along with his coffee, instead of jumping up from the table with his last mouthful of food still unswallowed. She didn't even feel an urge to sting him into a diatribe.

"Do you think you'd like me to come along with you?" asked Mary, yearning to go with him. So many years in this little moribund city of Holloman when there was so much to see outside it! Behind her passivity and her knowledge that she was neither so bright as Joshua nor so beautiful as Mama nor so necessary as James and Andrew and Miriam and Martha, a restless and bitter and frustrated spirit champed; alone among the Christians, Mary had an urge to travel, to see new places, experience new things. But being by nature a passive one, she couldn't come out and say what she wanted. She just lived her sterile life waiting for someone in her family to see it without being told; what she couldn't understand was that her very neutrality and passivity made her invisible to all the rest, that she hid her longings too well, and so no one ever dreamed they existed.

Dr. Christian smiled at her, shook his head emphatically. "No, of course I don't! I'll be fine on my own."

Mary said no more, nor let her feelings show.

"Will you be gone long?" asked the Mouse, looking down at her feet.

For her, so small and sweet and grey, he always had a special tenderness; so he gave her that wonderful special smile as he said gently, "I don't imagine so, dear Mouse. One or two weeks should do it."

Her eyes had lifted to drink in this benediction, eyes huge and wistful, teary-bright.

Andrew got to his feet immediately, yawning. "I'm tired! I think I'll go to bed, if you'll all excuse me."

James and Miriam rose too, glad someone else had suggested bed. Theirs was a good marriage, chiefly because it had brought an unexpected joy in its wake: wrapped in its sanctity they had discovered the deliciousness of skin against skin, body against body. And summer was their time, when they could sport in their bed for hours untrammeled by nightclothes and bedclothes. Perhaps intellectually Miriam preferred Joshua to James, but certainly in no other way imaginable.

"Lazy!" said Joshua, getting to his feet. "I'm going for a walk. Anyone else feel like it?"

Mama jumped up at once and rushed off to find some comfortable shoes, while the Mouse said in her shy little voice that she really ought to go with Andrew.

"Nonsense!" said Joshua. "Come with us. Mary?"

"No thanks. I'll clear up the kitchen."

For several seconds longer Martha dithered, her eyes traveling between Joshua and Mary, dismayed, apprehensive. "I won't come, Joshua," she said in the end. "I'll give Mary a hand and then I'd better go to bed."

. Mary looked at Martha a little grimly, then stretched out her hand and yanked the youngest member of the Christian family from her chair. It was not a gracious gesture, but as Mary's strong fingers closed over her own, Martha as always felt that hand plucking her from a sea of doubt and carrying her to safety.

"Thank you," she said as they reached the haven of the kitchen. "I never do know how to get out of difficult situations. And I'm sure Mama will want Joshua to herself."

"You're dead right," said Mary. She lifted her hand again, this time to tuck back behind one ear an erring strand of fine dun hair. So like a mouse's coat! "My poor little Mouse," she said. "But cheer up. You're not the only one who's trapped."

Mama and Joshua paced steadily through the still and tranquil night, arms linked, a feat he managed in spite of the difference in their heights by cuddling his mother's shoulder rather than her elbow.

"I'm glad Lucy's gone and you're free of the book," was her opening gambit.

"So am I, by God!" he said with great feeling.

"Are you happy, Joshua?"

When anyone else asked him that question he fenced, but Mama and he had been joint heads of the family for nearly thirty years, and on his side the bond between them was a mature one.

"Yes and no," he said. "I can see so many possibilities opening up, opportunities I really do welcome. That makes me happy. And yet I can also see problems. I'm a bit afraid, I suppose. Therefore I'm unhappy."

"It will work itself out."

"Nothing surer!"

"It's what you've always wanted to do. Oh, not write a book and become a famous man! I mean get yourself into a position where you can help a great many people. Judith is an amazing

154

woman, you know. I would never have thought of a book, not knowing your difficulties with the written word."

"Nor would I." He guided her across Route 78 and into the park. Enormous moths bumbled around the infrequent lights, the leafy trees sighed in a faint breeze, some unknown flower's perfume trailed elusively around the nostrils, and everywhere the inhabitants of Holloman walked the short summer night of the short summer. "You know, Mama," he went on, "I think that's what frightens me most of all. This afternoon I found myself thinking of Judith as the genie of my own personal Aladdin's lamp. I wish, and out she pops with all the answers."

"No! How could that be? It was chance, Joshua. If you hadn't gone to Hartford to sit in on that Marcus trial, you and she would never have met. But you did go to Hartford, and you did meet her. She's terribly important, isn't she?"

"Oh, yes."

"Well, there you are! She sees and knows so much we couldn't, living here in Holloman as we do. And she must know all the right people."

"Indeed she does."

"So doesn't it make sense?"

"It should. But it doesn't. There's *something*, Mama! I voice a wish, and she makes it come true."

"Then next time you see her, if that's before I do, would you ask her to grant me just one wish?"

He stopped beneath a light to look down at her. "You? What do you want you can't have?"

Her beautiful face laughed up at him, more beautiful because it laughed. "I want you and Judith."

"No good, Mama," he said, starting to walk again. "I respect her. Sometimes I even like her. But I couldn't love her. You see, she doesn't need love."

"I don't agree with you at all," said Mama stoutly. "Some people hide their feelings very well. She's like that. I don't know why. All I do know is that she's the right woman for you."

"Oh, look, Mama! A concert on the lake!" And he began to walk faster down the hill toward the ornamental lake, where four musicians on a moored pontoon were playing Mozart.

Mama gave up. There was no competing with Mozart.

VII

Summer swelled up on its own hot air, lush and oh so languorous, more ephemeral in these days when people were perpetually aware of its brevity and mortality, but no less hot, hot, hot; how could a place so arctically cold in winter be so tropically hot and humid in summer? But ice ages aside, that was a question Americans of the northern states had been asking themselves ever since the seventeenth century. The only real difference between a summer of the second millennium and one of the third millennium was its duration, shorter now by about four weeks.

In the evacuee cities of the north and midwest, summer had to be ignored while those who had made the arduous trek up from the south during the first days of April toiled to make up for their enforced winter idleness. And following an annual pattern apparent for some years now, the spring of 2032 saw fewer people than ever before return north, while more people than ever before relocated permanently in some Band A or Band B town south of the Mason-Dixon line, or west and south of the Canadian-Arkansas River.

When relocation had begun over twenty years earlier, no one who still had a job in the north wanted permanent relocation; but that state of affairs was now reversed, the list of applicants for permanent relocation grew ever longer, while a harassed government fell ever further behind in the number of permanent places

156

it could offer potential relocatees. Of course there were many who spurned federal assistance in relocating, just sold what they could in the north and bought afresh in the south. But because property in the north and midwest was fetching next to nothing, there were many indeed who could not relocate permanently until they received official help. Probably about the same number of new fortunes were made as old ones were lost; builders, housing developers and land speculators waxed fat while small northern businessmen and professionals waned lean. The warmest of the southern states fought desperate battles to curb the growth of trailer parks and shantytowns, dinning their woes in Washington's left ear while the skeletal remains of the northernmost states dinned their woes in Washington's right ear. All of which made the one-child family a crucial factor in the struggle to equilibrate. Oddly enough, many more people were prepared to defy the government in order to stay in the south all year round than defied the one-child family edict.

Excluding the area that once had housed the black and Hispanic communities, things came to life in Holloman after April Fool's Day. There were still more unoccupied houses by far than tenanted ones, but every block saw one or two dwellings with winter boards taken down and drapes flying proud as flags out of open windows. The streets had pedestrians, more of the suburban shopping malls opened, the frequency and number of buses increased, the few industries not permanently removed kept up production seven days a week. Winter grime was scrubbed and blown off everything, dilapidation lessened, the cinemas went back into business, so did a number of restaurants and diners and bars and ice cream stands. The roadways suddenly littered a modest number of solar-battery-powered electric carts that ambled quiet as the grave and slow as a snail on pleasurable errands. Those in a hurry or going to and from work or school caught buses and trolley cars, those going to the market or the park or the doctor crept there and back by electric cart. And a lot walked, of choice. Mentally the people might have been depressed and apathetic, but physically they had never been fitter.

However, by the end of September what little euphoria had trembled in the summer air above Holloman was dwindling away again. Two months before relocation would be completed, yet already the warmth was gone from the sun. Two months in which

157

to pack away things not wanted down south and wind up affairs and start the telephoning and queueing to see how and when the winter exodus would be conducted. While the glorious Indian summer that now came in September instead of in October worked its hot-day cold-night witchery on the trees and they turned red, yellow, orange, copper, amber, purple, Holloman thought only of how cold the nights were getting and shut out the pageant of the fall by boarding up its windows and doors. A dumb enduring hideously patient sadness came down with the first fog, and people began to tell each other how glad they would be to quit the place, preferably for good. Who wanted or needed this circus living, forever packing up and moving on? Who wanted living at all? The suicide rate commenced its soaring annual escalation, the acute psychiatric units at Chubb-Holloman Hospital and Holloman Catholic Hospital filled to overflowing, and the Christian Clinic was obliged to turn patients away.

The most cheering news to come out of Washington was that from the year 2033 onward, relocation of a temporary nature would be more realistic in terms of the weather; six months only in the north, from the beginning of May to the end of October, and six months in the south instead of four. Not that everyone arrived on the same day, anyway; such a massive movement of people took several weeks, though it was done with extreme efficiency given the conservation of oil, coal and wood, and with a minimum of red tape. No country in the world could do so much so quickly as the United States of America in the frame of mind to do. But this was far from cheering news to people like Mayor d'Este of Detroit; he read it correctly as the beginning of the end of winter relocation, and therefore as the death knell of the northern and midwestern cities. Places on the west coast like Vancouver and Seattle and Portland would last longer, being warmer, but eventually they too would perish. Those who insisted upon remaining in the doomed cities all through the depths of winter after winter relocation was phased out altogether (the estimate given for this was another ten years) would not be forcibly removed, any more than women who insisted upon defying the one-child family were forcibly aborted, or sterilized. Simply, they would receive no aid, no tax benefits and no welfare.

"I don't want to go south!" cried Mama when the family gathered in the living room to discuss this bolt from the Washington blue.

158

"Nor do I," said Dr. Christian soberly. He sighed. "But, Mama, we will have to. It's inevitable. Chubb has set itself a target for relocation, starting next year and finishing by 2040. Margaret Kelly phoned me today to tell me. She's pregnant, incidentally."

Andrew shrugged. "Well, if Chubb goes, it's the end of Holloman for sure. Where?"

Dr. Christian laughed silently. "Certainly not to any of those brash late entrants into the Union! They've purchased land outside Charleston, quite a swag of it."

"Well, we've got a while yet to think about where we'll go," said James. "Oh, Josh! Somehow when things happen you adjust, and once you've adjusted there's a sense of well-being again. You can tell yourself it's a false sense until you're blue in the face, but it doesn't cushion the shock when the next upheaval comes, does it?"

"No."

"What provoked this decision?" asked Miriam.

"I imagine the birthrate and the population have fallen more rapidly than anyone expected," said Dr. Christian. "Or—who knows? Maybe my friend Dr. Chasen and his computer have figured that now's the time to cut our losses with a vengeance. The whole phenomenon of relocation, if you'll permit me to call it a phenomenon, has had to be played by ear right along. It's never happened before, unless you can include the mass migrations of peoples out of central Asia. But the last of those occurred over a thousand years ago. One thing for sure. This isn't an irresponsible decision. So I guess we move."

"Our beautiful clinic!" said Miriam.

Mama was weeping. "I don't want to go, I don't want to go! Oh, please, Joshua, can't we stay? We're not poor, we can survive!"

He plucked a handkerchief from his pocket, passed it to James, who passed it to Andrew, who leaned over and took his mother's face in one hand and dried it with the other.

"Mama," Dr. Christian said patiently, "we elected to stay in Holloman because we felt it was those who didn't go south who would need us the most, and the people who relocated for the winter only too. But now we have to go south, because I imagine it will worsen there during the first few years of this new phase.

159

We go where we're needed, that's the real reason why our clinic exists."

Mama shrank and shivered. "It's going to be some shanty city in Texas, isn't it?"

"I don't know yet. Perhaps this publicity tour in November will give me the answer, if they send me to enough places. It's a good time to start looking, anyway."

Andrew put a kiss on each of Mama's eyelids, and smiled into her face with her own smile. "Come on, Mama, no more tears and chin up!"

"Oh!" gasped Martha, so suddenly everyone turned away from Mama to look at her.

"Oh?" asked Dr. Christian, smiling at her lovingly.

But she knew the love for what it was: a father for his youngest child, a brother for his baby sister. So she drew closer to Mary, who sat alongside her on the couch, and when Mary offered her a hand to hold she took it convulsively and held on to it tightly. "Mrs. Kelly," she managed to say. "Isn't it nice about her baby?"

"Yes, it's very nice," said Dr. Christian, and got up. He looked at his mother. "Don't mourn the dead, Mama. The little Mouse is right. Rejoice for the living."

He opened the front door, not boarded up yet, and went out onto the porch, closing the door behind him too quickly to permit of anyone's following him, a sure signal that he wished to be alone.

It was very still and very cold, but it was dry. Too many changes. He took the icy wood of the porch railing in his hands and leaned on them, watching his breath billow out from his mouth like the balloons in a comic strip. Not often these days did his family intrude upon his thoughts, but tonight was an exception. A reminder that though he had huge responsibilities to the community at large, he also had a responsibility for those beloved people sitting inside. I am receding from them, he thought; as fast as I go toward the faceless many do I leave them behind. Why can we not stay the same? Why is change? They are afraid, and they are sorrowful. They have reason for their fear and their grief. Yet I cannot summon up the old intensity of affection for them, I am too drained to bear with them as patiently and gently as I should!

The beast, the thing inside: it had the bit between its teeth

160

and it dragged at him remorselessly. His hands left the railing and went up under his sweater, plucked at his shirt and the meager chest that shirt harbored as if they could physically locate and tear away the thing that plagued and tore him so. He thought he would weep to ease his pain, and closed his eyes. But there were no tears.

God in Cursing: A New Approach to Millennial Neurosis saw the printed light of day in late September. A carton of complimentary author's copies was dispatched to Dr. Joshua Christian the day after the first batch of the first print run was packed in the huge printing plant Atticus owned outside Atlanta, Georgia. Atticus also owned a plant in southern California, which supplied the west of the country.

It was the most extraordinary sensation to pick up a well-bound and beautifully laid out book and see his own name on it, Dr. Christian discovered. He had never in his life experienced anything quite so unreal. The expected delight was just not there, for delight would have indicated reality, and about this book there was nothing real.

Of course he would have ample time to get used to the fact that the book did exist before he was obliged to embark upon his publicity tour, for publication day was scheduled sometime late in October. The ensuing weeks would see the book presented to booksellers across the nation by the Atticus salesmen (who had been busy with bound galley copies for six weeks already), after which it would be shipped off to bookstores in the specified quantities. The ensuing weeks would also see copies bestowed gratis upon the various people whose duty it was to read the book and review it for television and radio and newspapers and magazines and journals.

From the moment the book arrived in Oak Street, Holloman, life itself began to become unreal for Dr. Christian. He had no time of grace allowed him at all, for on the day after he received his advance copies, his sister buzzed him in his office.

"Joshua, I don't know whether I've got a really crazy patient on the line, or whether it's a genuine call," Mary said, voice sounding odd. "Maybe you'd better pick up and sort it out, okay? He *says* he's the President of the United States, but he doesn't *sound* crazy!"

Dr. Christian lifted up his telephone receiver a little gingerly. "Joshua Christian speaking. May I help you?"

"Oh, good!" said a deep and familiar voice. "My name is Tibor Reece. I'm not usually in a position where I have to announce who and what I am myself, but there are very good reasons why I'm phoning you in person, Dr. Christian."

"Yes, Mr. President?" What else did one say?

"Dr. Christian, I have read your book and I am impressed. However, I'm not phoning you in person just to tell you that! I have a favor to ask of you."

"Of course, Mr. President."

"Would it be possible for you to come down to Washington for a couple of days?"

"Yes, Mr. President."

"Thank you, Dr. Christian. I'm sorry to disturb your work, and I'm afraid the confidentiality of this matter makes it impossible for me to organize transport for you, or invite you to stay with me as my guest. But if you are willing to get to Washington under your own steam, I will arrange for a room to be held in your name at the Hay-Adams Hotel—it's comfortable and close to the White House. Can you bear with me through all these inconveniences, Dr. Christian?"

"Of course, Mr. President."

There was an audible sigh of relief from the telephone. "I will contact you at the Hay-Adams on—say—Saturday?"

"This Saturday will be fine, Mr. President." Did one have to keep on saying "Mr. President," or could one say "sir" occasionally? Dr. Christian decided that he would risk the occasional "sir" when he met the President. Otherwise how could one behave but stiltedly?

"Thank you very much, Dr. Christian. A further favor, if I may?"

"Certainly, sir," said Dr. Christian bravely.

"I would greatly appreciate it if you kept this matter to yourself. Until Saturday?"

"Yes, Mr. President." No use pushing his luck with the "sirs."

"Thank you again. Goodbye."

Dr. Christian sat, flummoxed, looking at the receiver he still held in his hand, then he shrugged, cradled it.

Mary buzzed on the intercom. "Josh? Everything okay?"

"Fine, thanks."

"Who was it?"

"Are you alone, Mair?"

"Yes."

"It really was the President. I have to go to Washington, but he doesn't want it spread around." Dr. Christian heaved a sigh. "It's Thursday afternoon, and he wants me down there by I presume Saturday morning. But the matter's confidential, so there will be no travel priorities for me this time. Do you think you can try to find me a seat on tomorrow's train?"

"Can do. Would you like me to come with you?"

"Good Lord, no, I can manage! But I guess I shouldn't say anything to the rest of the family, so what excuse am I going to find for a rush trip to Washington?"

"That's easy," said Mary dryly. "Tell them you're going to see Dr. Carriol."

"Why didn't I think of that? What a clever puss you are!"

"No, I'm not clever. It's just that sometimes, Joshua Christian, *you* are dumb!" And his sister cut off her end of the intercom with an angry squeal that hurt his ears.

"Well, I've sure done something, but I do wish I knew what," he muttered.

The confidentiality of the matter may have prevented the President from inviting Dr. Christian to stay at the White House, but the arrangements made for his accommodation in Washington were very nice, and when Dr. Christian presented his Totocred card for vetting, it was waved away. He had walked from Union Station using a street map, and was in his room waiting for Tibor Reece to call by midday Saturday.

The call came through about two o'clock, and something in the President's voice told Dr. Christian that this was not the first such call. Oh, dear! However, there were no overt or covert reproaches; the President just sounded extremely glad to find Dr. Christian had arrived.

"I'll send a car to pick you up at four," said Tibor Reece, and hung up so quickly Dr. Christian had no time to protest that he wouldn't mind the walk.

Nor did he have much chance to inspect the White House, for a servant conducted him swiftly through various corridors to what seemed a private sitting room; in retrospect his chief impression was one of disappointment. It couldn't compare for beauty or elegance with any of the European palaces or even stately homes he had toured via videotape during his schooldays. In fact, he thought it rather sterile and dreary. Maybe the brevity of its changing tenancies and the conflicting decorating ideas of its First Ladies precluded its acquiring either beauty or elegance? There was certainly nothing to rival the ground floor of 1047 Oak Street, in his humble opinion anyway.

President Tibor Reece and Dr. Joshua Christian did look very alike; each man recognized the fact in the moment of meeting. Their eyes were level, a welcome and most unusual occurrence. And their hands felt good intertwined, broad-based, long-fingered. Smooth-skinned, but still working hands.

"We could be brothers," said Tibor Reece, gesturing to a chair opposite the one from which he had risen to greet his guest. "Please sit down, Doctor."

Dr. Christian sat, deciding that the President's remark was not one he cared to comment on; he declined a drink, accepted coffee, and said nothing while the coffee was brought and dispensed. However, he was not at all uneasy, and his host sensed this gratefully; so often the President had to exert precious energy he could ill afford to squander in putting a guest at his ease.

"You're not a drinking man, Dr. Christian?"

"Only a good cognac after a meal, Mr. President. But I don't define that as a drinking man's habit. We got into it at home to warm up for bed."

The President smiled. "There's no need to apologize, Doctor. It's a very civilized habit."

And so within minutes they established a calm and mutually respectful rapport, more through their frequent silences than through the chitchat custom dictated. Finally the President sighed and put his cup down.

"Nitty-gritty time, Dr. Christian?"

"Yes, sir, I think so."

But Tibor Reece said nothing more for a moment, sitting with his hands clasped and frowning down at them. Then he made a little shrugging movement with his shoulders, and glanced up quickly.

"Dr. Christian, I have a personal problem of some import, and I'm hoping you can help me. After reading your book, I am sure you can."

Dr. Christian said nothing, merely nodded.

164

"My wife is very disturbed. In fact, after reading your book I'd call her a classic case of millennial neurosis—all her problems are caused by the times we live in."

"If she's very disturbed, sir, it may be that there's more to it than neurosis. I say that only because I can't allow you to hope I'm a universal healer. I'm only a man."

"Granted."

The President embarked upon his tale, never once stopping to remind Dr. Christian of the matter's confidentiality, though as he proceeded his disclosures became more and more harrowing, more and more humiliating. And more and more potentially dangerous to himself, if he had judged his man wrongly. In actual fact he was not relying entirely upon his own judgment; Dr. Judith Carriol had investigated this man with exquisite thoroughness, and nothing had uncovered a tendency to betray patients' confidences, or innate lack of principles.

Tibor Reece was a desperate man. His domestic blisses were nonexistent, conjugal relations were nonexistent, a proper degree of love and care for his daughter was nonexistent. And his wife's self-preoccupation was ever increasing. The possibility of a nationwide scandal was something he had lived with so long it did not concern him nearly so much as the purely personal aspects. Clearly what he really wanted was a healed wife rather than a cowed one.

"What do you want me to do exactly?" asked Dr. Christian when the story was told.

"I don't know, I honestly don't know. For tonight, just stay to dinner, huh? Julia is always home on Saturday and Sunday nights." He smiled wryly. "This is a Monday-to-Friday town, everyone splits for the weekend, even Julia's boyfriends."

"I'd be glad to stay for dinner," said Dr. Christian.

"She will take a fancy to you, Doctor. She does to any new masculine face. And you do look a bit like me." He laughed, the sound of a man who did not laugh enough. "Of course that may mean she hates you on sight! Though I doubt it. It wouldn't be in character. I shall arrange to be called away at the end of the main course, to give you an opportunity to be alone with her, and I'll stay away about half an hour." He looked at his watch. "Good God! It's way after five already! My daughter and I always meet here around five-thirty every day."

The girl came in on the echo of his words, escorted by a

woman uniformed like a British nanny. The woman did not stay, she merely bowed with great dignity to the President and went out, shutting the door firmly behind her. And there was the girl, too tall, too thin, too like her beaky sunken-cheeked father ever to be called attractive, though time and a good course of ballet or gymnastics might improve her carriage and her figure. Her name was Julia too, but her father called her Julie; she was about twelve or thirteen years old, definitely pubescent, and already close to six feet in height. Poor thing.

She behaved with gross immaturity, her antics more in keeping with a two-year-old. Her father had led her by the hand to his chair and placed her on his lap, where she sat playing with his tie and singing to herself tunelessly; it seemed she did not see Dr. Christian sitting watching, for she ignored him as if he wasn't there. She didn't speak. However, every so often she managed to sneak a quick glance at Dr. Christian, a furtive, purposive and calculating glance out of eyes that were unmistakably intelligent. The first time he caught that gaze Dr. Christian scarcely believed what he saw, but immediately he arranged himself so that he could watch her from under lids ostensibly directed elsewhere; for the instant her eyes encountered his, she had switched the intelligence off. And after several minutes of playing this game, Dr. Christian began to wonder if she might be a borderline case of autism. Certainly she was psychotic rather than retarded. Years before, he had come to the conclusion that the rich and the famous and the socially prominent were often less well served in the way of medical attention than many far less fortunately circumstanced people. So he wondered if the girl had ever actually been competently examined and tested, and he itched to send her to the Mouse for a couple of days. No one in the world tested better than the Mouse.

"Mr. President," he said after sitting observing father and daughter for perhaps ten minutes, "I wonder if it might be possible to see your house? I'm afraid I didn't look too closely at anything on my way in, and this is likely to be my only opportunity. Would it be too much trouble for someone to show me around?"

Tibor Reece looked intensely grateful. He picked up the telephone at his elbow, and within two more minutes had Dr. Christian organized, though on Saturday evening there were no professional guides on duty.

166

"Let's take it very slowly," said Dr. Christian to the house-keeper appointed as his escort. "I want to take the lot in!"

Thus it was close to seven o'clock when he returned to the sitting room, after driving the Presidential housekeeper to the brink of despair by poking and prodding and marveling and questioning with interminable thoroughness as he wandered from one room to another.

Julie had gone. Julia had come.

The First Lady's conduct followed a pattern Dr. Christian recognized at once, for he had encountered women like her many times before. No sooner was he ensconced on one end of a couch to which she had directed him than she was ensconced on its other end, body twisted to face him, one leg tucked under her, the whole pose designed not so much to reveal her physical charms to him as it was to irritate her husband, who from where he was sitting could not see precisely what or how much she was displaying to the guest. And whatever Dr. Christian said, she purred in answer, and whenever possible would emphasize her delight in his dismally undistinguished conversation by leaning across the vacant cushion between them to touch him lightly on the arm, or the cheek, or the back of his hand. In the days when people had smoked she would have made great play with his lighting of her cigarette, and use the hand that held it to punctuate her pleasure in him; to himself Dr. Christian thought with amusement that when smoking disappeared from the spectrum of human pursuits, so too did a lot of most illuminating body language.

A very beautiful woman, Julia Reece. Almost albino blonde, with rather prominent pale-blue eyes, a fine fair skin, and a magnificent white bosom left generously on show, but not to the point of indecency in a President's wife. She too was overly tall (which meant genetically the child probably hadn't had a chance), but she was Venus-shaped, a tiny waist separating the voluptuousnesses of chest and hips, and long lovely legs. She dressed well, very expensively too. And she was about fifteen years younger than her husband.

If President Reece had expected his dinner guest to shine verbally, he was doomed to disappointment. Though Dr. Christian held his end of the table discussion capably up, he said nothing even the most biased of auditors could have termed brilliant,

167

witty, profound or original. The presence of so unsympathetic and jarring a woman as Julia Reece he found not so much inhibiting as enervating; she possessed the disastrous habit of saying exactly the right thing to kill decent talk. Poor Tibor Reece! Either he had experienced an elderly man's fascination with young girls at a precocious age, or he had been caught like an unsuspecting fish. Dr. Christian thought it was probably the latter; Julia could conceivably behave very differently.

The consommé came and went, the salad came and went, and the roast chicken main course came. The promised urgent message was served just before the roast chicken remains were whisked away; Tibor Reece rose to his feet with an apology and a promise to Dr. Christian that he would return in time for coffee and cognac.

Which left Dr. Christian alone at the table with Mrs. Tibor Reece. He sighed to himself, feeling depressed.

"Do you really want dessert, Joshua?" she asked; she had called him Joshua from the moment of introduction, where her husband had preferred to retain his title and his last name, not because of any lack of warmth, but because to do so was a small courtesy Dr. Christian for one deeply appreciated.

"No," said Dr. Christian.

"Then let's go back to the sitting room, shall we? I don't suppose Tibor will get back, he rarely does, but we'd better give him an hour, for form's sake." This last was said in conspiratorial accents.

"Oh, most definitely for form's sake," said Dr. Christian.

As she passed him she glanced at him quickly, suddenly not quite sure of herself or him; but she put her chin in the air and stalked magnificently through the big double doors which led into the sitting room, far enough ahead of him to show him how deliciously her big bottom oscillated from side to side as she moved.

"I'll ring for coffee," she said, settling in her end of the couch and waving her hand at its other end, a signal that he was to sit there.

Instead, he chose a wing chair and turned it courteously so she could see him easily. He sat down, crossed his legs one over the other with the immense ease and comfort of the very thin, steepled his fingers like a pompous cleric and stared at her darkly over their tips.

"My God, you're a cold fish!" she said.

"So are you."

She gasped and showed her bottom teeth. "Well! That's sure straight to the point!"

"Yes, I meant it to be."

Her head tilted to one side, she lowered her lids and looked at him from under them. "What do you really think of me, Joshua?" she asked.

"Mrs. Reece, I am not sufficiently your friend to say."

That puzzled her, she had to mull it over. As a result, she changed her tack. Her face puckered like a sulky child's, and her eyes filled with genuine tears. "Joshua, I need a friend desperately!" she said. "Please, won't you be my friend?"

He laughed heartily. "No!"

The outrage was gathering fast, but she gave it one more try. "Why not?"

"I don't *like* you, Mrs. Reece," he said.

For a moment he thought she was going to slap him and scream for help while rending the bodice of her gown, but something in his face stopped her in mid stride; she swung round instead and ran from the room, weeping.

Thus when twenty minutes later Tibor Reece came in, he found Dr. Christian sitting alone.

"Where's Julia?"

"Gone."

The President sat down limply. "She didn't take to you, did she? Damn!" He looked around vainly for the after-dinner tray. "Haven't you been served with coffee and drinks yet?"

"I thought I'd like to wait for you, sir."

When Tibor Reece smiled his face lit up beautifully, it became ten years younger and very attractive. "I thank you, Dr. Christian! You are indeed a civilized man." He got up again and went outside, calling for some servant by name.

The cognac was a Hennessy, admittedly not Paradis (Dr. Christian had imagined it would be, given that his host was the President of the United States), but still a most acceptable XO served in properly warmed balloons, and the coffee was excellent.

"You can't help me with her, can you?" the President asked of his guest sadly.

Dr. Christian studied the amber contents of his balloon without speaking for a moment, then sighed. "Mr. President, no one can help you in this situation except you yourself."

"She's *that* bad?"

"She's that good. Sir, your wife is not any of the things you suspect—she's not a nymphomaniac, nor is she particularly neurotic. She is a spoiled brat who should have been shown that she is not the center of the universe when she was a child. It's too late now, of course. And I don't know what you can do to improve her disposition so far along in your marriage, either, because she has no respect for you. And that," Dr. Christian explained, burning his boats with a vengeance, "is no one's fault except your own. She craves attention, she insists on being the absolute center of any world she lives in, and she has no sense of duty or responsibility. So she takes a delight in trying to render you incapable of doing the job she now regards as her enemy. The only thing I can tell you that might relieve your mind a little is that I very much doubt anyone would ever be able to make an accusation of promiscuity against her stick. She's all show and no go, sir."

No man likes to be told by a relative stranger that he has made a bed of nails for himself with his own hands, but Tibor Reece was a gentleman, and he was fair-minded. So he swallowed it. With difficulty, but he swallowed it. "I see. You don't think then that if she read your book—?"

Dr. Christian laughed. "If you offered it to her, sir, I strongly suspect she'd throw it at your head! I may as well tell you that in your absence she and I had a falling out. I told her—not in so many words, perhaps, but plainly enough all the same—exactly what I thought of her. She didn't like the experience one little bit."

The President sighed. "That's that, then. There's never an easy way out, is there?"

"No," said Dr. Christian gently.

"I pinned all my hopes on you."

"Yes, I was afraid you had. I'm truly very sorry, sir."

"It's not your fault, Dr. Christian! I can see very well that it's mine—but I felt so sorry for her, so guilty myself—oh, well! Not to worry. Life goes on, as they say. *Do* have another brandy! Not bad stuff, is it?"

"It's very good stuff. Thank you."

Suddenly the President peered about, his expression a mixture of conspiracy and illicit glee. "There are very few private compensations for holding down this particular job, Dr. Christian, but one of them is that I am less likely than most men to get into trouble for smoking a cigar indoors. I am not going to ask you if you mind, because I don't give a shit whether you do. But— care to join me?"

"Sir," said Dr. Christian, "in answer I can but quote you the one bit of Kipling I know by heart—'a woman is only a woman, but a good cigar is a Smoke.'"

Tibor Reece shook with laughter. "By God, considering the circumstances, that's apt!" he said, and fetched cigars.

They got quite mellow on the third Hennessy, sitting back in their wing chairs puffing noxious clouds of smoke at the ceiling with open relish.

Dr. Christian then found the courage to say the one thing he had so far left unsaid.

"Mr. President, about your daughter."

Tibor Reece looked suddenly wary. "What about her?"

"I don't think she's a standard case of simple mental retardation."

"You don't?"

"No. She strikes me as possibly very highly intelligent. But she's either violently traumatized, or maybe biochemically psychotic. It's hard to tell on limited observation."

"What is this?" demanded the President, his voice showing his pain. "Do you take away with one hand and give with the other, or something? My God, my God, I can stand hearing the truth about Julia, but don't tamper with my daughter!"

"I'm not, sir. But I can't not try to help Julie. Who for instance has seen her? What actual evidence do you have that she's retarded? Was the birth hazardous? Was the early pregnancy adulterated by drugs? Is there a family history?"

The President looked blank. "Everything was fine through pregnancy and birth. And I doubt there's any history in my wife's family. There's none in mine, for sure. I guess I just left matters in Julia's hands. There have been doctors. Julia insisted from the beginning that Julie wasn't right, that's why she had her heart so set on another child."

"Sir, can you forgive me my failure with your wife, and grant me a very great favor?"

"What?"

"Let me have Julie tested."

The fair-mindedness came to the fore at once. "Why, of course

I will! What have I got to lose, tell me that?" He drew a deep breath. "What do you expect to find?"

"Nothing very consoling, sir, unfortunately. I think your daughter might be an autistic child. If she is, things won't be any easier for you, at least not right away. Nor will a diagnosis like that soften your wife's dislike of the child. But the cerebral potential is there, which it isn't in simple retardation, and the long-term results both in autism and psychosis of other kinds is very good these days. But all I want to do is test her properly. I may be wrong, she may be retarded. The tests will show us beyond any doubt."

"I'll send her to your clinic whenever you want."

Dr. Christian shook his head vigorously. "No, sir! I would much rather send my sister-in-law Martha here for a couple of days, if you don't mind. That way the testing can be done discreetly, and without the world knowing I'm involved. I have no desire to cash in on the illness of a President's child. In fact, I won't. If the test results indicate that Julie will benefit from some kind of active treatment, I'll give you the names of some very competent men."

"You wouldn't consider treating her yourself?"

"I can't, sir. I'm a clinical psychologist, which in this year of Our Lord 2032 means I do indeed have quite a lot in common with psychiatrists, but I specialize in neuroses, and one thing your daughter is not, is neurotic."

The President ushered Dr. Joshua Christian to his car in person, and shook him warmly by the hand at parting. "Thank you for coming."

"I'm sorry I wasn't of more help."

"You were a great help, actually, and I don't mean with my daughter. Dr. Christian, the company of a kind and a sensible man who isn't grinding an axe of his own is sufficient of a rarity in my life to have made this evening memorable. And I wish you well with your book. *I* think it's magnificent, and I mean that."

The President stood in the porch and watched until after the glistening red tail lights of Dr. Christian's car had been snuffed out by the driveway's curve. So! That was the surrogate Messiah manufactured by Dr. Judith Carriol to heal the lost folk of the third millennium. He couldn't in all justice say the man had fired him with wild enthusiasm, or indeed even that he had perceived the much-vaunted charisma. But there was *something*. A warmth, a kindness, a genuine and caring interest in his fellow men. A real man. Guts. Scads of guts, by God. He tried to visualize what sort of confrontation might have occurred between his wife and a man so incapable of compromise, and grinned. But the amusement faded very quickly.

What to do about Julia? Only two months until an election, so nothing right away. Oh, there had been divorced Presidents, even, late in the twentieth century, one who had survived a White House divorce to the extent of being reelected. Of course old Gus Rome hadn't made any mistake in the marital department. Sixty years of wedded bliss. The grin came and went. Old fox! They said when he was in his early twenties and so new in Washington he still smacked of the boondocks, he had cast his eyes around all the Washington wives; he picked Senator Black's wife Olive for her beauty, her brains, her organizational genius and her relish of public life, then simply stole her from the Senator. It worked, though she was thirteen years older than he. She was the greatest First Lady the country had ever known. But behind the scenes—oh, man, what a tartar! Not that he had ever heard old Gus complain. The public lion was perfectly content to be a private mouse. Gus do this, Gus don't do that—and he was so lost when she died that he abandoned Washington the moment her funeral was over, went to live in his home state of Iowa and died himself not two months later.

Well. Julia was no Olive Rome. Maybe he had been a bachelor too long. A couple more terms and he was through anyway; his inclinations leaned toward only one further term, for all he really wanted to do was go back to the beautiful house teetering on the treacherous cliffs of Big Sur, the house he saw too rarely, and there live quietly with his daughter, keep her from the madding crowd. Fish a little. Walk the leafy needly mossy paths. Imagine nymphs behind the rocks and all manner of dryads in the trees. Smoke cigars until his lungs were tarred better than a highway. And never have to lay eyes on Julia again.

"Shit, shit, shit!" hissed Dr. Judith Carriol, erupting into Dr. Moshe Chasen's cluttered office.

Startled was too mild; he was shocked. In all the years he had known her, he had never seen his chief in a royal rage before. And a right royal rage it was. Her eyes were big water-worn stones, basilisk-staring, and her whole body was visibly shaking.

He thought immediately of Dr. Joshua Christian and the newly titled Operation Messiah; surely nothing else had the power to rattle this woman!

"What's gone wrong?"

"That *bloody* fool!" She was so incensed she could find no stronger adjective. "Do you know what he did to me?"

"No," said Dr. Chasen, naturally assuming she was referring to Harold Magnus.

"He accepted an invitation from Tibor Reece to see that silly slut of a wife of his! Without telling me! How dared he? How *dared* he?"

"Judith, how dared who, for crying out loud?"

"Who does he think he is, gallivanting off to the White House without so much as a by-your-leave? What's he done? I will tell you what he's done! Fucked up everything!"

The truth was dawning. "Not Kublai Khan? Joshua?"

"Of course Joshua! Who else could be so unworldly?"

"My God!" Dr. Chasen's brain went connecting the wrong threads again and wove a picture of Dr. Christian falling victim to the First Lady's undeniable charms. Of course the whole of Washington knew she was frisky, but thought little of it; every man in public office had an Achilles heel, and the wife was almost as good a bet as a more illicit woman. Or man. Or whatever. "Well for God's sake tell me what's happened, Judith! Did someone like T.R. himself catch our Josh with his pants down in the First Lady's chamber?"

Dr. Carriol was beginning to regain her equilibrium, so she contented herself with casting her confidant a glance of withering scorn. "Oh, Moshe, how dumb can you be? Not *that!* T.R. asked him to come down to Washington and work a miracle cure on Jolly Jumbo Julia. And he actually went! Without telling me! So he screwed it up, of course. He went there without being briefed, he didn't know what the hell he was walking into, and there was sure no laying on of hands, I can tell you! Instead of having the hots for him, J.J.J. went right the other way. Probably he's so like T.R. to look at, how do I know? All I do know is that she's totally reversed the President's high opinion of Joshua and his book, and she is out to get Joshua no matter what!"

"Oh, shit indeed." But his brain was starting to function clearly again, so he asked, "How did you find out?"

"I fixed myself up with a date with Gary Mannering a couple

of weeks ago because I knew he was one of Julia's most faithful cicisbeos. Why else would I go out with the guy? He's a creep! The only way he could get it in would be if someone dropped it in for him. Like all her lotharios. The macho's a full molecule thick and the IQ's about six points higher than plant life, but the pedigree's faultless and the money's wall to wall."

Dr. Chasen was fascinated, never having seen this oddly feminine side to Dr. Carriol before. It embarrassed him, he couldn't really say why. Except that maybe if a man was saddled with a woman boss, he was more comfortable if she remained one of the boys at all times. This present mood of Judith's was too close to what he called powder-room stuff. "Why pick Gary Mannering? Why not an aide or an executive officer? I presume it's the President you want to know about, not Julia."

"An aide or an executive officer would smell a rat if I started asking questions about the President. And Joshua is not the kind of incendiary topic he'd save to discuss during working hours. He'd be much more likely to discuss Joshua casually over dinner. I mean, there's no secret our man is producing a book, and I know the President didn't intend to keep quiet about having read it. So the best way I could figure to keep tabs on what the President really thinks about Joshua was to get to know one of his wife's boyfriends. That simple, Moshe."

"My God, Judith, you're devious! So tell me the rest."

"Gary Mannering phoned me not five minutes ago and told me about Joshua's visit—and his effect on Julia. And I had to come somewhere to let off steam or the whole of this side of the building would have blown apart. It's too public up there in Magnus's corridor."

"Maybe the report is exaggerated? Too one-sided?"

Her rage was almost gone. "Could be, I suppose," she admitted grudgingly. "Let's hope it is! But how dared he, Moshe? How dared he make a move like that without telling me, without asking my advice?"

Dr. Chasen looked sly. "Do I detect just a tad of badly wounded ego, Judith?"

"Wounded ego be damned! It's *him!* He's like handling a greased pig. Oh, God, Moshe, what am I going to do? How long is it going to take the President to kill Operation Messiah before it's even off the ground? Here, wait a minute!" She grabbed at his phone and punched John Wayne's extension. "John? Has Mr.

Reece or Mr. Magnus been trying to reach me? Oh. Well, if you need me or if either of them should call, I'm in Dr. Chasen's office. Okay?" She hung up. "No word from the big boys yet."

"When was this supposed to have happened?"

"Saturday."

"It's Monday afternoon now, Judith. Plenty of time for the President to have contacted Kublai Khan and killed our beloved Messiah stone dead if he was going to."

"Not him! He's too deliberate, he'd think it over from all sides. No, Moshe, we've got to sweat for a few days yet."

Another line of thought occurred to Dr. Chasen. "Then how about getting the true story from Joshua?"

The second baleful glare in minutes daggered its way to Dr. Chasen. "How can I do that, Moshe? How can I do that and not give too much away? In some of his incarnations he's a dear, sweet, absent, bumbling fool, but in other incarnations he's the sharpest and most dangerously perceptive guy I've ever met. And I don't know if I'm ever going to know him well enough to pick when he's going to zip from one state of being to the other. Damn! Damn, damn, damn!"

Moshe Chasen saw what he thought was the light. "My God! I didn't realize!"

"Realize what?"

"You're in love with Joshua!"

She reared up and back with the speed and horrific menace of a cobra; Dr. Chasen literally shoved his chair away.

"I am not in love with Joshua Christian," she said, her teeth bared. "I am in love with Operation Messiah." And she turned on her heel and walked out.

Dr. Chasen picked up his telephone and punched John Wayne's extension. "John? If you're smart you'll dig yourself a hole and hide. The boss is on her way up, and she is not a happy woman."

His computer readouts had quite lost their usual allure; he finished pushing his chair back and sat for a long time just looking out his window. Shit. It sure was easier to deal with so many human beings they had to be reduced to nice anonymous ciphers. The big question was whether Judith could survive this first encounter with a flesh-and-blood statistic.

VIII

God in Cursing: A New Approach to Millennial Neurosis, by Joshua Christian, Ph.D. (Chubb), came out on Friday, October 29, of the year 2032, in hardcover and paperback simultaneously, both published by the Atticus Press, though the paperback bore the Scroll Books imprint.

The in-house gossip had reached boiling point by the end of June, the in-trade gossip was spreading from New York to London, Paris, Milan and Frankfurt by the end of July, and finally halfway through August the unprecedented wraps which had been kept on the book were broken by issue of the bound galleys to the Atticus sales staff for presentation to major booksellers. This edition of uncorrected proofs was limited to two thousand copies and of course not destined for sale, but because everyone confidently expected them to become collector's items later on, those lucky enough to be given one carried it everywhere with them, even to the toilet.

The whole publishing industry buzzed with the name of Dr. Joshua Christian, papers began to leak little articles about the book, and only the horrors of travel prevented droves of journalists from making premature forays to West Holloman. A few intrepid by-line hunters did, of course, but got little for their pains save Mama, who was more than a match for any journalist, and besides looked far too young to be the mother of a distinguished Ph.D. Truth to tell, she reveled in those early tastes of the fame to come, and in the compliments showered upon her.

After hot debate within the Atticus house, it was finally decided that the world was not to know very much about Dr. Joshua Christian until it watched the premier NBC talk show, "Tonight with Bob Smith," on the night of Friday, October 29. The Atticus publicity director was still walking on air, unable to believe that she had finally cracked the big one, number-one guest spot following right on the monologue; in the history of the show it had never been given to an unknown writer before his book was the talk of at least a big portion of the country. But from the moment the publicity director picked up her phone to begin the hi-there-how-are-you-dear-old-buddy-boy-have-I-got-a-guest-for-you routine, things happened with the kind of magic ease usually found only within the pages of children's books. One show after another agreed to give Dr. Christian its prime guest spot before the dazed publicity director had a chance to get into full stride—sure, sure, any day she wanted was fine, sure, sure, let us know later. And shows like "Tonight with Bob Smith," that never committed themselves to any untried guest without exhaustive pre-interviews, waived the rules of decades in order to accommodate Dr. Joshua Christian. There was not even one show that attempted to bluff the publicity director into granting an "exclusive." Unbelievable! Gorgeous! What was going on, for Pete's sake?

Of course the book was a runaway long before it was officially published, and it went into the *Times* as number one on both hardcover and mass market best-seller lists. The reviews were uniformly wonderful, many of them raves; *Publishers Weekly,* the *Kirkus Reviews,* and the *Times Book Review* all led with articles about *God in Cursing* and its author. But the most encouraging fact of all to the Atticus sales representatives who hawked their wares to booksellers all over the country under ghastly conditions of travel and accommodation was the response of these booksellers to *God in Cursing* once they had read it. They didn't gush, they didn't rave. They spoke of the book with extreme respect, and they refused to part with their own copies even if these were not the coveted bound proofs.

Not all the combined resources of NBC were sufficient to ensure that Bob Smith had read *God in Cursing;* Bob Smith refused to read a book whose author was likely to appear as a guest on his show. He believed that a writer guesting on his show was better approached fresh and uncluttered, and as a technique of interviewing it had stood up to the test of time remarkably well.

Atlanta, Georgia, was the home of all the national media networks. They had moved out of New York City in the eighties and nineties of the previous century, and out of L.A. soon after the beginning of the third millennium, driven from both places by prohibitive rents, airport hassles, unions, the cost of gas, and a multitude of other problems. Where they would go from Atlanta when its turn came not to need the networks they didn't know, but they figured there was always going to be somewhere to welcome them with open arms, and they were probably right.

Before he left for Atlanta and his appearance on "Tonight with Bob Smith," Dr. Joshua Christian was subjected to the horror of a major press conference for newspapers only; the periodicals, news magazines, Sunday supplements and the rest of the printed media were slotted into Dr. Christian's Atlanta stay, as was network radio. He acquitted himself at this press conference surprisingly well, undismayed by the exploding flashes and the questions fired at him from faces he could hardly see. But it was no occasion to provoke the Christian fireworks, which pleased the Atticus publicity director, who wanted him to save the big stuff for Bob Smith. However, she knew him well enough by this time not to make the mistake of telling him that.

There were mysteries about the man she couldn't fathom. For instance, how had Atticus managed to secure helicopter transport for him wherever he was scheduled to go? Even Toshio Yokinori, who held the Nobel Prize for Literature and was a top movie star into the bargain, could not command the like. Nothing daunted, the publicity director traveled with Dr. Christian by car from the Atticus offices on Park Avenue down to the old heliport on the East River, nervous as a hen with one chick, picking and clucking at a piece of fluff on his old tweed jacket and bemoaning the blueness of his beard shadow. He sat, the dear man, quite unruffled and unimpressed.

They flew him down from New York to Atlanta in a smart little helicopter that, had he known it, belonged to the President's fleet but had been repainted for this special assignment. So it could travel close to the speed of sound and was most comfortably finished inside. Never naive about the problems that beset his fellow men and women, he was naive enough personally to assume

179

that this mode of transport was the norm for Atticus authors (the publicity director had held her tongue); certainly he had no idea that the government of the United States of America was picking up the bill for the entire exercise, from helicopter to ground vehicles to hotels.

The speedy little mosquito of a thing made one stop en route, in Washington, to pick up Dr. Judith Carriol.

He was desperately glad to see her. Mama had wanted to come, of course, and James had valiantly volunteered, but with him away on what he was staggered to learn would be a ten-week publicity tour, neither of them could be spared. Mary also offered her services, dour and darkling; she was refused on the same grounds. So he had hoped that maybe Lucy Greco would go with him to Atlanta, or failing her, Elliott MacKenzie, or the publicity director. To board the helicopter alone was a little daunting.

He had never flown. By the time he was old enough to wish to fly, planes were virtually grounded save for a very few flights classified as imperative and always booked out by those whose jobs or needs gave them priority. The people traveled by jam-packed train or bus, town to town, state to state, border to border.

"Oh, Judith, a miracle!" he said, squeezing the hand she held out to him as she settled into the other half of the back seat.

"Well, I thought you might be grateful for a friendly face, I had some leave coming, and Elliott very kindly said I could serve as your official escort and unofficial friend. I hope you don't mind that it's me."

"I'm delighted!"

"Bob Smith tonight, huh?"

"Yes."

"Have you watched his show at all?"

"No, never. I thought it might be a good idea to watch it last night, but Andrew advised me not to. He's been tuning in to all the shows on the list Atticus sent me, or the ones we receive, anyway. And he said it would be better for me if I just went on and did everything cold."

"Do you always take his advice?"

"When Drew advises, which isn't often, it's smart to take heed."

"Nervous?"

"No. Should I be?"

"No. It's a piece of cake, Joshua."

180

"All I care about is the opportunity to reach people. I hope Bob Smith has read the book."

"I hope he hasn't," she said, knowing full well he hadn't. "*You* tell Bob Smith about millennial neurosis! There's nothing more boring than having to listen to two people in the know trade questions and answers. They assume too much, and they take too many short cuts."

"You're right. I never thought of that."

"Okay!" She wove her fingers through his, pressed their palms together, turned to smile at him. "Oh, Joshua, it is good to see you!"

He didn't answer, just leaned his head back against the seat squabs behind him, closed his eyes and permitted himself to enjoy the extraordinary sensation of being shot through the air like a projectile.

Serious talk shows were a thing of the past. So for that matter was any kind of serious dramatized television unless it was musical, classical or at least safely historic. Shakespeare and Molière were very much in vogue. Even the much praised shows hosted by Benjamin Steinfeld and Dominic d'Este were only serious in that they purported to discuss the issues of the times; in reality they did so in ways that could cause their viewers neither grief nor rage. Everything media was geared to minimizing trauma and stifling a genuine spirit of inquiry. Television especially glittered and scintillated, fell over itself wisecracking and dancing, laughing and singing.

"Tonight with Bob Smith" came on air at nine and lasted for two hours, and after fifteen years it still held the vast majority of the country in thrall. The moment that fresh, happy, freckledy face came on camera grinning almost from one jug ear to the other below its wild thatch of bright red hair, "Tonight" was a headlong frolic of gags, sketches, zippy guests, song-and-dance acts, and more zippy guests.

The format of the show dated back to long before Bob Smith had been born; spontaneously witty and attractive host with indefatigable slightly long-suffering sidekick, opening monologue, number-one guest spot, song or song-and-dance, number-two guest spot, comedy sketch, number-three guest spot, song or song-and-dance, number-four guest spot, and so on and so on.

Usually there were between four and eight guests, this

number depending solely upon how Bob Smith felt any one guest was faring with himself and the studio audience. He was a past master at the art of cutting a guest short, and right royal in a decision to can the last few of the hopefuls still waiting back in the green room because a guest was doing better than anticipated when the show was put together.

His real name was not Bob Smith, it was Guy Pisano, and he owed his fair urchin face to some nineteenth-century Visigoth who marched over the Brenner Pass and kept on going south to Calabria. The network think tank chose his name because Bob was the most popular male first name and Smith the most common last name; it had no race or creed connotations, and it conjured up an irresistible image of Everyman. His sidekick, Manning Croft (real name Otis Green), was cute, black, hip and sassy, an exquisitely dressed and thoroughly up-to-the-minute version of Rochester or Benson. He knew his place on Bob Smith's "Tonight" and he never never exceeded it, though inside himself he dreamed of one day hosting his own show.

Andrew had advised Dr. Christian wisely not to watch; had he seen the show, he might well have decided to cancel his entire publicity tour and gone on quietly practicing in Holloman, trusting to his and Lucy Greco's written words to reach the masses he so longed to help. Or then again, depending upon who looked at the vexed question, perhaps in the light of what followed, Andrew's advice was not wise at all. As it was, he drove in a large black car in blissful ignorance of what was in store for him, Dr. Judith Carriol sitting beside him, from the Atlanta helipad all the way down Peachtree Street to the NBC studios, multi-storied and made of pink mirrored glass in a grandiose plaza that also housed the buildings of CBS, ABC, Metromedia and PBS.

"Tonight with Bob Smith" occupied two whole floors, its studio rising through both of them on the north side of the NBC building. Dr. Christian was greeted most respectfully in the ground floor lobby by a casually dressed young lady who explained that she was one of the show's fifteen junior or assistant producers. As she conducted the Doctors Carriol and Christian up thirteen floors in an elevator and then through a warren of subfusc passages, she chattered away to the clipboard she carried, some of her words occasionally reaching the ears of her charges, dutifully following.

Finally, a little over an hour before the show was scheduled to

182

begin taping, Dr. Christian was settled with Dr. Carriol in the green room. Later on he would become a green room expert, and would in retrospect deem the "Tonight" green room far and away the most commodious and tasteful specimen of the genus any-where. The chairs were roomy and comfortable and came from Widdicomb, there were coffee tables littered around it carrying vases of freshly cut flowers, it had no less than six gigantic video monitors placed so that every chair had an unobscured view, and a mirrored mini-cafeteria with a uniformed nubile maiden in attendance graced one wall. Declining all but coffee, Dr. Christian subsided into the first chair he came to and gazed around with the appreciation of one who took an interest in decor and interior design.

"Why do I feel like whispering?" he asked Dr. Carriol, smiling with a bubbling amusement he couldn't suppress.

"It's an inner sanctum," she said with an answering smile.

"Yes, of course." He looked around again, but differently. "There's no one here but us."

"You're the first guest. They always ask that guests be here at least one hour before their time slots. So just wait, the others will come."

They did. To Dr. Christian it was an education he really enjoyed acquiring, watching his fellow guests. No one arrived alone, some had quite an entourage, and he could tell the very famous ones because of a sudden electrical curiosity that galvanized those already present. They were essentially connoisseurs of themselves, more star-struck than any mere mortal watching at home. There was no interparty chatting; each designated guest kept his or her distance from all save his or her companions. But the eyes slid round assessing, the ears flapped to eavesdrop, the hands lifted and fluttered and drummed and scratched as if yearning for something valid to do with themselves. A kind of guilty privilege oozed out of everyone, mixed with the subtlest drop of twitching twisting fear. This venue, Dr. Christian concluded at the end of his observations, was colossally important to all these people.

Half an hour before the show began, another young female assistant producer came to take Dr. Christian "down to Makeup," as she phrased it; he followed her docilely, leaving Dr. Carriol behind looking superbly at ease and making everyone else in the green room feel slightly wrong somehow.

In Makeup he felt like a wart or a wen, sitting in a dentist's chair while a taciturn elderly man muttered about dark bases and big pores and proceeded to gild this most unpromising lily.

"Gingerbread!" said Dr. Christian suddenly.

The hands stopped; the makeup man looked at him in the mirror as if he suddenly saw his subject as a human being for the first time.

"Gingerbread?" echoed the makeup man.

"I was thinking of myself as a lily, but that's patently ridiculous," explained Dr. Christian. "A lily I shall never be, I toil too hard. But I might just qualify as gingerbread."

The makeup man shrugged, lost interest in the mind under the face, and finished deftly with this inappropriate guest.

"There you go, Doc!" he announced, whipping his drape off with the flair of a magician.

Dr. Christian eyed himself ironically in the mirror, ten years younger, skin a lot smoother, eyes debagged and quite mysteriously larger. "Thirty instead of forty! Thank you, sir," he said, then ambled back along endless corridors with his third different assistant producer guide.

"I haven't enjoyed myself so much in years," he said to Dr. Carriol, sinking back into his chair. "You know, this is a revelation."

She studied him with approval. "They've certainly made you look more your age! Very spiffy!"

That was the end of any conversation. On the monitors the empty studio had acquired an audience in his absence, and since it was being warmed up by Manning Croft, it laughed with increasing frequency and ease.

He didn't see Bob Smith, because just as the opening chords of fanfare announced that the tape was rolling and the show beginning, a different young female assistant producer came and collected him from the green room.

Amid urgent whisperings they positioned him at the edge of a praline-colored curtain so heavy with silk that it hung straight and somnolent and graceful.

"Wait here until we cue you, then take a step out onto the stage, stop, turn and smile at the audience—a *big* smile, please!—then walk on over to the podium. Bob will rise to shake your hand and you will sit down in the chair on his right. The minute another guest is announced, you move out of the chair and sit on the nearest end of the long sofa, and every time a new

184

guest comes on, you move down one more space on the sofa. Got it?"

"Got it!" he said gaily, too loudly.

"Sssssh!"

"Sorry."

The preliminary repartee between Bob Smith and Manning Croft was over amid giggles from the audience, and Bob Smith stepped alone into the middle of the huge polished space between where Dr. Christian stood behind the edge of the silk curtain and where the vacant podium waited with its stunning backdrop of a sunset Atlanta shimmering in the brilliant studio light.

Dr. Christian didn't hear the monologue, for a man edged up next to him, grasped him urgently by the arm and introduced himself as the producer of the show.

"It's a pleasure and a privilege to have this exclusive, Dr. Christian," he murmured. "Uh—have you ever been on television before?"

Dr. Christian said no, and was subjected to a soothing sotto voce rundown on how easy it was as long as you just remembered to concentrate on Bob and ignore the cameras.

The monologue was winding up, the audience was ecstatic. The producer, still clutching Dr. Christian's arm, tensed.

"Be bright, be cute, be witty—and make *Bob* look good," said the producer, changing his grip and thrusting Dr. Christian out into the glare of the stage.

He remembered to pause and smile at the audience after his initial step forward, then he walked across the long empty space between the edge of the curtain and the podium. Now ensconced behind his desk, Bob Smith rose to his feet, leaned over to shake Dr. Christian's hand, and with a broad smile welcomed him to the show. Dr. Christian sat down and twisted to gaze at the eager chirpy face to his left, wondering why they couldn't be permitted to face each properly. It was damned awkward having to sit twisted into an artificial pose.

Bob Smith held up a copy of *God in Cursing*. The Atticus art department had produced a wonderful jacket, white with scarlet lettering and a jagged raised bolt of silver lightning running through title and author's name from the top right of the cover to the bottom left. The monitor screens filled with it, dramatic, telling.

The star of the show was not a happy man, though this did not reveal itself even to his guest, the source of all the trouble. A serious subject, a serious doctoral guest, and a serious implication, all rolled up into the number-one spot on his show. Never before had every one of his perfectly valid objections been swept aside by the network chiefs; in vain he had protested that Dr. Christian ran counter to the whole philosophy of the show, that the entire country would switch channels five minutes into the number-one guest spot, that they were going to lay the biggest egg in the history of Bob Smith's "Tonight." His producer and his producer's bosses merely nodded all the way through his protests, then told him Dr. Christian went on no matter what, and he would just have to deal with Dr. Christian as best he could.

So at the end of his monologue he had announced that he was going to introduce a book and its writer first off and that both were a bit away from the usual slant of the show, but he felt both were so important he must draw the attention of the country to them. He ended by looking into the camera very seriously, adjuring his audience to keep watching while giving an unspoken impression of intense excitement and anticipation.

Minus his usual infectious grin, Bob Smith waited until Dr. Christian had disposed of his plethora of bones within the inadequate recesses of the guest chair. After which he held the book up to the camera, turned to Dr. Christian, and said, "Dr. Christian, what *is* millennial neurosis?," feeling an utter fool.

Nor did Dr. Christian behave like the normal guest. He didn't smile, he didn't make it easy for his host, he didn't focus all his attention on his host. Instead, he seemed to fix his gaze on some point quite high in the rigging which hung above the stage; his chin was raised, his hands loosely linked on his crossed knees.

"I was born literally at the dawn of the third millennium," he said, staccato, "only days from the end of the year 2000. My father and mother had four children. I am the eldest. We children are each not more than a year apart in age. While my youngest sibling Andrew was still newborn, our father froze to death in his car somewhere on the Thruway in upstate New York. He was going to see a patient on consultation. My father was a psychiatrist. Somewhat unorthodox, but beginning to be very respected all the same. He died in January of 2004, but he wasn't dug out until April. He was one of several thousand who died in that same storm on the same stretch of road. It was the worst winter in the

186

history of the country to that time. And we ran out of petroleum. The seas were ice, we didn't have enough icebreakers to keep the harbors and the sealanes clear, we couldn't keep the roads and the railbeds clear, the blizzards were so continuous between January and April that we couldn't get enough planes into the air, and all across North America above the fortieth parallel, people died. That winter of 2004 was the first of the great shocks which were the devastation of us."

He lowered his head and looked into the lens of the camera with the red light glowing, so naturally that the action was remarkably professional; and in the control cubicle hung sponsonlike on the wall one story up, a frisson of shock and excitement passed down every spine. Something was leaping out of the screens concentrated upon him, a most extraordinary projection of power and compulsion.

"The third millennium was not Armageddon," said Dr. Christian. "None of the things the doomsday merchants had been predicting for a century actually came true. We didn't have the war to end all wars. We didn't perish in flames. Instead, the glaciers were on the move, and so were the people. All over the world's northern hemisphere the people began to move south. Where there was sun. Where it was still warm. Where the winters were endurable. A mass migration bigger than any other human migration this planet has seen.

"Some hard decisions were taken. That nowhere could men and women be permitted to procreate indiscriminately. That fossil fuels must be stringently conserved. That further expansion of any kind must not merely come to a stop, but must actually be reversed to the point of contraction. The alternative was to reduce global population by nuclear holocaust, slaughter ourselves back into equilibrium with the shrinking chilling environment. If after nuclear holocaust what was left might still be called an environment.

"We were wise enough to see this millennial message from God, yes, but the people were driven out of the Promised Land into the wilderness in ignorance and fear. There was just too much to be done, and not enough intelligence to go round. All too often the laws had to come first and the explanations afterward. All too often the explanations were tendered in language beyond the comprehension of the many. All too often the news was imparted to the many with the irresponsible and exaggerated drama the yellow media have made their trademark. And—this is the tragedy of third millennial humankind—all too often our emotions and our drives pushed us where common sense and farsightedness *screamed* we shouldn't go."

The studio audience was very still. No one even coughed. Nothing Dr. Christian had said so far was news to them, but he spoke so sincerely and so strongly that they listened to him like Celtic tribesmen to a master bard. He had the bardic witchery that was part wording, part rhythm, part cadence, part voice, and wholly the intangible ability to bind his listeners with the spell of himself.

"It is the children who bite deepest, it is the children we suffer most. Though we are not alone in this. The people of every land endure the same fate, the people of every land feel the same sorrow. A man wants a son, but has a daughter instead. Behind him there stretches a son tradition all the way back to the dawn of history. Or a couple have a son and want a daughter. A woman overflows with maternal longings and simply wants to have lots and lots of babies. Even those whose mating preference lies with their own sex experience a strong urge to reproduce. Only in a relative yesterday there still existed one of the most basic human tenets—populate or perish. Only in a relative yesterday some religious institutions held that any attempt at curtailing progeny was against the teachings of God and a sure precursor of eternal damnation."

He couldn't sit still on that ridiculous chair facing the wrong way a moment longer; he got up from it and strode into the middle of the stage, the bulk of the lighting behind him and the audience visible to him at last. Off-camera, Bob Smith was gesturing frantically to his gaping floor manager to produce a chair. This, when found, Bob carried himself to the middle aisle, and there sat down on it. Since the show was taped between six and eight in the evening, eastern time, a full three hours would have to elapse before watchers across the country could see the unimpressionable Bob Smith carrying his chair, could see him sit like a freshman college student experiencing his first truly brilliant lecturer. Manning Croft decided to be less formal, thereby providing a nice contrast to Bob, and just sat down cross-legged on the floor among the feet of the front row.

"Inside most of us there is a strong love of hearth and home as well as of children," said Dr. Christian, voice soft, "and the three

188

go together. The hearth is the source of warmth and family focus, the home is the shelter and family protector, and the children are the natural reason for the existence of the family. Man is an essentially conservative creature who dislikes being uprooted unless the place where he lives becomes utterly untenable, or some new place becomes equally alluring. This country was founded on emigrants who came looking for religious freedom, the space to pursue new kinds of living, greater earthly comfort and riches, and emancipation from the shibboleths of ancient custom. But having settled in this country, back came that love of hearth and home. Take me. My ancestors came from the Isle of Man and Cumberland in Britain, the fiords of Norway, the mountains of Armenia and the southwestern plains of Russia. In the United States of America the succeeding generations of my family prospered. The United States of America became the homeland, for where else could the seed of such disparate racial strains have become intermingled, and what could they have in common save this new homeland?"

He stopped, looked around the audience as if to discover how many different kinds of faces comprised it, nodded to himself, and suddenly—for the first time—smiled. Not any smile; the special smile that loved and embraced and comforted and distinguished.

"I still live in Holloman, Connecticut, in the house where I grew up, near the schools I went to and the great university I chose to attend. After the cold came down, I weighed the alternatives and I deliberately elected to be cold in winter. For outside of a lack of heat and rationed amounts of electricity and gas, my home still offered me a degree of comfort and heartwarming familiarity no southern relocation apartment ever could. But as a result of my ancestors' industry, I have a certain amount of money, and my personal needs are minimal. I can for instance well afford to pay my federal and state and city and goods taxes even though they are at an all-time high and my choosing to remain in Holloman gives me no relief. I decided not to exercise my right to have one child by being vasectomized. Now, a full fifteen years after my family made the decision to remain in Holloman, we face the fact that we will after all have to leave Holloman. Yet—yet it might truly be said of me that I am *happy*."

In the green room there was silence too. Dr. Carriol covertly watched the other guests to see who was restless, who thought it was high time Dr. Christian got the hook, but no one moved. No one even commented upon the fact that the tapes were running without thought of commercial breaks. All attention was focused on the monitors.

"Most people in this age of our world are not happy," said Dr. Christian, "and the deep and wretched misery in which they dwell today is what I call millennial neurosis. Do you know exactly what a neurosis is? Well, I define it as a reversible negative mental state or attitude. Its cause may be tenuous or even entirely imaginary, in which case it is said to be grounded in a person's own inadequacies or insecurities. Then again, the cause of a neurosis may be real. Valid. Inescapable. As with some physical peculiarity or illness, as with other concrete factors severe enough to warp or maim the psyche. Millennial neurosis is caused by reality. Millennial neurosis is *not* imaginary! In itself it is real. And God knows it is valid! We keep telling ourselves that we are adult, grown up—mature and responsible people. But inside every last one of us there lives somewhere at the core a little child. That child cries when it doesn't understand why it cannot have what it wants. That child has the power to create psychic havoc within its adult host. And it often does. It can also end up in ruling its unknowing adult host."

His voice changed, lost its crisp clear definitive delivery and became louder yet more tender, stronger yet more loving, a most extraordinary and compelling transmutation, akin to the difference between a diamond and rich red gold. And as did his voice, so did he change in himself.

"Why *do* you cry so?" he asked. "I who have never needed to cry for myself can tell you, you the cause of the only tears I shed. You cry for the children you cannot have. You cry for the impermanence of your homes. You cry for the freedom to do as you want and live as you want. You cry for a kinder, warmer earth. You cry because the concepts of God fostered in you are concepts you can accept no longer, that you do not understand and therefore cannot draw comfort from."

Across the country no one watched as yet except in the White House, where via a special land line permanently installed between Atlanta and Washington (more secure and interference-free than satellite), President Tibor Reece and Secretary for the Environment Harold Magnus sat in comfortable chairs in the Oval Office watching the actual recording of Bob Smith's "Tonight." And they watched very closely indeed, hypersensitive to every

190

nuance in Dr. Christian's words and voice, waiting for any indication that the winner of Operation Search was going to turn out to be disappointing, or plain unsatisfactory, or even subversive. So far, so very good, however.

"Natural griefs," said Dr. Christian, "are just that. They result from the loss of someone or something that can never come again. Death. Innocence. Health. Youth. Fertility. Spontaneity. When living conditions are normal, the mind has mechanisms which deal with natural grief. And never forget that grief *is* natural. Time is the greatest friend, and to keep busy accelerates the passing of sufficient time. But we in the millennial neurosis situation are surrounded by perpetual, remorseless reinforcement of our grief. Time is never given the chance to do its healing work. Many of us my age and older have multiple brothers and sisters, so we know the joys of large families. We have cousins galore, we have aunts and uncles. Our children have no brothers and sisters, and their children will have neither aunts, uncles, nor cousins. Many of us are still journeying between old homes and new, or have left old homes permanently for new homes less well built, smaller, less private—or perhaps we have gone from a slum dwelling of the north to a shanty in the south. Many of us have been made redundant, so we do not even have the solace of useful work. But none of us actually starves, or even endures a particularly monotonous diet. None of us is as badly off as the northern Europeans or the central Asians. Nor do we suffer an indifferent government. The law of the land is mercilessly just, cruelly impartial, and no citizen can escape the fate of all citizens. Yet nothing do we suffer that fires our emotions. Everything we suffer only serves to quench them. And thus—millennial neurosis."

He stopped, not because he was drained, or uncertain where he was going. He stopped because he was a natural orator, and his instinct said it was the right moment to stop. No one stirred.

He went on. "I am an optimist," he said. "I *believe* in the future of Man. And I believe that everything happened, happening, will happen, is both a necessary part of the ongoing evolution of Man, and an inescapable part of the pattern God weaves. I believe that to despair of the future of Man is an insult unendurable to God."

He drew a deep breath, and his next words rolled out in a thunder that set the sound-volume indicators in the control room climbing frenziedly. *"God is!* Accept that first, and only then question what and who He is! It is said that as a human being grows older and therefore closer to his grave, he comes to believe in God because he fears to die. I do not agree! Belief replaces skepticism as a man or woman grows older because that man—or woman—in simply living out life has begun to see a pattern. Not a pattern affecting the race, but a pattern inside the limitations of his own little single humble life. The chances, the coincidences, the truly astonishing relevancies. Youth cannot see the pattern because youth is too young. Not enough years, not enough data.

"God is! That much I know. I cannot find it in me to condemn any form of religious belief or observance, but for myself, I can believe in none. I must tell you that about myself, for you must not be under any misapprehension about me. The only reason I stand here now comes out of my conviction that I can actively help all those who suffer from millennial neurosis. I have already helped many who live in my town of Holloman, but I am only a man, one man. So to reach all of you I have had to write a book, a book which speaks in the same way I do in person. Therefore you are entitled to know what kind of man I am. And what kind of believer. I am not a religious man, if by that you envision a man who observes an established religious regimen. Yet I believe in God! *My* God. Not anybody else's God. And God is the crux of my life, my therapy, my book. So—" he drew a huge breath—"here I stand speaking of God, here I stand in this bizarre—" his shaking hand swept round him—"setting speaking of God! To faces I cannot see, to people I will never know."

His head went forward, his chin dropped, that chameleon voice performed yet another change, from a lion roaring to the quiet sadness of long grief.

"Every one of us needs a bulwark against the loneliness of life. For life *is* lonely! Sometimes intolerably so. Sometimes indescribably so. Inside each one of us a human spirit lives alone, intensely individual, perfectly formed no matter how imperfect the mind and body housing it might be. To me that spirit is the only part of a man or a woman God created in His image, for God is not a man or a woman, He is not a human being, He probably doesn't even live in our infinitely small segment of the sky. I do not think He wants or needs us to love Him, or propitiate Him, or personify Him in any way. Times have changed. Human nature may or may not have changed, though I think it has, and for the better. We are not quite so quick to hurt each other, we are not quite so ignorant of each other. But many people have abandoned God, thinking God has not changed, God has not moved with the times, God has not given us the credit we are due. That is a completely false set of assumptions. What has not changed is the formal and institutionalized *human concept* of God. God has no need to change, because God is not a being Who can be defined in our human meaning of the abstraction we call 'change.' The third millennium has shown us Americans especially the dangers of naivety, the wholesomeness of skepticism. But never, never be skeptical about God! Be skeptical about the men and women who have presumed to define and describe God. They are just men and women, and they can offer little if any proof that they are any better qualified to define and describe God than the rest of us. The main reason such vast numbers of people have abandoned God in the last hundred and fifty years is not actually to do with God at all. It is to do with human beings. People have given me all kinds of reasons why they have abandoned God, and in every case those reasons are actually based not in God but in human rules, regulations, dogmas and the like.

"Do not abandon God! *Turn* to God! There is your bulwark against loneliness! To understand and feel the pattern. To know individual personal existence is a vital part of the pattern. To go forward not into chaos or random chance, but into a further phase in the history of our race, its ceaseless groping after the truth and the goodness which is God. Not our truth! Not our goodness!"

He began to walk, which created a frenzy among cameramen, floor staff and the control room, unable to predict his peregrinations. He didn't even notice, let alone care.

"We are not God's children except in a purely biological sense, because we belong to ourselves. It is our right as human beings to belong to ourselves. God gave us not His laws but the ability to make our own. And if God expects anything at all of us, then He simply expects us with patience and endurance and strength to overcome every obstacle not He but we ourselves and our environment keep putting in our way. This is not God's world. It is *our* world! He gave it to us! I cannot believe in a proprietorial God. We have made this world what it is, not God. We should blame Him as little as we should praise Him. I like to think that when we die the best part of us goes back to God, not necessarily as the entity we call self, but as the part of God already in us, that lonely spirit. But I don't know, and I can't tell you. I just believe that inside me is a little drop of God to fuel me, keep me going. What I do most certainly know is that here is where I am right now, here in this world made by me and my fellow men and all our ancestors. Here is the world I have participated in creating. The world which is therefore my responsibility, as it is all men's responsibility."

"The book!" cried Bob Smith from his chair, spellbound, yet sufficiently possessed of himself to dislike the way his show had been wrested from him.

Dr. Christian stopped pacing and turned to look down on Bob Smith from his great height, eyes blazing, nostrils dilated, the makeup on his face standing out like a mask in which those eyes dwelled like alien fires.

The remark had dragged him back to where he was, why he was there, what he was supposed to be doing.

"The book," he said, and it might as well have been, "Which book?" He paused, searching. "The book. Yes, the book! I called it *God in Cursing* because that is the crucial phrase from a line or two of a poem by Elizabeth Barrett Browning which appeals to me. It is biblical in that it refers to the severance of God and Man, that time when Man was driven from the Garden of Eden with God's curse ringing in his ears. God cursed Man with the choice between good and evil, with bringing forth—and up!—his children in pain and travail, with wresting a living from the earth by the work of his hands, with the cycle of life and death. The poem itself was written as a hymn to work. '*Get leave to work . . . for God, in cursing, gives us better gifts than men in benediction.*'

"It is my opinion," he went on with no apology in his tone, "that all myth and legend and archaic theology including Genesis is allegorical and was originally intended by its writers to be interpreted allegorically. To me, God in cursing us actually gave us the gift of ourselves. We were handed the entire responsibility for our collective and our individual destinies. Like any good parent, He kicked us out of His nest to make our own way in our own infinitesimal segment of the sky.

"The dawn of the race of Man and Man's power to reason was a very long time ago, as long before recorded history as the waxing and waning of several ice ages. The millennia have passed in endless progression, though about the last five of them only do we know very much. And now we stand on the brink of a new

194

millennium. Facing the same old problems. Facing some new ones too. Good and evil are. They cannot change. But work used to be the lot of every man, and now it is rapidly becoming an aristocratic privilege. Men nowadays are more often paid not to work. And the greatest pain our children can inflict upon us is their dwindling number, in our having to wrap up the whole of our urge to immortality within the frail person of one single child per family, give or take the winners of the SCB lottery, and they have their own pains, poor souls."

Some shifted in their seats to hear Dr. Christian's evident sympathy for two-child parents; Bob Smith, who had two children and would gladly have kept his family to one child had he dreamed of the repercussions, was suddenly moved to like this strange and terrifying man. Even to forgive his usurpation of the show.

"Millennial neurosis is loss of hope in the future and faith in the present. It is a perpetual feeling of futility and lack of purpose. It is a dull and utterly unproductive fury turned in upon itself. It is depression often to the point of suicide. It is apathy. It is believing in nothing, from God to our country to ourselves. It is also a Tantalus situation, where most of us living—the average age of all Americans is now up beyond forty—can look back to kinder days, days when we chafed and caviled at restrictions on our liberty so minor by comparison that we would all happily give an arm or two for the chance to go back to then. Therefore millennial neurosis is not only loss of hope in the future and faith in the present, it is love of the past. Because—well, who could want in his heart to live in our present?"

"Since we don't have any choice but to live in the present, Doc, how about giving us some answers?" called Manning Croft.

Dr. Christian looked at the black man sternly and gratefully, pleased to be reminded where he was, what his purpose was. He gave his answer quietly, with tender strength.

"Turn to God, first of all, and understand that the more persistent in the face of adversity any human being is, the richer will be his pattern of life, the happier he will be contending with his life, the bigger his spirit or share of God will grow, and the easier he will face his death. And learn to be busy with hands and mind, for then grief is less unbearable. Acquire a taste for beauty in the world around you, in the books you read, in the pictures you see, in the house you inhabit, in the street where your house is, in the town where your street is. Grow all kinds of living things, not to replace the children you cannot grow, but to keep your brain and eyes and skin constantly exposed to the adventures of growth and life. And accept the world for what it is while doing everything in your power to make it a better place. Do not fear the cold! The race of Man is greater than the cold. The race of Man will be here when the sun warms again."

"Dr. Christian, do you think what we are going through right now is really necessary?" asked Bob Smith.

In the White House two men sat up straight in a hurry, and in the green room Dr. Carriol crossed her fingers and shut her eyes and wished she had someone to pray to. But how could one pray to the God of Joshua Christian?

"Oh, yes, it is necessary," answered Dr. Christian. "For which is worse, to elect to possess one whole and perfect child, or to run the risk of littering broods of genetically warped quasi-children because the only way left to give ourselves that kind of freedom is nuclear war? Which is worse, to run out of gas in a blizzard in upstate New York within the splendid isolation of personal wheels, or travel to Buffalo packed shoulder to shoulder in a warm safe train? Which is worse, to keep on reproducing at the rate we were reproducing, and find our cities squeezing our available arable land to the point of inadequacy, or to limit our reproduction and thereby our industry and our urban sprawls to a size which will allow all of us to live comfortably in the icy times to come?"

He looked around him slowly, suddenly—visibly—weary. And the audience was weary with him, yet not tired of him any more than he was tired of them.

"Remember that we are the ones who must suffer most, for we are the ones who remember different times. What is alien to us will be normal to our children. What you have never known you cannot miss, except as an exercise in abstract thinking. And the very worst disservice we can do our poor solitary children is to fill them with longing for a world they will not know and cannot know. Millennial neurosis is exactly that. A phenomenon of our generation, the millennial generation. It will not endure, if we have the strength to let it die with us. For when we go, it *must* go."

"Dr. Christian, are you saying that the only certain cure for millennial neurosis is the passing of our generation?"

196

This came out of the audience somewhere in the dimness; the floor manager nixed a suggestion from upstairs that he swing a camera in the direction of the inquirer, for Dr. Christian had embarked upon his reply without hesitation.

"No. I am not even saying that with the passing of our generation, millennial neurosis will cease. All I am saying is that we owe it to our children to *let* it die with us! As for more positive ways of combating it, I outlined those to Mr. Croft, so I won't repeat them now. But all of it is in my book, better said, because more logically said." The rare sweet smile was aimed into that section of the audience where the almost invisible woman sat. "I get carried away, you know, and that means I forget how to be logical. I am only a man, and not even a very perfect specimen, I'm afraid. I have struggled to give you an imperfect man's imperfect ideas about what ails us, about God, about ourselves. And I only offer these ideas because I have found that they have helped the people who have turned to me for help."

"Hey, Doc, you say we ought to keep busy," said a male voice from the audience. "But these days it takes money to keep busy."

"I don't agree," said Dr. Christian. "There are many ways to keep busy that cost a minimum of hard cash. Growing things need not be expensive, except in time and care. There are hobbies which can yield a small income if done well enough, community projects, grants from local government bodies as well as from state and federal bodies. There is, I venture to say, not a town in this whole country not well endowed with books—borrowable books, I mean. I'm preaching, I know, but keeping busy is a *habit!* And like all habits, it needs a lot of practice before it becomes ingrained. In my family we can always tell when my mother is really worried or upset, because she scrubs the floors on hands and knees. That's a form of keeping busy. Let me tell you, for acutely worrisome situations, it's a therapy that's hard to beat. Sporting activities are wonderful for those who enjoy sports, and nowhere these days is without public sporting facilities. You must keep busy! And you must teach your children to keep busy! The most soul-destroying thing a man or woman can do is lie around and think, unless the thinking is productively designed and directed. Otherwise all that happens is self-analysis, self-preoccupation and self-destruction." He stopped for a moment, then asked, "What do you like to keep busy at that takes a lot of money?"

"I like to count it, Doc! I used to be a bank teller before banks got self-service money dispensers, and phased us tellers out."

Dr. Christian's face creased into laughter. "Then I suggest you learn to play Monopoly," he said. He sobered abruptly, opened his mouth to speak about the problem of redundancy, and found himself confronted by a determined Bob Smith.

"How about we go back to the desk and sit down, Dr. Christian?" he asked, putting his arm as high around the sloping shoulders in their shabby tweed coat as he could reach, and steering his guest into a turn toward the empty podium. "I guess there are still a lot of people including me who want to ask you questions, so let's have a proper question-and-answer time, huh?"

So they sat down in their original places, with Manning Croft on the near end of the long sofa. Dr. Christian was near exhaustion, sweating and trembling from the enormous effort he had put into that long impassioned speech.

"Are you trying to form a new religion?" asked Bob Smith seriously.

Dr. Christian shook his head vigorously. "No! Oh no! I'm simply trying to offer disillusioned people a more mature and acceptable idea of God. As I emphasized, it's just my own view of God, so I can't say how good or bad it might be. I'm not a theologian, by training or by inclination. It isn't God Who matters to me in fine detail. People matter. So what is important to me is that people start thinking about God again, and start believing in Him. Because Man without God is a purposeless speck of protoplasm coming from nowhere and going nowhere, not responsible for himself or his world. He's an accident, a wart on the skin of the universe, a nothing. Therefore I believe that if a man cannot believe in any of the assorted concepts of God offered to him by the various religions of the world, he should find God for himself, and owe his God to no one but himself."

"You can't have God without a church!" cried a big bass voice from the audience.

Dr. Christian raised his whole forehead. "Why? What is really important, God or a church? No human being should feel he has to go to or belong to a church in order to believe in God! Because the word 'church' has two meanings. It can be the house of worship in which religious ceremonies are conducted. Or it can be a religious institution which has come to formulate a method of worshipping a defined God, in which case it has lands, invested wealth and human personnel to care for. Personally I don't like either kind of church much, but that's purely an individual choice I have made. The cardinal mistake would be if I shut out God from my mind and spirit because I cannot take up membership in a church. Don't you see how depressing it is that people automatically equate refusal to conform to some orthodox religion with nonbelief in God, or with intrinsic wickedness? But *I* ask, which is more important, God or a church?"

"Are you saying we should leave our churches?" asked Manning Croft.

"Oh, no! *No!* If any human being can find God in either kind of church, it is a wonderful thing. I'm not saying that to minimize the shock of my own avowed nonconformity, or to curry favor with devout practicing churchgoers. I'm utterly sincere in saying I envy them their faith. But I *cannot* subscribe to what I do not believe in, and I cannot agree that my disbelief is evidence of personal wickedness or lack of grace. If I did subscribe to what I cannot believe in, I would be the most contemptible type of human being known to Man or God—a hypocrite. Nor am I here to proselytize *anyone,* even an atheist! I'm here simply saying that I want people to go back to God, because there is a God, and that God must continue to be a part of humanity for the rest of the time of humanity. It appalls me that there are many people who believe God is a concept we should abandon, that we will never attain maturity as a race until we have abandoned Him. I could not abandon God! Nor will I let my patients abandon God! Nor will I let you who listen to me now abandon God! *Because I have seen the patterns*—in the world—in other people—and in myself."

In the green room Dr. Judith Carriol sat back with a big voluptuous sigh of sheer pleasure. Her man had come through his ordeal with his colors flying, and it was going to be all systems go right down to blast-off. He would do it! He would give every man, woman and child in this country something to hang on to. Somewhere to go outside of themselves. Oh, the bliss! Oh, the *relief* of this moment! Not that she had ever seriously doubted him. Only that she was a skeptic about everything, including God. Sorry about that, Joshua! Yes. All systems were go right down to blast-off. Hmmmm . . . Blast-off. What an interesting word! Blast-off? Something for the future. Something absolutely gargantuanly astronomically cosmic, in concept and in execution. "Tonight with Bob Smith" was not blast-off. It was no more than an engine check. Blast-off was still in the future somewhere. A bang to end all bangs. *Millennial!* The progress of Dr. Joshua Christian could not be let fizzle out, it could not be let die away in an anticlimactic series of repeat performances of tonight's fireworks on "The Dan Connors Show" and "The Marlene Feldman Hour" and "Northern City" and the rest. Oh, he would have to go that route, yes. But he would have to cap this first bombshell appearance in some other way than by mere repeat performances.

"Well, you certainly picked the right man for the job, Mr. President," said Harold Magnus affably.

"*I* picked him? Oh, Harold, give credit where credit's due, you can afford to!" cried the President. "You brought her and her Operation Search to my attention in the first place, you gave her the money and the staff and the equipment to arrive at Operation Messiah, so a big slice of the credit must go to you. But it's Dr. Carriol's baby, no one else's."

"Yep." The Secretary for the Environment was in a mood to be magnanimous. "I have to give her this, she's no fool, Judith Carriol. But God, does she frighten me!"

The President turned his head. "*Does* she?"

"To death. The coldest-blooded woman in the world."

"Interesting. Now I find her not only an extremely attractive woman, but a most charming and caring human being." The President used his remote-control panel to switch off the television set, and rose to his feet. "I'm on my own for dinner. Can you join me?"

Under Tibor and Julia Reece's rule the White House food was little better than mediocre, so in actual fact the gourmet side of Harold Magnus would have preferred to dine at Chez Roger, the newest and best of Washington's many French restaurants. However, the ambitious side of Harold Magnus was quite willing to forgo langouste and canard, in order to eat littlenecks and rib roast with the boss.

"Julia not going to join us?"

The President for once didn't seize up like a robot in a rainstorm at mention of his wife; he merely shook his head and kept on strolling down the corridor. "No. I believe she's going to Chez Roger tonight."

Shit. Lucky lucky Julia! "How's Julie-girl?"

"She's marvelous," said the President, sounding pleased. "There's been a change of direction in her diagnosis, and she's away at a special school. I miss her, but every time I go to see her, I can also see improvement."

They dined in Tibor Reece's private study, at a small table for two, on the expected littlenecks and rib roast. The clams were tough and the beef too well done, but Harold Magnus pretended both were delicious. When the equally predictable dessert of strawberry shortcake was placed in front of him, he plucked up the courage both to eat this indigestible mess, and to ask Tibor Reece a question.

"Mr. President, aren't you concerned about the terrific emphasis Dr. Christian is obviously going to place on God?"

Tibor Reece blotted his lips with his napkin, placed it to one side of his empty dessert plate, leaned back in his chair and thought a while before he replied.

"Well, it's pretty revolutionary God-talk, and he's sure no trained theologian, but I agree with Dr. Carriol. If this man can offer the people a hope of divine purpose without railroading them into a formal religious persuasion they apparently don't want, I can't see the harm in it. I'm actually a God-fearing man myself. I was born an Episcopalian, and I'm happy to admit that I still draw great comfort from my church and my beliefs. God has saved my sanity on too many occasions for me to take God lightly, that much I can tell you! Yes, I think Dr. Christian and *God in Cursing* are going to be a good thing for the country."

"I wish I could be so sure, sir. I mean, think of the antagonism he's going to rouse among the organized churches!"

"True. But how powerful are they today, Harold? Hell, they can't even get together a decent Washington lobby!"

Harold Magnus grinned. "There speaks the politician." He huffed a little to help the strawberry shortcake down. "There's one comfort, at any rate. The man's a patriot."

"On that score there's no worry at all, I agree." The dark, habitually saturnine face lit up in a glorious smile. "Oh, Harold, doesn't that give you your answer? It should! God is definitely an American!"

"Tonight with Bob Smith" had been running for perhaps six minutes that night when Dr. Millie Hemingway's telephone rang, and kept on ringing until she came grumbling out of the bathroom still hitching up her clothing.

"Millie," said the voice of Dr. Samuel Abraham, "turn your TV onto NBC. You've got to see Bob Smith." And he hung up immediately.

She did as she was told, and in the moment of coming to life her television screen filled up with the face of Dr. Joshua Christian, animated, intense.

"My God!" she said, and sat down limply in a chair. "I don't believe this!" she said a minute later, when a white notice ran through the bottom of the picture announcing that tonight's "Tonight" would be run without commercial breaks or station identification.

The wraps kept on Dr. Joshua Christian had been very thorough, especially for shielding premature news of him from people like the Environment think tank chiefs, too concerned with their own projects and affairs to be devout newspaper readers or television watchers anyway.

Yet there he was, the man Operation Search had dragged up from the primordial ooze of total obscurity. But it was only an exercise, a drill!

Dr. Millie Hemingway watched on to the end, enthralled and appalled. Her phone rang again just as she turned the television set off.

"Millie?"

"Yes, Sam, it's me."

"What's going on?"

She shrugged, though her questioner could not see it. "I don't know, Sam."

"It was an exercise!"

"Yes."

"But it can't have been!"

"Now, Sam, don't jump to conclusions. Just because one of the final candidates crops up now doesn't mean it wasn't an exercise. I think it's just as valid to assume that we did a better job on Operation Search than even we dreamed of. We were after the people who could influence a nation. And Moshe found this guy. We all laughed because he didn't seem a likely bet. But obviously Moshe was right, and we were wrong. That simple."

"I don't know, Millie. . . . I tried to phone Moshe, no reply. No reply all night."

"Oh, Sam! Go to bed, and stop speculating." Dr. Millie Hemingway hung up.

Chance. Coincidence. Further evidence of Moshe Chasen's undeniable brilliance, if they had needed further evidence. That was all it was. My God, Dr. Christian was powerful! He came out of that screen three-dimensional. Moshe was right. Charisma. And what he said made a lot of sense. Patterns. He couldn't know of course that he himself was a perfect example of his own contentions.

Dr. Moshe Chasen watched "Tonight" in his office, with the phone switched off.

All he said was, "That's my boy!"

IX

On the night of Friday, October 29, 2032, Dr. Joshua Christian became famous. *God in Cursing: A New Approach to Millennial Neurosis* sold out its enormous first printing within a month, and continued to sell at the rate of 100,000 copies per day. Everyone everywhere clutched the white volume with the red lettering and the silver bolt of lightning across its front, and everyone everywhere was actually reading it.

By overwhelming popular demand, the Bob Smith show on which Dr. Christian originally appeared was rebroadcast a week later after a huge advertising campaign, and the whole nation watched. This time the show's usual sponsors were accommodated in three long commercial breaks, one at the very beginning of the show, one between Dr. Christian's solo speech and the question-and-answer period, and the last at the end of the show. Though "Tonight" had not lost revenue on its first broadcast; Environment picked up the tab.

And soon that gaunt sunken face with the piercing dark eyes could be seen on the cover of every magazine and periodical; it was stamped onto T-shirts, and its first edition as a poster, with the single word BELIEVE printed beneath it, sold out in a day.

Dr. Moshe Chasen had managed to evade his colleagues on the night Dr. Christian appeared with Bob Smith, but he knew he had only postponed the inevitable confrontation. So when he came in to work the following Monday and found two notes on his secretary's desk, he sighed, scratched his head, and invited Dr. Abraham and Dr. Hemingway down for morning coffee.

"Did you watch 'Tonight' last Friday, Moshe?" demanded Dr. Abraham before his bottom was into a chair.

"As a matter of fact, I did," said Dr. Chasen. "Judith sent me a message that I'd find it interesting."

"Oho!" cried Dr. Hemingway. "Judith knew, did she?"

It gave Dr. Chasen enormous pleasure to lean back in his chair and imitate Dr. Carriol at her most supercilious; he tried to drive his brows into his hairline and drawled, "My dear Millie, when have you ever caught our esteemed chief napping?"

That stymied both of them, since it was unanswerable.

"Actually," Dr. Chasen went on, his tone indicating that he thought he should take pity on them, "she's a great friend of the publisher at Atticus, and they've got Dr. Christian under contract. I believe Atticus used Judith as one of the first readers of Dr. Christian's book while it was still in manuscript."

"So last Friday's 'Tonight' show was no surprise to you, huh?" asked Dr. Abraham, still skeptical.

"None at all."

"Then why didn't you warn us?" asked Dr. Hemingway.

Dr. Chasen grinned wickedly. "I couldn't resist not warning you. What surprises me most is that you didn't see him when he was here in Environment earlier this year."

They both sat up. "*Here?*" bleated Dr. Abraham.

"That's right. After Judith read his book, she invited him down to talk with me about relocation."

That took the wind completely out of their sails; they stared at Dr. Chasen with the expressions of two children discovering far too late that they had missed out on a treat.

"I never realized you were so close-mouthed," said Dr. Abraham feebly.

Well, Sam, I am, thought Dr. Chasen to himself; and I wouldn't have told you now about his visit to Environment, except that it's not impossible that someone noticed him here, and it might get back to you. This way, you've been offered an explanation you must accept whether you want to or not.

"It *was* an exercise, wasn't it?" asked Dr. Hemingway.

"Yes, Millie, it was," said Dr. Chasen gently.

Dr. Abraham shook his head, unconvinced. "I don't know," he said. "Something sounds fishy to me."

Dr. Joshua Christian spent a week in Atlanta, mostly shuttling back and forth between the buildings with the pink and blue and grey and gold and black mirrored walls that formed the semicircle of Media Plaza. He spoke with Dan Connors and Marlene Feldman and Bob Smith again and Dominic d'Este and Benjamin Steinfeld, with Wolf Man Jack VI and Reginald Parker and Mischa Bronski on radio; he gave long interviews to all the important newspapers and magazines, he did several signing sessions in several big Atlanta bookstores. Times had changed; Atlanta was now the most influential book town in America, and rapidly eclipsing New York City as the nation's cultural capital. Part of this was due to the fact that it had already passed the five million population mark, and was besides the hub of a large constellation of Band A and Band B relocation settlements.

He went from strength to strength. Even Dr. Judith Carriol was amazed at the smallness of the opposition to his ideas; logic said it was because he did not deny God, therefore could not be dismissed as evil or corrupt save perhaps by those who felt their particular brand of belief in God was the only one that mattered to God. But privately she considered the main reason for his instantaneous, positive effect on people to be the extraordinary power within the man. It came across undiluted on television or radio, it reached out, it embraced, it infiltrated a long way farther down than skin. He *made* people believe in what he said, working through their emotions and their instincts, their pain and their sense of isolation. The concept of the universal truth had always intrigued but simultaneously baffled her; he projected it, yet still she could not fathom its nature.

However, Atlanta was only the beginning of Dr. Christian's publicity tour. Both the Environment think tank in the person of Dr. Judith Carriol, and the Atticus Press in the person of Elliott MacKenzie, felt that Dr. Christian should be *seen* by as many people as possible. So where most author tours concentrated upon mass exposure via the mass media, Dr. Christian's tour deliberately included a large number of public appearances in the bigger relocation towns, in the established cities, and in any areas felt to be either sensitive or influential. After two slightly unpleasant experiences in Atlanta when he was scheduled to sign copies of his book in stores, signing sessions were abandoned; he had drawn so many people into the stores that chaos reigned, and he had to be removed in a hurry. Instead, he was slotted into formal appearances that were advertised as lectures and to which admission could only be gained by ticket. These tickets were free of charge, but had to be applied for.

No one, least of all Dr. Carriol, could know ahead of time how well Dr. Christian would take the grind of a full publicity tour; how quickly the novelty would wear off and the enervation set in. However, she had prepared herself as well as possible by doing some research first; she had made it her business to talk to several major writers, a brace of movie stars, and to the three biggest public relations firms in the people-pushing business. And from every person she saw she learned much the same thing; that a publicity tour rapidly became a grind to its star, that in the end the star would become almost maddened by so much brief contact with so many people all asking the same questions, and that sometimes the star would even pack up and go home without notice or apology.

However, Dr. Joshua Christian displayed no sign of ennui, exhaustion or disillusion. He kept right on talking to any soul who would talk to him, he actually welcomed people when they recognized and accosted him, he signed his book cheerfully whenever it was thrust under his nose, he handled the occasional nut or antagonist with professional tact and smoothness, and with journalists of all sorts he was brilliant.

The worst of it was that the publicity tour kept getting longer. As the book was read by more and more people and his name reached the proportions of a genuine household word, town after town flooded Atticus with requests for a visit from Dr. Christian. Understanding the exigencies of remorseless public exposure, Elliott MacKenzie turned all these requests down, until a discreet message came from Washington that Dr. Christian should where possible visit all these clamoring places. At least twice a week Dr. Carriol would receive word from Atticus that two or three more towns had been added to their agenda.

One week had become two, two became three, and three became four; a month on the road, and still Dr. Christian went from strength to strength, apparently capable, thought Dr. Carriol with tired horror, of going on forever. Once they had quit Atlanta the "on the road" nature of a publicity tour made itself felt, for every night (and sometimes during the day as well, when they were scheduled to visit several smaller communities in one day) the helicopter picked them up and whizzed them to a new town, they slept all too briefly in their strange beds, then by eight in the morning at the latest they would commence the new day's round of engagements, continuing from one engagement to another without let until helicopter time arrived again.

Outside of the major cities most of Dr. Christian's engagements fell into the lecture category, and these functions he relished enormously. He would give a fifteen-minute set speech, never the same, and follow it up by at least an hour of question-and-answer time. His appetite for people awed Dr. Carriol, who had never seen this side of him, any more than perhaps anyone else ever had. Not content with the personal exposure he invited through his question-and-answer periods, he refused to hold himself aloof from the crowds who flocked to hear him, even on one memorable occasion sharply rebuking a concerned local official who attempted to give him a brief respite by ordering the crowds away. Unafraid for his person, undaunted by his reception, he would arrive at a lecture venue and at once dive into the mass of waiting people, talking away, questioning, having a ball. Only how *could* the man be having a ball? Absolutely fed up with being civil to hosts of strangers and dredging up the appropriate small talk, longing for peace and quiet and time on her own, Dr. Carriol could not understand how her charge managed to sustain his mood of what looked very much like real euphoria. Anybody's people-palate ought to be cloyed! But apparently Dr. Joshua Christian was a bottomless pit when it came to people.

Of course not all of his public appearances went well, or even smoothly; Dr. Christian refused to prepare his speeches, insisting that if they were not spontaneously extemporaneous, he would lose his effect on audiences. But that led to a certain amount of unevenness, compounded by the fact that he was not consistently logical, nor always able to resist the wild emotions which had a tendency to come roaring up out of his buried deeps. Luckily television and radio sobered him a little; he did at least stick to the subject and answer the questions properly. Be grateful, said Dr. Carriol to herself, for small mercies. And only let me continue to find the strength to trail around this huge country in his wake!

While Dr. Christian continued his ever-extending and ever more triumphant tour of the United States, his publisher was trying to decide when (or if) Dr. Christian might be free to tour South America and the Eurocommune. In both continents *God in Cursing* was selling enormously well, despite the loss inevitable in translation, and the ideological differences. The Russians rumbled a little at first, then wisely piped down while they debated how much editing *God in Cursing* was going to need before it could be circulated through the many Soviet states; glaciation was worst in this biggest, most landlocked and northerly of the world's major powers, and a concept of God which could be allowed to exist side by side with Marxist philosophy was not to be sneezed at.

The Christian family of course had been following their Joshua's progress with minute attention to its national import, and huge attention to Joshua himself. His brothers did at first manfully strive to keep some degree of detachment, but after a week succumbed to the mood of joy and pride which the Christian women exuded from every pore.

"He's wonderful!" cried the Mouse after watching "Tonight with Bob Smith."

"Of course he is," said Mama complacently.

"He's *wonderful!*" cried the Mouse after watching Benjamin Steinfeld's "Sunday Forum."

"I always knew he was," said Mama complacently.

Only Mary kept her own counsel. The pain in her was not easily classified enough to be called simple jealousy; to herself, she thought she suffered because somehow it was always Joshua who made it impossible for her to be happy. But when as the secretary she opened the Atticus cylinder containing Joshua's poster, down which was stuffed the T-shirt—ah, that was the last straw! She hid emotions, poster and T-shirt until after dinner that night, when she threw them onto the coffee table without a word and sat back to watch, trembling.

To do the family justice, no one was quite pleased, even Mama. Andrew's distaste showed clearly, as did James's bewilderment.

"I suppose it was inevitable," Andrew said after a long moment. He shrugged. "I wonder what Joshua thinks?"

"Knowing Joshua," said Miriam, "he hasn't even noticed. Everyone around him could be wearing one of those T-shirts, and he still wouldn't notice. He never does notice much to do with himself—he wears highly selective blinkers, you know, and they blot out anything to do with himself."

"You're quite right," said James. "Poor Joshua!"

"It *is* a compliment," said Mama feebly.

But it was Martha's face tipped Mary's precarious balance; the poor Mouse sat burning to take the poster for her own, yet didn't have the courage to do so.

"It's disgusting!" Mary hissed, leaping to her feet. "Oh, you fools, you idiots! They're *using* him! They don't care about him, all they care about is what they can milk out of him, and you're right, Mirry, he's blind! He's a donkey that will pull their cart as long as they dangle the carrot! Can't you see how they're using him? All of us? And when they're finished—" she pushed impatiently at her tears—"they'll just kick him to one side. It's disgusting!" She turned to Martha, shrinking away in terror. "Grow up, damn you! Grow up! Does he love you? Does he love any of us except Mama? No, he doesn't! Why don't you love someone who loves you back? Oh, *why* don't you?"

She made a grab at the poster to tear it up, but Martha was too quick for her. The poster was removed from the table, rolled up, and passed reverently to Mama.

"Go to bed, Mary," said Andrew tiredly.

She stood a moment longer looking down at all of them, then she turned and left, not running; she would not give them that satisfaction.

"Oh, why is she such a difficult girl?" asked Mama, distressed but helpless, for she didn't honestly know what was the matter with Mary, nor therefore what to do about it.

"She's jealous of Joshua," said James. "She always has been, poor Mary."

"Well," said Mama, picking up the T-shirt and poking it down inside the poster, "I think the best thing we can do with these is burn them."

Martha got up. "Give them to me, I'll take them down to the incinerator," she said colorlessly.

But it was Andrew who reached out and plucked the roll off

210

Mama. "No, I'll do it," he said. "You, my Mouse, can make me a mug of hot chocolate." He lifted wry brows at James and Miriam. "I'm sure the plants won't mind a little puff of warmth from Joshua!"

That was perhaps the most depressing of the Christian family's early reactions to Joshua's sudden fame. It was followed very shortly by the most euphoric, heralded by the arrival of Elliott MacKenzie on the back stoop of 1047 Oak Street. He was armed with a proposal.

However, he waited until after Mama served him an excellent dinner, using the time to observe the various Christian faces, and wondering how their fair placid beauty could ever interlock with Joshua's dark turbulence.

"Joshua is going to be literally months touring around the United States," he said over coffee, "and I have an enormous market abroad, especially in Europe and South America. England, France, Germany, Italy and the Netherlands are clamoring for a visit from Joshua, as are all the states south of Panama."

They sat listening attentively, proud but a little puzzled.

"Anyway, I have an idea I'd like to put to you," he went on, "though there's no need to give me an answer right away. You've always supported Joshua in the clinic, you're a very close-knit family and I guess you know Joshua, his work and his ideas, better than anyone else." He paused, turned to James in particular. "James, would you and Miriam consider touring the Eurocommune on Joshua's behalf? I know Miriam is a very fine linguist—which actually Joshua is not—and that gives you a very great advantage. It's not the same as Joshua, but in all honesty I don't think that matters." Then he turned to Andrew. "I've got a job for you too, if you're interested. South America. Would you and Martha take that on for Joshua? I know you speak fluent Spanish, and we'd put you through an intensive course of Brazilian Portuguese before you go."

"How do you know what languages we speak?" asked Mary, staring at Elliott MacKenzie so painfully that he shifted uncomfortably in his palest-pink chair.

"Joshua told me, when he had dinner at my place. He's terrifically proud of all of you, you know. And I think it would delight him to realize you were taking his work into other countries."

"It's a very hard thing to decide," said James slowly. "Usually

211

Joshua's here to make the decisions. Couldn't we contact Joshua—by phone if it can't be arranged any other way—and see what he thinks?"

"Well, I hate to remove Joshua's authority, but honestly he's got so much on his plate at the moment that I think it would be much better if you didn't bother him," said Elliott MacKenzie delicately.

"I'll go," said Mary abruptly.

Her brothers both turned to stare at her, astonished.

"*You?*" asked James.

"Yes. Why not me?"

"For one thing, Drew and I are married, we have wives to help us. For another, we have the necessary languages."

"Please let me go!" she whispered.

Andrew laughed. "We haven't even decided yet if anyone is going, Mair. But Jimmy's right. If any of us go, it will have to be the married couples. You and Mama must stay here to look after things." His eyes rested thoughtfully on Martha, who sat with lids lowered and face blank. "Actually I'm very tempted, Elliott," he said, turning to smile at the Atticus publisher with a great deal of his oldest brother's sweetness. "A couple of months in South America might do my wife the world of good."

So it was that Dr. Christian's mother joined him in Mobile, Alabama. As reason for her sudden unheralded appearance, she gave out the news that all work in the clinic had had to be discontinued because of the head of the clinic's meteoric plunge to fame.

"Oh, you've no idea what it's been like!" she said to her son breezily. "People everywhere! They don't come for treatment, they just seem to want to look at our houses and have a cup of coffee and talk to us because we're your family. It's like trying to move around with a million newborn chicks all over the floor! We can't work. But it's quite all right, dearest," she said with great earnestness because he stood there so still and quiet, "we've all found other work to do. Mr. MacKenzie is sending James and Miriam to Europe because the book's out there, and everyone's screaming for you. Only you can't go because you've got here to do, and anyway, you don't have the languages. Then because Andrew speaks such beautiful Spanish, Mr. MacKenzie is sending him and Martha to South America. The book's out in South

America too. So there I was! Out of a job! James and Miriam and Andrew and Martha have already gone to New York for briefing or coaching or something, and they won't be back. So—anyway!—I told Mary she would have to look after the houses and the plants, because *I'm* going to come along with you!"

His stillness broke into a huge jerky shudder. "But—my work!" he gasped.

Mama rattled on nervously. "Well, of course it goes on, dearest Joshua, but it just can't go on in the clinic any more is all. It's going on throughout the country, and in other countries as well. You can rest assured James and Andrew will work very hard for you abroad! You see, after Mr. MacKenzie went back to New York we had a family talk, and we all decided that the best thing we could do for you in the circumstances was to help publicize the book."

"What have I done?" he asked, of no one.

Mama had not given Dr. Carriol time to divert this thoughtless relaying of information it had been decided to keep from Dr. Christian for the moment; impotent but seething, Dr. Carriol deemed it best to hold her tongue until Mama ran down. Now she tried to step in and repair the damage.

"You're doing it," she said soothingly. "Joshua, you are doing what you most wanted to do! You're actively helping millions of people to recover from the depression of decades! There's a whole new mood in the country, and it's entirely due to you."

He turned his poor shriveled face to her piteously, desperately. "Is it, Judith? Is it really?"

She took hold of his hands, squeezing them hard. "My dear, I would not mislead you about something so important! You're in the midst of working a great miracle."

"I'm *not* a miracle worker! I'm just a man doing a man's best!"

"Yes, yes, I know. I meant it metaphorically."

"Why did it have to be like this?"

A huff of breath in a little sigh came out of her, half exasperation, half frustration. "Look, in a month you've gone from utter obscurity to absolute fame. How could you know what it was going to be like? No one could have known, including me! Certainly I for one never thought of what might happen in Holloman. But in spite of the clinic's closure, you're moving forward in ten-league boots."

"Is this then my life's work, Judith? But this isn't real! This

won't last, it can't last! It was never intended to last! The clinic—"
He stopped, so moved he could not finish.

"Joshua, when this is over you can reopen your clinic. That's
so easy! What's happened in Holloman isn't going to last either.
James and Andrew will come back, you'll all be together again,
the clinic will reopen, and your life will resume some normality.
Of course you won't ever be entirely free from the effects of *God
in Cursing*, but I don't suppose you want to be. You will be able
to continue your work in Holloman! Mama's news just seems such
a catastrophe because of the life you're leading at the moment,
because you feel if you were there the clinic wouldn't be closing.
Calm down and *think* about everything! What you're doing now is
the most unreal existence in the world—constantly traveling,
constantly meeting new people, constantly giving of yourself in
ever-increasing amounts—but you never thought it would be
easy, Joshua. So how about giving everything a little time? Let
yourself work through this period of transition, and then reorganize yourself. Don't you say in your book that change means
reorganization? And that reorganization takes time and patience?
Work?"

He tried to laugh, a tight little rustle of noise, a face too
twisted for success. "I'm a poor subject for my own preaching,
that's the trouble. I can only listen to it inside my own head. And
my own head is beginning to be a pretty bad place these days."

"Joshua, it's late," she said, her voice dropping half an octave
with unconscious solicitude. "We have a six o'clock start in the
morning, because this is Mobile, and there's a breakfast show. Go
to bed."

He went, but there was no euphoria tonight. For the first
time since he had started on his tour, Dr. Carriol knew him to be
depressed. God damn Mama! Why is it that certain women are so
sure of their maternal ground that they refuse to think with anything higher up than their own uteruses? During all of Dr. Carriol's desperate attempts to mend what Mama had made, Mama
sat looking adorably bewildered and innocent, her eyes traveling
from Joshua to Judith and back again as if she didn't really understand what was going on. But how could she not understand?

Obviously she didn't understand, for when he started to leave
the room she got up to follow him, to fuss and cluck.

Dr. Carriol put out a hand to detain her rather roughly.

"Oh no you don't! I want a few words with you," she said

214

grimly, and hustled Mama from the sitting room in the opposite direction from Joshua's room, to her own room—and had Mama thought of accommodation? Did she think she could share a room with dear Judith? And how had she got all the way to Mobile? Not with the help of Atticus, for sure! Oh she knew she was doing the wrong thing, all right. But it didn't stop her doing it, thought Dr. Carriol, eyeing her sourly.

"What's the matter, Judith?" Mama quavered. "What is it? What have I done?"

"The last thing in the world your son needed was to be told a lot of garbage about his clinic closing down and his brothers taking off for foreign parts."

"But it's all true! Why shouldn't he know? I thought he'd be pleased!" Mama whined.

"When he came back to Holloman with all this touring behind him was time enough to tell him. Why do you think I haven't told him? At the moment he is under incredible strain, Mama! He's traveling without letup, he's not getting enough sleep, and he's draining every reserve of energy he's got by talking to people nonstop and signing hundreds of books and letting people shake him by the same hand he signs with—Mama, *why* did you come? Don't you understand that your presence is just another burden he's going to have to pick up and carry as well?"

Mama gasped, her magnificent bosom heaving. "*I* am his mother!" Another gasp. "I—I—I have been entirely responsible for him since he was four years old! I know what a strain he's under, that's why I came! Believe me, *Doctor* Carriol, I'll be a help to him, not a burden!"

"Oh for God's sake, Mama, don't get the shits with me," said Dr. Carriol tiredly. "I know what I'm saying, and so do you. Be honest! You were sitting up there in Holloman with the clinic in ruins and your other sons taking off for exciting tasks in exciting places, and you felt left out of everything. If concern for Joshua's welfare was really what was driving you, you would have sent Mary down here and stayed behind yourself in Holloman to do the fortress-holding. That is a good girl you sit on all the time, poor Mary! Be honest! You were feeling left out and you were dying of curiosity, your apple-of-the-eye firstborn has gone and got himself famous, and you know *you* did it, and so you decided you were going to have some of the excitement. You're a very beautiful woman, you're still in the prime of life, and people are going to look at you. They're going to admire you. They're going to congratulate you on producing Joshua. They're going to accord you a lot of the credit."

"*Judith!*"

"Look, Mama, the wounded martyr act doesn't cut any ice with me at all, so don't bother. I'm the one has to care for him while he's crazily barnstorming his way round this enormous country, and he doesn't need you to worry about as well as himself. Because he will worry about you—whether you're busy destroying all his good work by prattling on about the joys of having four children while he's trying to convince people that the ideal number of children is one, whether you're feeling as fucked and bedraggled as he is, if you've had enough to eat because he hasn't, if you're bored, if you've been left behind in some radio station or newspaper office—that's the truth of it, Mama!"

The only possible refuge was tears, so Mama trotted the tears out. Genuine tears too, for she really hadn't thought to question her motives for coming to join him, and now that someone she trusted and admired as much as Judith Carriol had pointed them out to her with such disastrous clarity, she was not only devastated but ashamed. Ashamed too of her unthinking treatment of Mary, the dowdy spinster who never got any of the attention and never got any of the bonuses.

"I'll go home first thing in the morning, and send Mary down," she grieved.

"No, it's too late for that. You're here now, so here you stay," said Dr. Carriol with weary resignation. "But I'm warning you, Mama! Keep a low profile. Don't open your mouth—and don't keep it shut looking like a martyr either. Content yourself with looking like the ravishing fallen angel you are, and don't do *anything* to increase his anxieties."

"I won't, Judith, I promise I won't!" She was cheering up second by second. "And I will be useful, honestly I will! I can do all his washing, all your washing—"

The laugh she hadn't known she still possessed came tumbling out of Dr. Carriol. "Oh, Mama! Who has time or facilities to do washing? We move on too fast for hotel laundries, and the rooms are too cold to wash in a bathroom basin—we don't do it. Every day while he's waiting for us, our pilot goes and buys the few bits of fresh clothing we need, for himself too. And since you're join-

216

ing the ménage, you'd better give Billy your size in underpants and bras before you run out, or you'll be wearing dirty ones."

Mama blushed. She actually blushed.

Dr. Carriol gave up. "Here, you'd better have my room," she said, picking up her single suitcase from where it still lay unopened. "I'll go down to the desk and see about another one. Where's your bag?"

"Downstairs," whispered Mama wretchedly.

"I'll have it sent up. Goodnight."

After the bag came Mama went to bed, and cried herself desolately to sleep.

Dr. Christian was in bed too, but neither tears nor sleep came to heal him. Where had all the pleasure gone, so swiftly, so suddenly? Oh, he had enjoyed this past month! He had found it supremely satisfying to move freely among so many pain-racked people, watching their faces as they listened to him speak, knowing that indeed his inner promptings had not led him astray, that he could indeed help. The days had fled in joyous activity, he hadn't needed to count his energy because it flowed through him in rivers of fire impossible to quench. Such an adventure to whip through the air from town to town with Billy the pilot, silent and smart and Service, guiding his craft wherever he was bidden. So many questions, so much that people yearned to know—and there he was, magically enabled to help them through the offices of Fairy Godmother Carriol. It had been so *easy!* A landbound seal finding the water at last. He had frolicked in his natural element, so happy, so content. The people had received him, the people had not rejected him.

But ever in the back of his mind had lain Holloman, his dear beloved clinic, the work he would go back to in a relatively short time, even if only to begin planning the removal of that clinic to some desperately needy place in the south of the country.

Not true. Not there. He closed his aching eyes. Think, Joshua Christian! Think! He had spoken of change and of patterns, of the future's viability and the present's uncertainty and the past's mortality. So was this trouble not a part of the pattern too, was this direction not intended to guide his ignorant feet? He had taken himself and he had deliberately altered the conditions of his life.

And once conditions have been altered, something entirely different must emerge.

Be optimistic, Joshua Christian! How lovely and how very satisfying, that James and Miriam and Andrew and Martha were to be a positive part of all this newness. Fitting. They had always been shoulder to shoulder with him—so why not now, in this altered condition? Be positive, Joshua Christian! It is for the best. It is meant. It is a part of some pattern shaping itself so subtly and so secretly that you cannot as yet so much as glimpse its nature. But you will! You will.

He concentrated upon sleep. O sleep close mine eyes! O sleep heal my pain! O sleep show me that I am mortal man! But sleep was far away, it curled through the brains of those he helped.

From Mobile the augmented Christian ménage moved to St. Louis. Mama behaved herself beautifully, making friends with Billy the pilot immediately, and endearing herself to him by coyly handing him her vital statistics in a sealed envelope.

"What color do you like?" he whispered.

She smiled at him angelically. "White, thank you."

On the surface St. Louis went very well, and out of it came one of the most charming of the little allegories with which Dr. Christian peppered his talks. Luckily it was preserved for posterity on videotape, for it occurred during a morning show on one of the local television stations.

The hostess was lightweight and terrifyingly gushing; very pretty, very blonde, quite young. Dr. Christian was the most important guest she had ever collared, so an acute attack of nerves made her just the slightest bit patronizing. And since she was not equipped to patronize him on an intellectual level, she concentrated on his masculinity and his childlessness.

"Doctor, I'm interested in the way you defend those who have been lucky enough to obtain a second-child approval," was her opening gambit. "But it's awfully easy for you to be magnanimous, isn't it? I mean, you're not married, you have no children, and—uh—well—you can never feel like a mother, can you? Do you honestly think that you're in a position to condemn the attitude of all the poor women who haven't been lucky in the SCB lottery when they hit back at the lucky few?"

He smiled, sighed, leaned back for a moment with his eyes

218

closed, then opened them and stared straight into her soul, which was not very far down.

"The worst feature of the SCB lottery is the means test placed on all applicants for second children. Who is to say which group in the community will make the best parents of two children. A certain amount of material comfort is good, I suppose, especially since education is so prohibitively expensive after secondary school. But we can't run a country entirely on graduates, especially when the average age of the manual tradesmen in the country is far higher than the average age of teachers or computer technicians. We need our few young to become plumbers and electricians and carpenters as well as sociologists and surgeons.

"The means test has added an extra element of unnecessary rancor to the SCB lottery. Unlucky people can always level a charge, no matter how ill founded, of collusion, bribery, string-pulling, whatever. Because the means test weeds out those not in a financial or social position to have influence."

Mortification had already set in with his hostess, it showed in her too-bright eyes and her uneasy pose; now he increased it by raising his voice slightly, and letting it show his disapproval.

"But that wasn't what you really asked, was it? You asked what qualifications I have to condemn the way the unlucky applicants treat the lucky ones, so I gather you yourself condone the means test. And quite clearly you condone this abhorrent attitude of malignity and revenge."

He leaned forward in his chair, dropped his head, put his arms on his knees and stared down at his hands loosely folded between his legs. So his voice was very low, though quite audible.

"What qualifications do I have?" he asked. "No, indeed I can never be a mother. But I am the parent of two cats, the maximum number the law allows me. Both neutered as kittens, since I had no wish to apply for a breeder's certificate. Yes, I am the parent of a male cat named Hannibal and a female cat named Dido. Beguiling creatures, Hannibal and Dido. They love me very much. But do you know what they do with most of their time? They don't wash themselves. They don't hunt mice and rats. They don't even tuck their paws under their bodies and doze the hours away. My cats are ledger keepers. A his ledger and a hers ledger. And they scribble, scribble, scribble. A typical day's entry from Hannibal's ledger might read something like this: 'Dad put *her* plate of food down first this morning. *She* got four pats to my three when Dad came in for lunch. When Dad came in for dinner tonight he picked *her* up and ignored me. And *she* got to sleep on Dad's bed while I was forced to make do with a chair nearby.' Dido's ledger for the same day might read more like this: 'Dad put more food on *his* plate this morning. When he left for the clinic after lunch Dad gave *him* six pats and me none. Dad sat with *him* on his knee for half an hour after dinner. And when Dad went to bed he put *him* on a special chair while I had to make do with the bed.' Yes, my cats do that every day of their lives. They waste their days watching each other to see how much of my attention each gets. Weighing me up—and to the last tiny scruple! And every slight, real or imaginary, is entered in their ledgers. Scribble, scribble, scribble."

He lifted his head and looked straight at the camera. "So all right. I can put up with this kind of mean-spirited pettiness from my cats. Because they are cats. They are a lower form of life than I. Their manners and their ethics are based on instinct and self-preservation. In a feline brain there is little room for any image outside the self. And when it comes to love, the feline instinct is to keep a ledger."

His voice changed, freezing his hapless interviewer to her marrow. "But *we* are not cats!" he roared. "We are far higher creatures than cats! We have feelings we can discipline, or learn to discipline. We can apply logic to our baser emotions and cancel them out. Our brains are big enough to accommodate far more than just ourselves. And I say this to you! If our spirits are so mean that we must qualify love by keeping a ledger, then we are no better than cats. Any loving and caring relationship, be it husband and wife, parent and child, friend and friend, neighbor and neighbor, countryman and countryman, human being and human being—*any* loving relationship that counts how much is given against how much is received is doomed! That is animal thinking! And—" he turned to his interviewer so quickly she shrank away—"in my humble, completely unqualified opinion, it is beneath our dignity as men and women. To weigh one's own sorrow against another's joy and punish that other person for his joy versus our own sorrow—anathema! Do you hear me, woman? *Anathema!* I say to everyone, not only to you, cast it out!"

ABC bought the segment from this small unaffiliated local station and showed it cross-country that night on their evening news. With two immediate results. The first was a joint directive from Congress and the President to the effect that the Second Child Bureau would abolish its means test at once. The second was an indignant flood of letters to Dr. Christian from cat lovers who felt cats were much nicer, more loving and more worthwhile than any human being, including Dr. Christian. There were two further results, much slower in surfacing; it became less socially condoned to persecute parents with second children, and the little allegory passed into the Christian myth where some very much more important things he said were quite forgotten.

"I never knew you had any cats, Joshua!" shouted Dr. Carriol to Dr. Christian that evening in the helicopter as it whipped them from St. Louis to Kansas City.

"I don't," he grinned.

She didn't comment for a moment, then she said, "No wonder Mama looked stunned! But I must say she handled it very well. Mama!" she shouted into the front seat, leaning forward. "What a terrific actress you are, you villain! Telling that poor squashed girl after we got off the air all about Hannibal and Dido! A ginger and a stripey, for crying out loud!"

"Well, I did think of making them Siamese!" Mama shouted back, twisting her head to laugh at her son. "But then I decided that if ever Joshua should decide to keep cats, he would *never* keep a breed! Waifs and strays, that's Joshua!"

"You're bound to be asked a lot more about Hannibal and Dido, Joshua. What are you going to say?"

"Oh, I'll field the questions to Mama. I've appointed her the real expert on Hannibal and Dido."

"Ledger-keeping cats! Where on earth did you dig that one up?"

"A friend," he said tranquilly, and would say no more.

Mobile and St. Louis marked the emergence of what Dr. Carriol later catalogued as Personality Three in the changing parade of Dr. Joshua Christian. Personality One was the old original Dr. Christian of purely Holloman days. Personality Two was the happy, fulfilled, intolerably energetic, people-guzzling Dr. Christian of the first month after *God in Cursing* was released. The new personality was bewildered and slightly numbed, but still capable of flashes reminiscent of Personality Two; Personality

Three was also more enclosed, more obdurate, more Messianic. But none of her knowledge of those three Dr. Christians prepared Dr. Carriol for Personality Four, waiting in the green room for an appearance still months away in the cold impenetrable future.

He never spoke to her about his feelings on learning of the closure of the Holloman clinic, the dispersion of his brothers and sisters-in-law across the face of the globe in his service; all she had to go on in assessing the importance of this as a cause of the emergent Personality Three was his initial reaction when Mama had broken the news. He was shocked, most definitely. Dismayed too. Brokenhearted? That she did not know. Oh, she could reason shrewdly enough that like most people shot to sudden fame, he had never thought about its personal consequences, either for himself or for those around him; he had probably assumed that when the tumult and the shouting died down he would be at liberty to go quietly back to where he was before it all started. Besides which, the man had a natural humility and some sound skepticism about himself. It was possible he thought that despite his aspirations his success would be modest, or at greatest a flash-in-the-pan thing, quickly up, quickly down, quickly dead. But to turn overnight not into the object of a fantasy-based adulation, but into a super-guru, reverenced, thanked, respected—ah, that was a very different adjustment to make.

So there were more than enough reasons to account for the emergence of Personality Three, which Dr. Carriol called the super-guru. And, in retrospect, more than enough for the emergence of Personality Four as well.

Inside himself Dr. Christian had abandoned any kind of self-analysis. His circumstances had simply turned him into a sponge, doomed to sop up every scrap of the hugely strong and pervasive emotions he now encountered on every hand.

During the first few weeks he had indeed fared best, for his self-image was partially anaesthetized by the shock of sheer novelty and the remorseless travel, so many different faces and places. Then he stood outside himself enjoying himself, at a distance from the shabby, ugly, too-thin, too-dark scarecrow of a man who always seemed to be surrounded by people. And beneath the fantastic joy, all his reveling in this astonishing success, beneath the pleasure of knowing his aspirations fulfilled, a pool of sorrow waited. He so singularly unhandsome was told he was the handsomest man this or that woman had ever seen, he so unaware of his switched-on dynamo of a self was told how magnetic he was, what charisma he had, how mesmeric and hypnotic and electrifying and powerful and and and . . . The adjectives and the metaphors tumbled one on top of another into the formidable recesses of his brain like bits of glitter down a chute in a sequin factory.

So how he felt, and what he thought, and who he became, and where he went, all were taken care of without his knowing volition. The tides of the sea of idolatry in which he found himself swimming, poor seal out of his element again, carried him hither and thither, too strong to fight against. The best he could do was try to remain afloat.

The second and third engagements of the day in Kansas City were in close proximity to each other, a radio station four blocks from another radio station. When Dr. Christian emerged from the first of the two, WKCM, his chauffeur-driven car was drawn up right outside the main entrance. Wherever he went such a car was laid on for him, not a real limousine, because the days of the limousine were long over, but a big comfortable government car nonetheless, all evidence of its legitimate owner removed.

Mama had trained herself to leave wherever her son was two or three minutes early, so she would be installed within the car by the time her son came out. It was Dr. Carriol's practice to march Dr. Christian briskly and with great determination through the knots of people who always gathered outside, and thanks to this uncompromising escort service, all Dr. Christian was able to do was smile and wave and call a few greetings before Dr. Carriol had him safely inside the car, and the car moved immediately away.

But this morning he balked. The gathering waiting on the sidewalk outside Station WKCM was large enough to be called a crowd, thanks to the detailed itinerary the local morning newspaper had printed along with its front-page article about Dr. Christian's visit to Kansas City. Half a dozen policemen had cleared a wide lane through the middle of the three or four hundred people who would otherwise have completely blocked Dr. Christian's path from the doors of the radio station to the doors of the waiting car. It was shockingly cold, between a temperature of 25 degrees Fahrenheit and a strong wind, yet the crowd waited.

Dr. Carriol looked through the glass of the foyer's outer wall and locked her fingers firmly around Dr. Christian's upper arm. "Come on, we've got to be quick," she said, pushed open the doors, and almost frogmarched him out.

The moment he appeared the crowd sighed; some of the people in it began to call his name and reach out to him. But he was no movie star, and they knew it. No one rushed forward, no one pushed, no one commenced a movement which would have ended in his being mobbed.

Halfway across the sidewalk he balked. And angrily he wrested himself from Dr. Carriol's grasp.

"I must speak to these people," he said, turning to his left, where the crowd was thickest.

Dr. Carriol got her hand on his arm again, again was shaken off.

"I will speak to them," he said.

"Joshua, you can't!" she cried, not caring how many heard her. "You have an appointment in five minutes at WKCK!"

He laughed, approached a policeman and touched the padded navy nylon of his parka almost caressingly. "Officer, you don't mind if I talk to these good people, do you?" he asked, and in his next breath called to the crowd, "Where is WKCK?"

A dozen voices answered him; the policeman moved aside.

Dr. Christian laughed and spread wide his arms. "Come on, walk me to WKCK!" he shouted.

The crowd closed around him, but respectfully, awed and delighted and solicitous for his welfare. Uncertain as to how they should proceed, the police tagged along behind as Dr. Christian and the crowd walked away.

Dr. Judith Carriol found herself alone.

Mama wound down the car window and stuck her head out. "Judith, Judith, what's the matter?"

Dr. Carriol swung round and strode to the car, shook her head at the driver preparing to alight, and climbed into the back seat unassisted.

"Drive us to WKCK, please," she said curtly. Then she turned to Mama. "He's decided to walk, if you can believe that. In this weather! He wants to speak to the people. And he's going to be late. *Shit!*"

He was late, half an hour. But such was his reputation that the radio station happily shuffled its programs around to accommodate him, and the newspaper which was next on his schedule scrubbed a formal interview in favor of attaching a reporter to the swelling crowd which escorted Dr. Christian from the second radio station to the town hall, where he was to give a luncheon speech. Word was spreading as WKCK ecstatically broadcast Dr. Christian's unorthodox behavior, with the result that people came from every direction.

Impotent, Dr. Carriol seethed in the background, only poor Mama available to listen, and since Dr. Carriol was not a pointless talker, Mama listened to her thunderous silence. And shivered, not merely from the cold.

But it was not until they checked into their new hotel in Little Rock that Dr. Carriol had a chance to voice her displeasure in the privacy it demanded. Thanks to the continuous addition of new towns to Dr. Christian's tour agenda, so far their progress had been in the nature of a will-o'-the-wisp; north today, south tomorrow, north the day after, east of the Mississippi one day, west of it the next. So after she finished chewing Dr. Christian out, Dr. Carriol intended to telephone Harold Magnus and ram a giant flea down *his* ear. To the effect that, while Dr. Christian seemed willing enough to take on the extra load, several of the best people in Section Four must start plotting a logical route immediately. Places like Kansas City and St. Louis were too far north; from Little Rock the tour must go southward and westward, thus avoiding the worst of what was promising to be a terrible winter.

But first things first. And her primary target was Dr. Joshua Christian.

They had been given a suite for him, with two more rooms alongside it for the women, and Billy, independent of his own wise choice, on a lower floor.

The moment the door of his sitting room closed behind the porter and Mama, she prepared for battle.

"Just what did you think you were doing today, Joshua?" she demanded.

In the act of walking through into his bedroom, he stopped and turned back, genuinely puzzled. "What was I doing?"

"This walking business! Shoving yourself into the middle of a crowd, for God's sake! You might have been shot!"

His face cleared. "Oh, that! I don't know why I didn't think of it before, Judith."

"What?"

"Walking among the people. It's so obvious I could kick myself! It's with flesh-and-blood people that I do my best work. Oh, radio and television are fine in their place, but I've done the most useful of them already in Atlanta. These local stations aren't nearly as important as the local people. Today I did more good walking and talking to the people who came in person to see me than I could have done on a hundred local media shows."

She was flabbergasted, could find absolutely nothing to say in reply; she just stood staring at him.

He laughed at her expression, came across to her and took her tight pugnacious chin in his hand. "Judith, please don't spoil everything by making a scene! I know, I know, you're a punctuality nut, and you like every little *i* dotted and every little *t* crossed well ahead of time. But if you want me to go on with this tour, its nature has got to change. I saw that the moment I walked out of WKCM to find all those people waiting for me in the freezing cold. I'm not doing this tour to give media ratings a boost, I'm doing it to help the people. So why am I insulating myself from them? Why am I spending my time looking into little glass lenses and talking into little wire meshes? Why am I traveling in a car? Oh, Judith, don't you understand? They came to wait for me in the *freezing cold!* Hoping I'd do just what I did, acknowledge them with more than just a regal smile and wave. When I walked among them, they blossomed like crocuses after a thaw. Today I—I really felt as if I accomplished some good. I didn't feel guilty or uncomfortable climbing into a car when they have none—I walked among them, and I was one of them. Judith, I loved it!"

Her rage was all gone. No use fulminating when the reason made so much sense. What a long way up it was to his face! And what a comforting face it was, not beautiful, not sexy, not synthetic. "Yes," she said, her voice sad. "I understand, Joshua. And I'm sure you're right."

To gain victory so easily rattled him; he had girded his loins for a real scrap, so now he didn't know what to say. Instead of saying anything at all, he swung her off her feet and waltzed around the room carrying her, he laughing uproariously while she squealed and struggled.

Mama came in while this was going on, and almost wept with

joy. It was all right, they were still on good terms, whatever resentment Judith had cherished was gone.

The sight of his mother sobered him. He put Dr. Carriol down immediately and brushed his palms together awkwardly. "I've just won," he explained lamely. "Mama, from now on I am going to walk through every town I visit."

"Oh, my God!" Mama tottered to a chair and collapsed.

"It's all right, I don't expect you and Judith to walk," he said soothingly. "You can travel in the car."

Dr. Carriol gathered her tattered dignity about her and attempted a rearguard action. "That's all very well, Joshua, but you have to be sensible too," she said. "You'll have to do a little radio and television, and the worst feature of all towns is that the main television stations are miles out. So you'll have to compromise by using a car to go to any venue more than a mile from the rest."

"No, I'll walk. No car for me."

"Look, be reasonable! We're five weeks into a national tour and we've got at least another ten weeks to go. Every day the tour gets longer, every day the powers-that-be decide it will be good policy if we include this goddam town and that goddam town. . . . Joshua, it's got to end as quickly as it possibly can, or we'll both be dead from exhaustion! I'm already losing the war with Washington—" She broke off, aghast at her own indiscretion.

He never even noticed. "This is not a publicity tour! It's my life's work! It's what I was born to do! I was pulled out of Holloman and that other life *to do this!* I thought you said you understood!"

"Of course I understand," she said, but she missed the change in his outlook since Mobile and Mama's news. "You're right, Joshua. You—are—right! Okay!" She put both hands to her head. "No, not another word! Let me think! I have got to think." And she went to a chair to sit, to compose herself, to *think*. "Okay. We're in Little Rock, and we can't go north again. Winter's here with a vengeance. So we'll move south. We've got some relocation towns to do in Arkansas, then we'll head for Texas, after that New Mexico, Arizona and California. Let's say twelve more weeks, maximum. But instead of spending one day in each town, we'll spend two, so you can walk without exhausting yourself. And we'll can the north completely."

This horrified him. "No! That's not the way at all! Judith, we have to go north into the winter! The people who have stayed behind are going to need me more than anybody down south, whether they're on relocation or they've been in the south for generations. The northern cities and towns aren't dead yet, Judith. But after Washington's decision to make relocation six months instead of four, it's obvious they are going to die. So this year, hard on that news, think of how many people up there in the northern winter are trying to face a truth they haven't been able to cope with so far. They'll be afraid, they'll be depressed, they're feeling the ground has been cut from under them. No way do we go south! North it is, or nothing. Christmas in Chicago. New Year's in—I don't know—Minneapolis or Omaha."

"Joshua Christian, you're raving mad! You *can't* walk up there in winter! You'll freeze to death!"

Mama added her mite, pleading tearfully, while Dr. Carriol tried the more logical approaches.

But to both women he turned a deaf ear, a walled-up heart. North he would go or nowhere. Walk he would.

So north they went from Little Rock, working ever further into the depths of the worst winter the world had ever seen. Even on the Gulf coast there had been snow already; the northern cities were feet deep in it, and enduring one blizzard a week. But he walked. Cincinnati, Indianapolis, Fort Wayne. And he was right. The people turned out to meet him, and the people walked with him.

At first Dr. Carriol tried valiantly to walk with him, as did Mama. But neither she nor Mama had his reserves of fuel, for they weren't interested in burning themselves up or out. So while he walked, if possible she and Mama had themselves driven, or if not, they sat and waited for him in their hotel. They knitted, they chatted, they read. And they waited.

The new schedule had stretched each town to three days instead of the old one, and after a while Dr. Carriol and Mama admitted it was easier on them, if not on Joshua. They got to sleep longer, didn't change beds so often, and from Dr. Carriol was removed the burden of keeping unfaltering vigil during the media appearances Dr. Christian had almost entirely eliminated from his daily round. Billy the pilot was equally pleased at having more time between flights; he did his own engineering, and now he knew he could keep his little bird flying like a bird.

And slowly, incredibly, Dr. Christian worked his way toward the southern tip of Lake Michigan. His appearance had changed somewhat. He remained cleanshaven and he liked to keep his hair short, but instead of the shabby beanpole in tweeds of the "Tonight" show, he was now a polar explorer. He walked very fast. Five miles an hour on a good day when conditions favored walking. By walking fast he kept no more than twenty people around him at a time; they would stride alongside him for perhaps two hundred yards, then fall away, and be replaced by others waiting along his well-publicized and well-prepared route.

The efficiency of all the local city authorities in keeping Dr. Christian's path physically clear may have given Dr. Christian a false impression of general conditions in the north, an impression reinforced by the cessation of the blizzards that had come one after another earlier in the winter. For in Decatur he announced that he was going to dispense with the helicopter.

"I'm going to walk from one city to another," he said.

"God Jesus in heaven, Joshua, you *can't!*" Dr. Carriol literally screamed. "Decatur to Gary at Christmas? You'll freeze to death! And if you don't freeze to death, you'll be weeks on the road! What happens if a blizzard catches you? You know we have to gear everything around blizzards, from flying to walking. Why the hell do you think we've given ourselves so much time all of a sudden? Oh, Joshua, Joshua, *please* be sensible!"

"I walk," he said.

"Oh no you don't!"

Dr. Carriol's raised voice penetrated through Mama's wall; she came in timidly, afraid of what she might learn but convinced it was worse to stay in her own room wondering.

Dr. Carriol turned to her at once. "Do you know what this— this *idiot* wants to do? He wants to walk from Decatur to Gary! And what happens if he's caught in a blizzard? Are we supposed to hover above him all the way to snatch him up? Mama, doesn't this son of yours have any sense? You talk to him! I give up!"

But Mama didn't talk. The image of her husband's frozen, perfectly preserved body rose up in front of her as clearly as if it had been yesterday they called her to Buffalo to go through the countless corpses in search of Joe. Only in her mind the frozen body wasn't Joe; it was Joshua.

Memories pushed and crushed and squashed, memories of the

229

thousands of others like herself plodding from one stiff cold thing to another, the muffled sobbing, the sudden keening of an identification, the hideous hope that maybe—just maybe—the loved one wasn't there after all, but still snowed in in some lonely farmstead. Until the moment. The face.

She went into hysterics, screeching, howling, yammering, beating herself against walls and furniture like a great golden moth. Neither her son nor Dr. Carriol could get near her, they had to stand by helplessly and let her bruise and break herself into the relative calm of huge and stormy weeping.

It sobered him; from somewhere very dim and ancient he grasped at a memory, of his father. Of his father who—who froze to death in a blizzard?

"We'll use the helicopter between cities," he said to Dr. Carriol abruptly, and went into his bedroom.

Thanks! thought Dr. Carriol, left to cope with Mama. If that isn't typical of a man, even a man as different as Joshua Christian!

So violent had the hysterical seizure been that Mama was still partially insensible when Dr. Carriol and her son loaded her into the helicopter. Obtaining medical help in strange towns was difficult in this weather, and perhaps in a way it was better for Mama to run the full gamut of physical distress. Certainly by the time Billy helped her alight in Gary and passed her tenderly to her son, she was able to speak without hiccoughing her way into a fresh storm of tears.

"Dearest Joshua," she said to him as he helped her across the ice to shelter, "you can only do so much. You're only a man. Flesh and blood and bones. So do a sensible part of what you'd like to do, because that's all you *can* do."

"But I'm missing the farmers!" he pleaded.

"Not all of them. It's amazing how many manage to get into whichever town you're visiting. Don't forget that your book is out there in the farmlands. It's going to all the places you'd never be able to reach if you lived to be two hundred years old and kept walking the whole time."

Billy the pilot, hand firmly under Dr. Carriol's elbow to help her keep her footing, followed mother and son across the ice at a discreet distance.

He was of them yet not of them; still a serving member of the armed forces with the rank of master sergeant, he had been seconded to the President's helicopter fleet three years before.

When Dr. Christian was allotted government transportation, Billy was handed over to Dr. Carriol because he was engineer as well as pilot. The days were long gone when parts and repair services for machines as sophisticated as helicopters could be found in most places.

And much to his surprise, Billy had found himself enjoying working for this mad bunch of people. Instead of buzzing placidly around the Washington skies or taking Presidential VIPs south somewhere, he was really *flying* the bird. Not to mention acting as errand boy, purchaser of underwear and outerwear, mechanic—it sure was an interesting life. After Mama joined the party Dr. Christian transferred himself into the spare front seat alongside Billy, leaving the two women together in the back; and, as is the wont of men thrown together, they became friends despite their very different backgrounds and outlooks.

On the ground Billy kept himself very much to himself. He didn't dine with them, he didn't travel in the car with them, he didn't stay in the same hotel as them if he could help it. And all his spare time he spent with his beautiful bird. Tonight he knew something was very wrong, of course, but it went against the grain to ask. However, the formidable Dr. Carriol was a kind of Service person, so when he found himself escorting her, he did nerve himself to ask.

"Ma'am, what's up?"

She didn't try to sidestep. "Dr. Christian is being a little difficult," she said. What an understatement! "He wanted to walk from Decatur to Gary."

"You're kiddin'!"

"I wish I was. You probably know from the articles about Dr. Christian that his father perished in a blizzard. So when Dr. Christian told his mother he planned to walk from town to town in future, she went off the deep end. I'm glad she did. It brought him to his senses. I hope!"

Billy nodded. "Thanks, ma'am." They had reached the small building at the edge of the helipad, and Billy gazed around its unwelcome interior. "Here we go again!" he said, but to himself. "Gary, Indiana, on Christmas Eve. Man, I gotta be crazy too!"

X

As Dr. Joshua Christian in Wisconsin and Minnesota walked through forty-below weather during January of 2033, Dr. Carriol chanced a separation and flew back to Washington. It was high time she checked at first hand what the current feelings were in the corridors of power about Dr. Christian; besides which, she knew she must have this break, or break down. Billy got her as far as Chicago, where she caught one of the scheduled priority flights out of Chicago bound for Washington. Thank God for Alaska! And the Canadians! So much experience and equipment meant things could be made to function in all weather save the worst blizzards—at least on a limited scale.

Moshe Chasen met her at the airport. There was snow on the ground here too, but compared with where she had come from its six inches were a mere powdering, and the temperature was in the high twenties Fahrenheit, a real heat wave. And to see dear old Moshe's big broad rugged face almost triggered tears. My God! What's the *matter* with me? Am I so tired? Am I so at my wits' end?

Dr. Chasen had followed the soaring star of Dr. Christian with bated breath ever since Dr. Carriol had filled him in about Operation Messiah. Proud as if the man had been his own son (his own son was a marine biologist living in Haiti), he reveled in the twin feelings of self-vindication and his candidate's vindication. What a man! Did he have charisma, or did he have charisma?

However, when the first month of Dr. Christian's progress became the second month and Dr. Chasen realized that the tour was going to be very long, then realized that the tour was going north into this terrible winter, he began to experience twinges of doubt. After that he worried. What was with Joshua, trying to do what no man could do? Yet Joshua kept right on doing it! And what was with Judith, to let him do it?

"Shalom, shalom!" he cried, kissing Dr. Carriol on either cheek and tucking her arm through his.

"I didn't expect to be met," she said, blinking.

"What, not here to greet my Judith? *Meshugge!* The ice has got into your brain."

"You are absolutely right, it has."

He had a car, evidence of her increasing importance; oh, that was a consolation!

Until they reached her house in Georgetown they did not speak again, Dr. Chasen contenting himself with sitting and occasionally squeezing her hand, sensing her despondency and appalled that he sensed such an alien mood in her. Judith Carriol despondent? He hadn't thought it possible.

What paradise it was to walk into her own dear house, flop down in one of her own dear chairs, look at her own dear pictures on her own dear walls.

"All right, Judith, what's going on?" Dr. Chasen demanded after Dr. Carriol had prepared them hot toddies.

"How can I tell you when I've given up asking myself the same question?"

"Whose idea was it, this walking through the snow?"

"His, of course. I'm pretty hard-driving, Moshe, but even I couldn't push another human being to that kind of self-torture!" she said tartly.

"I'm sorry, I'm sorry! I didn't really think you were capable of it, but on the other hand I didn't think he was, either. He struck me as more sensible."

She laughed, not a happy sound. "*Sensible?* Moshe, he doesn't even know the meaning of the word! Oh, he did once, but that was a long time ago. B.B."

"B.B.?"

"Before Book."

The phone rang. Harold Magnus, impatient and edgy.

"The President wants to see both of us tonight," he said.

"I see." She debated whether to ask, decided she had better. "Is he displeased, Mr. Magnus?"

"Hell, no! Why? Is there any reason he should be?"

"Not at all. I'm a little distraught at the moment—weeks and weeks on the road get to you, you know. Especially if you're not calling the plays, but just running interference."

"Wisconsin and Minnesota in January? I'm not surprised. Would you like a special heating allowance to put some warmth back into you, Judith?"

The first gesture of genuine thoughtfulness the man had ever made her! And the first time he had ever called her by her given name. Sufficient evidence to deduce the President was anything but displeased.

"Believe it or not, I'm inured to the cold," she said, and laughed, again not a happy sound. "Thank you for the offer. I may take you up on it about next June." Another laugh, more a dry cackle. "It's going to take that long to thaw out enough to feel heat."

"Meet me here at five-thirty," Harold Magnus commanded.

She hung up and turned to Moshe Chasen. "A royal summons to the White House. Six o'clock, I presume."

Dr. Chasen drained his glass and rose. "Then I'd better get out of your hair. You'll want to bathe and change."

"I'll see you tomorrow, Moshe. We can talk better then. Take the car and have the driver drop you home. By the time he gets back here I'll be ready."

"Are you sure I should use your car for myself, Judith?"

"Positive! Go, go!"

Tibor Reece was grinning from ear to ear. "Well, my dear Dr. Carriol, your Operation Messiah has certainly given the people of this country a boost! I am delighted."

"So am I, Mr. President."

"Who gave him the idea to walk? Brilliant!"

"He thought of it all by himself. I'm healthy enough to tell myself I'm a very dedicated person, but going where he is—I would never have dreamed of walking."

Harold Magnus pursed his rubbery lips, blew through them in a way which made them audibly vibrate. It was an irritating habit, but the only one who ever had the courage to tell him so was his wife, and he never took notice of her, let alone believed anything she said.

"I wonder if you fully realize what you've just said, Dr. Carriol?" he asked. "Walking is crazy! You don't think he's heading that way, do you?"

Tibor Reece had one great weakness; he always interpreted the deeds and reactions of others in terms of himself. Since he was no altruist and possessed superb political acumen, it rarely got him into hot water, but it was there just the same, waiting for the right opportunity to trip him up. "Nonsense!" he said vigorously before Dr. Carriol could formulate a reply. "It's the exact right thing to do. In the same situation I would have done it myself." He put his glasses on and turned to a sheaf of papers lying on his desk. "I won't keep you, but I did want to thank you personally for Operation Messiah. I think it's working magnificently, and I congratulate you both."

Today there was no question as to whether Dr. Carriol would walk back to Environment; today she had her own car and driver, waiting just behind the Secretary's vehicle.

"I want to see you in my office," he said as he separated from her at the edge of the driveway.

"I want to see you too, sir."

Of course Mrs. Helena Taverner was on duty when Dr. Carriol walked into the Secretary's suite of offices. Dr. Carriol gave the woman a smile and looked at her watch pointedly.

"Don't you ever go home?"

Helena Taverner laughed, blushed. "Well, he keeps such odd hours, Dr. Carriol, that's the trouble. And I live quite a way out. If I'm not here, he wrecks every system I've got looking for something. So I have a couch in my private rest room, and I use it."

"As long as you do," said Dr. Carriol over her shoulder.

Harold Magnus was behind his desk, waiting.

"Right. Total candor if you please, Dr. Carriol."

"You shall have it, Mr. Secretary."

"You're not a bit happy about the situation, are you?"

"No."

"Why? Tangible evidence aside from the walking?"

"Difficult to answer. After all, I christened it Messiah myself, so why should it worry me if he does indeed show signs of becoming Messianic?"

"Is that the crux of it?"

She sighed, sat back, lifted her head and thought. As she did Harold Magnus watched her narrowly, aware of subtle changes in her; she was not so snakelike, not so physically disturbing. Whatever had happened out there on the road in middle America had sucked her brittle.

"I am a trained psychologist," she said. "Also a trained data statistician. Also a trained sociologist. However, I am not a psychiatrist, nor have I ever studied mental states on a one-to-one basis. I'm purely a group expert, and when it comes to predicting group behavior in almost any given situation, I doubt I have an equal within government, possibly outside it as well. Yet one-to-one unsettles me. So I am aware that I may not be interpreting Dr. Christian's thought processes correctly, you must understand. However, I'm sure you can appreciate why I don't want to bring in a psychiatrist to help me decide what's wrong with Dr. Christian."

"Oh, indeed I can!" he said with feeling.

"All I can tell you is how *I* feel. And my feelings about the man are that he is no longer quite stable. Yet—the actual concrete evidence is minimal. Delusions of grandeur? Aaaah . . . If so, not obvious. Ideas of reference? Haaah . . . I would say definitely not. Loss of touch with reality? Ummm . . . I would have to say no again. And yet—and yet—there *is* a change. Given the events of the past few months, it may be a logical change. His current behavior might be bizarre, but his instincts are right on target, and his instincts guide his behavior enormously. So there you are, back to square one again. Is he, or isn't he? All I can tell you is that I have made it my business to get to know him very well. And I am developing bad vibes."

Her answer panicked him. "My God, Judith, are we going to fall flat on our asses with this?"

Her given name again! Well, well. "No," she said, sounding sure. "I will never let it get to that stage. However, I do think we—you and I—should make some contingency plans. Just in case. And we should be ready to act when and if it becomes necessary."

"I agree wholeheartedly. What do you suggest? Do you see any hint of what direction he's going to fly in if he does come apart at the seams?"

"No."

"Then?"

"I would like half a dozen—I don't honestly know what to call them, except what they call them in the movies! Heavies? Heavies will do, anyway. Half a dozen heavies close enough at hand to carry out my orders within five minutes maximum. No matter what those orders might consist of."

"Shit! You're not thinking of *killing* him?"

"Of course I'm not! Anything but! To create a martyr would be disastrous. No, I just want to be prepared at all times to bundle Dr. Christian away to an appropriate institution at a minute's notice, that's all. Which means the men you find me ought to be trained psychiatric nurses used to dealing with extreme violence and irrationality. They'll have to have top security clearances, and they can't be genuine Christian cult followers. The last thing we want is any kind of public scene. So these men will have to be really on the ball, ready if I snap my fingers to whip Dr. Christian out of wherever he is before those around him even understand what's happened, and long before Dr. Christian himself can make a fuss."

"You'll have the men on the plane to Chicago with you, but from there on they'd better have their own helicopter. It would also be best if you saw them yourself here in Washington and briefed them thoroughly. But don't worry. I'll find you the right men for the job."

"Good. Good!"

"That's short-term. What about long-term?"

"I doubt there is a long-term, because of one thing I am absolutely sure. He will never last the distance of the tour he plans to make. It keeps getting longer and longer, no thanks to our good Mr. Reece, I might add. And, incidentally, I wonder what might have happened to Operation Messiah if he'd lost the election last November? I was so busy I never even remembered to vote! Anyway, the White House keeps adding towns to his itinerary, and after we left Chicago, Dr. Christian began looking at the maps as well. Now *he's* adding towns!"

"Shit!"

"Yes, Mr. Secretary, cartloads of the stuff. At the rate we're going, and given that from now until the end of March the blizzards are going to slow us down a lot, it is going to take Dr. Christian another *year* to finish his tour."

"Shit!"

"Yes, but you're sitting pretty in six inches of nice wet Washington snow. I'm the one with Dr. Christian. And frankly, I do not think I stand a chance of lasting another year on the road. Luckily, I don't think I'm going to need to last. Because he won't last, sir. I know it in my bones. He is going to break into a million little pieces, and I just hope when it happens that he's in Casper, Wyoming, not in the middle of Madison Square Garden—" She broke off abruptly, knotting up with the beginnings of an idea, an amazing idea, an idea that took her breath away.

"So what do we do?"

"Actually I think his mood is better since Christmas, in spite of the new business of his picking yet more towns. When we left Decatur, en route for Gary, he announced he didn't think it was right to fly from town to town. He felt he ought to walk."

"In winter?"

"Right! I dealt with it, or rather his mother did. She earned her keep that night, I don't begrudge the expense of toting her around too. You remember his father died in a blizzard? Well, when Mama found out he was planning to walk from Decatur to Gary, she went bananas. Right off her head. It was just the shock he needed to bring him to his senses. Since then, he's definitely been more amenable to reason. Thank God!"

Harold Magnus held up his hand to silence her, and pushed his intercom buzzer. "Helena? Some coffee and sandwiches, please. And bring your pad with you when you come, I want you to find some men for me."

The break was welcome, the food also; even if he had to eat sandwiches, Harold Magnus made sure he ate the best. As a result, Helena Taverner was obliged to keep breads and spreads in the little kitchen off her private rest room.

However, it wasn't the break, the food or the coffee which caused Dr. Carriol's spreading sensation of utter, happy, peaceful well-being. Washington and her own milieu were responsible. Suddenly she was back where she belonged, her mind was functioning the way it used to, her emotional and physical exhaustion had subsided. In short, she was feeling her old self again. And she understood how insidious, how dangerous, Dr. Joshua Christian was to the ego and persona of Dr. Judith Carriol. All those weeks of being in close proximity to him had shifted the center of her being the way an irresistible gravitational field played with the light of the very stars in the firmament. What was more, she now realized how much she detested this bending effect, how uncomfortable and miserable she was when drawn into his sphere of influence. This was her life, this was her natural métier. Washington! Environment! And she began to wonder if she actually hated Joshua Christian; if she was continuing to grow in hatred of him

238

with each day more she was forced to pass in his company. Her own private black hole.

Harold Magnus had given Mrs. Taverner her orders to begin negotiating with the mental health arms of the various Services in search of Dr. Carriol's heavies; now he was ready to finish his discussion with the chief of Section Four.

"You were saying that you don't think he stands a chance of lasting the distance," said the Secretary, sliding down in his chair and watching Dr. Carriol over the rim of his glass; he was concluding his scratch meal with a fine old malt whiskey.

"Yes. Oh, I think he'll continue to do well as long as he's in the north. What worries me is when he moves south again. At our present rate of progress, he'll hit the thirty-fifth parallel around the first of May. And May further south will see gigantic crowds wherever he goes. I can't be sure how he's going to react with so many people going wild around him, but I imagine it will give his Messianic zeal an enormous boost. If he was a cynic, or he was in it for the money, or if this was a simple power trip, there'd be no problem. But, Mr. Secretary, he is utterly sincere! He thinks he's helping. Well, of course he is helping. Immeasurably. But can you even imagine what it will be like when he hits L.A.? He'll insist on walking, and there'll be millions of people out to walk right along with him—" She broke off, caught her breath audibly. "My God! My God!"

"What? What?"

"An idea. The germ of one, anyway. Leave it for a while, it's growing. Back to what I was saying. May. May is the cutoff point. We *must* finish Dr. Christian's public appearances in May. It may be that after some first-rate treatment he'll come right again, in which case he can resume his tour where he leaves off."

"What are we going to do? Just pull him out and issue a statement to the effect that he's sick?"

"I was thinking that, but not any more. Mr. Magnus—what if we could finish with a bang instead of a whimper? It's been nagging away inside me ever since he went on Bob Smith, the germ of an idea. Blast-off!, I thought then. Not an endless publicity tour, but a long countdown to some cosmic blast-off. Think of it, Mr. Secretary! A super-super-super last public appearance!"

A grin was spreading across the Secretary's face. "My dear Judith, you are wasted as a mere back room boy. At heart I suspect you are an entrepreneur. Because you're right. He ought to go out with a bang. A cosmic public appearance."

"Washington," she said.

"No! New York City!"

"No! No! A walk, Mr. Secretary! *A walk!* The one he has been dying to do ever since Decatur! A walk from one town to another, all the goddam way on foot. New York City to Washington, D.C., in May. It's going to take some organizing, but let him have what he wants. Let him walk! From New York City to Washington in the spring, with the leaves coming on the trees, and those who have had to come back from the south just slipping into a new routine—man alive, what a walk! And for once we'll let him have his head. He can draw the people in all the way, from the Battery end of Manhattan to the banks of the Potomac. The march of the millennium." She stiffened, suddenly all snake, eyes staring, reared back to strike. "Oh! Oh! That's what we'll call it, of course! *The March of the Millennium!* At the end, he can address the crowd from the steps of the Lincoln Memorial, say, or some place else near the monuments, where there'll be plenty of room for the people to gather to hear him. And after it's all over—we put him into temporary retirement in a nice quiet sanatorium."

"God! My God!" The Secretary for the Environment sat awed and a little frightened. "A march that size, Judith? We'd have a riot on our hands!"

"Nope. Not if we're properly prepared. We'll need lots of military assistance, that's for sure. To organize shelters along the way, first-aid stations, canteens, rest rooms, that kind of thing. And keep order. This country loves a parade, Mr. Magnus! Especially one they can participate in. He can lead the people to the seat of the people. From where so many came in as immigrants over a hundred years ago to where they put their government. And why should they run riot? The atmosphere will be high carnival, not general strike. Have you ever seen a walkathon or a marathon or a cyclothon on a cool crisp sunny weekend in New York City? Thousands upon thousands upon thousands of people, and never a trace of trouble. They're happy, they're free, they're out in the open air, they've left their griefs and their problems at home right alongside their wallets. For years all the experts have been insisting that the reason New York City has taken glaciation, the one-child family, lack of private transport and the rest so well is that New York City's local government has offered New Yorkers an alternative life style. So there you are. The March of the Millennium will be a cosmic walkathon, led by The Man himself. Face it, he's led the people out of a wilderness of pain and futility. He's given them a creed to live by that suits the times and suits them. So let him lead them in the flesh! And while he's walking from New York City to Washington, we can also organize a dozen other giant walks in other major centers across the country. Dallas to Fort Worth, for instance. Gary to Chicago. Fort Lauderdale to Miami. Mr. Magnus, it will work! The March of the Millennium!"

She had achieved the impossible; she had set Harold Magnus on fire with an impossible dream. "But will he do it?" he asked, not quite able to abandon all caution.

"Try and stop him!"

"Your people—the Section Four think tank. We'd better get them started on the logistics at once. I'll see the President myself and sound him out. If he says it's go, it's go. Though I can't see him turning the idea down. Being reelected for a third term seems to have given him a new lease on life; he's tasting success and he's beginning to see the history books calling him an even greater President than Gus Rome. Maybe his divorcing Julia helped too. I never thought he'd do that! Anyway, anyway. The March of the Millennium . . . A whole country on the move, literally and figuratively, to tell the rest of the world that it's finished with depression, it's gonna *get there!* Oh, man alive, what a beautiful, beautiful thing!"

She got up, wincing. "I had planned to stay a couple of days in Washington, but on second thought, I think I ought to get back to him, like yesterday. He's the one at the center of the scheme, so it behooves me to keep him from flying apart until next May. However, I will try to pay a flying visit to Washington every weekend, if that's all right with you."

"Good idea. Things go better in Section Four when you're around, though I must say John Wayne is a good administrative replacement. If he had your brains on the theoretical side, he'd do fine."

"Then I'm very glad he doesn't have my brains."

He looked startled, then chuckled. "Well, sure! I hope Helena can find your heavies tonight."

"I'll leave the moment I've briefed them, anyway."

"Judith?"

"Yes, Mr. Magnus?"

"What if he doesn't last until May?"

"Then the March of the Millennium goes ahead just the same. Why shouldn't it? Under those circumstances, we'll call it a vote

241

of confidence in him by the people. You know, a kind of giant get-well card."

He giggled. "Hallmark, eat your heart out!" Then, so typical of the man, he felt morally obliged to display a token revulsion. "You know, Judith, you are the coldest-blooded bitch I've ever met."

Sat-is-fac-tory, Judith Carriol! You have just ensured the entire future of your career in Environment. No one will ever be able to knock you off this pedestal! Your grading is going to go up at least two notches this year. For the first time in over eight years that gross complacent ruthless old glutton Magnus has called you Judith! You are *in!* You are made. He's to the place where he's got to rely on you more than he does on himself. You will finally enjoy the in-service status your masculine predecessor in Section Four automatically enjoyed. Amazing how in this day and age, they can still find valid reasons for putting a woman down. Only not this woman! Not forever. This woman is better than the whole goddam male establishment of this town, and she is well on her way to proving it. This time next year you will have your own car driving you permanently to and from work, and you will have all kinds of perks, and you can go to the occasional art auction at Sotheby's, and—

She stopped dead on the K Street sidewalk outside her entrance to Environment, where on her return from the White House her car and driver had been parked. Waiting for her to come out. Waiting to take her home. The driver had known his orders. It was close to nine o'clock. It was below freezing by ten degrees. It was just beginning to blow and snow. She was dressed for riding in a car, not waiting for the bus. And that fucking old bastard Magnus had sent her car away. On purpose? Of course on purpose! To put her in her place. Oh, I will get you for this, Harold Magnus!

Halfway to the bus stop she was struck by the funny side of it, and burst out laughing.

By the time Dr. Carriol caught up with him, Dr. Christian had made it to Sioux City, Iowa. Her stay in Washington had been longer than she wanted, for the psychiatric nursing heavies had taken time to round up, and she couldn't leave until they were properly briefed. Then she was delayed in Chicago for another day by a worse blizzard than usual, even for that icy Pur-

242

gatory-on-Michigan. Luckily her six heavies—good men too, thank God—were whisked out of Chicago in their chopper minutes ahead of the blizzard. She, waiting for Billy, ended up waiting thirty-six hours.

Dr. Christian's day had just about ended, along with his visit to Sioux City. So he and Dr. Carriol planned to meet at the airport, where he and his mother would join her and Billy, and fly onward in the helicopter to Sioux Falls in South Dakota.

All the way from Chicago to Sioux City, Dr. Carriol fought her apprehension and her detestation of this mission, this way of life Dr. Christian had foisted on her. How very lovely Washington had been, how cozy and welcome her house, how glad to see her everyone from John Wayne to Moshe Chasen had been. Between "Tonight with Bob Smith" in Atlanta and the too-short visit to Washington just over, ten weeks had gone by. Ten incredible, exhilarating, sickening weeks. Ten weeks too many of Joshua Christian.

Why then be so anxious to see him again? Why worry what he was going to say when they met?

The Christians had not yet arrived when she and Billy landed, so she told Billy to put the machine under shelter, then come inside to wait in the warm. Given Joshua's fits and starts, he could be hours yet. It was snowing lightly as they entered the inhospitable small building which was all places like Sioux City had left in the way of airport facilities. No planes came to Sioux City any more; the actual landing strip was kept up only as part of the national emergency-defense network.

Dr. Christian came in about half an hour later, carrying a gust of snow with him, clad in his arctic explorer gear, and followed by about fifty or sixty people who apparently had walked with him in spite of the weather. Well, nothing new in that! Wherever he went, they came out to walk with him in any weather short of an actual blizzard.

Though Dr. Carriol stood up and waved, Dr. Christian did not notice her and Billy against the far wall. He was too involved with his followers, who crowded around him as he stood half a head taller than any of them, one or two clucking as they brushed melting white flakes from his arms and shoulders. But though they did crowd round him, Dr. Carriol noted (as she had noted many times before) that they had given him air space. A tiny indication of their awe and reverence. No one tried to mob him, tear at him and his clothes, as they might have done were he an actor or a pop star. It was enough to be close. Too much to touch.

He swept off his hood and the scarf muffling his face, ripped off his big gauntlets and tucked them into the nearest pocket in his jacket. And stood, head thrown back, *regally*.

A woman went down on her knees before him, her face as she looked up suffused with blatant but sincere adoration. Fascinated, Dr. Carriol saw him reach out one long sensitive hand and lay it lightly, tenderly, on top of her head; it dropped to her cheek, its fingers trailing across her glowing skin, then lingered in the air in front of her face, and made a movement which was almost a blessing. An intense and shocking love mushroomed out of him and wrapped itself all around his companions. His people. His disciples.

"Go now," he said, "but remember I am always with you. Always, my children."

And they went, like little sheep, back into the swirl of snow outside.

On the short ride to Sioux Falls, Dr. Carriol shrank into her seat with her face turned obdurately away from Mama. Mama had started to greet her ecstatically in the airport building, and then seen something in her face which was terrifying.

An unusual silence filled the busy vehicle as it rose into, then above, the clutching snow, its frequency-sniffing black wet nose homed in with two-yard accuracy on a beacon in Sioux Falls.

Billy was in no mind to talk, for though conditions and in-air winds were not bad, he disliked night flying these days; the mountains were looming ever closer as they moved westward. His instruments were superb, he could see the height and contour of every upthrust in the land on the big phosphorescent screen just above his right knee, and provided altimeter and the rest were exactly calibrated, he knew they were as safe as at ground level. Still, he was in no mind to talk.

Dr. Christian was happy, and in no mind to talk. How glad they had been to see him today! How glad every day. The pattern on the loom of time which spelled out his destiny was shaping, shaping, growing, growing. Still obscure in its overall picture, but beginning to reveal some of the details. So long they had waited for him! So long too he had waited, though that was an infinitude of shortness in comparison.

Mama was in no mind to talk. What was the matter with Judith? Why had she looked so? Oh, there was trouble coming! How to discover its direction, how to run for cover? They had committed some frightful sin in her absence, she and Joshua, and Judith's cool lustrous brain had condemned them without trial.

The cool lustrous brain certainly put Dr. Carriol in no mind to talk. It was not cool. It was not lustrous. A huge awful outrage and anger had blasted coolness to white heat, lustrousness to incandescence. *Think!* She had to think! But thought, useful productive thought, was impossible. So she turned her face away from the other occupants of the little cabin, and turned her heart away as well.

When they walked into the motel which offered a haven to the few visitors Sioux Falls could expect at this time of year, Dr. Carriol pushed Mama to her room as she might have shut an animal out for the night, and rounded on Dr. Christian grimly, purposefully.

"Joshua, please come to my room," she said curtly. "I want to talk to you."

His tired slow footsteps followed her sharp thudding ones the short distance from the foyer to where her room was; when she closed her door and shut them in together he sighed, and he smiled his sweetest, most special smile just for her.

"I'm so glad to see you! I missed you very much, Judith."

She scarcely heard him. "What was the meaning of that little exhibition at the Sioux City airport tonight?" Her voice came grinding out from between clenched teeth.

"Exhibition?" He stared at her as if she were receding from him at light-speed. "What exhibition?"

"Letting those people kneel to you! Letting those people adore you! Touching that idiot woman as if you had the right— *and* the might!—to bless her! Just who do you think you are? Jesus Christ?" Her hands writhed, coiling their fingers in upon each other fruitlessly, then she reached out to grasp at a table to steady herself, to keep herself upright, and the table began to shake, to rattle. "I have never seen such a filthy, disgusting exhibition of sheer egomania in all my life! How dare you? How *dare* you?"

His skin had gone grey, his cold-festered lips worked in and out like uncomfortable new covering on old dry teeth.

"She—she didn't! She—she wasn't! She knelt for help! She— she *needed* something from me, and God help me, I didn't know what! So I touched her because I didn't know what else to do!"

"Bullshit! Fucking crap! You're not merely on an ego trip, Joshua Jesus Christian Christ! You're on a god trip! And it's got to stop! It's got to stop right this minute! Do you hear me? Don't you *dare* let anyone kneel to you! Oh, don't you *dare* let people worship you! You are no different from any other man, and don't you ever forget that! If there is any reason in the world why you are where you are and who you are on this day, that reason is *me!* *I* put you here, *I* created you! And I did not put you here to act out a second coming, to cash in on the fortuitous coincidence of your name by encouraging people to remember you not as one of themselves but as a divine being! The reincarnation of Jesus Christ in the third-millennial person of Joshua Christian! What a mean, shoddy, despicable trick to play on these hapless people! Trading on their need and their credulity! It's got to stop! Do you hear me? It has got to stop this instant!"

She was foaming at the mouth, actually foaming at the mouth; she could feel the bubbles clinging all around the corners of her lips, and sucked them in with a long hiss.

And he stood looking at her as if she had found the magical plug at the back of his bronze heel, upstoppered the tide of ichor that had kept his titanic will pushing him on from town to town without feeling the cold, the exhaustion, the despair.

"Is that truly what you think?" he asked, whispering.

"Yes!" she said, unable to stop herself from saying yes.

His head shook slowly from side to side. "It isn't true!" Shaking, shaking. "It isn't true! It—isn't—true!"

She flung away from him to look at the wall. "I am too angry to continue this discussion! Kindly go to bed! Go to bed, Joshua! Go to bed and sleep like any—other—mortal—human—*man!*"

Usually a tirade helps, when the object of such bitter, overwhelming rage is on hand to berate. Not tonight. Not in Sioux Falls. Not Joshua Christian. At the end of it, after he had stumbled from her room, she actually felt worse. More and more angry. More filled with more emotions than she had ever suspected she possessed. She couldn't go to bed. She couldn't even sit down, let alone lie down. So she stood with her scorching forehead against the freezing wall of her motel bedroom and wished herself dead.

Dr. Christian's room was quite warm; these good kind people had somehow managed to give him what they thought he would most need. Warmth. But he didn't think he would ever feel warm again. Is that true, what she said to me? Can it be true? Why was I ever born, to have to listen to that? It isn't true! It *can't* be true!

The legs which drove like pistons up and down day after day and had long grown used to putting forth in abnormal effort suddenly would not could not did not hold him up. He collapsed to the floor and lay there, divorced from all sensation save the terrible grief of understanding how badly he had failed.

They didn't need a god! They needed a man! The moment divinity invaded a man, he ceased to *be* a man. No matter what the books said or how sacred the books were supposed to be, he, Joshua Christian, *knew* a god could not suffer, a god could not experience pain, a god could not be at one with the people he was god of. Only as a man could anyone help Man.

Through a dense foggy wall he plucked feebly at memory, tried to picture a woman on her knees to him, and after what Judith Carriol had said, it seemed to him looking back that she must indeed have knelt to him in adoration. And it also seemed to him that he had indeed responded to her adoration as a god would have responded. Accepting it as his right. A man would have repudiated it with horror and rebuke. No, no! He hadn't interpreted the incident that way at the time! He had merely seen someone so bowed down with her pain that she could no longer remain on her feet—her *pain* had driven her to her knees, not her love! Help me! she had cried without a voice, help me, my fellow man! And he had reached out a hand to touch her, thinking that his were healing hands, and could help.

But if in truth she had knelt to worship him, then everything he had done was in vain. Everything he had done was a blasphemy. If he was not one of them, if he was not a man as they were men, then what he did and could do had no meaning. If he was not one of them, and therefore one with them, he offered them ashes. And if he was not one of them, but was one above them, then they had used him to steal an essence they could not hope to find for themselves. They were little better than vampires, and he was their willing victim.

His body jerked, writhed, shuddered. He wept desolately. He was broken. Broken man or broken idol? What did it matter? He was broken. And there was no one to pick up the pieces, no one to put him back together again. For Judith Carriol had abandoned him.

247

In the morning he looked very ill. Aghast and ashamed of her wild outburst, Dr. Carriol suddenly realized that though he had often looked tired to death, never before had he looked ill. When her fury finally quit her in the middle watches of the night, she knew that she had fatally tampered with powers she neither understood, nor respected. Had she respected them, she could never have been made so angry. She realized that what had enraged her to the point of madness was the knowledge that this puppet king, this image of her creation, was usurping powers for himself that she had not granted him, and did not consent to grant him.

After the physical chill of her room permeated her flesh so deeply that her anger curled up and shriveled up and died away, she understood her mistake. What bothered her was not his usurpation of powers she did not consent to grant him; what bothered her was that she had begun to think of herself as the one with the real power, and he had simply shown her beyond any shadow of a doubt that what lay within him could not by definition be anything she was capable of creating. When the king-maker is unmade by the king, towers fall, fortresses crumble. All in the mind. Her mind. His mind.

How to repair the damage she had done? She didn't know, because she couldn't even begin to divine what the damage was. Nor was the matter one she could discuss with him in the beautiful cool sanity of reason and logic; it lacked both. Nor could she attempt an apology. He would not even understand why she was apologizing.

For the first time in her life, Dr. Judith Carriol was forced to admit that what she had said and done could not be mended, at least by herself.

Mama scuttled into breakfast sideways like a wary crab, took one look at Dr. Carriol's face and gasped, then looked at her son, and began to flutter and keen. Dr. Carriol put an end to that with a single glance. Mama sat silent, eyes down.

"Joshua, you're not well this morning," Dr. Carriol said very crisply and calmly. "It might be better if you didn't try to go out on foot today. Use the car."

"I will walk," he said, easing his lips back from his teeth painfully. "I will walk. I have to walk."

And walk he did. Looking so ill that Mama sat huddled in the car and let the tears fall down her face unheeded and untended.

He talked, he advised, he listened, he comforted, he walked again, he spoke in the town hall with great power and feeling, but not about God. When asked questions about God, he answered evasively if possible, otherwise as shortly as possible, giving as his reason a new dilemma within himself that had to be sorted out. Hearing this, Dr. Carriol tensed. Wished with might and main and heart and soul that she could turn back the clock. Cursed her stupidity, her lack of control, the emotional weaknesses she hadn't known she possessed. Not that any local person in Sioux Falls recognized the difference in him, for no local person had seen him in the flesh before, and even so ill, so cast down, he had an enormous presence. The gulf between what had been glorious spontaneity, and now was merely iron determination, was lost on the pitifully small remnant of the population of Sioux Falls who had stayed there during the winter of 2032–33.

On he went: North Dakota, Nebraska, Colorado, Wyoming, Montana, Idaho, Utah. On and on and on in hideous cold, always walking, walking as if his life depended upon it.

But the spiritual ichor that had warmed him outward from the center of his soul had bled away when Dr. Judith Carriol pulled out the stopper. And in the new bleak ice of his soul, his body began to crumble. It ached. It itched. It cracked. It festered. It bled. Every passing week saw some new external evidence of his internal disintegration. Abscesses. Boils. Rashes. Bruises. Cracks. Blisters. He told no one, he showed no one, he sought no medical aid. At night he ate as little as he ate during the day, then dropped like a stone on his bed, and closed his eyes, and told himself he slept.

In Cheyenne he fainted, and it was many minutes before he came round fully. No, no, there was nothing seriously wrong, a weakness that had come and gone, that was all.

And oh the grief. The terrible sorrow.

Not Billy, not Dr. Carriol, not Mama was able to plead, to remonstrate, to reason with him; even to bully him. He simply mentally removed himself from them, and from all external evidence of who or what he was. As far as Dr. Carriol could ascertain, he was even ignorant of the pending March of the Millennium, for whenever someone mentioned it to him, his face did not change, did not register interest. He was a walking machine, a talking machine.

And he began to speak continuously about his mortality. More and more he protested that he was only a man, that he was a very poor and imperfect specimen of the breed, that he too was doomed to die.

"I am a man!" he would cry to anyone who would listen, and then he would search their eyes feverishly for a sign that they believed him; and when he imagined that they looked upon him as a god he would preach them strange sermons going round and round in ever-decreasing circles, all to do with the fact that he was a man even as they were. But of course those who heard him did not hear him; it was enough to see him.

He continued to walk, and the people walked with him, not understanding his pain. Not understanding how intensely he resented this burden of responsibility they were thrusting upon him. Oh, how could he get it through their thick heads that he was just a man, and he couldn't work miracles, and he couldn't heal cancers, and he couldn't raise the dead, and he couldn't, couldn't couldn't couldn't. *Anything!*

So walk on, walk on, Joshua Christian. Hold back the tears. Don't ever let anyone know what you are suffering. How you feel. Is this truly sadness? Is this the bottom of grief, or have I still further to fall? Walk, walk. They need *something!* And you, poor man, are all they have managed to find. Dreadful. Oh why can they not be made to see that all they have found is another man? A fellow man. A yellow man. A Jell-O man. A hollow man. A minnow man. That was fun! How many more? Any more? Yeah, plenny more!

He walked because it was something to do. It mechanized his pain, it drove his pain from one part of him to another, and that was better oh that was much much better than bearing his pain alone in one dark unmoving place. The dark unmoving place of his soul.

And the greatest of Joshua Christian's many tragedies was that no one saw how vastly his humanity had grown, eclipsing even his encroaching dementia; for he was more a man, not more than a man.

XI

In Tucson, on an early May day with the mountains glowing in the sun and the air stilly cold, Dr. Judith Carriol tried to tell Dr. Joshua Christian about the March of the Millennium.

His mood seemed to improve after he came to Arizona, colder in May than the state used to be by far, but lovely yet, and able to penetrate even Dr. Christian's obdurately walled-up mind. So Dr. Carriol coaxed him to take a drive with her to see an exquisitely laid-out piece of parkland between the fringe of Tucson and the Band A relocation town of Hegel.

This parkland had been randomly but artfully planted with groves of silver birch, clusters of flowering almond, magnolia and azalea. The birches were fluffed with palest lime, azaleas congealed whole slopes with a Japanese mosaic of color, the magnolias were pink and white and muted purple, the almonds were massed with white blossom, and daffodils smothered the ground in a display of blatant narcissism that would not have shamed the Cambridge Backs.

"Sit here with me, Joshua," she said, patting a redwood bench warm from the sun.

But he was too enchanted, wandering this way and that, cupping a magnolia bloom in his hands, marveling at the way a dead beech had been persuaded to give tenure to a wisteria vine whose heavy bunches of lilac flowers trailed drifting in a little wind.

But after a while he needed to communicate his delight to an understanding fellow creature, so he approached the bench and then sat down, sighing. "Oh, this is wonderful!" he cried, moving his arms to embrace the scene. "Judith, how much I have missed Connecticut! In all its seasons, but in spring most of all. Connecticut in spring is deathless. The dogwoods on Greenfield Hill below those enormous copper beeches, the weeping cherries, the prunus, the apple blossom—yes, it is deathless! A hymn to the return of the sun, the most perfect overture to summer. I see it in my dreams!"

"Well, you can be in Connecticut in time for all that."

His face changed, closed up. "I must walk."

"The President would prefer that you rested until the fall, Joshua. It's vacation time, the wrong time for you and your work. You keep saying you're only a man. Well, a man must rest. And you haven't rested for nearly eight months."

"That long?"

"Yes, that long."

"But how can I rest? There's so much still to do!"

Now. Careful, Judith. Slow. Find exactly the right and proper words. Only were there any right and proper words left for him these days? "The President has a special request to make to you, Joshua. He wants you to rest during the summer, but he feels also that the people would like this long tour of yours to finish in a very special way."

He nodded; whether he heard was debatable.

"Joshua, would you be willing to lead the people in a walk from New York City to Washington?"

That did penetrate. He turned his head to stare at her.

"The winter is finally over, and spring is here for those parts of the country that see a real spring any more. And the President feels that with the severity of the winters increasing, the length of the summer shortening, and the mood of the people still frail in spite of all your good work . . . Well, he feels you could really jolt them into a—a summer mood, for want of a better description. You could do this by leading as many of them as would be willing to walk on a pilgrimage to the center of government. And he feels that New York City is a logical starting place. It's a long way, it's going to take days. But after it's over you can rest for the whole summer knowing you've—oh, how can I describe it?—finished your long tour with a colossal upsurge of enthusiasm?"

252

"I'll do it," he said at once. "The President is right. The people need some extra effort from me at this stage, my ordinary walking isn't enough any more. Yes, I'll do it."

"Oh, that's splendid!"

"When?" he asked, indicating that he had really heard.

"A week from today."

"So soon?"

"The sooner the better."

"Yes. Well." He ran his hand across his hair, which he now wore in a short crew cut to save time drying it of a morning; where he had been was no climate to venture out in with damp hair. Not, Dr. Carriol suspected, that this was what had motivated him to cut it so; rather he seemed to have developed an instinct for every kind of self-punishment, everything unflattering. The crew cut did not suit him at all; it accentuated his jailbird pallor, his concentration camp emaciation, and it made what was actually a very thick head of hair look thin and dull.

"We'll leave for New York right after we've finished here in Tucson," she said.

"Whatever you say." He got up, walked off toward a cluster of bee-besieged almond trees.

Dr. Carriol stayed where she was, hardly able to believe that it had been so easy.

In fact, if one could only set aside his growing mental oddity, all of it had been ridiculously easy. His book still sold in the hundreds of thousands, and those who bought it not only read it, but kept it to treasure. No one had ever tried to molest him. No one even harangued him! And wherever the lunatic fringe was dwelling in these days when admittedly little was left to attract the lunatic fringe, they had avoided Dr. Christian like the plague. How great was the measure of his success, how many people had turned to his concept of God, could be seen in the way some very important personages had climbed on his bandwagon, from television greats like Bob Smith and Benjamin Steinfeld to political greats like Tibor Reece and Senator Hillier. The Second Child Bureau was minus its means test. Relocation was in the midst of massive change. And, on a less earth-shaking scale, a letter from Moshe Chasen relayed two bits of Washington scuttlebutt, the first to the effect that President Reece had dumped Julia after talking to Dr. Christian, the second that it was Dr. Christian responsible for the radical—and apparently very successful—change in the treatment of President Reece's daughter.

Well. Dr. Carriol slapped her hands upon her thighs, an I-give-up gesture. Perhaps no one would ever be in a position to evaluate exactly what had grown between Dr. Joshua Christian and the people he had elected to serve. Even in the foreseeable future. He was the brightest object in the sky, a comet to whose glittering tail she was tied like the merest tin can. All she saw and felt were the cooled sparks spinning in his wake.

To Moshe Chasen had been given the job of organizing the March of the Millennium. Oh, not in the flesh. On the computer his wife always reckoned he should by rights have married. But Dr. Chasen was growing steadily more worried, not by the March of the Millennium, which was a piece of cake logistically speaking; by what was happening to Dr. Christian—and to Judith Carriol. The promised meeting the day after he had picked her up from the airport the previous January had not eventuated, nor did the weekend visits to Washington John Wayne had told him she planned to make. She never wrote, and when she phoned she vouchsafed no real information. The only lengthy communication he received from her was a coded computer telex sent from Omaha in which she detailed the format of the March of the Millennium and gave him his instructions. Section Four was suffering somewhat in her absence, for she was unique, they had all come to understand that. John Wayne kept the administrative end up and Millie Hemingway was pinch-hitting on the ideas end, but without the serpentine presence of Dr. Carriol some vital zip and snap and fizz was definitely missing.

Of course they all knew where she was, and somehow too they all knew her mission was at the President's behest. A lot of correct arithmetic had gone on after Dr. Joshua Christian popped out of the Holloman woodwork to take the country by storm, especially on the part of those who had worked on Operation Search. The name Operation Messiah was never bruited, so the leaks were not so much leaks as the inevitable exchange of snippets of knowledge between friends in Section Four. Millie Hemingway had clammed up a week after Dr. Christian commenced his publicity tour, and poor old Sam Abraham had been shipped to Caracas on a special teaching mission. But their chief researchers were still around Environment in Dr. Chasen's own employ. Loyal people, but people were still people.

Then came the March of the Millennium. The whole concept not only staggered Dr. Chasen, it appalled him. A brilliant, blatant bit of hype was how he read it. Then, his hands poised to screw up the yard-long computer telex Dr. Carriol had sent from some Omaha keyboard direct to his own terminal, he changed his mind. Hype it was in her brain, the clever devil, but in the hands of Dr. Joshua Christian it would take on a dignity and importance in keeping with its breathtaking size. He would obey orders for Joshua, not for Judith. For Joshua he would whack out a dream of a failproof plan. For Joshua. Not for Judith. He loved her as the ideal boss, always; as a friend, sometimes; as a child, never. He also pitied her, and he was a man whom pity moved unbearably. For the sake of pity he would perform Herculean tasks; for the sake of pity he would forgive what love would find unforgivable. A devout Jew but nonetheless the most Christian of gentlemen, his sins were purely sins of omission and due to thoughtlessness or lack of perception. Yet in the matter of Judith Carriol he sensed what no one could have perceived: the impoverishment of a spirit that in order to survive had set up its self as a totality.

However, his worry did not prevent his getting down to work on planning the March of the Millennium. What he produced was forwarded to Millie Hemingway, who annotated it, and added to it, and then forwarded it to Judith Carriol by coded computer telexes. Dr. Carriol had done the final work during the hours she spent sitting in cars or hotels waiting for Dr. Christian to return from his walks. And the result was indeed millennial in its scope, its care, its vision.

The privilege of announcing the March of the Millennium was given to Bob Smith, who broke the news on his special birthday edition of "Tonight" at the end of February, 2033. Bob had adopted Dr. Christian as his own creation. Every week on his Friday show he had a film clipping of where Dr. Christian was, complete with mini-talks to those who had spoken to Dr. Christian while he walked. There was a new "Tonight" backdrop to the guest podium, a giant illuminated map of the United States, with Dr. Christian's tracks wandering all over its southeastern and middle and northwestern sections in emerald green, and the towns he had visited lit up in starry crimson, with the states he had touched pale shimmering pink, versus the dull white of states he had still to visit.

All through March and April the publicity built up, carefully orchestrated by the Environment think tank, which had bought time on all the networks. The spirit of the March of the Millennium was extolled, the difficulties of marching explained in meticulous detail, along with exhaustive descriptions of the various facilities available en route. Brilliantly produced one-minute commercials showed exercise programs to fitten up prospective marchers, meditation programs to get marchers into the right mood, medical programs to aid potential marchers in making the decision whether to march at all. Every supermarket and department store was inundated with bits of paper and instructed to place them free of charge on every counter; these bits of paper included maps of the march route, maps showing the various transportation schemes to get marchers from home and back home, leaflets of advice on what to carry, what to leave home, what shoes to wear, what clothes to wear, what headgear to wear. There was even a wonderfully stirring theme melody in two-four time, entitled simply "The March of the Millennium," and composed on commission by Salvatore d'Estragon, the great new operatic musical genius, whose well-earned nickname at the Met was Spicy Sal. A satyr he might be, decided Moshe Chasen after hearing the composition, but there was no doubt it was the best piece of musical patriotism since Elgar wrote his "Pomp and Circumstance" series.

They brought Dr. Joshua Christian to New York City in the middle of May, while the wind still moaned up the sunless streets and the last ice still lingered in every patch of perpetual shade, for it had been a very long, cold winter. He refused to make the short trip from New York to his home in Holloman, though Mama begged and begged. All he did after he arrived in the city was sit in the window of his room high in the Pierre and count the paths he could see winding through Central Park, then count the people he could see walking those paths. And walk, of course. He hadn't given up walking.

"Judith, he's so sick!" said Mama after he had gone to bed on the first night after they arrived. "What can we do?"

"Nothing, Mama. There's nothing can be done for him."

"But a hospital—surely there's some kind of treatment he could have?" Though she asked it hopelessly.

"I don't know that sick is the right word, even," said Dr. Carriol. "He's just—gone away from us. I don't know where he's going, and I don't think he knows either. But can you call that a sickness, even of the mind? His is not like any mental or physical illness I've ever heard of. And one thing I do know. Whatever it is he suffers from has no cure outside of himself. After the March is over I'm hoping he will agree to go away somewhere for a complete rest. He has not stopped in eight months."

Even as she spoke to Mama, Dr. Carriol knew perfectly well that Dr. Christian was indeed going to rest after the March. It was all arranged, the private sanatorium in Palm Springs, the bal‐ ₐ₊ ₑed regimen of diet and exercise and relaxation. A week out of Sioux Falls she had sent the heavies back to Washington; she could tell beyond a doubt that they were not necessary. Curse herself for that insane outburst of rage she might, but undoubtedly it had served one purpose; it had capped the well of fire in Dr. Christian that until then had seemed in perpetual threat of eruption.

James and Andrew and their wives were scheduled to come to New York to make the March of the Millennium, but Mary arrived from Holloman first, with the same end in mind. The moment Mama set eyes on her only daughter she was hideously reminded of Joshua, for she saw a person changed out of all recognition—growing, yet not growing familiarly; bedeviled, but not by familiar devils.

And then hard on Mary's heels the others arrived. Both the younger brothers had mushroomed in self-confidence and initiative, separated for the first time from their too-powerful senior sibling and their suffocatingly single-minded mother. They had tasted the very special freedom of being at liberty to alter Joshua's ideas to suit their own ideas, secure in the knowledge that the changes they had wrought were safely abroad and would therefore never be drawn to Joshua's attention. Oh, Joshua's ideas were wonderful, but they didn't always fit the foreign mentality any more than his choice of words always fitted the foreign language. Big clumsy clever Miriam had grown in concert with James, but Martha the Mouse came back still Martha the Mouse.

Of course when they arrived at the hotel, Joshua was out

walking somewhere; the first ecstasies of reunion between them and Mama were over by the time he returned. Dr. Carriol had absented herself too, aware that the last place she wanted to be when Joshua walked in was there amid the Christians.

So Mama had a small breathing space between the younger children and Joshua. It was not a happy respite. She stood wondering where her family was at this moment, versus where it had been at the same time two years earlier. Long before Joshua had his restless winter, long before he went to the Marcus trial, long before he produced Judith, long before the book. It's the book. It's all the fault of that wretched book. *God in Cursing!* Never was a book more aptly named. God has cursed the Christians. And God has cursed me. But what have I done to deserve His curse? I know I'm not very bright, I know I'm a rather wearing woman and I get on people's nerves, but what have I done to deserve His curse? I brought up my dear children alone, I never gave in, I never cried for mercy, I never stopped looking into the future, I never took time out for myself to find a lover or a husband or so much as a hobby, I never turned my face away from trouble and pain. Yet here I am, cursed. I shall have to spend the rest of my life on this earth in the company of my one daughter, and that will be hell, for she hates me as much as she hates Joshua, and I don't even know *why* she hates us!

Joshua just walked in and stood looking at the little knot of his family clustered against the brilliant backdrop of sky through a window, aureoles fuzzing their silhouettes, faces invisible. He said nothing.

The eager chatter died instantly. The faces turned. The faces changed.

And then, before anyone could gather together an expression of joy and welcome, Martha fainted. The giant pair of hands Dr. Christian used to fantasize as delivering a stunning clap had materialized. She didn't moan or sway or sweat or gag. She dropped to the floor as from a blow.

It took quite some time to bring her round, and by then everyone had his or her reaction to Joshua well under control, could disguise their distress by pretending it was distress for Martha. This Belsen victim could now be appropriately greeted as a long-lost and intimidatingly famous brother. But the Mouse they had to take away, Mama fussing and clucking until Mary just lifted her aside and shut the bedroom door in her bewildered face. Shut her in the sitting room with James and Andrew and Miriam and Joshua. Shut her in with her ruined world.

"Are you all coming with me to Washington, then?" asked Dr. Christian, stripping off his gloves and unzipping his parka, laying them on a table.

"You couldn't keep us away with a team of horses," said James, and blinked quickly several times. "Oh, dear, I must be tired!" he exclaimed. "My eyes are watering terribly."

Andrew turned away, yawning and rubbing his face. Then he cried with an exaggerated start, "What am I doing here, can you tell me? I should be with poor Martha! You'll excuse me, Josh? I'll be back."

"I'll excuse you," said Joshua, and sat down.

"Yes, indeed, we are certainly walking!" cried Miriam with great heartiness, thumping James on his bowed back with loving gusto. "You walked through Iowa and the Dakotas, we walked through France and Germany. You walked through Wyoming and Minnesota, we walked through Scandinavia and Poland. And everywhere the people came, just as they did here. It's so beautiful, dearest Joshua! A miracle."

Dr. Christian looked at her out of alien black eyes. "To call what we do miraculous is a blasphemy, Miriam," he said harshly.

A silence fell; no one knew what to say to break its dreadful clutch.

At which moment Dr. Carriol opened the outer door and walked in. Even not knowing what exactly to expect, she was startled to find herself descended upon by a loudly yelping Miriam and an unusually demonstrative James, with Mama fluttering just behind them, and Joshua sitting limply in a chair watching the gyrations as if they were happening on a very old, very dim, silent piece of celluloid.

Mama ordered coffee and sandwiches, Andrew came back, and they all sat down except Joshua, who chose that moment to go to his room, for what purpose he didn't say. Nor did he come back. But they said nothing about him to Dr. Carriol. Instead, they concentrated upon the March of the Millennium.

"It's under control," she said. "I've tried for weeks to persuade Joshua to rest up beforehand, but he won't hear of it. So the walk starts the day after tomorrow. On Wall Street. And he'll walk from Wall Street mostly up Fifth Avenue, crossing to the West Side at 125th Street and taking the George Washington Bridge into Jersey. Then down I-95 to Philadelphia, Wilmington, Baltimore and finally Washington. Once he's on I-95 we've worked out the perfect way to keep him apart from the crowd yet very much among it. We've had a high wooden boardwalk constructed down the median divider, and we'll let the people walk on either side of him, but below him on the road itself. All normal truck and bus traffic will use the Jersey Turnpike. I-95 is better for our purposes anyway, because it goes through the cities rather than around them like the Turnpike."

"How long do you think it's going to take?" asked James.

"Hard to tell. He walks very fast, you know, and I can't see him consenting to having his mileage planned ahead of time. He outdistances most people quickly, which I imagine he wants to do, as it gives new people a chance to be with him all the time. I don't honestly know, because he's never discussed the actual technique of his walking with me. Anyway, we've got a comfortable camping complex geared up to follow him, and as soon as we have an idea of when and where he's going to finish each day, we'll put the camp down as close by as we can. A park or some other public land. There's plenty."

"What about the people?" asked Andrew.

"We estimate most people will only want to stay with the March for one day, though there's bound to be a nucleus who will stick with Joshua right to Washington. New people will join the March all the way down I-95, and we're going to make sure these people have a chance to walk with Joshua for a mile or so before he outdistances them. Transport is laid on every inch of the way, so people dropping out will be able to find their way home fairly easily. The National Guard is looking after food and shelter and medical emergencies, while the Army will have the responsibility of keeping people moving in an orderly manner. We have no idea how many people will actually turn up to march, but we're catering for several million. Oh, not all at once—all told. However, I think the first day will see a minimum of two million people turn out to march at least some of the way."

"If Joshua is going to walk on a high pathway, won't he be a sitting target for assassins?" asked Miriam quietly.

"That," said Dr. Judith Carriol with great deliberation, "is a risk we've decided to take. Joshua refuses to walk between two shields of bulletproof plexiglass, which is what we originally

260

planned. He also refuses to cancel the March, and he refuses an escort on his walkway. He says he'll walk alone, and unshielded."

Mama mewed softly, reaching out a hand to Miriam, who took it comfortingly.

"Yes, Mama, I know," said Dr. Carriol. "But there's no point in concealing this from you, you're better prepared. And you know Joshua! Once he makes up his mind, there's no shifting him. Even the President couldn't shift him on this."

"Joshua is too proud," said Andrew between his teeth.

Dr. Carriol raised her brows. "Be that as it may, I for one don't have any kind of feeling that he'll be attacked. Wherever he's gone, Joshua has always been a calming influence, and I couldn't begin to count the number of people he's moved amongst quite fearlessly and without any protection. Never a hint of an assassin! Hardly a crackpot. It's astonishing. Public response to the March has been uniformly good too. It's along the lines of an old-time Easter festival, I suppose, though it's too late in the year for Easter. But the winters are much longer than they used to be. Easter was the original New Year, the welcome to spring and the rebirth of life. So who knows? Maybe with spring coming later and later as the centuries pass, we'll end by changing Easter to coincide with the new date of spring."

James sighed. "It's a new kind of world, for sure. So why not?"

On the night before the March was scheduled to begin, the family split up early. Mama was the last one to go, after which Dr. Carriol enjoyed sole possession of the big sitting room in the Christian suite.

She went to the window and looked down on Central Park, where the first contingents of marchers were setting up camp, those who had come in from Connecticut, New York State, and even farther. Down there she knew there were mummers and minstrels, dancers and clowns, puppets and buskers and bands, for she had been walking herself; Central Park was harboring the biggest gathering of *commedia dell'arte* the world had ever seen. Though it was cold it was not wet, and the mood of the campers was eager. They talked to each other freely, they shared what they had, they laughed a lot, they showed no fear or suspicion of strangers, they had no money, and they had no cares. For two hours she had moved among them, watching and listening, and it

261

seemed to her that though of course he was not forgotten, some-where along the way to this gigantic starting point, those who had congregated in the park had abandoned all thought of actually seeing Dr. Christian himself. Everyone she had quizzed there felt that if they really did want to see Dr. Christian, they were better off to remain at home and watch the March on television. Those who had come in person had come to be a physical part of the March of the Millennium.

"It's *my* idea! I thought of this!" she wanted to shriek to them; but didn't; merely hugged her secret triumph.

She had asked many how they were going to get home again, though she knew better than almost everyone that the Army had mobilized to undertake the most massive transportation of people in the history of the country. Simply, she wondered how many of these willing walkers had actually absorbed the weeks and weeks of preparatory messages. But no one seemed concerned about getting home again. They just figured they would, sooner or later; worry about getting home again was not going to be allowed to spoil their great day.

Dr. Joshua Christian had probably the least idea of anyone as to what was happening; how big his march was, how colossal an undertaking, how terrifying it might be if things went wrong. He was going to walk from New York City to Washington, D.C., and further than that he couldn't think. Wouldn't think. Dr. Carriol had told him that he would be expected to make a speech at the end of the march on the banks of the Potomac, but he wasn't dismayed or fearful. Words came so easily to his tongue, now as before. If they wanted him to speak, he would speak. Such a lit-tle, little thing to do. Why did these little things he did mean so much? To walk—what was that except the most natural activity of all? To talk—how easy. To hold out his hands in comfort—a noth-ing. He could offer no real solace. That they could only find within themselves, among themselves. Yet wasn't that what they had been doing all along? He was merely a sounding board, a catalyst of the mass mind, a conductor of spiritual currents.

These days he felt ill all the time. He walked in a most dread-ful pit of physical and mental pain. Though he had told no one, nor showed anyone, he was indeed disintegrating. The bones of his feet and legs were beginning to flaw, jarred by the last months of walking without caring, walking without inner warmth. He had learned to tuck his hands inside his parka pockets when he walked, for in the first months when he had held them down his sides, his shoulders had begun literally to give way in their sockets. And his head was sinking into his neck, and his neck was sinking into his chest, and his chest was sinking into his belly, and his belly and his chest and his neck and his head were all sitting lumped on top of his creaking pelvis. When the fire had gone out because the vital ichor was all drained away, he had ceased to care for himself; too often he didn't bother to don the fresh underwear Billy bought faithfully, too often he forgot his socks, or he donned his trousers without noticing how the thermal layers beneath had rumpled and crinkled into hard little tubes along his skinny legs, around his skinny sides.

It didn't matter. Nothing mattered. He knew this great walk would be his last. And he had given up trying to think of what he was going to do with himself when he could no longer walk. The future had no future. When a man's work is done, when a man has burned himself out, what is left to him? Peace, brother, his soul answered tranquilly. Peace in the longest, soundest sleep of all. How beautiful! How eminently to be desired!

Lying full length upon his bed in that last night before the March of the Millennium was due to begin, he worked the miracle of his mind upon his poor macerated body, softened to mush by the sweat he generated inside his polar garments. But cease thy complaining, O bones, leave off thy rawness, O skin, be gone from me with thy sharp pain, O spine, unknot thy ropy sinews, O muscles. I will lie in sweet oblivion, I will taste no more pain, I am not me, I am not anything, I am blankness, I am nonexistent. Lead weights of coins for Cheiron be on my two eyelids in readiness, stick fast my lashes, roll, O balls of my two eyes, within thy orbits, roll up and out of this conscious living agony. . . .

Just after the sun was risen on a chaste cushion of sweet and cloudless air, and the tops of the skyscrapers around Wall Street flashed golden and pink and copper, Dr. Joshua Christian commenced his last walk. With him were his two brothers, his sister, his two sisters-in-law, and for the first few blocks his mother too, until her fashionable shoes forced her sore little feet to tiptoe quietly into the back seat of a car parked round the corner, under orders to trail the VIP walkers in case of distress. An ambulance also trailed the VIP walkers, in case of extreme distress.

Liam O'Connor the Mayor of New York was walking and fully expected to finish the march, for he had been in training for weeks and had been quite an athlete in his youth. Not to be outdone, Senator David Sims Hillier VII was right in there beside the Mayor, also intending to walk to Washington. Governor Hughlings Canfield of New York, Governor William Griswold of Connecticut, and Governor Paul Kelly of Massachusetts were all walking, so determined to finish that they had been training since Bob Smith announced the March back in February. Every New York City councilman was walking, so was the commissioner of police, the fire chief, and the city comptroller. A large group of city firemen was walking in uniform, the American Legion had gathered outside the Plaza Hotel to join the March, and the band of the one remaining Manhattan high school was present, complete with cheerleaders and every other student to boot. Black Harlem's remains were assembled around 125th Street, and what was left of the Puerto Rican West Side was gathered at the entrance to the George Washington Bridge.

It was cold and there was a fairly sharp wind blowing from around the corners to pounce on the marchers, but on this occasion Dr. Christian elected to walk with his head unhooded and his hands ungloved. He made no ceremonious start; he simply appeared from out of the hallowed portals of the bank where he had waited since well before dawn, strode out into the middle of the street without seeming to notice anyone, and kept on walking. His family moved in a group just behind him, the waving smiling dignitaries came next with the high school band to give them a tune, and then the thousands who had cheered Dr. Christian's appearance tacked on obediently as the waiting police gave them leave to begin.

Dr. Christian was quiet and a little stern, looking neither left nor right; he lifted his chin and aimed his eyes at a point somewhere between the CBS and ABC camera vans as they cruised along in front of him, having outmaneuvered NBC for the crown of the road. The media were under strict orders not to get in Dr. Christian's way at any time, nor to attempt to interview him as he walked. No one broke the taboo, especially after the first four blocks, when no walking journalist had the breath left for questions. Dr. Christian was walking very fast, as if the only way he could finish was to commence with a winding up that would allow him to coast later.

Ten thousand, twenty thousand, fifty thousand, ninety thousand . . . Ever growing, the crowd came out of every side street as he passed to latch on behind, fed into the back ranks of the walkers by the soldiers and police who lined the way shoulder to shoulder, saluting Dr. Christian very gravely as he came abreast of them, a continuous undulation of moving arms that went for miles. Their buttons and buckles and badges gleamed, their uniforms were freshly cleaned and pressed, they looked and felt wonderful.

From SoHo and the Village issued a great stream of colorful people dancing to every musical instrument they could find, feathers in their caps, scarves floating in divers hues, beads and sequins and ribbons and fringes and braids glittering. A few precious helicopters hovered vibrating like dragonflies around the south end of Central Park, the cameras they contained picking up Dr. Christian as he emerged from the canyon of Fifth Avenue with half a million people behind him spreading east and west along Madison and Park, Sixth and Seventh, moving two hundred abreast with eyes shining and teeth braving the Manhattan spring wind.

And they tumbled out of Central Park in his wake, the out-of-towners who had camped and talked and laughed all night, pouring along and singing as they went. Those within hearing of the jazz bands strutted and cavorted, those near guitar-playing and lute-playing minstrels tried to follow their lays, whole hundreds dipped and rose like gangling birds in a ritual dance, while others marched militantly left-right left-right in time to brass bands, and some in the vicinity of flutes and pipes seemed to float. They walked on stilts. They hopped on pogo sticks. Some balanced on their hands. Many many just walked and enjoyed those who preferred more unusual locomotion. There were Harlequins and Pierrots, Bozos and Ronald McDonalds, Cleopatras and Marie Antoinettes, King Kongs and Captain Hooks. A group of over five hundred came dressed in togas and had a Roman general in full triumphal regalia perched atop a sedan chair they carried on their shoulders. Martial arts clubs came in their white baggy gear with various colors of belts. Horses and bicycles were outlawed, but there were wheelchairs galore with fox tails fluttering from the ends of makeshift wands and tinsel streamers bedizening their chrome utility. An organ grinder strolled tunefully along with his monkey on his shoulder, the monkey squealing and grimacing, the organ grinder singing in a cracked tenor voice. Three frock-coated gentlemen with stovepipe hats flaunting moth-eaten peacock feathers skittered along on unicycles because no one had thought specifically about unicycles and the frock-coated gentlemen won their argument with the police. A fakir on a bed of nails was carried by a saffron-wrapped, shaven-headed band of disciples, his hollow belly filled with water lilies. Several Chinese dragons a hundred people long weaved and caterwauled amid rattles and drums, cymbals and firecrackers. A black man seven feet tall clad in all the feathered beaded glory of a Zulu prince stalked through the crowd bearing his assegai, its tip rendered impotent by a block of cork painted and feathered to seem the skull of an enemy killed in battle.

Dr. Christian's pain-racked sobriety broke as he came up Fifth Avenue toward the Metropolitan Museum, where a big group of prospective walkers clustered. They began to pelt him with flowers—daffodils and hyacinths, a few last crocuses plucked dying from the grass, roses and cherry blossoms and gardenias. He turned aside from his determined onward plunge and crossed the great wide avenue to where they stood behind police and soldiers, and he reached his hands between crusty uniforms to take theirs, laughing at their joy, stuffing the flowers he had managed to catch behind his ears, in his pockets, between his fingers. Someone stuck a crown of big daisies lopsided on his head, and someone else flung a garland of begonias around his neck. He went on to the steps of the museum adorned the prince of spring, with their flowers all dredging his brain his flaring brain in perfume. Mounting the steps, he flung wide his arms, and his shouted words were picked up by the vigilant loudspeaker microphones the March's high command had commissioned just in case, his shouted words were relayed instantly to the walking masses and stilled them in their tracks, and they listened raptly.

"People of this land, I love you!" he cried, in tears. "Walk with me into this beautiful world! Our tears will make it paradise! Throw off your sorrows! Forget your griefs! The race of Man will long outlast the coldest cold! Walk with me holding the hands of all your brothers and sisters! For who can mourn the lack of brothers and sisters when every man is every man's brother and every woman his sister? Walk with me! Walk with me into our future!"

Then on he went amid a profound roar of cheers, the flowers

266

falling one by one on the road behind him, gathered up by those who saw them tumble so, and pressed between the pages of Joshua's book for all their browning tomorrows.

On he went, the grotesqueness of his body disciplined into the long swinging rhythmic stride that ate up miles and defeated those who meant to keep up with him.

He crossed the George Washington Bridge at noon and led three million people into New Jersey, a vast walking singing mass that had found a rhythmic cadence of its own, and squeezed itself across the two levels of the bridge with tranquil ease. They were following this pied piper of their dreams they cared not where, and worried not at all. Such a beautiful unique momentous day, on which they knew no trouble, and no pain, and no ache of the heart.

It was here in New Jersey that the true genius of the March of the Millennium's high command displayed itself, for as Dr. Carriol had said, he would walk the whole length of I-95 from New York to Washington atop a low-fenced elevated walkway that straddled the highway's median divider and raised him far above the throngs who marched down both sides of the road.

"Hosanna!" they shrieked. "Hallelujah! Bless you all of your days for loving us! God keep you and thank God for you, Joshua Joshua Joshua CHRISTIAN!"

And they spread like a slow and sluggish delta of hairy brassy ball bearings, an ocean of bobbing heads, through the slag heaps and ancient industrial wastelands of dying New Jersey, through the old boarded-up towns of Newark and Elizabeth, through the green dairy meadows and the plaited strands of railroad yards, with Dr. Christian at their head atop his walkway and all their cares forgotten somewhere behind them. They helped one another, they passed the exhausted out of their ranks very tenderly, they slowed down and dwindled away and followed him no more, passing the torch to those who waited to pick it up.

Five million people walked that first day, never so many again, glad and free, lame and purged, happy and together.

Dr. Judith Carriol did not march. She remained inside the Pierre suite to watch the start on television, chewing her lips and feeling her purpose trickle away between her legs like a slow haemorrhage. When the head of the vast procession passed by beneath the hotel she leaned from a window and she watched it painfully, her eyes fixed on Dr. Christian's bare black brush of a head. The sight of those assembled moving masses left her breathless; she had never before comprehended how many many people the world contained. Unable to understand the nature of genuine suffering, now she began to grope after it consciously, stimulated and annoyed by her own bewilderment. Yet her kind of intellect would never be capable of assessing quality; only quantity.

And they walked on and on and on below her, half a day long, three-quarters of a day long, until the sun began to die, and the city crashed headlong into a hugely bellowing silence.

The moment this desolation happened she went downstairs, crossed Fifth Avenue and entered the park, where a helicopter waited to take her to New Jersey. She would join her incubus at his night camp, wherever that might be.

In the White House it was a ragged day, for the President's temper was ragged. He fretted at the nightmare thought of something going wrong, of that human sea going berserk for no good reason any one of the March's high command could predict, of some kind of magnetic eddy forming amid the unnumbered multitudes and dashing heads together like so many eggs, of a black speck of hatred festering undetected somewhere and erupting through the human cells in bloody waves of violence, of one lone fanatic bringing the sights of his rifle to bear on Dr. Joshua Christian as he strode defenseless and exposed along his boardwalk.

Naturally he had assented immediately to the concept of the March of the Millennium when Harold Magnus brought it to him, but as time went on and the March grew more irrevocable, he became more and more frightened of it, and wished with ever-increasing frequency that he had not given his consent. When, just after May arrived, Harold Magnus twitted him about his jitters, he grew snappy and defensive; he had been informed of Dr. Christian's refusal to be protected. He demanded more and more proof from Environment, the Army, the National Guard—and anyone else he could find—to the effect that every contingency was planned for and covered in quintuplicate. Only the piles of evidence deposited before him stiffened his original resolve. Yet still his presentiment of disaster persisted, now focused on Dr. Christian's vulnerability, because this was the one contingency beyond control.

So on this commencement day he fretted and he fretted. More positive behavior was utterly denied him, for the March of the Millennium, Dr. Christian's fame, and the amazing success of the Christian philosophy abroad, all conspired against his acting positively. For the first time since the Delhi Treaty the leaders of the world were gathering in Washington, for the first time since the Delhi Treaty it seemed as if real amity might be achieved between the United States of America and the other major powers. So much was riding on the broad thin shoulders of the man his video monitor showed him striding along with credible swiftness, mile after mile, hour after hour, a perfect target for an assassin. And he knew if Dr. Joshua Christian came crashing down with his blood flying that America would receive a blow more crippling than Delhi. For her own people and the people of the world would point once more to the senseless destructive anarchistic element that dogged her and flawed her. Oh, too much to pin on too little!

He had denied everyone access to him since dawn, sitting with Harold Magnus for company, chafing and starting up in a panic whenever it seemed to him that the panning cameras might have focused on a possible nucleus of trouble. He had chosen Harold Magnus for sole companion because if anything did go wrong, he had someone on hand at whom he could lash out with complete justification.

It awed him. It terrified him. It made him understand for the first time what the reality of abstract millions was actually about. There they were in the flesh, genuine millions, his faceless masters and his responsibility. There they were, *five million* little blobs of heads spewing across the face of a New Jersey countryside without end, and every one of those blobs housed a brain that had voted for him or against him. How had he ever dared to presume to govern them? How had his predecessors ever dared? How had he ever been deluded into thinking he could control something so astronomical? How could he ever again nerve himself to act? He just wanted to run away and bury his own blob of a head where no one would ever find it. Who was Joshua Christian? Why had he come out of a nameless obscurity to this utter dominion? What right did a computer have to determine living fates? Could the man on the boardwalk truly be so selfless he didn't understand the awesome possibilities that ocean of flesh was offering him? I am afraid, I am so afraid! *What have I done?*

269

Harold Magnus was aware of the doubts tormenting Tibor Reece, but he experienced none of them for himself. He purred. What a sight! What a fucking miracle! What a triumph for himself, to orchestrate a happening of this magnitude! Oh, what a thing to do! Nothing disastrous was going to happen, he was sublimely confident of that. And he swallowed all of it greedily, the visual offering that came in on the monitors from New York, plus the nine other marches going on across the country, shorter versions of the March of the Millennium designed to finish in a day or two at most—Fort Lauderdale to Miami, Gary to Chicago, Fort Worth to Dallas, Long Beach to Los Angeles, Macon to Atlanta, Galveston to Houston, San Jose to San Francisco, Puebla to Mexico City, and Monterrey to Laredo. He gorged himself on the sight of all those millions of walking people, he gobbled up dreams and hopes and aspirations, he frolicked and basked and gamboled, a lone whale soaking in the richest sea of human plankton soup ever made. Oh, what a *clever* boy am I!

Moshe Chasen watched at home with his wife Sylvia, and his emotions were much closer to those roiling inside Tibor Reece than to the careless rapture of Harold Magnus.

"Someone's going to get him," he muttered, the moment he saw Dr. Christian climb onto his high walkway and begin his march down I-95.

"You're right," said Sylvia, no comfort.

He rolled his eyes toward her in anguish. "You were not supposed to agree with me!"

"So I'm your wife, so I argue a little! But when you are right, Moshe, I agree with you. Maybe it just goes to show how seldom you are right."

"Swallow your tongue, woman!" He clutched his head in his arms and rocked it. "Oi, oi, what have I done?"

"*You* done?" Sylvia took her eyes away from the television screen to look at him. "What's with this *you* done, Moshe?"

"I have sent him to his death, that's what I've done."

Her first impulse was to deride this statement; then she decided on a different tack. "Come on, come on, you look as happy as Benny in search of a home! He will be fine, Moshe."

But Dr. Chasen was beyond cheering up.

Darkness had fallen an hour before Dr. Christian finally came down off his walkway and parted the cheering crowds all around him. He had walked for over twelve hours without letup, no break for food, no pause to relieve himself; he had even waved the offered drinks away. Not good, thought Dr. Judith Carriol, waiting in the walled-off compound of tents in which he and his family and the walking dignitaries were to stay for the night. *He has become a complete fanatic, with the superhuman strength and endurance of such men, the indifference to his own bodily welfare. He will burn himself out very soon. But not before he makes it to Washington. Such men never burn out untimely.*

What security measures were possible and feasible had been implemented to protect him, of course; above his head hovered several helicopters that were not in any way connected with the media, though they purported to be. They were there scanning the crowds ceaselessly, ever alert for the flash of a gun barrel or the trajectory of a missile. The boardwalk was actually some protection, in spite of its nakedness, for it was well elevated and it kept him remote. Anyone intent on killing him would, if in the crowd, have to lift his weapon up and thus display it to those around him, and if removed from the crowd, would have to be several floors high in a building. Not one such place had been left unscoured if it was within accurate shooting range of the highway.

When Dr. Christian came into the big tent allocated to him and his family, Dr. Carriol came forward at once to help him out of his parka. He looked totally exhausted, as well he might. When she suggested he visit the toilet, he nodded and disappeared in the direction she indicated, but was back again within a minute.

"We've set up whirlpool baths for all of you," she announced in general. "Nothing better to iron out the kinks."

"Oh, Judith, it was wonderful!" said Andrew, cheeks pink from the breezy day.

"I'm bushed, but I'm so happy I could cry," said James, flopping into a chair.

None of them had walked with the single-mindedness of Dr. Christian; he and he alone had gone without food or drink, rest or respite. Every two hours the official marchers had been whisked from the highway to enjoy an hour's break, then were transported to a point ahead of the March so they could rejoin it when Dr. Christian arrived.

"Here, boys, let me get you a drink," said Mama from behind laden tables.

But once he returned from the toilet Dr. Christian simply

stood without moving or speaking, staring in front of him as if nothing he saw had substance, or needed substance.

Mama had begun to notice this peculiar behavior and was preparing to make a fuss, so Dr. Carriol got in first. She walked across to him and took him gently by the arm.

"Joshua, come and have a bath," she said.

He followed her to one of the rooms tacked onto the end of the tent, wherein whirlpool tubs had been placed. But once inside the especially big cubicle reserved solely for his use, again he stood without moving.

"Would you like me to help you?" she asked, a sudden alarm knocking at her ribs.

He didn't seem to hear her.

Silently she stripped off his clothes, while he stood docilely still and unprotesting.

What she saw when he was naked sucked everything out of her but the pain that came squealing to fill the vacuum up.

"Joshua, does anyone know?" she summoned up the strength to ask, her faintness dissipating.

At last he did seem to hear; he shivered, shook his head.

She inspected him minutely, incredulously. His feet were enormously swollen, the toes partially eaten away from frostbite. All up the front of his shins a network of deep cracks oozed redly. The insides of his thighs were bloody meat, every hair rubbed away along with the skin. Both armpits were abscessed, so were his groin and perineum and buttocks. And he was smothered with bruises, old bruises and new bruises and bruises halfway between.

"My God, man, how have you kept going?" she cried, to fuel her self-defensive anger. "Why haven't you asked for help, in God's name? You're quick enough to give it!"

"I don't honestly feel anything," he said.

"Well, it's the end. You can't walk tomorrow."

"I can walk. I will walk."

"Sorry, no way."

And he rounded on her, took her between his hands and cracked her viciously against the wooden side of the tub seething with vile bubbles like an acid bath in a horror movie. And as he spoke to her with his face thrust into hers, he cracked her again and again into the side of the tub.

"Don't you presume to tell me what I can do and what I can't do! I will walk! I will walk because I must walk! And you will say nothing. Not one word to anyone!"

"It's got to stop, Joshua. And if you won't stop it, then I must," she gasped, unable to break free of him.

"It will stop only when I say so. I walk tomorrow, Judith. I walk the day after tomorrow. I walk all the way to Washington to keep my appointment with my friend Tibor Reece."

"You'll be dead long before you get there!"

"I'll last the distance."

"Then at least let me get you a doctor!"

"No."

She moved angrily within his hold, twisting and beating at him with her hands. "I *insist!*" she cried.

He laughed. "The time has long passed when you could control me! Do you honestly think you do still control me? You don't! You haven't since Kansas City. From the moment I began to walk among my people I have listened only to God, and only done God's work."

She gazed up into his face in dawning fear and sudden understanding. He really was mad. Perhaps he had always been mad, just hidden it better than anyone she had ever met. "You must stop this, Joshua. You need help."

"I'm not mad, Judith," he said gently. "I see no visions, I have no communications with unearthly powers. I am more in contact with reality by far than you. You are a hard, ambitious, driving woman, and you have used me to further your own ends. Do you think I don't know that?" He laughed again. "Well, I have turned the tables on you, madam. I am going to use you to further *my* ends! Your power trip is over, so is the subtle manipulation. You will do as you are told, you will obey me. If you don't, I'll destroy you. I can! And I will! It's no concern of mine if you don't understand what I'm doing and why I'm doing it. I have found my life's work, I understand how to do that work, and you are my assistant. So no doctor! No word to anyone."

The eyes of a madman. He *was* mad! What could he do to her? How could he destroy her? And then she thought, Why am I bothering to defy him? If he wants to kill himself on this march, then let him do so. He'll make it to Washington, he's mad enough and single-minded enough. That's all he has to do to serve *my* ends! I was going to phase him out anyway. And maybe I'm overreacting to the sight of all that—that—insane self-flagellation.

273

The heart and the guts and the gizzard inside are fine, it's only the outside of him and the tips of him that are maimed. He'll live, after a period in the hospital. I was shocked. I was thrown out of myself by the sight of what he has the power to do to himself. It's not the extent of the injuries, it's the horror any sane person must experience at sight of what a madman can do to himself in the name of a purpose, or his God, or any other obsession. He wants to walk to Washington? Let him walk to Washington! It is very much to my advantage that he does. So why am I defying him? If not to achieve this cosmic undertaking, why did I consent to exile from my home and my real work for months? *He is wrong!* Still I—use—him.

"All right, Joshua, if that's the way you want it, that's the way it will be," she said. "But at least let me do something for you. Let me find some ointment to ease the pain, okay?"

He let her go immediately, as if he knew full well the nature of the debate she had just had with herself, as if he had been sure all along that she would keep his secret. "Go and get it, if you must," he said.

So she helped him up the little flight of steps and over the side of the tub, into the roaring bubbles. Truly he did not seem to be in pain, for he sank down into the below-blood-heat isotonic solution of bone-healing salts with a sigh of what sounded like genuine pleasure, and no agony crossed his face.

When she emerged from the cubicle his family turned to her quickly; for a sick moment she thought they must have heard what passed between her and Joshua. Then she realized that the sound of the air being forced through the water in the tub must definitely have drowned out any words they said, for the family's faces held only concern, normal concern.

"He's soaking," she said lightly. "Why don't the rest of you follow suit? I just have to slip out for a moment. Mama, I've found something of real value you can do for Joshua."

"What? What?" Mama asked eagerly, poor thing relegated to cipher maternity.

"If I manage to get hold of some silk pajamas, do you think you could stitch the pants inside the trousers he'll wear tomorrow? He's a bit chafed, and luckily I don't think it's cold enough for thermal underwear. The polar outer gear is probably too much too, but it's comfortable and lightweight, and with some silk for lining he should do better."

274

"Oh, poor Joshua! I'll rub some cream into his skin."

"No. I'm afraid he's not really in a mood to be ministered to, Mama. We're going to have to be sneaky, like the silk pants. I'll be back as soon as I can." And she slung her good roomy bag over her shoulder before she left the tent.

A Major Withers was in permanent charge of the nightly rest camp. Dr. Carriol had already been introduced to him in New York, so he knew she was in effect his commanding officer on this exercise. She had deemed him a particularly wooden-headed stickler for duty and detail, but when she asked him to find her as many pairs of pure fine silk pajamas as he could, one pair at least tonight, he didn't flinch. He simply nodded and disappeared.

In the hospital tent she asked curtly for supplies to treat chafing and boils, not daring to go into detail; she was given powders and ointments, stuffed them into her bag along with dressings, and returned to Dr. Christian in the bath.

He was not in pain. That had finished at the moment in which he was garlanded in flowers, a sign of such love and such faith that he knew himself vindicated. They had come in their millions to be with him on his last walk, and he would not disappoint them. Not if it cost him his health, his last sane action. Judith had never really believed in him, only in herself, but *they* believed in him. And he had never done anything for her; it had all been for them. The walking was easy, once the flowers drugged his pain. After the kind of conditions he had endured through the winter, pulling his feet in and out of deep fresh snow, treading across rough razoring ice, the March of the Millennium was more a waltz. Especially once he ascended the special walkway they had built for him; all he had to do from then on was open his legs wide in front and behind, and keep those legs moving steadily down the soft, never-ending, level path which stretched away in front of him. Which was narcotic in itself, so steady, so changeless, so unfraught with footfall perils. He ate up the miles, he felt on that first day as if he could have walked forever. And the people had followed, freed, happy.

The effect seeing his body would have on Judith Carriol had not entered his mind, for he was indifferent to it himself, and the pain was gone. Nor did he ever bother to look at himself in a mirror, so actually he had no real idea how horrifying his appearance was.

Aaaaah! Not to worry. She had come to heel as he had known

she would, once he refreshed her memory about how much to her advantage it would be to let him finish the March. He leaned his head back against the side of the tub and relaxed deeply. Lovely! So peaceful to be lapped by something churning even more violently than he himself.

At first Dr. Carriol thought he must have died, for his head was back at such an angle he was surely not using his windpipe to breathe. She made a noise of alarm so loud it penetrated the roiling bubbles; he lifted his head, opened his eyes and looked at her dimly.

"Come on, I'll help you out."

To touch him with a towel would certainly exacerbate his injuries, so she stood him to dry in the warm and well-ventilated room, fairly free of steam because the water in the tub was barely warm. Afterward she laid him on a stretcher covered with several thicknesses of cotton sheeting. Originally she had arranged for a masseuse, out of the question now, of course. Still, the stretcher was useful. It seemed better not to tamper with the healing effect of the salty bath and the subsequent dryness, so she left his chafing and cracking and frostbite alone, contenting herself with smearing a combined steroid and antibiotic ointment over his— abscesses? carbuncles? They weren't boils, for each was enormous in size and many-headed.

"Stay there," she ordered. "I'll bring you some soup."

Mama was busy sewing when she emerged into the main room of the tent, but the others had all vanished, presumably to bathe or nap before dinner.

"Oh, how clever of Major Withers to deliver them straight to you! I wonder where he got silk pajamas so quickly?"

"They're his own," said Mama, biting off the thread between her little white useful teeth.

"Good God!" She laughed. "Who would have thought it?"

"How is Joshua?" Mama asked, so offhandedly Dr. Carriol knew she suspected he was quite ill.

"A bit miserable. I think I'm just going to give him a big bowl of soup, nothing else. He can sleep where he is, it's comfortable." She moved to the table where food had been spread out, took a bowl in her left hand, a ladle in her right. "Mama?"

"Yes?"

"Do me a big favor, will you? Don't go near him."

276

Mama's large blue eyes filmed over, but she swallowed her disappointment valiantly. "If you think it's best, of course."

"I do think it's best. You're a gallant soul, Mama. It's been an awful time for you, I know, but as soon as Washington's over we'll send him away for a long rest, and you can have him all to yourself. How does Palm Springs sound, huh?"

But Mama just smiled and looked sad, as if she didn't believe a word of what she was being told.

When Dr. Carriol came into the cubicle bearing her bowl of soup, Dr. Christian sat up and swung his legs over the side of the tall stretcher. Now he looked very tired, but not exhausted, and he had wrapped a cotton sheet around himself sarong-wise to hide the worst of his wounds, which were from the chest down or hidden in his armpits. Even his toes were beneath the edge of the sheet. Prepared for Mama, no doubt. She handed him the soup without a word, and stood watching while he drank it.

"More?"

"No, thank you."

"You'd better sleep in here, Joshua. I'll bring you your fresh clothes in the morning. It's all right, the family just think you're terribly tired and a bit irritable. And Mama is busy sewing a silk lining into tomorrow's trousers. It's not that cold, you'll be better off with silk than thermal stuff."

"You make a very capable nurse, Judith."

"Only so far as my common sense takes me. After that I'm lost." The empty bowl in her hand, she looked at him, on eye level because she was standing and he was sitting. "Joshua, *why?* Tell me why!"

"Why what?"

"This secrecy about your condition."

"It's never been that important to me."

"You *are* mad!"

He tilted his head to one side and laughed at her through his eyelids, his mouth straight. "Divine madness!"

"Are you serious, or are you putting me on?"

He lay down on his narrow bed and looked at the ceiling. "I love you, Judith Carriol. I love you more than any other individual human being in the world," he said.

That shocked her more than seeing his body, shocked her into sitting down abruptly on the chair near his stretcher. "Oh, sure!

After what you said to me less than an hour ago, how can you now say you love me?"

His head turned on the flat pillow and he looked at her so sadly and strangely, as if her having to ask that of him was but one more disappointment. "I love you because of those things. I love you because you need to be loved more than any other human being I have ever met. I love you therefore in the full measure you need. And I do love you that much."

"Like an old ugly disfigured cripple! Thanks!" She leaped up from the chair and rushed from the room.

The family was back; God protect me from these Christians! Why could she never seem to find the right thing to say to him any more? How could he expect to get a genuine reaction from her when he gave her news like that at a time like this? Damn you, damn you, damn you, Joshua Christian! How dare you presume to patronize me?

She turned on her heel, went back into his cubicle, walked up to him as he lay with eyes closed, grasped his chin in her fingers and pushed her face down to his. Six inches away. His eyes opened. Black black black is the color of my true love's eyes. . . .

"Stick your love!" she said. "Shove it up your ass!"

In the morning Dr. Carriol assisted Dr. Christian to dress, though more accurately he assisted her. He had crusted over on the worst areas of chafing and cracking, but she didn't think this beginning of a healing process would survive the day's march. Tonight she would have a better arrangement in the bath cubicle, a proper bed for one thing, and some sort of active exhaust system to suck stray wisps of steam out of the air. He never said a word while she dressed him, just sat and stood and turned and put his legs in and held his arms out in automatic response to the commands of her hands. But no matter how he might deny it, he was in pain; when it caught him unprepared he shivered like an animal, and when what must surely have been a stab of agony pierced him, he jerked like an epileptic.

"Joshua?"

"Mmmmmm?" Not the most encouraging response.

"Don't you think that somewhere along the line each of us has to make a definite decision about life? I mean, where we are going, whether we're going to set our sights big or small, on something personal or something grander?"

He didn't answer; she wasn't even sure he heard, but she went on doggedly anyway.

"There's nothing personal in this, I'm just doing a job I happen to be good at doing, probably because I don't let anything or anyone get in my way. But I'm not a *terrible* person! Truly I'm not! You could never have gone among the people if I hadn't made it possible, don't you see that? I *knew* what the people needed, but I couldn't give them what they needed from myself. So I found you to do what had to be done. Don't you understand that? And you have been happy, haven't you? In the beginning you *were* happy, before the bugs started crawling around inside your head. Joshua, you can't blame me for what's happened! You can't!" The last two words came out despairing before they were even uttered.

"Oh, Judith, not now!" he cried wretchedly. "I don't have the time for this! All I want is to walk to Washington!"

"You *can't* blame me!"

"Do I need to?" he asked.

"I guess not," she said dully. "But—oh, I wish I was someone else! Haven't you ever wished that?"

"Every second of every minute of every hour of every day I wish it! But the pattern must be finished before I finish."

"What pattern?"

His eyes came to life as briefly as the sputter in a lit stick of incense. "If I knew that, Judith, I would be what I am not—I would be more than a man."

And he went out to walk.

He walked, millions followed. From Manhattan to New Brunswick on the first day, though never so far so fast again as that, and never with so many people. Through Philadelphia and Wilmington and Baltimore he walked, to the outskirts of Washington, D.C., on the eighth day.

Those who walked with him were shyer after the New York marchers went home, though some of the gaudy ebullient New Yorkers did go all the way with him. And never were there less than a million people on the move. Down 1-95 on his boardwalk he went, followed on high by helicopters, led by the network television vans, with his family right behind him, and that cheery waving dog-tired little band of government dignitaries in the vanguard of the crowd. From New Brunswick on, the Governor of

New Jersey came; the Governor of Pennsylvania joined up in Philadelphia, where Dr. Christian spoke briefly. At his age and weight the Governor of Maryland had opted to attach himself to the reception committee in Washington, but the Chairman of the Joint Chiefs of Staff, nineteen U.S. senators, over a hundred U.S. congressmen, and half a hundred assorted generals, admirals and astronauts were slipped in among the walking VIPs as Dr. Christian strode through the drab red-brick and half-finished ambitious public works of Baltimore, abandoned for good at the turn of the century.

He walked. Dr. Carriol did not know how, but he walked. And each night when he stopped she ministered to the slowly dissolving ruin of his body, each night Mama sewed a fresh pair of pure silk pajama pants inside his next day's trousers, each night the family tried to keep their spirits up when Dr. Christian was removed from them by his jealous guardian, who, had they only known it, was chiefly concerned to keep from them any idea of Joshua's condition and pain.

Dr. Christian himself had ceased to think after New Brunswick. The pain had stopped in New York, the thinking in New Brunswick, and the walking would stop in Washington. All he kept in his mind was Washington, Washington, Washington.

Something in his brain betrayed him. Not the conscious part, for it understood very well that he had only arrived on the outskirts of Washington, at a place called Greenbelt. The last night's bivouac. Yet here he let his guard down, he relaxed as if he had actually gone all the way to the Potomac. Instead of going straight into the cubicle which housed his whirlpool tub and his bed, he sat with his family in the tent's main area, talking and laughing like his old self; instead of drinking a bowl of soup, he made a good meal in the company of his family, veal stew and mashed potatoes and string beans, with coffee and cognac afterward.

He was in severe pain; Dr. Carriol had acquired sufficient expertise by now to see the little telltale signs of it, the way his eyes did not focus so much on faces as on whole walls, with faces in their middles somewhere, the muscular spasms that followed a wrong movement (for the family's benefit he called them cramps), the stretched lifeless look of the skin over his cheeks and nose, the inconsequence of his conversation.

In the end she had to order him to bath and bed, at which point he went with her willingly.

No sooner had she turned on the air feed to the tub and firmly closed the canvas flap across the entrance to the cubicle than he rushed to the toilet she had added to the facilities after New Brunswick. He vomited until he had nothing left to vomit, painfully, dreadfully, racked by paroxysms that seemed to come all the way up from the calves of his kneeling legs. Until he was sure he was finally done he refused to move, then had to be helped to his bed; he sat on its edge hunched over, breathing stertorously, his face so drained and strained it was the color of a black pearl.

The explanations and the recriminations, the accusations and the exculpations, all were finished in New Brunswick. Since then Dr. Christian and Dr. Carriol had drawn very close, fused by a bond of pain and suffering, united in the face of the world to preserve his secret at any cost. She was his servant and his nursemaid, the only witness of his battle to continue, the sole human being who understood how frail was his hold on the self he called Joshua Christian.

So now she held his head against her belly while he labored to drag a little air into his lungs, then when he was easier she sponged his face and hands, held a cup and a basin while he rinsed his mouth. In silence. In conjunction.

Only when he was undressed and put into clean silk pajamas with all his wounds anointed did he speak, slowly, indistinctly.

"I will walk tomorrow," was what he said.

Further speech was not possible, he shivered too much. The skin of his lips was blue.

"Can you sleep?" she asked.

The ghost of a smile around chattering teeth. He nodded and closed his eyes immediately.

Until she was sure he did indeed sleep she remained with him, sitting quietly on a chair and never letting her eyes wander from his face. Then she rose to her feet and tiptoed out to telephone Harold Magnus.

Finally freed from his White House exile, he was about to sit down to a very late and much anticipated dinner when Dr. Carriol rang.

"I have to see you at once, Mr. Magnus," she said. "It cannot wait, and I mean that."

He was not displeased, he was furious, but he knew Judith Carriol better than to argue. His home was across the river in outer Arlington, which made the Department of the Environment closer by far to Greenbelt; besides which, he loathed seeing staff in his home, and he loathed rushing a dinner. "My office, then," he said curtly, and hung up. The dinner was Nova Scotia smoked salmon followed by coq au vin, so it had better wait until he returned. *Fuck!*

The Department of the Environment had been built after extreme petroleum rationing was instituted, so it had no helicopter pad, and its roof had long been sacrificed to a growing colony of store rooms for the accommodation of paper. Therefore Dr. Carriol decided to travel in from Greenbelt by car, commandeering one of the vehicles reserved for the use of the dignitaries walking with Dr. Christian. The distance was not great, but the journey took nearly three hours. Washington had filled up with people waiting to join the last leg of the March of the Millennium, the people were in high carnival mood and spilled everywhere across the roads, even camping in them. Though there were more cars in Washington than anywhere else in the country, no one had respect for the sanctity of roads any more. The car crept where the crowd was thickest, constantly sounding its horn, zigzagging between clumps of sleeping campers and occasionally having recourse to the sidewalk. It irritated Dr. Carriol but did not unduly worry her, for she knew Harold Magnus would be having much the same experience, and he had to come a long way farther. No point in getting to Environment way ahead of him.

As it happened, the crowd was considerably thinner on the Virginia bank of the Potomac, and Dr. Carriol had underestimated the distance from Greenbelt to Environment versus the distance from Falls Church; it took Harold Magnus a mere two hours. However, when he arrived he was in one of his meanest moods, chiefly on account of the dinner left behind uneaten. For eight days he had been tied to Tibor Reece's side, unable to leave the White House. He hated staying at the White House; the President was not an eater and was currently a bachelor, so the meals were infrequent, deplorably dull, and of one course only, with no seconds offered. Even in the middle of the night he had been unable to sneak away, for Tibor Reece was determined to have a whipping boy on hand if anything happened to Dr. Joshua

Christian. So Harold Magnus had taken to raiding the candy machines in the White House's staff cafeteria, and during the eight days of his exile he had consumed enormous quantities of Hershey bars, M&Ms, and Good and Plentys, vainly trying to fill up his empty corners, equally vainly trying to sweeten his disposition. But on this night, his last, the Secretary had rebelled. He phoned his wife and ordered his favorite dinner, then he refused the White House fare when it was offered. At nine in the evening he went home, his excuse the grand reception to be held on the morrow; he told the President he had to look over his clothes.

When the Secretary erupted through his outer office doors at a little after two in the morning, Mrs. Helena Taverner's face lit up. She had literally been filling his position all through his White House incarceration, and it was beating her.

"Oh, sir, I'm so glad to see you! I need decisions, directives and signatures desperately," she said.

He kept on going, waving at her over his shoulder to follow him into his office.

Sighing, she gathered a large sheaf of papers together, her notepad and pencil, and joined him.

They worked for an hour, the Secretary occasionally looking at the clock on the wall behind him, as he wore no watch.

"Where the hell is she?" he demanded as they finished.

"It's bound to be slow going, sir. She's coming in on the March route, and I imagine it's solid people," soothed Mrs. Taverner.

But Dr. Carriol arrived not five minutes later, just as Mrs. Taverner was settling herself back at her own desk with yet more work to do. A look of understanding passed between the two women, then a smile.

"That bad, huh?" asked Dr. Carriol.

"Well, he's been stuck at the White House for eight days, and the food isn't what he likes at all. But his mood's on the upswing since he's been back in his own chair."

"Oh, poor baby!"

Indeed his mood had improved; dinner would be eaten later if not sooner, Helena hadn't made too many mistakes in his absence—he really ought to remember to give her a nice gift sometime—and his White House exile was over. He greeted Dr. Carriol with huge affability, a corona corona jammed in one corner of his mouth, his paunch gaily sheathed in a pink-and-green brocade waistcoat.

"Well, well, Judith, this is more like it, eh?"

"Yes, Mr. Secretary," she said, taking off her coat.

"Greenbelt tonight, then a final stroll to the Potomac tomorrow morning. We've got it all set up, a solid Vermont marble platform that will form a base of the Millennial memorial later on, loudspeakers on every street corner and in every park for miles around, and *some* reception committee! The President, the Vice-President, Congress, every ambassador, Prime Minister Rajpani, Premier Hsaio, loads more heads of state, movie stars and television stars and college presidents—*and* the King of England!"

"The King of Australia and New Zealand," she corrected.

"Well, yes, but he's really the King of England; it's just that the Commies don't like kings." He buzzed Mrs. Taverner and asked for coffee and the drinks tray. "You will join me in a glass of brandy, Judith? I know you're not a drinker, but I heard from the President that Dr. Christian had converted you to a little cognac with your coffee, and I'm not averse to it myself."

When she didn't reply he eyed her more closely, fanning a cloud of heavy aromatic smoke away from her vicinity. "My cigar worrying you?" he asked with unwonted concern.

"No."

"What's the matter? His speech not up to scratch? He does know he's expected to speak—doesn't he?"

Her sigh came up from the bottom of her belly. "Mr. Secretary, he's not going to speak tomorrow."

"What?"

"He's—ill," she said, choosing her words with extreme care. "In fact, he's mortally ill."

"Oh, bullshit! He looks great! I've been watching him the whole goddam way with the President ready to have my balls if anyone picked him off, and I can tell you I watched the guy like a hawk! He looks great. *Ill?* Walking at the rate he does? Bullshit! What's really the matter?"

"Mr. Magnus, you must believe me. He is desperately ill. So ill that I fear for his life."

He stared at her in gathering unease, beginning at last to believe her, but he couldn't repress a final protest at the injustice of her news. "Bullshit!"

"No, the truth. I know, because I have to deal with him every

284

night and every morning. Do you know what his body looks like under all that gear? He's a mass of raw flesh. He wore away his life trudging through the north in winter. He's losing significant amounts of blood where he's got no skin left. He's in the kind of pain that causes near dementia. His sweat glands are great lumps of stinking pus where they've burst, and great lumps of agony where they haven't. His toes are dropping off. Drop—ping—off! Hear me?"

He went faintly green, gagged, stubbed his cigar out in a hurry. "God Jesus!"

"He's done, Mr. Magnus. I don't know how he walked this far, but it's his swansong, believe me. And if you want the man healed instead of dead, you'd better help me prevent him walking to the Potomac tomorrow."

"Why the hell did you keep this to yourself? Why wasn't I told?" He was bellowing so loudly he didn't notice his secretary open the door, then shut it again quickly without coming in.

"I had my reasons," said Dr. Carriol, unintimidated. "He will live and he will be all right, provided he's taken somewhere very quiet and very isolated, given the best medical attention we can command, and we don't waste any time organizing it." She was feeling better by the second. How nice it felt to dominate Harold Magnus.

He made up his mind. "Tonight?"

"Tonight."

"All right, the sooner the better. Shit! What am I going to tell the President? What's the King of England going to think? Come all that way at great expense and no one to say hi to! Shit! What a shlemozzle!" He peered at her suspiciously. "You're *sure* the man's done?"

"I am sure. Look at it this way, sir," she went on, too tired and too—heartsick?—to care whether she successfully kept the ironic contempt out of her voice. "The rest of the bunch are in great shape. So they should be! They haven't walked all winter, they've trained all winter, and they haven't walked the whole way to Washington, like him. Senator Hillier, Mayor O'Connor, Governors Canfield, Griswold, Kelly, Stanhope and de Matteo, General Pickering, et cetera, et cetera, are all in fantastic form, lapping up the attention. So why not let tomorrow be *their* day? Dr. Joshua Christian was the driving force behind the March of the Millennium, yes, but the cameras and the eyes of the world have been fastened on him for eight days now, with everyone else—no matter how important—aware he's taking a back seat to the Man of the Millennium. And let's face it, Dr. Christian doesn't give a shit about the King of England or the Emperor of Siam or the Queen of Hearts, any more than the King of England really gives a shit about Dr. Joshua Christian. So let Mr. Reece and the senators and the governors and all the rest have tomorrow for themselves. Let Tibor Reece be the one to climb that platform and address the crowd! He adores Dr. Christian; he won't deliver a speech that will fail to do justice to the occasion. And the crowd won't care at this stage who addresses them. They've been a part of the March of the Millennium; that's all they'll want to remember."

His brain had followed this line of thought with somewhat less than its customary precision and flawless self-interest; he hadn't slept properly for eight days, he hadn't eaten in many hours, except candy, candy, candy, and he was feeling just a little queasy.

"I suppose you're right," he said, blinking. He yawned. "Yes, it should work. I'd better see the President right away."

"Whoa, there! Before you go off half-cocked, I want some decisions from you as to where and how we take Dr. Christian. Palm Springs is out, I arranged that before I knew how sick he was. It's also too far. What worries me most is secrecy. Wherever we take him can't be vulnerable to local speculation or gossip. We don't want any rumors leaking out about the shocking state he's got himself into walking among the people; it would make a martyr of him. He must be treated by a small, hand-picked group of doctors and nurses in a place fairly close to Washington, but where no one will find him. Of course the doctors and the nurses will have to be service personnel with top security clearances."

"Yes. Yes. We certainly can't afford to make a martyr out of him, living or dead. We have to show him to the people in a year's time or whenever, fit and well and ready to go."

Dr. Carriol raised her brows. "So?"

"So—where? Any suggestions?"

"No, Mr. Secretary, not a one. I thought you might know of somewhere, as you're from Virginia. It can't be too far away because we don't know what the medical team will really have to contend with, so they'll have to be able to get extra staff or equipment from their usual base of operations—I guess they'll be from Walter Reed?"

He nodded.

"Yet it must be an isolated place," she insisted.

He plucked the dead cigar out of the ashtray, looked at it, then reached for a fresh one out of the humidor placed shamelessly on his desk. "The best cigars," he said, getting himself puffing, "have to be rolled on the inside of a woman's thigh. These"—*puff*—"are"—*puff puff*—"the best."

Dr. Carriol looked at him more alertly. "Mr. Magnus, are you all right?"

"Of course I'm all right! I can't think without a cigar is all." He sat and puffed some more, then he said, "Well, there is one possible place. An island in Pamlico Sound, North Carolina. Deserted these days. It belongs to the Binkman tobacco family. Fallen on hard times, of course. Didn't think to diversify. Must have been the only tobacco family that didn't diversify." He puffed on.

Get *on* with it, man! Dr. Carriol wanted to scream, but didn't. She sat as patiently as she could.

"One of the Parks and Wildlife people brought it up with me just before the March. Seems the Binkmans want to donate it to the nation as a designated park, if they can't sell it. It's already a bird and wildlife sanctuary, has been for years, but the Binkmans just don't have the money to use the place any more, and they're desperate to unload it while it's still in good condition. There's an interesting old house on the island that they used as a summer home for—hell, centuries, nearly! They've just fixed the house up because they thought they had a firm offer for house and island, but the sale fell through a couple of weeks ago. And unless they get rid of it, they're facing a massive tax bill. Hence the offer to Parks. I think what they're really hoping for is that the nation will buy it for a Presidential retreat; it's ideal. But with the March taking up all the President's attention, I haven't brought the matter up with him yet. There's no one in the house or on the island, but Parks assured me it all works. There's water and proper plumbing and a 50 kVa diesel generator to provide power. Would it suit your purposes?"

She stretched, shuddered. "It sounds ideal. Does the place have a name?"

"Pocahontas Island. It's a bit the Cape Hatteras side of Kitty Hawk and about in the middle of that end of the sound. Only about a mile long and half a mile wide. I guess it's really a sand spit that's stayed above sea level long enough to green up. It's on

287

the charts, Parks says." He buzzed Mrs. Taverner. "Damn the woman! Where's my coffee and cognac?"

They appeared very quickly, but when Mrs. Taverner went to leave just as quickly, he detained her. "Hold it, hold it! Dr. Carriol, do you have sufficient medical knowledge to give Helena some idea of what doctors we need and what equipment they'll need?"

"Yes. Mrs. Taverner, we need a vascular surgeon, a plastic surgeon, a good general physician, a shock and exposure specialist, an anaesthetist, and two class A nurses. All with top security clearances. They will need everything necessary to treat shock, exhaustion, exposure, severe frostbite with what I suppose is gangrene or some other form of necrosis, chronic malnutrition maybe, some degree of kidney failure, a full gamut of drugs, plenty of wound dressings, the appropriate surgical instruments to deal with abscesses and debridement of tissue—oh, and we'd better throw in a psychiatrist too."

This last requisition made him squint narrowly at Dr. Carriol, but he made no comment beyond a grunt.

"Got all that?" he asked Mrs. Taverner. "Good. I'll tell you what to do with it after Dr. Carriol has gone. And get me the President on the phone now."

Mrs. Taverner paled. "Sir, do you think you ought? It's nearly four in the morning!"

"*Is* it? Well, too bad. Wake him."

"What shall I tell the aide on duty?"

"Something, anything, I don't care! Just do it!"

Mrs. Taverner fled. Dr. Carriol rose, poured the coffee and the cognac and put the Secretary's in front of him before returning to her chair.

"I didn't realize it was so late. I must get back to him. Damn the crowds! If you don't mind, I'll arrange to go back by helicopter. And I think it would be best to get Dr. Christian straight into the helicopter—before dawn, if possible—and down to Pocahontas Island. He's used to traveling with Billy, our pilot, so it won't alarm him. I'll go with him, of course. The medical team can meet us at Pocahontas. At the rate I'm going they'll make it there before us anyway. At least they will if you get moving." This last was minatory.

"I can assure you, Dr. Carriol, that I intend to get moving! It is no part of my plan to endanger Dr. Christian's life," he said with great dignity. He picked up his brandy balloon, grimacing at the small amount of liquid Dr. Carriol had poured into its bottom. "I like my drinks Texas style," he said, drained the glass in a gulp and held it out. "A decent one, if you please."

His secretary buzzed while Dr. Carriol was busy with the decanter.

"Sir, they're wakening Mr. Reece. He'll call back."

"All right. Thanks." He took several rapid gulps of his replenished cognac. "You'd better get going, Judith."

She looked at the clock behind him and pulled a face. "Hell! It will be five before I get back, even by helicopter. Just as well double daylight savings has put the dawn back quite a bit. Now don't forget to instruct the medical team properly, and tell them they will be met at Pocahontas Island by their patient. Oh, we had better have someone along who can deal with a diesel generator."

"Dammit, you're worse than my wife! Stop fussing! The place will be in perfect working order—hell, they're expecting the President to look it over! God Jesus, will I be glad when this zoo is a thing of the past!"

"Me too, Mr. Magnus. Thank you. I'll keep you informed."

As she left him, Harold Magnus was on his feet pouring a third cognac, and preparing to light up another thigh-rolled cigar.

In the outer office she paused by Mrs. Taverner's desk to call Billy and arrange that he meet her at the Capitol helipad. "How I wish Environment had a pad!" she said as she hung up. Then she looked at Mrs. Taverner closely. "You are absolutely beat!"

"I am indeed. I haven't been home since Dr. Christian left New York City."

"Literally?"

"Yes. Well, Mr. Magnus has been at the White House, so someone's had to keep things going, and you know him. He's never been one to trust deputies or delegate authority."

"He's a bastard. Why do you put up with him?"

"Oh, he's not so bad when things are nice and calm. And this is one of the few top-graded secretarial positions in the federal service."

"You'd better go in to him—but not until after he gets his call from the President, okay?"

"Okay. Good night, Dr. Carriol."

Four in the morning, thought Harold Magnus, drinking his third cognac at a gulp. He blinked, yawned, his head swimming. Shit. Brandy never went to his head! Oh, God help him if things continued to go wrong! He didn't feel his best, he really didn't. Too much candy, not enough proper food. But fuck the doctors, he did *not* have diabetes! Four in the morning. No wonder he wasn't feeling his best. No dinner. Fuck Dr. Judith Carriol. Fuck Dr. Joshua Christian. Fuck the doctors. Fuck everything. Thinking about doctors and his own state of health made him remember Dr. Christian's plight. He reached to buzz Mrs. Taverner to come in and take her instructions. But she beat him to it; she buzzed first.

"Mr. Reece is on the line, sir. He doesn't sound happy."

The President wasn't happy. "What the hell are you waking me up for?" came his voice, sleepy and crotchety.

"Well, Mr. President, if I am kept awake and from my dinner by the state of the nation, why the hell should you sleep? It's your nation, not mine!" he said, and giggled.

"Harold? That is you?"

"Mi mi mi mi mi mi! Of course it's me!" sang Mr. Magnus. "It's four A.M. and I'm a gem!"

"*You* are drunk."

"God Jesus, I must be!" The Secretary fought hard to regain some control. "I apologize, Mr. President. It's been too long between food and this brandy is all. I'm sorry, sir, I am truly sorry."

"You had me wakened to tell me you're drunk and hungry?"

"Of course I didn't. We have a problem."

"Oh?"

"Dr. Christian isn't walking. I've had Dr. Carriol here this morning, and she tells me he's mortally ill. So it looks like the March of the Millennium is going to have to end without its leader."

"I see."

"However, the rest of the important marchers are in good shape, so with your permission I intend to let them lead the March in. Oh, with his family right in front, naturally! But we need someone to give Dr. Christian's oration, and I think it can be none other than you."

"Yes, I agree. You had better come to the White House later this morning, say at eight. I'll arrange to get Dr. Carriol here too.

I want to find out what's the matter with poor Dr. Christian for myself. And, Harold, lay off the sauce, will you? It's a big day today."

"Yes, sir. Of course, sir. Thank you, sir."

Gratefully the Secretary for the Environment cradled his receiver. His head wouldn't stop going round, he felt really dreadfully ill, he was so druggily tired he fancied he might never be able to get up from his desk. And without knowing he actually did so, he laid his head, so heavy, so dizzy, so glutted with sugary blood, so exhausted, he laid his head down on his desk and he slept immediately. Or rather he passed into the altered state of consciousness indicative of a very severe hyperglycaemia.

In the outer office Mrs. Taverner's desk was empty. She had taken advantage of the President's phone call and visited her private rest room. On the way out again she thought she might just sit down on the edge of her couch for a moment, because her legs were shaking with a mixture of exhaustion and frayed nerves. But the sitting became lying. She fell at once into a dreamless sleep.

Somehow on the previous night Dr. Christian had felt he must make an effort, must spend a little time with his dearly beloved family. He knew he had neglected them badly ever since *God in Cursing* was published, he knew he had been grossly unfair in his treatment of them; it was not their fault that the practice and the clinic in Holloman had disintegrated, it was his fault. Yet he had blamed them. And he had grown out—not of loving them, maybe, but certainly of liking them. Poor things, so desperately dependent upon him, so eager to please him, so pathetically cast adrift by his conduct since they had all gathered in New York City to support him.

So he had made the effort, sat and talked to them, even laughed and joked a little. He ate the food Mama plied him with, he gave words of advice to James and Andrew and Miriam, he smiled with special sweetness on the little Mouse, and he even tried to conciliate Mary. Alone among them she did not like him, he was really not sure why; but he admitted there were many possible reasons.

Oh, he had paid for giving them those hours! Was it just the food that sat undigested and lumpish in his belly, was it just the food he had to vomit up? Or was it them as well? The pain of bringing it up was excruciating, the act unendurably long. How could one love one's executioners? How could one love one's betrayer? Between lying down and sleeping he asked himself those and other questions over and over again, but thought was ever-increasingly difficult and he knew himself to be wandering in strange mental lands.

Sleep had not come until after Dr. Carriol got up and left him. He couldn't sleep with her watching, so he feigned it. Only after she was gone did he work his little personal miracle, will sleep to come. And admit that ever since she had begun to minister to him he had been more comfortable, better equipped to deal with the nightly upsurge of pain.

He slept very freely and deeply and contentedly until four in the morning, like a last sleep; no dreams came to plague him, no sounds penetrated.

But not very many minutes after four o'clock he rolled over and squashed his right arm up against his side, compressing the tennis-ball-sized mass of unrelieved necrosis in that axilla; it tried to condense itself out of the way without success, swilled around the great nerve-laden arterial trunk that supplied his right arm and hand with blood, swilled around the great bundle of fibers that supplied his right arm and hand with feeling and movement, and both these swollen infected ropes of tissue screamed in agony.

He leaped to sit bolt upright in his bed, the huge cry swallowed in his throat before it could howl out of his gaping mouth, and he rocked himself back and forth and back and forth in sweating horror, so transfixed with agony that for perhaps ten minutes he wondered if it was possible for a human life to snuff itself out from pure pain.

"My God, my God, take this away from me!" he whimpered then, rocking back and forth, back and forth. "Haven't I already suffered enough? Don't I know I am only a mortal man?"

But the pain rolled on and on. He catapulted from the bed to walk the floor in a frenzy, his bare black festering toes unable to guide his feet along a steady path. And so afraid was he of screaming aloud that in the end he knew he must find a place to go where a scream would not matter.

Like a shadow he passed through the darkness of the outer canvas room, into the night. Limping and staggering, stopping each few agonized paces to rock his pain like a baby.

A tree reared up in his path; he reached out to grab it, held on to it, slid slowly down it until he crouched on the grass at its spreading base, and there he held his arms around his head, rocking back and forth.

"My God, grant me tomorrow!" he gasped, fighting, fighting. "Not over yet! Only tomorrow! My God, my God, do not leave me, do not forsake me!"

Though it may not be possible to die from pure pain, it is certainly possible to become demented from pure pain. Crouching there at the base of the tree, Dr. Joshua Christian yielded up his reason. So gladly! So gratefully! So very easily, now he no longer had the strength to struggle. He went quite mad. Mad in the fullest sense of the word. Free at last of the chains of logical thought, emancipated at last from the fetters of conscious will, he floated into a perfect and blissful limbo of unreason, of madness, racked at last beyond endurance, an animal creature huddled there in touch with the earth that was formed and firm, warm and welcoming as his mother.

I never want to see another helicopter again as long as I live, thought Dr. Judith Carriol as her vehicle approached the temporary helipad marked out in the grass of the park just comfortably outside the palisaded compound in which the various Christians and governmental dignitaries were accommodated.

An expert by now, she leaped from the grass bubble and ran across the grass without waiting more than a second after the pontoons touched the ground. In the act of entering the tent she stopped, realizing she would never find the light mechanism; she retreated back outside, turning toward the perimeter of the compound. The high palisade was policed by a hundred men.

"Sentry!" she called.

"Ma'am?" He loomed out of the darkness.

"I need a flashlight."

"Yes, ma'am." He disappeared.

Half a minute later he was back, a flashlight beam bobbing up and down in time to his smart steps. With a snappy salute of respect he handed it to her and went back to his post, where a small dim puddle of light on the ground gave him his point of reference.

With the flashlight held well down toward the wooden floor, Dr. Carriol passed silently through the tent, and peeled the flap across Dr. Christian's private cubicle away. The scant furnishings within slid uneasily in and out of the enveloping blackness as she directed the beam uncertainly toward the bed. There! The light came gliding up a leg, spilled across the tossed heap of coverings. He wasn't there! He wasn't in his bed!

For a moment she stood not knowing which was best, to flood the whole damned tent with light, thereby rousing everybody, or to commence a stealthy systematic search. The decision came in seconds, disciplined and cool. If he was cracking she had to get him out quietly, before anyone understood what was the matter. Mama was pretty close to cracking herself. Yes, too close to the wire now to risk bringing it all down.

So she prowled the tent in absolute silence, roving back and forth across every foot of it with her flashlight, into every backroom cranny, under the tables, behind the chairs. He was not there. He was not inside at all.

"Sentry!"

"Ma'am?"

"Would you fetch me the officer of the watch, please?"

He came five minutes later, five minutes during which she waited in static panic, steeling herself not to move.

"Ma'am?" He leaned closer. "Oh, Dr. Carriol!"

Major Withers himself. That was a break. "Thank God for a familiar face!" she said. "Major, you understand that I have Presidential authority, do you not?"

"Yes, ma'am."

"Dr. Christian is missing from his bed, and he is not in the Christian tent anywhere. You may take my word for that. Now it is absolutely imperative that no fuss be made, that no hint be given to any other occupant of this compound that we have trouble. But we have to find Dr. Christian! Quickly and quietly and with no more light than we can help. When we do find him, I want no attempt made to approach him. No matter who finds him, I want that man to report immediately to me. *Only* to me! I am going to stand here without moving, exactly where I am now, so I can be located without delay. Understood?"

"Yes, ma'am."

Again a wait, a long and painful wait, with the precious minutes galloping away into the coming dawn. Once she looked down at her watch by the light of the flashlight, and saw that it was nearly six. O God in heaven, let them find him! Let him not be out there on the other side of the palisade among the crowd! She

294

had to get him away before the compound woke up, before the people outside woke up. Helicopters coming and going were bad enough. Thank God in this power-deprived day and age for two-hour daylight saving! They had a few more minutes before it became light enough to see. Across the grass little jerky jets of light flickered in and out of shrubbery and trees as a hundred men moved through the darkness.

"Ma'am?"

She jumped. "Yes?"

"We've found him."

"Oh, thank God for that!"

She followed after the major with her shoes hushing in the grass, *shish shish, shish shish,* quick and flawless in their rhythm. Good girl, Judith! You're calm. You'll save it yet. Just keep calm no matter what they've found.

The major pointed into the blackest patch of shrubbery.

She approached slowly, not playing her light around in case it frightened him.

There he was! Huddled at the base of a great beech tree with his head wrapped in his arms, very still. She came up to him and knelt down beside him.

"Joshua? Joshua, are you all right?"

He didn't move.

"It's Judith. What is it? What's the matter?"

And he heard her. He heard a well-known human voice and understood that he was not yet dead, that this vale of tears was still his for the taking. But did he want to take? No! He smiled secretly into his arms.

"I hurt," he said, like a child.

"I know. Come!" She slid her hand in under his left elbow, and got both of them to their feet quite easily.

"Judith? Who is this Judith?" he asked, looking at her. Then he looked beyond her to where the dim thready outlines of a dozen men towered against a sky that dreamily cherished the first tiny hint of daybreak.

"It is time to walk," he said, remembering the only fact he had carried from sanity into madness with him.

"No, Joshua, not today. It's over! The March of the Millennium is over! This is Washington. Now it's time for you to rest and be healed."

"No," he said, more strongly. "Walk! I walk!"

"The streets are too crowded to walk, it's impossible." She no longer knew the right things to say to him, she could not follow his thoughts.

He stood stubbornly still. "I walk."

"Then how about walking with me a little way, just as far as the fence? After that you can go off on your own, okay?"

He smiled, began to obey, smelled her fear, and backed off. "No! You're trying to trick me!"

"Joshua, I wouldn't do that to you! I'm Judith! You know me, I'm Judith! Your own Judith!"

"Judith?" he asked, his voice rising incredulously. "No! Judith? No! You're Judas! Judas come to betray me!" And he began to laugh. "Oh, Judas, most beloved of all my disciples! Kiss me, show me it's over!" He began to weep. "Judas, Judas, I want it to be over! Kiss me! Show me it's over! I cannot endure this pain. This waiting."

She bent forward and hovered on tiptoe with her face an inch from his cheek, her eyes closed, almost tasting the smell of his skin, which was stale and malodorous. Then her lips made the last enormous journey, and came to rest at one side of his mouth, his mouth bitten to shreds. "There," she said. "It is over, Joshua."

And it was over. The only kiss he had ever asked her for. What might have happened to Judith Carriol and Joshua Christian if he had wanted to kiss her? Probably nothing different.

It was over. He held out his hands to the soldiers. "I am betrayed," he said. "My own beloved disciple has betrayed me to my death."

The men moved forward, surrounded him. He began to walk in their midst. Then he turned to where she followed, and said, "How much did they have to pay you in this day and age?"

Over. Over. Over. "A promotion. A car. Independence. *Power!*" she said.

"I could offer you none of those."

"Oh, I don't know. They're all thanks to you, really."

Through the trees and bushes. Out of the palisade to the waiting helicopter, blades whipping idly. One man leaped in first and held out his hands to Dr. Christian, who took them and made the upward step easily with his long legs; the man leaned over him and buckled him securely into half the back seat, shoulders and hips, a good restraint harness, actually. Billy had been waiting with his engine turning over ever since she had alighted, thinking she would only be gone a very few minutes, and aware that to start the engine afresh would make more noise than idling and then taking off.

Dr. Carriol waited until the man in the back seat jumped out, then prepared to climb in herself. In midstep she detained the soldier, gestured him back into the helicopter. "I might need you, Private. Buckle in beside Dr. Christian, would you? I'll go up front with Billy."

A captain came running across the grass, pushed between the soldiers and ducked up to the helicopter. "Dr. Carriol!"

She leaned out, impatient to be gone. "What's up?"

"Message from the White House, ma'am. Been waiting for you for some time. The President wants to see you in the White House at eight on the dot."

Damn! What next? Her watch said six-thirty, it was now quite light, and the crowds some distance off (kept off deliberately) were stirring, their rest terminated by the noise of the helicopter. She swung round to face the pilot. "Billy, how long will it take us to get where we're going?"

He had brought the appropriate charts with him from his base, so his course was plotted. "Gotta gas up first, ma'am. Sorry, I would have gone and done it already, but I kept thinkin' you must be comin' any second. So—oh, about an hour, I guess. Half an hour comin' back, plus whatever time you wanna spend on the ground."

Ten minutes on the ground at Pocahontas Island at least, more very likely. What to do, what to do?

Ambition won. Sighing, she unlatched her harness and swung her legs out of the bubble. "Billy, you'll have to take Dr. Christian down on your own and then come back for me." Frowning, she turned her head to study Dr. Christian, who sagged limply, eyes closed, held upright by his harness. The soldier with him in the back seat. Could he be trusted? Would Joshua stay quiet, or would he have another fit of wanting to walk? Would he become violent? Maybe she ought to send Major Withers instead. She looked down at the small group of men and studied the major's face as intently as she had Dr. Christian's, saw something she didn't really like in it. The captain, then . . . No. No. Back to the private already strapped in. A strong lad, in training. Good enough at his age to have been picked for this VIP guard assignment. Quiet and steady face. What lay behind it? Was he discreet? Oh, for God's sake, woman, decide! Decide! The medical team would undoubtedly already be there, of course, that was a help. Yes, of course, of course . . . It was only a matter of the journey down. He'd be all right.

"Billy," she said to the pilot, "you'll have to go without me, I daren't risk being late to see the President. Get Dr. Christian down to the rendezvous as soon as you possibly can, okay? Find the house I told you about and put your bird down as close as you can get to it." She turned to the soldier. "Can I trust you, Private?"

He stared at her out of wide grey eyes. "Yes, ma'am."

"All right, then. Dr. Christian is sick. We're taking him to a special place for treatment. He's physically ill, not mentally ill, but he's in such terrible pain he's a bit deranged—only temporary, you understand. I want you to look after him on the way down. And when Billy lands I want you to escort Dr. Christian to the house there. Don't wait to scout around; the less you see, the better for yourself. There will be doctors and nurses waiting for Dr. Christian. So just take him to the house and then get the hell out. Got it?"

He looked as if he was prepared to die to bring off this most important mission of his life successfully; and probably for the chance to ride in a helicopter.

"Got it, ma'am," said the soldier. "I am to look after Dr. Christian on the flight, then escort him to the house. I am not to wait. I am not to look around. I am to go straight back to the bird."

"Good man!" She smiled at him. "Not a word to a soul, even your commanding officers. Orders of the President."

"Yes, ma'am."

She gave Billy an affectionate pat on the arm and climbed out. Then, leaning into the back of the craft, she touched Dr. Christian on the knee.

"Joshua?"

He opened his eyes and gazed down at her; a vestige of sad sweet reason flickered, went out.

"You'll be fine now, my dear. Believe me, you are going to be fine! Sleep if you can. And when you wake up, it will all be over. You can start to live again. Nasty old Judas Carriol will be out of your life forever."

He made no answer, seemed not to know she was there.

She swung round and ducked out of range of the rotors, then stood with the soldiers as the helicopter lifted itself off the ground in its languid, death-defying fashion. It ascended very slowly to about two hundred feet, clear of every obstacle in the vicinity, then the turbine engines began to shriek, and it shot forward, jet-propelled.

Dr. Carriol suddenly realized that the ring of silent men around her was gazing at her with that curiously wooden expression well-trained troops adopt at the inexplicable gyrations of High Command. She set her lips.

"Nothing happened here this morning," she said. "I mean *nothing*. You've seen nothing, you've heard nothing. And that order will change only if your new orders come from the President. Understood?"

"Yes, ma'am," said Major Withers.

Billy the pilot looked at his fuel gauge, did a swift calculation, and nodded. He loved Dr. Christian. All those months of ferrying him around the country had cemented his awe and admiration for this incredible and incredibly nice man. They never seemed to understand how hard it was on the poor guy, plodding from one place to another without a break. So here he was getting his break at last, but too late to be in shape to finish what he started. However, Billy figured there was one final good turn he could do Dr. Christian before their paths diverged. There was fuel at Hatteras, it was a defense-warning station. So he could go straight on down to this Pocahontas Island, give Dr. Christian over into medical care for his much needed and long overdue rest, then he'd fly on to Hatteras and gas up there instead of farting around forever filling out forms at one of the bases down along his route.

"Cheer up, Doc!" he shouted over his shoulder. "We'll get you there quick as a shake of an ant's dick!"

Dr. Carriol trudged across the grass toward the Christian tent, her feet obeying her; wonderfully obedient feet she had! They traipsed one after the other to the entrance flap, they led her rocking through it, and into a tiny crowd of waiting Christians.

Mama pounced first, trembling. "Judith, Joshua is gone! He's started the March without us!"

Dr. Carriol plodded to the first chair, sank into it and looked up at them, eyes glazed with weariness, face haggard. This morning she looked her age. "Martha, honey, is there any hot coffee? I must have something stimulating to drink, or I'll never last the distance."

Martha went to a table where a steaming carafe stood, poured a mug full and gave it to Dr. Carriol. She did the task it seemed grudgingly, face sullen; ever since setting eyes on Joshua again in New York City she had been different, looking at Dr. Carriol with loathing as this outsider took complete charge of Joshua, shutting *them* out.

"Mama, sit down," said Dr. Carriol gently, sipping at the fluid in her mug and wincing. "Ow! That's hot!" She leaned forward limply. "I'm afraid Joshua hasn't started without you, it's you who must start without him. He's all right, but he's ill. I've known it ever since New Brunswick, but he wouldn't listen to reason and I felt I couldn't betray him—" She broke off, remembered pain pouring through her. Betray. He had called her Judas. Insane he might be, but still it hurt. Betray. Was that what she had done all those months and months ago in frozen Hartford? She tried the treacherous—oh apt adjective!—word again, stumbled again. "Betray him." No, she was *not* going to cry. Never cry. "He wanted to walk. And I let him. You know Joshua. He wouldn't be talked out of it, and he wouldn't let me tell anyone else. But this morning he—he—he just wasn't able to walk any more. So the President has set up a special hospital for him alone, where he can be treated and rest in absolute peace and quiet. I've just shipped him off by helicopter."

Mama cried, of course; Mama had done a lot of crying in the months since she arrived in Mobile to be with Joshua, share his triumph. She would have done better by herself to have stayed in Holloman. Mary wouldn't have done all that fruitless and impotent suffering. That fresh beauty of hers had diminished little by little to the middle-aged relics of perfect bones; nothing much was left now to suggest how dazzling and young she had been a year ago. *Only a year ago?*

"Why didn't you tell us?" asked Mama through her tears.

"Mama, I wanted to, believe me! I've not kept him from you for kicks, or to suit some design of my own. He has always dictated our behavior, including mine. He didn't even want me to find out he was ill. What I do know is that more than anything he wants you to finish the March for him. Will you?"

"Of course," said James gently. Dear, gentle James!

300

"It goes without saying," said Andrew stiffly.

But Martha turned into a tigress. "I want to go to him! I insist on going to him!"

"That is quite impossible," said Dr. Carriol. "Joshua is in a special hospital under Presidential security. I'm sorry, but what goes for Mama must go for you too, Martha."

"This is some plot!" cried the young woman fiercely. "I don't believe a word you've told us! Where is he? What have you done with him?"

Andrew got up quickly. "Martha, stop being silly. Come with me at once."

She began to weep, but her husband was scant of sympathy; he grasped her hand by the arm and marched her into their own cubicle, where everyone else, uncomfortable, could hear her weeping and protesting more and more desperately.

Andrew came out. "Sorry," he said, and looked toward his sister. "You pipe down too. Enough! Not a word! Go and cry on Martha's shoulder if you must, but don't stay here looking like a dying duck in a rainstorm!"

Mary turned and left immediately; and within moments Martha's stormy grief was quieter, the two voices, one teary and hiccoughing, the other low and tender, merging indistinctly.

Dr. Carriol sat blinking, intrigued despite her exhaustion.

"It's all right, Judith," said Andrew, sitting down next to Mama and taking her hand. "Martha has always had a bit of a crush on Joshua, you know, and it makes her very silly occasionally. As for Mary—well, Mary is Mary."

"It's none of my concern," said Dr. Carriol feebly, and tried her coffee again to find it cooled enough to drink. "I'm just terribly glad you've all taken this so well, and that goes for Martha too. I can't blame her. It must look as if I've usurped family authority in dealing with Joshua."

"Nonsense!" said James, his arm about Miriam, who didn't bounce or say much these days. "We've just expected that when all of this is over, you and Joshua will marry. Which does give you many rights."

It didn't seem worthwhile to disillusion them, so she merely nodded and smiled her thanks.

"What about me?" wailed Mama. "*I* can't march! And I don't feel right, sneaking in on the last day in a car!"

"Then how about if I set up a ride for you in one of the television vans?" asked Dr. Carriol. "That way you'll be at the speaker's platform first. So you can take your seat next to the King of Australia and New Zealand and look him right in the eye."

This suggestion appealed, but couldn't console her. "Oh, Judith, why can't I go to Joshua? I wouldn't be in the way, I promise I wouldn't! Haven't I been good all these months, just as you told me? Please! Oh, *please!*"

"The moment he's well enough to be moved to some place less security-mad than where he is now, you'll see him and you'll be with him, I promise. Be patient, Mama. I know you're very worried, but, honestly, he couldn't be in better hands."

Major Withers saved them a lot more of the same from Mama when he poked his head around the tent entrance flap. "Dr. Carriol, your chopper is waiting."

Dr. Carriol dragged herself to her feet, anxious to be anywhere except where she was. "I have to go. The President wants to see me urgently."

And even as she said those magical words and watched their effect on the Christians, she felt a small thrill of pride in her accomplishments.

But there was one more thing to do; she looked across not at James but at Andrew, who seemed to have assumed the senior role in the Christian family now that Joshua was *hors de combat*.

"I should tell the VIPs that Joshua won't be leading the March this morning," she said. "Andrew, you'd better come with me and talk to them as well."

He moved to her side at once, but glanced back to James and Miriam and Mama. "It's better if Martha doesn't march," he said to them. "Mary can take her back to Holloman on the train today."

James nodded sadly.

"If they can wait here for a couple of hours, I can most likely set up a helicopter for them," said Dr. Carriol, anxious to make what amends she could.

But Andrew shook his head positively. "No, thank you, Judith. It's best they take the train. The last thing my wife needs is to sit around for half a day nursing her grudges. And I might say the same for my sister. Coping with the train will keep them occupied, and the long ride home will cool them off. The only thing I'd ask is if they could have a car to take them to the station."

And that was obviously that.

302

XII

Dr. Carriol need not have worried. The passenger strapped into the back seat gave no trouble to his fascinated escort, or to Billy. Quietly he sat with his head hanging and his eyes closed, not as if he slept, rather as if he waited in passive consent for something yet to come.

The miles passed away, and gradually in the pearly new sky the land below acquired features—little towns and villages, many fields, roads bereft of traffic. Gradually salt marshes and swamps crept into view, tossing seas of silvery plumes with arrow-straight tidal channels and exposed mud flats between; the occasional sight of a fishing boat lying on its side like a dying horse lent the scene an abandoned look, as if everything was present except people.

They flew over Kitty Hawk, where the Wright Brothers had made their pioneer flight, zoomed across the head of Albemarle Sound with the long thin sandy thread of land out to their left that held the Atlantic back, over a vast expanse of salt marsh and into the top waters of Pamlico Sound. Just south of Oregon Inlet the island came into view, a flat, lozenge-shaped piece of ground smothered in bald cypress.

Billy checked the chart spread out in his lap, overflew the island to verify that it was the correct shape and size, then did a run to locate the house. There it was, on the northern tip, in the

303

middle of a huge clearing. Bright green grass, domestic trees, a yellow rash of daffodils someone must once have planted in the days when daffodils bloomed in April, and a huge grey house.

An interesting-looking house, thought Billy idly. Made of some grey stone, with a grey slate roof. And it had a big grey courtyard in its front, enclosed by a high grey stone wall which embraced and became contiguous with the walls of the house. He eyed the courtyard curiously, wondering how it could possibly have a pattern to it, a crisscross herringbone paving far too large and straight to be flagging. Well, the soldier could tell him later. He dropped his bird as neat as you please about fifteen feet from the double wooden doors that cut the courtyard wall in half, and formed the only entrance to the house complex, as if in its early days it had fortified itself against siege.

"Okay, this is it!" he shouted into the back seat. "But make it snappy, will you, soldier? I'm awful low on fuel."

The private undid his belt and leaned over Dr. Christian, touching him gently.

"Sir! Dr. Christian, sir! We're here! If I get you out of this harness, do you think you can manage okay?"

Dr. Christian opened his eyes, turned his head to stare at the soldier, then nodded gravely. When his feet touched the ground he stumbled and fell, but the soldier was out behind him in a flash, scooping him up before his body actually made contact with the grass.

"Take it easy, sir. You just lean against the old bird here for a minute while I open them gates, okay?"

The soldier ducked and loped over to the gates, gave them an experimental push and stood back in satisfaction as they swung easily inward. He returned to the helicopter and took Dr. Christian's arm, pressing down on it to force that too-tall body to stoop sufficiently clear of the whipping rotors, then ushered his charge toward the gates.

"Get a move on, will ya?" screamed Billy behind them. "I don't dare stop this fuckin' thing, but we are just gonna make it to Hatteras!"

So the soldier increased his pace, and Dr. Christian kept up with him obediently. Ahead of them across the courtyard loomed a twelve-foot-high archway that receded in a short wide tunnel to what was obviously the front door. Not breaking his pace, the soldier got Dr. Christian to the single step below the door, and pounded on it.

"Hey!" he shouted. "Hey there inside, we're here!" He put a hand on the big brass handle that jutted from the extreme middle left of the door, and pushed it down. The door opened inward without a sound to reveal a long wide hallway, very white and stark and unadorned, its floor made of diamond-shaped black and white marble tiles with small red inlays at all their angles. A real bare-looking place was the soldier's thought, for classical simplicity was not familiar to him.

"Best of luck, Doc!" the soldier said, and gave Dr. Christian a friendly shove in the back that sent him stumbling up the step and into the hall, where he stood facing away from the soldier, looking around him in what seemed wonder.

"You just go on in, Doc," the soldier said. "They're in there waitin' for ya!"

At top speed the soldier turned and ran back across the courtyard, through the gates. A careful and properly trained man, he paused to shut the gates firmly, then leaped into the helicopter, which took off the moment Billy decided his only remaining passenger was far enough in not to fall out again.

"Okay?" he yelled, but this time with a fair chance of being heard, for the soldier had settled into the seat beside him and was preparing to enjoy the rest of what might be his last as well as his first helicopter flight; his unit was always moved by truck.

"I guess it's okay! I didn't see anyone, but I sure didn't hang around either!"

"Hey, kid, the flagging in the courtyard!" Billy yelled. "What's it made of, huh?"

The soldier stared, then laughed. "Shit, man, I was in such a hurry I never looked!"

On thundered the helicopter, sou-sou-east for Hatteras, scant miles away. Below them the pellucid waters of Pamlico Sound shimmered, sliding and changing.

"Wow!" roared the soldier suddenly, peering down, his face awed. "Holy shits, will you look at them fish?"

A school of large black streamlined shapes was moving beneath the surface of the water, not as fast as the thing in the sky above them, but very fast, as if even in their swimmy world they

305

could hear the thing above them, and it was a pterodactyl predator big enough to dive snatching for them, gobble them up.

Billy and the soldier were so busy trying to work out whether they were sharks or dolphins or mini-whales that they didn't notice one of the great rotor blades shear itself off and scream at a thousand miles an hour away from them and the fish, arcing its way down a flat trajectory to the sea with the lethal efficiency of a discus. The bubble in the sky jerked, shuddered enormously, and fell. It was only a short distance, perhaps two hundred feet. A rotor blade tip hit the water first, flipped the little craft upside down and spun it reeling along the surface like a skipping stone. When it stopped, it didn't stop, it was still traveling far too fast in a downward direction. So it merely cleaved its way cleanly beneath the water, ploughed up and then burrowed into the sea bed, and settled amid a cloud of dust and sand and weed, buried from all inquisitive eyes. Neither man emerged to pop to the surface, which skittered in a little wind and kept its secrets, licking at itself like a satisfied cat.

The hall was very cold, and so glaringly white that Dr. Christian shut his eyes for a moment before tilting his head to look up. Above him the ceiling was not a ceiling but a great curving canopy of milky glass that welcomed the entry of a pure pale light, sending bars of black shadow to muddle the perfect geometry of the floor from its dark supporting rib cage of steel. There was no staircase, only four arches down each long pristine wall, their recesses sealed by huge wooden doors that seemed black with a venerable age. At the very end of the hall was a white arched alcove, and in it stood a seven-foot-tall bronze statue, a late-Victorian copy of the Praxiteles "Hermes Holding the Infant Dionysos," the beautiful enigmatic face of the god looking out at nothing because no one had painted in his eyes, and on his curved arm there rode a sweet fat reaching baby, also blind. In front of them was a small square pool of aquamarine water, on which floated one perfect deep-blue water lily with a yellow throat and three serene green leaves.

"Pilate!" Dr. Christian called, his voice rolling and echoing. "Pilate, I am here! Pilate!"

But no one came. No one answered. The black doors stayed closed, the man-god and the baby-god stayed bronzely blind, the water lily shivered in suddenly vibrating air.

306

"*Pilate!*" he roared, and back roared his own voice, "-ilate -ilate -ilate!," dying away.

"Why do you wash your hands behind my back?" he sadly asked the statue, and turned and walked away through the still-open front door.

In the arched tunnel he gazed about, big-eyed, searching for the guards in mail and sandals and helmets, with pila at the ready, but they too were evading him.

"You're hiiiiiiiiiiiding!" he called coyly, and stooped, and pranced a little. "Come out, come out, wherever you are!" he sang, then chuckled away to himself, and capered clumsily.

Craven legionaries! They knew what was coming, that was why they stayed in hiding. No one wanted to shoulder the blame, not Jews, not Romans. That was the trouble. Always had been the trouble. No one ever wanted to shoulder the blame. So in the end, as ever, it had been left to him. He must shoulder it all, he must take the world on his back and carry it to his cross, there to die of its awful weight.

He ceased his dancing and prancing and walked unsteadily out into the courtyard, bare and drab and austere and grey. Grey its walls, grey its floor, grey the sky above it. Various shades of grey. Ah, but that was the *world!* He stood in the very center of the world, and it was grey in the end as it had been grey in the beginning, grey the color of no-color, grey the color of grief, grey the color of desolation, grey the color of the whole world.

"I am grey!" he announced to the greyness.

But being grey, it didn't answer. Grey was speechless.

"Where are you, my persecutors?" he cried.

But no one answered, and no one came.

He walked shivering in his wispy silk pajamas, for no one in Washington had thought to provide him with a coat. And the crusted blood between his thighs broke away against the fabric and let the meat below bleed an androgynous ooze; his bare feet dragged across the grey paving and left browning prints behind. The prints went first to one wall and then to the other, back to the house walls and out again into the middle of the courtyard, an aimless walk to an involuted Calvary that was nowhere save inside the greyness of his broken mind.

"I am a man!" he shrieked, and wept inconsolably. "Why will no one believe me? I am only a man!"

He walked. This way and that, he walked. And with every step he cried aloud, "I am a man!"

But no one answered, and no one came.

"My God, my God, why?" He tried to remember the rest of it, but couldn't, and decided it would do very well as it was, a simple simple question, the first question, the last question, the only question. "Why?"

But no one answered.

Against the wall where it joined the house on one side there was a small stone shed, its wooden door closed. And in there, he suddenly knew, they all were hiding. Every last one of them. Jews and Romans, Romans and Jews. So he crept shuffling stealthily across to it, noiselessly unlatched the door, and flung it inward with a cry of triumph.

"I caught you, I caught you!"

But no one was inside hiding. The shed was almost empty. It held some shelving on which rested a few tools, all new-looking: several hammers, a big spike mallet, a set of chisels, two saws, two short lengths of heavy chain, a single-bladed axe, some long iron rail-tie spikes, some nails, a coil of stout rope, a big pocket knife left carelessly open, another coil of rope, but much thinner, almost like twine. There were gardening implements too, but these were much older than the tools, relics not of the recent repairs but of the days when this house knew much laughter from many children. And resting against the far end wall from the door were six or seven wooden beams, each the same size and shape. About eight feet long, a foot wide, and six inches deep.

He had stumbled on the place where indeed in days gone by the gardener had kept his treasures, and where too the owners of the house had stored a few spare wooden beams, in case the peculiar flagging of the courtyard ever needed to be repaired. For the courtyard was paved with ancient wooden railroad ties, laid with their narrow sides down in a perfect herringbone pattern. It was wonderful flagging, for the wood was so hard it was not susceptible to rot during its useful life on the rail bed; when the seas threatened to overrun the island in the great king-tide storms which happened once or twice in every lifetime, this flagging would endure. And the salt had soaked into the fiber of the wood and helped to petrify it, so that never had it actually been necessary during the tenanted years of the house to use any of the spare ties. These spare ties, nearly two hundred years old, had not fared so well, sheltered from the annealing salt spray by the dim little shed; they had softened, and at last were beginning to decay.

Dr. Christian gazed at the beams, and understood. Not for him the solace of companionship, not for him a stout, Roman-made, well-engineered cross, and a helping hand onto it. He was doomed to do it all alone. The silent absent accusing crowd had sentenced him to crucify himself.

The ties were dreadfully heavy, but he could manage to move them. First he dragged one out into the courtyard, then another, and laid them down on the selfsame wooden paving to form a T. He returned to the shed and took the spikes, the iron spike mallet, the hammers, the axe, the chisel and two saws. His idea was to weld the ties together at the junction of the T by driving several spikes through at an angle from one tie to the other. But it couldn't be done. The moment he positioned his spike and drove down with the mallet, the recoil from the blow pushed the two beams apart.

For five minutes after he gave up this plan he just stood howling and wailing, plucking at his spiky hair, his ears, his runny nose, his gaping mouth.

Then he set out to cut one beam down at its top end, halving its thickness there in a rabbet, from six inches down to three inches. Using the bigger of the two saws, he cut a narrow groove through the top three inches of wood a foot below the end of the beam. Then he took hammer and chisel and split the wood away between the groove he had made with his saw and the end of the tie. It worked, for the grain of the wood was with him, but it was so slow, and it hurt. The axe might do the job better and faster. He picked it up and swung it. The head snapped off the handle immediately, flying to land with a huge clang some feet away, where it sat with its hollow handleless mouth laughing at him. No short cuts; for him, the hard way. Back he went to hammer and chisel, striking the broad flat end of the chisel with the hammer again and again, chipping long slivers of wood away. And so he fashioned a thinner end to that tie, a foot long and three inches deep.

The second beam was more difficult, for in this one he had to gouge a foot-wide rabbet midway down its length, in which he could lock the thinned end of the first beam, rabbet into rabbet. And he was in pain, he was in pain. It lanced through his armpits and his groin every time he drove down with the hammer on the chisel. The sweat ran down into his eyes and it stung and it burned, he bled from his poor split fingers into the fresh-hewn wood, and his toes where they braced his feet against the ground as he knelt stuck to it, and he knew if he looked he would see their bones. He didn't look. He wouldn't look.

But it was like all work. Work the great healer, work the panacea. Work took the mind off more ephemeral pain, it made dwelling upon one's wrongs impossible, it gave direction to confusion and it answered purpose. Work had true integrity. Work the curse was the greatest of all blessings.

He labored on, whimpering, sobbing, wandering an abyssal ocean of pain.

And in the end he had two beams, one with its middle section halved in thickness, the other with an end section halved in thickness. He laid the one with the middle rabbet on the ground and lifted the one with the thin end over it, and joined the two rabbets together simply by resting one tie on top of the other. He fixed them permanently together with two spikes, though swinging the mallet was one long curve of agony that pinned him on an axis of time eternal. And he brought the mallet down so hard and strong and true on the splayed ends of the spikes that when he was done he found he had nailed his cross to the paving beneath it. He wept then, kneeling and rocking back and forth, but after a little while he grew calmer, and applied the same will to this new horror that he had to walking through the depths of winter. He fetched the axe head, wedged it underneath his cross and hit its flat hollow rear with the mallet. The cross came away, shifting a few inches sideways with the force of the blow.

But now that he had made his cross he found that there was nowhere to take it, no convenient hole in the ground dug by a KP legionary with his Marius-issue shovel. No secure place where he could prop it against a wall and be sure it would not tumble over under his weight when he mounted it. Somewhere, somewhere . . . If he had made his own cross—and he had made his own cross—there had to be somewhere he could fix it upright.

He found his answer at the beginning of the arched tunnel which led to the front door. In the middle of the top curve there was a great iron hook, where maybe in the old halcyon days of tobacco and tobacco kings they might perhaps have hung a brazier or a beacon.

310

Back he went to his cross, picked up the axe head, wedged its blade deep into the join of his two interlocking rabbets midway between the two spikes holding the ties together. One blow from the mallet, and the axe head was embedded in the join so deeply even his weight plus the weight of all that wood could never budge it.

The thicker rope he cut with the pocket knife, making himself a loop by threading it through the handle hole in the axe head. He knotted it and reknotted it and knotted it again, then used the ten feet of rope still dangling from the knot to drag his cross over to the arch. The hemp bit into his shoulder like a dull blade, his back humped itself, his legs and his feet and his toes pushed, pushed, pushed, all to pull.

A chair. He couldn't go any further without a chair. Into the house, through one of the black wooden doors. Here was a dining room, with a black wooden table like a monks' refectory table, along each side of it a backless wooden bench. They were too heavy and too long; he could not manage to drag a bench through the doorway and turn it within the hall on his own, not now that his purpose was nearing its end, and his fevered burst of strength was dying too.

In the fifth room he entered he finally found what he was looking for, a low backless stool, very big and square of seat, but only about fifteen inches high; a good height for the doing, a bad height to reach the iron hook. Getting the stool outside was so hard, took a long time considering the amount of time he had devoted to making his cross, a far harder task. His strength was running away. But he couldn't let himself be beaten now. Babbling and swaying, he called on all his last reserves, drumming his fists against his skinny sides in anguish, the tears running to join the sweat seeping into his writhing mouth.

Finally he positioned the stool beneath the hook in the tunnel entrance. And climbed upon it, and threw his rope's end through the curve of iron above.

The cross moved when he pulled on the rope, it came up off the ground at its top end where the T-junction was, and the buried axe head held without moving. Hauling on the rope, he stopped the upward progression of his cross while it still lay at an angle, knotted the rope to hold it there, and went to climb down from the stool. He fell, grabbing at the long vertical of the cross as it flashed by, then lay beneath it looking up at it, rocking uneasily.

"I am a man!" he said fretfully, levering himself slowly upright again.

In the shed he took the coil of thin twinelike rope and some of the nails and the pocket knife, still sprung from its sheath. Back to the cross. He drove two nails into each end of the horizontal top beam, first measuring the length of his arm against each side to ensure that the nails would sit on each side of a wrist. He bent the nails over outward, and fixed a loop of twine between them.

One last task, and all would be ready. Done the way it had surely been done in reality two thousand years before, almost to the day. No man's weight could be held by mere nails, his flesh and small bones would tear apart; the Romans didn't make simple physical mistakes like that. The occasional nail they might have used to immobilize, but they tied their condemned to their crosses. As he would tie himself.

He removed both top and bottom of the flimsy pajamas, humming a little under his breath in happy pain-racked triumph, for he had shown the hidden watchers how a man could do the impossible. Yes, he had shown them, Pilate and his tiny army of practical Roman clerks, the high priests and the synod, the people. Let them watch now! Let them see how a mortal man with no more god in him than any other man could make and go to his dying!

Standing on the ground, he finished hauling up his cross, and when it was fully upright the end of its vertical beam was neatly balanced on the wooden paving with which it was by nature one. He held the rope in his hand and clambered upon the stool; the cross was indeed so perfectly balanced that he didn't even need to steady it while he edged to stand on the stool, muscles groaning. The nether ends of the horizontal crosspiece just cleared the archway on either side. He hadn't considered the possibility that they might be too long, so finding now that they weren't was a confirmation of this most perfect of all patterns. Pulling the rope just taut, he wound it round and round itself in a hangman's noose, and knotted it securely. But he didn't cut off the surplus six feet of rope that still dangled from the end of the noose holding his cross to the iron hook.

He had positioned his stool this time so that it just brushed the front of the vertical upright. Facing his cross, he brought the

312

spare rope down behind the left-hand arm, pulled it through beneath the arm to the front of the cross, linked it very loosely over the front surface of the upright, pushed it back under the right-hand arm, and tied it with many knots to the left-hand side of the same rope. His cross now had a sagging piece of rope along its front just below the junction of the T.

He turned around to place his back against the wood and look out across the courtyard, then bent his knees and worked his head inside the loop of rope, tucking it securely under his chin before straightening up. With arms outstretched he slid his hands beneath the twine at each end of the crosspiece; these loops were far too loose to hold his arms without their sliding out the moment they had to take any weight. But he had reasoned that also in this most insanely logical of all madnesses. His fingers groped for and closed over the excess twine, and tightened it until it bit into the skin cladding his wrists.

"Into Thy hands I commend my spirit!" he cried out in a huge brazen voice, and kicked the stool away.

The whole weight of his body dragged down immediately upon those three pieces of rope, the one across his throat and the two at his wrists, and he let his body feel its weight. Oh the pain was not so bad! No worse than pressing his arms down on top of the massive lumps of pus at their roots. No worse than Judas Carriol's kiss. No worse than all those endless miles of walking, walking, walking. And oh so much easier to bear than the pain of the burden, the grief of his calling, the long sorrow his mortality had been. No the pain was not nearly so intolerable as that!

"I am a man!" he tried to declare, but man that he was, he could not for the rope which cut off speech and let only the thinnest trickle of air go down into his heaving laboring bursting lungs.

And in his tormented mind the courtyard filled with people. His mother was there, so beautiful, kneeling looking up at him with the marmoreal restraint of perfect sorrow. James and Andrew, Miriam and Martha. Mary. Poor, poor Mary. Tibor Reece and a fat man he knew was Harold Magnus. Senator Hillier and Mayor O'Connor and governors all. And Judas Carriol, smiling as she trickled a silver stream of perks and promotions from one serpentine hand to the other. The gates he looked directly at flew open with a clap of thunder, and there beyond stood all the men

313

and women and pitifully few children of the world with their hands stretched out to him, crying for him to save them.

"But I cannot save you!" he said to them within his slow, greying mind. "No one can save you! I am only one of you. I am a man. I am only a man. Save yourselves! Do that and you will survive. Do that and the race of Man will live forever!" And the last word he knew was "forever."

He died not from the rope around his neck but from the weight of his body dragging down so heavily as he wandered closer and closer to death and farther and farther away from consciousness of his burden, dragging down so heavily that he could not lift the webbed tissues on the bottom of his chest against this intolerable weight of himself, and so could not push the used-up air out of his lungs. He died gently asleep, a grey man on a grey cross in a little grey corner of the big grey world.

It rained a little, greyly, and washed away the blood that spattered him, put a sheen on his colorless grey skin.

He had been on the island for exactly three hours.

XIII

The last stage of the March of the Millennium began on that fine Friday morning in May with Andrew and James, Miriam between them, at the front of the cavalcade. They led the marchers out of the compound and into the road, followed by a bevy of waving, smiling governmental and military chiefs. No one had been too upset at the idea of stealing this last day's thunder from the absent Dr. Joshua Christian, which may have accounted for the sheer width of the smile on the face of Senator David Sims Hillier VII, who somehow had managed to place himself alone in the road just behind the remaining Christians, and several paces in front of anyone else.

All along the way as the people waited for the leading procession to pass by so they could tag on in its wake, the crowds gave that curious collective sound which is not a moan nor yet a sigh, but lies somewhere between. For Dr. Joshua Christian was not there, and grand as this climax was, it could not be the same without him.

Ever afterward in her more cheerful moments, Mama stoutly maintained that *she* led the March of the Millennium into Washington and down to the banks of the Potomac; for she was the most senior Christian of all, and she rode in the back of the ABC van as it ambled along in front, filming the faces and striding legs of the vanguard.

Exactly at eight Dr. Judith Carriol arrived at the White House and was shown immediately into the Oval Office, where Tibor Reece already sat watching his video monitors. The March was due to arrive at the specially constructed Vermont marble platform at noon sharp, so he had still several hours in hand before he would have to leave. He was sitting by himself.

"I'm sorry, Mr. President, I must be early," Dr. Carriol apologized when her eyes failed to find Harold Magnus.

"No, you're punctual as always, Doctor. May I call you Judith?"

She flushed, made a deprecating gesture with her hand, very gracefully and expressively and not at all reminiscent of snake or spider. "I would be honored, Mr. President."

"Harold is late. The March, no doubt. They tell me it's well-nigh impossible to move out there on the streets for the hordes of people everywhere." The President's dark mournful Christian-esque face lit up with amusement. "And I just can't see Harold Magnus walking, somehow."

"No, sir, nor can I," she said demurely. Dr. Christian's plight had slipped into the background of her thoughts, their forefront being taken up with the pleasantnesses she was at this moment drinking in. Thank you, Harold, for being late! I might never have got to see him alone otherwise. And I *like* him! Why couldn't Joshua have had his detachment and good sense? They're so alike in face and body. Still, a Tibor Reece couldn't achieve the oneness with his people that Joshua Christian did. The comparison is pointless and invalid.

"What a grand thing this has turned out to be," said the President warmly. "Truly the most memorable experience of my life, and I am humbled to think it happened during my incumbency." His Louisiana origins showed in his voice when he was moved, so he sounded suddenly very southern gentleman, the more recent California twang he had adopted to catch more votes quite gone. "There is so little an American President can do to show his appreciation to those who have served him so faithfully and well, Judith. I can't create a peerage for you like the Australians, I can't grant you a dacha and paid vacations at premier resorts like the Russians, I can't even overturn the ironclad rules of the federal public service by bumping you up a couple of grades overnight. But I do thank you, and I can only hope my thanks are enough."

316

His eyes, dark as Joshua's and as deeply set, rested upon her extremely affectionately.

"I've just done my job, Mr. President. I'm well paid for it, and I love doing it." God in heaven, which were the proper platitudes to mouth? And where the hell was Harold Magnus?

"Sit down, sit down, my dear girl! You look exhausted." The President of the United States of America fetched her a chair and handed her into it courteously. "A cup of coffee?"

"Sir, that I would appreciate more than a peerage!"

And he fetched it himself, on a small silver tray with creamer and sugar bowl alongside a big full china cup.

She drank it down thirstily and would have liked another, but didn't dare ask for it.

"I am very fond of Dr. Christian," Tibor Reece said, and sat down himself. "Please tell me about this illness."

She told him only as much as she thought he ought to know, therefore she was not nearly so frank as she had been to Harold Magnus; it was still more than enough to perturb the President, however, on a personal rather than a national level. This he confirmed when she had finished by saying:

"He came to see me at my invitation before *God in Cursing* was released, and I have rarely enjoyed an evening more than I did in his company. He is a *man!* I had a few personal decisions to make at the time, and he was a great help to me in making them, though in the one case he declined to offer positive help. Very intelligent of him! It was a decision I had to make, that no one else could have. But in the matter of my daughter—he put me onto exactly the right people to help her, and changed her life. She's doing about a thousand percent better now."

So that was what it had all been about! How amazing. All that spleen she had poured on Moshe Chasen, and for what? All that boredom too, dating Gary Mannering. Serves you right, Judith Carriol!

"Yes, that's Joshua," she said out loud.

"I remember that when his name came up as our choice for Operation Messiah—prophetic of you, Judith!—you implied that you and he had established a very close relationship. I am so sorry that you've had to bear the burden and the worry of his illness, as well as the March of the Millennium. And why didn't you let me know this morning that you were planning to accompany him for treatment? I would have understood."

"In retrospect I realize that, sir. But at the time it was—well, it was pretty hectic. Hard to make the right decision, so many things seemed to be happening. Still, he's in the best hands, and I'm flying to join him straight from here." And she let her large strange eyes look into his.

He cleared his throat, shifting his chair so he could see the video monitors more comfortably; she followed suit, and they sat watching the progress of the marchers through a bunting-decked, brilliantly sunny Washington. Waiting in vain for Harold Magnus.

By nine he hadn't come. Something was definitely wrong. Dr. Carriol got to her feet.

The President looked around at her, raising his brows.

"Mr. President, I would like to go across to Environment. It isn't like Mr. Magnus to be so late without letting anyone know. Would you excuse me?"

"I'll phone," he said, not about to tell her that at four o'clock that morning his Secretary for the Environment had been silly drunk.

"No, sir, you carry on watching. I'll go over." She had to get to Environment herself, because she knew something was wrong. Very wrong.

Of course there were people milling everywhere around the White House, waiting for the President to emerge. Dr. Carriol went to the helipad and asked her pilot to put her down as close to Environment as possible, preferably closer than the Capitol landing area. The pilot scratched his head, then elected to set her down in K Street right outside her entrance, hovering down slowly enough to permit the few people in the vicinity to scatter safely.

It was the greatest public holiday in the history of the country, so of course Environment was closed, but when she got up to Section Four she found little John Wayne at his desk, working busily.

"John!" she cried, tossing off her coat. "Have you seen or heard anything of Mr. Magnus?"

He looked up, looked blank. "No."

"Come on, then. He was supposed to be at the White House over an hour ago, and he hasn't turned up."

Mrs. Taverner's desk was unoccupied, the small telephone multi-line console on it flashing every light it could; Harold Magnus disliked bells, so it was not wired to ring. No doubt the White House was trying to get him too.

"Find Mrs. Taverner," she said to John Wayne curtly. "I believe she has a couch in her private rest room, so look there first and the hell with your natural modesty." She went on into Harold Magnus's office.

At some stage he had transferred himself, still hovering between sleep and coma, from his desk to the big comfortable sofa against the far wall. And there he lay on his back, one foot trailing off, a big old-faced dribbling snoring baby.

"Mr. Magnus!" She bent down to shake him. "*Mr. Magnus!*"

The level of sugar in his blood had been falling slowly during the hours between the last time Dr. Carriol had seen him and this moment, but it still took a good two minutes to rouse him.

Finally his lids lifted, fluttered, opened, and his eyes goggled up at her like two boiled skinned gooseberries, pale greenish grey.

"Mr. Magnus, will you wake up?" she asked for the twentieth time, tight-lipped.

The glaze in his gaze cleared gradually; at first he did not seem to recognize her.

"Shit!" he yelped suddenly, struggling to sit up. "God! Oh, God, I feel awful! What time is it?"

"Nine-thirty, sir. You were supposed to meet with the President at eight. He's still waiting for you, but he won't wait much longer. The March is due to end in a couple of hours, it's on schedule, and he'll be leaving on schedule."

"Shit! Oh, oh, double shit!" he whimpered, grinding his teeth. "Get me coffee! Where is Helena?"

"I don't know."

At precisely that moment John Wayne buzzed to tell her he had found Mrs. Taverner, and in what condition.

"Bring Mr. Magnus some coffee, would you?" Turning, she leaned against the edge of his desk, folded her arms, crossed her ankles, and watched her boss ironically as he sat on the edge of the sofa, pressing his fingers into his fat stubbly cheeks so deeply their tips quite disappeared.

"Didn't feel well," he mumbled. "S'funny! Just—passed out! Never done that before, even on ten drinks."

"Have you got a change of clothes here? Something suitable for the ceremony of the century?"

"Think so." He yawned enormously, eyes watering. "Uh! Gotta think! Gotta *think!*"

John appeared with the coffee.

"How's Mrs. Taverner?"

"She's all right. Contemplating suicide. She's never collapsed on the job before, she keeps telling me."

"Tell her in this situation my sympathy is entirely with her, and no job and no boss are worth killing yourself over. Why don't you send her home?"

As John went from the room Dr. Carriol bore a mug to the sofa and handed it to Harold Magnus, who drank it down black and sugarless at a gulp in spite of its heat. He held out the mug.

"More."

She obliged, pouring coffee for herself also.

This time he sipped it. "Oh, what a day! I still don't feel a hundred percent well."

"Poor old you!" said Dr. Carriol, not sympathetically. "I don't suppose you know that Mrs. Taverner passed out too? With a damned sight more justification, I might add! You flog that good kind loyal woman to death."

Perhaps luckily, there was a tap on the door. Mrs. Taverner appeared, looking bandbox neat; she had used ten minutes to best advantage.

"Thank you, Dr. Carriol, I will go home if Mr. Magnus will give me permission. There's only one thing—what do you want done about that list of doctors and equipment you gave me last night, ma'am?"

All the color fell out of Dr. Carriol's permanently colorless face, mocking at degrees. For a moment Mrs. Taverner thought the chief of Section Four was going to have an epileptic fit, for she went utterly rigid, her eyes rolling up in her head and her lips drawing back from her teeth; she even made strange and horrible noises in her throat. Then she struck so fast Mrs. Taverner did not see her cross the space between desk and sofa; she simply was there at the sofa. With one hand she lifted the bulk of the Secretary for the Environment clean off his behind, then put her other hand on his other arm, and shook him fiercely.

"Pocahontas Island!" she said. "The medical team!"

Her words sank in. "Oh—my—God! Judith, Judith, I didn't do it!"

"Get John," said Dr. Carriol to Mrs. Taverner. "And you can't go home now. We've got work to do." She brushed the Secretary away like a noisome insect and went back to the desk to pick up the phone, but before Mrs. Taverner made it through the outer door she was summoned back. "Helena, go outside and get me Walter Reed Hospital, the duty administrator."

Dr. Carriol knew by heart the number which connected her with the President's helicopter squad. She dialed it. "This is Dr. Carriol speaking," she said quietly. "Where is Billy?"

"Hasn't checked in yet, ma'am. Hasn't radioed either, and we can't raise him."

Her head was thumping. Or maybe it was her displaced heart? "He went on a special job for me at six-thirty this morning, but he should have been back in Washington by eight-thirty at the latest. However, he did say he had to refuel."

"We know, ma'am. We understand his destination was classified, but he requisitioned charts and possible fuel depots between Washington and Hatteras and Raleigh. We've already gone the whole route and he hasn't checked in anywhere to refuel yet. But no one's reported a May Day even on the ham bands, so we kind of assumed he must be landbound at his destination with an empty tank and a bum radio."

"Very likely, as he seems to have decided to do my job before refueling. If he did run out of fuel in midair he could get down safely, couldn't he? I seem to remember that actually happening in Wyoming a few months ago, when he was coming to pick us up."

"Oh, sure!" said the phone heartily. "That's the great thing about those birds, they can land anywhere. And he'd have enough warning to get down, ma'am."

"Then we must assume he's stuck at his destination rather than somewhere en route. There's not a soul where he was going and no telephone either, so if his radio isn't working he'd have no way to contact us." She glared across at Harold Magnus sourly. "Thank you. If you hear anything, let me know at once. I'm with the Secretary for the Environment in his office. No, no, don't get off the line yet, man! I need one helicopter big enough to carry about eight to ten people and several hundred pounds of medical equipment. Top priority. Hold it for me until I give you the word."

"Can't do it, ma'am," said the phone. "All available craft have been earmarked by the President himself for lifting VIPs down to the Potomac for the ceremony."

"Fuck the ceremony and fuck the VIPs!" said Dr. Carriol. "I want that helicopter."

"I'll need the President for this one," said the phone laconically.

"You'll get him. So start moving now."

"Yes, *ma'am!*"

Another line was flashing. "Yes?"

"Walter Reed, Dr. Carriol, the duty administrator."

She held the phone out to Harold Magnus. "Here, you take this one," she said curtly. "It's your mess."

While Harold Magnus spoke to the duty administrator at Walter Reed, huddling with Mrs. Taverner and John Wayne over the list Dr. Carriol had dictated some hours earlier, Dr. Carriol went into the outer office and asked to be connected with the President himself.

"Trouble, Judith?"

"Big trouble, Mr. President. We have an emergency situation. Dr. Christian apparently is stranded on Pocahontas Island in Pamlico Sound without the medical attention he should have had hours ago. Your helicopter squad can't provide me with a suitable craft to get this medical attention to Dr. Christian without your personal okay. The ceremony has swallowed all the craft in the area. Please will you get in touch with your squad HQ and okay my request for priority?"

"Hold on." She could hear him relaying instructions to someone, then he came back on the line. "What's up?"

"Mr. Magnus had a slight heart attack just after I left him in the early hours of this morning. I'm afraid it happened before he organized the medical attention I had arranged with him to be sent to Dr. Christian. God, that's about as clear as mud, but I guess you know what I mean. I'm going down to Pocahontas Island with the medical team immediately. There is definitely some kind of problem down there, because his helicopter pilot hasn't made contact with base since he left Washington at six-thirty this morning."

"So Harold had a heart attack, huh?" Was it her imagination, or did the President sound ever so faintly satirical?

"He collapsed in his office, sir. I've got an ambulance coming from Walter Reed."

"Poor old Harold!" This time the Presidential voice was blatantly sarcastic. "Keep me posted, will you? It's good to know there's someone in Environment with a level head."

Ouch, Harold! "Thank you, Mr. President."

Back into the inner office, where she waited for her chief to conclude his arrangements with Walter Reed.

"There, that's done!" he exclaimed, mildly jaunty now that things were getting back under control. "I can leave this mess with you from here on in, can't I? I've got to get changed for the ceremony."

"Oh, no!" said Dr. Carriol with steely calm. "I have just covered your great bare ass with the President by informing him you had a heart attack—minor only, of course—this morning. So you are going to look very sick, and be taken by ambulance to the Walter Reed Hospital as soon as I can spare someone to get it organized."

He did turn green and he did look very sick. "But I'll miss the King of England!" Then his expression became dangerous. "What did you want to run off at the mouth to the President for?"

"I didn't have any choice. There isn't a helicopter to run the medical team down to Pocahontas, so I had to have an executive order. That meant he had to know about the fuckup. Sorry, Mr. Magnus, but I did not create the fuckup. You did. So no ceremony, that's your punishment."

And never again, she thought, walking out to leave him and Mrs. Taverner and John Wayne gaping after her, never again will Harold Magnus be in a position to send my transportation away and leave me to wait ill clad in the snow for a bus.

By the time the big Army chopper took off from Walter Reed Hospital bearing Dr. Judith Carriol, Dr. Charles Miller (a vascular surgeon), Dr. Ignatius O'Brien (a plastic surgeon), Dr. Samuel Feinstein (a general physician), Dr. Mark Ampleforth (a specialist in shock and exposure), Dr. Horace Percy (a psychiatrist), Dr. Barney Williams (an anaesthetist), Miss Emilia Massimo (a general nurse) and Mrs. Lurline Brown (a nurse specialist intensive care), it was eleven-thirty. All of the medical team held high service rank, and all had top-flight security clearances.

Before the helicopter took off, Dr. Carriol briefed the team, thanking them for giving up their time, and assuring them that while Dr. Joshua Christian was extremely seriously ill, she very much doubted that more than two or three of them would have to remain with the patient longer than twenty-four hours. For those obliged to remain, she said with a smile, there would be a flight

323

to Palm Springs and a few weeks in the southern California sun to compensate. All food and other supplies for Pocahontas Island would be flown in by Presidential helicopter, as domestic staff could not be engaged. The pilot of the Army craft which flew them down could be relied upon to start the diesel generator up. With them they carried a day's rations of food and drink in thermal containers, a large amount of medical equipment, including a hospital bed, and several drums of diesel fuel in case the fuel on the island had gone off.

They flew over the same terrain Billy had negotiated some hours before, the pilot and Dr. Carriol watching the ground closely for evidence of a crash. As they left Washington well behind, the sky began to cloud over until a general overcast existed, but it was stratus cloud and not dangerous for a helicopter at routine altitude. And by the time that Pocahontas Island came into view, it seemed fairly certain that they would find Billy and his bird on the ground.

Then the shock; circling the house and buzzing the whole strip of land revealed no sign of Billy or the helicopter. Dr. Carriol's pilot shrugged.

"Beats me, ma'am, but it sure looks as if they never got this far," he said, hovering over the precise spot where Billy had landed.

"Go down anyway. I want to have a look."

It was by now after twelve-thirty, for the big Army machine was a slower, more conventional helicopter than Billy's bird.

"I'd bet the generator will be in that shed under the edge of the trees," said the pilot, pointing to a spot about four hundred yards away from the house. "Generators make a racket, especially if there's no wind, or it's blowing from the wrong quarter. I'd rather have you all out before I go take a look, because the ground's swampy and I don't have pontoons."

"Thanks for waiving the rules about carrying diesel as well as passengers."

"The President asks, I waive."

The medical team disembarked and got their equipment out quite handily; the pilot lifted his machine a few feet into the air and idled on over to the generator shed.

Everyone was standing around looking to her for a lead, so Dr. Carriol took the initiative and moved to the double gate in the courtyard wall, tugged the plank bolt back and gave both leaves of the gate a push. They swung inward without a squeak until they bounced against stop bolts in the ground.

"Man, this place must have been riddled with malaria in the old days!" said Dr. Ampleforth. "Why build a house here?"

"From what I remember, the whole of the east coast even up as far as Massachusetts was riddled with malaria," said Dr. Carriol. "And I guess they coped. I for one think it isn't a bad place to build—you'd be king of all you surveyed."

She led the way inside. All seemed quite normal, for the grey man on his grey cross hung in the dense noonday shadows plugging up the mouth of the tunnel to the front door.

Still leading, Dr. Carriol walked briskly into the open space of the courtyard and headed for the house, the team in a clump behind her, unsure of themselves, unsure of this peculiar and sudden mission.

About halfway, and her mind finally grasped what was in the archway. She stopped abruptly.

"Oh, my God, my God!" came from someone.

She started to walk again, her feet groping feebly after traction on the grey paving of herringboned railroad ties that heaved and shifted in great undulating waves from one wall to another and another.

About eight feet away, and she stopped again, extending her arms sideways to prevent anyone behind her from moving forward. "Stay where you are, please."

He hung with the bones poking out of his tattered toes, just barely clear of the ground, all his weight yearning for contact with that ground, only his head with the rope cut into its neck just beneath the jawbone and his hands with their fingers still tightly clutching onto the rope loops around his wrists preventing his weight from achieving its aim. His face jutted far forward over the noose, which had cut so deeply into his neck in trying to help his body reach the ground that it was level with his ears. So he looked not up, not straight ahead, but downward, his eyes half open. All the cruelest work of the rope had been done after he died, for his face was no more congested than the rest of him, his tongue was inside his parted lips, those lips were not swollen, and his eyes did not start out of their orbits. The respiratory arrest which had killed him had simply starved his tissues of oxygen, and so all of him had gone the color of weathered wood. The bruises, for instance, hardly showed.

325

It would be many weeks before Dr. Judith Carriol would be able to face the emotions the sight of him had aroused in her, let alone catalogue those emotions. During the time when she did physically stand there gazing on him, she felt only an extraordinary sense of fitness, of inevitability, of a pattern completed save for a few final strands which would add satisfying but quite unnecessary finishing touches.

"Oh, well, done, Joshua!" she said, smiling. "Beautifully and perfectly done! A better end to Operation Messiah than I could ever have dreamed of."

The white nurse was weeping, the black nurse on her knees keened thin and mournful, the doctors were shocked to silence.

Judith Carriol was the only one with a voice. "Judas!" she said, turning the word over on her tongue in wonder. "Yes, some things *are* immutable. I did indeed give you up for your crucifixion."

In Washington it was all over too. The March of the Millennium concluded amid a Roman holiday, two million people spilling through the streets and parks of Washington and Arlington, holding hands, touching each other, weeping, singing, dancing, kissing.

The President was waiting on the banks of the Potomac to welcome the Christian family, the U.S. senators, the Mayor of New York, the governors and the service chieftains and all the motley rest. He spoke from the white marble platform raised on high where Dr. Joshua Christian should have been, after which the King of Australia and New Zealand, the Prime Minister of India, the Premier of China and a dozen other heads of state all spoke, just a few graceful words each that were too brief to bore and too well phrased to offend anyone. They thanked Dr. Joshua Christian for giving new hope to the people of the world, they marveled at the human spirit behind the March of the Millennium, they praised various versions and professions of God, and they praised each other.

About one o'clock, when all the prominent heads of state, politicians, movie stars and other dignitaries were gathered in a specially erected marquee near the Lincoln Memorial to refresh themselves after the ceremony and before they went to rest up for the night's Millennial Ball, an aide approached President Tibor Reece, drew him a little away from the King, and whispered in his ear. Those who were watching him saw him stare at his aide in obvious shock, part his lips to say something, then think better of it and just nod his thanks. After which he went back to his conversation with His Majesty, but as soon as possible he excused himself and quietly slipped out of the marquee. He went back to the White House, and he waited there for Dr. Judith Carriol.

She arrived not long after two o'clock, in the fastest of the Presidential helicopters; after he received her message in the marquee, Tibor Reece had dispatched it to Pocahontas Island to fetch her.

When she entered the Oval Office the President's initial reaction was to think that she appeared remarkably calm, considering the magnitude of this calamitous event; but then, as he had grown to know her better, he had decided she was a most admirable kind of woman, incapable of panic, incapable of emotional excess, warm without being effusive, and above all one who esteemed her intelligence far ahead of her looks. So he had come to like her enormously, contrasting her with the very different Julia perhaps more often than he realized.

"Sit down, Judith. I can't believe it! Is it true? Is he really dead?"

She passed a hand over her eyes; the hand shook. "Yes, Mr. President, he is dead."

"But what happened?"

"Due to Mr. Magnus's illness, the medical team was not sent to Pocahontas Island. As far as we can gather, the helicopter which took Dr. Christian down there early this morning dropped him off without realizing nobody was there. It must have taken off again, because it isn't anywhere on the island, but it and Billy and the soldier who acted as Dr. Christian's escort have literally vanished off the face of the earth. The Coast Guard, the Navy and the Air Force have been searching for it now for two hours, and there isn't a trace. It's as if it had been—spirited away." She shivered uncontrollably, the first time he had ever seen her unable to discipline herself.

"It may have gone down in the sea," he said soothingly.

"If it did, there should have been an oil slick. And its course was entirely over shallow water, where it should be seen on the bottom. The weather was overcast in the area but basically fine and clear all along the route. Helicopters navigate by landmarks, so there's no reason to suppose it was off course the way a high-flying plane might stray. Billy armed himself with the charts before he left his base to pick me up. You know Billy, sir! The best."

"Yes."

"That helicopter is gone, I tell you."

The President decided it might be politic to alter the trend of Dr. Carriol's thinking away from the missing aircraft, and he had besides a bone of his own to pick. "So it's thanks to Mr. Magnus's—heart attack—that Dr. Christian was left alone to die of neglect."

Dr. Carriol glanced up, stared straight at him, her strange green eyes glittering not wetly but demoniacally. "Dr. Joshua Christian," she said with a slow relish, "was crucified."

"*Crucified?*"

"Or more accurately, he crucified himself."

The President lost color, his lips moving soundlessly, his brain formulating so many questions that his speech mechanisms went into chaotic overload. Finally he grasped hold of a simple query and managed to articulate it. "How, for God's sake, could he do a thing like that?"

She shrugged. "He was demented, of course. I knew that this morning when I went back to the March compound to take him down to Pocahontas Island. And I'd been watching the signs and symptoms grow ever since—oh, as far back as a month after his book was published. But today he was supposed to go straight into the hands of doctors and nurses, and I had no reason to think he hadn't. I'm not saying his madness was the permanent kind. I think it was more a derangement brought on by his extreme overload of work in the beginning, and later by physical suffering too. Frostbite, chafing, abscesses and the like. In the normal course of events he should have recovered from his dementia along with his bodily ailments. After a summer's rest, he should have been quite back to his normal self."

"So what happened, for God's sake?"

"Apparently he arrived on Pocahontas Island to find himself totally alone. He made himself a cross out of two old railroad ties—we found the tools he had used scattered around the courtyard attached to the house. The courtyard, I should explain, is paved with old railroad ties similar to the two he used to make his cross. There were chips of wood all over the place, from his work of joining the beams together. He couldn't nail himself up, of course, so he tied himself up. He used a stool to position himself, and kicked it over. And he hung there with a piece of rope tied around the cross holding his neck, and two more pieces around his wrists. He died of respiratory arrest, which also appears to have been the chief cause of death back in the days when a lot of people were crucified."

The President looked stricken, as indeed he was. The images Dr. Carriol was conjuring up were not anything he could associate with the man who had spent an evening at the White House, relished his cognac, quoted Kipling, smoked a cigar, and behaved in the most human manner.

"It's blasphemy!" he said.

"In all fairness to Dr. Christian, no, sir, it is *not* blasphemy. Blasphemy implies a state of mind sufficiently organized to want to mock. Dr. Christian was quite demented, and the conviction that one is Jesus Christ is very typical of organically based dementias. His own name—his extraordinary position—the adulation he received wherever he went—some people did actually worship him, you know. All these memories and experiences were cemented in his brain, and when his thought processes disintegrated, it was quite logical for his particular loss of contact with reality to take a Jesus Christ form. What *I* find unbelievable is the fact that he actually managed to do this thing, crucify himself. Physically as I've said he was extremely ill—worn out, and on the verge of permanent crippling. All that walking in subzero cold. He went among the people, Mr. President! Just like Jesus Christ. And he was a truly good man. Just like Jesus Christ."

The implications of what Dr. Carriol was telling him were beginning to sink in; Tibor Reece sat up straight, and broke out in a heavy sweat. "What happened to his body?"

"We took it down at once."

"And the cross he made?"

"We put it in a small stone shed within the courtyard. As I said, the paving is made of these old railroad ties, and the owners of the house kept five or six extra ties in the shed in case they needed to replace any paving. Dr. Christian found these spare ties, and he used two of them to make his cross. So we just put his cross back with the others."

"Where's his body now?"

"I instructed the medical team to take it to Walter Reed with them and put it in the mortuary with extreme secrecy. Dr. Mark Ampleforth, who was chief of the team for its duration as a team, is waiting your personal instructions."

"How many people—saw him up there?" An expression of extreme distaste glimmered, was wiped away out of respect and affection for the dead man, who he was *assured* had genuinely gone mad; yet not for all the respect and affection in the world could he bring himself to say, "How many people saw him hanging on the cross?"

"Just the medical team and me, Mr. President. Luckily I had sent the helicopter pilot over to start the generator. After we found Dr. Christian, which was immediately, I kept the pilot away from the area. He knows Dr. Christian is dead, but he thinks the cause of death was simple illness."

"Where are the medical team now? Who are they?"

"They're back at Walter Reed. They're all service officers of high rank and they're all security-cleared. I made sure of that before we went down to Pocahontas."

What to do? What to do? Dr. Judith Carriol watched imperturbably as Tibor Reece assembled all the alternatives and assessed their relative merits. He would not have the medical team eliminated, that she knew; it was the kind of thing you might have done to obscure people, or unconnected people, or fewer people; but not even the President of the United States of America could arrange to have concrete boots made for eight high-ranking officers in his own armed forces. No matter how cleverly it was done, every nosy nose in the District of Columbia and surrounds would start twitching. Besides which, a long and senior Washington career had made Dr. Judith Carriol very skeptical about the occasional sensationalist allegations of murder in high places. She did not believe it existed, certainly among politicians. Politicians were just too careful of their own necks to contemplate running such an appalling risk. For murder was always a risk.

No, the kind of thinking Tibor Reece was doing (her interpretation was absolutely right) ran along the lines of whether the horrific nature of Dr. Christian's death could successfully be suppressed, and if it could not, what was best to do about it?

He decided to aim for suppression, for a general cover-up; the watching Dr. Carriol smiled inwardly. Good! Good! That was the sensible and prudent course to take. Tibor Reece would invite the medical team to the White House, ostensibly to talk to them about their vain but heroic attempt to keep Dr. Christian alive, and while he had them there, he would personally request of each of them that he or she maintain an utter silence about what they found on Pocahontas Island. Naturally they would all pledge their silence. But she wondered if the President understood how implacable an enemy time was going to be; probably not. Though her bald and frank description of the manner of Dr. Christian's death had horrified and disgusted Tibor Reece, she knew he had actually little comprehension of what a sight had met the eyes of those who saw the manner of Dr. Christian's death. The horror would fade. The shock would dissipate. But no one who saw him hanging there could ever forget the sight. The crucifixion death of Dr. Joshua Christian was going to haunt every one of those eight people so long as each of them lived. By the time Tibor Reece could gather the eight members of the medical team here in this room, and request their total silence, they would already have talked. Not in general. Not to superiors, or fellow officers, or professional colleagues. They would have unburdened themselves to those they loved, because what they had seen could not be endured without a cathartic sharing of the experience with a loved one.

The President had managed to file his personal feelings about Dr. Christian's death; now he could really begin to think about its implications for the country, for the world, for his government.

"All along we agreed that the one thing we could not have on our hands was a martyr," he said grimly.

"Mr. President," said Dr. Carriol, "Dr. Christian's death resulted from a series of cosmic events, events beyond our control. And he was a law unto himself. Had he not been, he could not have done what we set him up to do. Why should he be accounted a martyr? Martyrs are made, they're the victims of persecution. But no one *ever* persecuted Dr. Christian! The government of this country has worked with him in everything, from providing transport for his travels to the March of the Millennium! Facts you can point to with pride, facts that indicate loud and clear how appreciative of Dr. Christian this government was and is. Sir, please approach the problem of Dr. Christian's death bearing those facts in mind! Martyrdom isn't an outcome you need worry about."

He put his chin on his hand, chewed his lips, then looked across at her wryly. "Martyrs," he said, "come in two types. The persecuted variety, and the self-made variety. He's the self-made martyr. You must surely admit, Judith, that there is such a creature—look at half the world's mothers."

"Then we must try to ensure the people don't look at him in that light," she said, and rose to her feet. "You don't need me now, Mr. President. If you don't mind, I ought to get across to Walter Reed and see Mr. Magnus."

He looked startled; clearly he had forgotten the existence of the Secretary for the Environment. "Yes, certainly! Thank you, Judith. Please convey my regards to Harold, and tell him he can expect a visit from me tomorrow morning." Tibor Reece's fine dark eyes held a dangerous gleam.

How he knew it Dr. Carriol didn't understand, but somehow the President did know that Harold Magnus was shamming.

That night, as a weary but delighted nation thought about settling back into the weary routines of everyday life, the President commandeered all television and radio stations for a special broadcast. The time was eight o'clock, the hour at which the Millennial Ball had been scheduled to commence; it had of course been canceled.

Comfortably ensconced in her own living room, her shoes off, her feet and body wrapped in fleecy lightweight warmth, Dr. Judith Carriol turned on her small television set. It was approaching the end of the longest day of her life.

No matter how rational a person one was, she thought, still the brutal severing of a link that had been sometimes suffocatingly close for months on end, a link that had joined a whole set of intellectual and emotional chains into a circle, a link that had brought her so much she had always wanted and not a little pain as well—still the brutal severing of that link must hurt. Had Dr. Joshua Christian been her evil genius, or had she been his? A bit of both, probably. Well, Tibor Reece's speech to the nation would mark the complete conclusion of the chapter in her life called Joshua Christian.

After she left the White House to see Harold Magnus in his sickbed at Walter Reed, the horrors of the day had gone on unabated. When she got all the way to the hospital through the delirious crowds which clogged Washington, she found the Secretary for the Environment denied all visitors. His luck had held; apparently he was indeed a very sick man and had indeed sustained some kind of genuine seizure after she left his office. No doubt this would be communicated to the President and all would be forgiven. Damn! Still, she availed herself of the opportunity to see Dr. Mark Ampleforth, discovering that the President had already been in touch, and moves were afoot to disguise the manner of Dr. Christian's death.

As she rejoined her car for the return trip, hoping to go home, a message was relayed to her from the President; he wished her to break the news of Dr. Christian's death to his family. And would she kindly do it at once, please, before the news broke and they heard it less kindly? Also please tell them that a car would fetch them to the White House at seven in the evening so that the President could personally convey his sympathies to them.

Dr. Carriol had dragged herself, aching and hating, to the Hay-Adams Hotel, where the Christian family was staying. She found them a little bewildered; following the marquee reception things had somehow seemed to fizzle out, and they could find no one to tell them how Joshua was. Oh, the reception had been impressive, as had the actual ceremony concluding the March of the Millennium, but for them all of it had been an anguish because Joshua was not with them. Oh, it was very nice to talk in person to the King of Australia and New Zealand; he seemed a most amiable fellow, was possessed of exquisite manners and never said anything out of place or contentious. Very nice too to exchange nods and smiles and bows and banalities with so many prime ministers and presidents and premiers and chairmen of this and that, ambassadors and governors, senators and congressmen. But Joshua was not there. *Joshua was ill!* All they really wanted was to be allowed to see Joshua. Where it seemed all everybody else wanted was to prevent their seeing Joshua.

So when about six that evening Dr. Judith Carriol appeared, she was greeted by the Christians in the manner of a returned prodigal. She who they assumed would marry Joshua had become their only channel of communication with him. The events of the past few days had thinned their ranks from six to four and flattened any rebellion in them, but worry was rapidly fanning indignation into anger. Andrew may have condemned his wife's behavior to Judith, but Martha's words had sunk into Mama's brain; now Mama wanted answers.

Had Judas been obliged to talk to Mary and the others after Jesus' death and before he, Judas, went out to hang himself? Judith. Judas. Judas. But there had to be a Judas. There always had to be a Judas! Without Judas, humanity would not need saving. For it was the Judas element that justified all the pain of birth and death and everything that happened in between, pain and pain and yet more pain. Judas was he or she who owned high ambitions but needed the talents of others to achieve success. Judas was he or she who rode upon the back of another's genius. Judas was profit and loss, emotional blackmail, manipulation, despair, self-righteousness, the purest of intentions, the basest methods, exculpation. Judas was not betrayal! Many a Judas never needed to betray. And Judas was not an aberration. Judas was the norm.

"Joshua is dead," she said, before the fermenting Christian anger could surge over her.

And they had been expecting it after all. They had known. James moved closer to Miriam, Andrew to Mama. And they simply looked at Judas Carriol. No one exclaimed, or wept, or evidenced disbelief. But their eyes—oh, their eyes! She closed her own so she could not see.

"He died," she went on in a calm and level voice, "at about ten o'clock this morning. I don't think he died in much pain if any pain. I don't know. I wasn't there. His body is at Walter Reed Hospital. He will be given a full state funeral in five days' time, and with your permission he will be buried in Arlington National Cemetery. The White House is taking care of all the arrangements. President Reece is sending a car for you in a very little while, because he wants to see you."

To her genuine and naive surprise, she discovered that the hardest thing her life had yet called upon her to do was now to open her eyes and look at them. She *had* to open her eyes and look at them. She had to be sure they accepted this most uninformative account. They probably thought they would get more from the President, but she knew they would not. No one was ever going to tell them how Joshua Christian died, or for what reasons.

She did open her eyes and she did look directly at them. They gazed back at her without suspicion or criticism. That was just not fair!

"Thank you, Judith," said Mama.

"Thank you, Judith," said James.

"Thank you, Judith," said Andrew.

"Thank you, Judith," said Miriam.

Judas Carriol smiled very slightly and sadly, got up and left them alone. She never saw any of the Christians in person again.

Now, alone at last and able to shed the outer trappings of her public image, Dr. Judith Carriol watched the shimmering screen in front of her as it filled with a picture of the exterior of the White House, then that dissolved, and the Oval Office came into view. It too vanished; the President had chosen to broadcast from his private sitting room. He was seated at one end of a small sofa,

with Mama beside him on his right hand looking exquisitely, se-
renely, heartrendingly beautiful in a pure-white dress with a sky-
blue stole draped across her shoulders and through her arms.
James and Miriam were also to the President's right, Miriam on a
chair and wearing white, James standing behind her with his
hand on her shoulder. On the President's left, but standing oddly
alone behind and beyond the sofa on which his mother sat with
the President of the United States of America, was Andrew. All
three men wore dark-blue sweaters and trousers. Whoever had
posed them thus was brilliant at his job. It worked. The impression on any viewer was immediately momentous and profound.

The camera zoomed in slowly on the President's face, drawn
and very serious, truly Lincolnesque; or would tomorrow's adjective be "Christianesque"?

"At ten o'clock this morning," said Tibor Reece, "Dr. Joshua
Christian died. He had been suffering from a grave illness for
some time, but he refused to have treatment until after the
March of the Millennium was over. He made a conscious decision, in full possession of the medical facts about his condition."

He paused, then went on, "I would like to quote, if I may,
from the speech Dr. Christian made only the other day in Philadelphia, during the March of the Millennium. It is his last speech
and the one I personally think his greatest."

The piercing deep-set eyes subtly changed; to Dr. Carriol, an
expert, it was obvious he was now reading from a prompting device positioned exactly in front of him and at his eye level.

"'Be quiet. Be still. Have hope in the future. Hope stemming
from the knowledge that you are not alone, you are not abandoned, for you are an essential part of the congregation of souls
called Man, and an even more essential part of the congregation
of souls called America. Hope stemming from the fact that you
have been entrusted by God with a mission, to preserve and il-
luminate this planet in the name of Man. *Not* in the Name of
God! In the name of *Man!* Hope for tomorrow, for tomorrow is
worth hoping for. No tomorrow will ever come that will see the
light of Man extinguished, if you as Man work to preserve that
light. For though it came originally as a gift from God, only Man
can keep it burning. Remember always that *you* are Man, and
Man is Man and Woman united.

"'I offer a creed for this third millennium. A creed as old as
this third millennium. A creed summed up in three words—faith,
and hope, and love. Faith in yourselves! Faith in your strength

and your endurance. Hope in a brighter and better tomorrow. Hope for your children and your children's children, and their children. And love—ah, what can I say about love that you, all too human, do not already know? Love yourselves! Love those around you! Love those you do not even know! Waste not your love on God, Who does not expect it and does not need it. For if He is perfect and eternal, then He needs nothing. You are Man, and it is Man you must love. Love wards off loneliness. Love warms the spirit no matter how cold the body might be. Love *is* the light of Man!'"

Tibor Reece was weeping openly, but the four Christians sat and stood around him dry-eyed, utterly composed. Yet no one watching made the mistake of thinking them without grief.

"He is dead," the President continued through his tears, "but he died knowing he had lived better than most of us. How many of us know ourselves to be truly good, as he was? I have chosen to speak to you tonight in his own words, because I have absolutely none of my own to offer you that can sum up so well what Joshua Christian stood for. He was faith. He was hope. He was love. He has offered you a creed for this third millennium, a creed which is a restatement of the unquenchable spirit in Man and Woman, a creed which can offer all of you a positive and ongoing philosophy of life in the midst of this cold, hard, unrelenting third millennium. Hold on to his words and hold on to your memories of him, the man who said the words. And know that as long as you do, he who insisted always that he was only a man can—never—truly—die."

That was the end of it. Dr. Carriol switched off her set before the network she had chosen to watch could come on with its frantically collated two-hour special on the life and the work of Dr. Joshua Christian.

She got up, went through to her kitchen, and opened her back door. There was a floodlight, hardly ever used because it devoured far too much electricity, but nonetheless a most necessary adjunct for a woman living on her own, illuminating as it did her entire backyard with dazzling efficiency.

Throwing the switch now, she walked outside. A very neat scene. A high brick wall around the yard, and a padlocked gate which led into the side passage. Fieldstone flagging instead of grass. No garden beds, but many shrubs and bushes, and three larger trees. First a weeping cherry, its drooping branches past the full glory of its pale-pink blossoms. Then there was a silver birch, its lime-green leaves still half furled, fresh and young. And a huge, very old dogwood in white flower, its branches spreading so perfectly it belonged in a Japanese composition; and it had a ghostly, carven serenity about it, all its flowers turning their faces upward, laid on with the unerring instinct of a master builder greater than any mortal man. In legend, Judas hanged himself from a dogwood. And, then as now, it would have been in flower. How *beautiful* to die amid such perfection!

Someone in the next house was weeping inconsolable tears for Dr. Joshua Christian, who had come to save the race of Man and died as kings had died in the beginning of the human experiment, a sacrifice to placate the gods and preserve the people.

"You will look for me in vain, Joshua Christian!" she said, not to herself, but to the dogwood tree. "I have a lot of living to do yet."

She switched off the floodlight, went inside and shut the kitchen door. In the backyard in the moonlight the dogwood blossoms glowed up into the still cold silver vault above, a patient, dreaming loveliness.

Of all the people who heard the President's broadcast, and though it seems an excessive thing to say, Dr. Moshe Chasen mourned for Dr. Joshua Christian more deeply and more painfully than anyone.

The moment Tibor Reece uttered his first words, Dr. Chasen burst into a paroxysm of grief, keening, wailing, weeping, tearing at himself; his wife could do nothing to console him.

"It isn't fair!" he said when he was able. "I meant him no harm! It isn't fair, it isn't fair! What is the pattern? Why is the pattern? I meant him no harm!"

And he wept again.

The President sent the Christians back to Holloman by helicopter, promising them that he would bring them back to Washington the following Wednesday for Joshua's state funeral and the interment at Arlington. They were transferred from the Holloman airport to 1047 Oak Street by car, and they arrived in the early hours of Saturday morning. James let them in, into the welcome pure white light that streamed down on the springtime flowering glory that was the Christian living room. The plants had not suffered in Mary's absence, for Mrs. Margaret Kelly had volunteered to come in and care for them, and she had not fallen down on her word. The air was sweet and very softly quiet.

"I don't suppose Mary and Martha will be home until at least tomorrow," said James.

"Oh, poor things! To think that they'll hear without us there to help them," said Mama, who had not shed a tear.

"I'll make some coffee," said Miriam, disappearing to the kitchen because she was unable to sit down, unable to let herself think, unable to look at those three beloved faces.

"What are we going to do?" asked Mama, not of James but of Andrew, standing near her with his hand on her shoulder.

"We carry on. The work isn't finished, it's only begun. So we carry on."

James shivered. "Oh, Drew! It will be so hard without Joshua to guide us!"

"No. It will be easier."

"Yes," said James after a moment. "Yes, it will!"

They sat, the mother and the two brothers, in a perfect understanding.

Mary and Martha were on a train when they heard the news. Though at the time Mary had not appreciated Andrew's high-handed treatment of herself and Martha, she had had time to cool down while she struggled to catch the train, especially because she was coping with Martha as well; now that they were safely on board, she found herself more inclined to thank Drew than to hate him.

The train dawdled, as trains had a habit of doing, and because of the March of the Millennium it was nearly empty. At nine in the evening they drew into Philadelphia, and stopped yet again. The platform was utterly deserted, it lay there in all its stagnant dreary indignity, swept clean of humanity, but not of humanity's detritus. Beautifully and ornately painted on the waiting room's outside wall was a huge despairing cry from some human soul beyond Joshua Christian's help: GRAVITY SUCKS! Oh, poor mortal bird! thought Mary from out of her aching heart; you too?

The station's public address system was reeling out words in a professional announcing voice that came across loud and clear, emanating not from the station master's office but from the local NBC radio affiliate.

Mary and Martha sat alone in their long carriage and heard the voice talking about the dead Dr. Joshua Christian.

338

Martha slumped against Mary, heavy and limp, but not fainted. Mary put her arms about the toneless shoulders and listened to the loudspeaker voice without surprise. The train started again almost at once, as if the man who operated it preferred to be somewhere away from that remorseless public address system.

I knew, thought Mary. I knew this morning that I would never see him again. And I didn't want to be with *them* when they heard. Let the boys and Miriam deal with Mama. I shall resign. I cannot bear any more. All I truly wanted was to travel, and they denied me. *He* denied me. The only person I have ever loved does not love me, can never love me. *He* claimed her without even wanting her.

"Oh, Mary how can I live?" asked Martha, her face folded against that spare flat unstimulated bosom.

"The same as the rest of us," said Mary. "Forever in his shadow."

Dr. Charles Miller, vascular surgeon, to his wife, while preparing for bed: "He *crucified* himself, I tell you! And I keep asking myself, is that how we made him feel? Is that truly how we made him feel? As if he had to die for us? Oh, God! Oh, God!"

Dr. Ignatius O'Brien, plastic surgeon, to his male lover, in an Arlington studio apartment: "I don't think my flesh will ever stop crawling! At first I thought he was still alive, because his eyes looked down with such a world of bitter pain and knowing life in them— I tell you, I cannot believe that his eyes have died along with the rest of him."

Dr. Samuel Feinstein, general physician, to his spinsterly middle-aged secretary in their Walter Reed office: "Well, at least this time they can't blame it on the Jews, Ida! If I was a Christian I'd probably know right off whether what Dr. Christian did was blasphemy or martyrdom, but I don't and I never will. But do you know what really scared the shit out of me? The Carriol woman standing there with a big smile on her face saying something like, 'Well done, Jay See! I couldn't have dreamed up a better end to the operation myself, Messiah!' Oh, Ida, do you suppose he *was?*"

Dr. Mark Ampleforth, specialist in shock and exposure, to his eighteen-year-old fiancée, during a meeting originally planned to discuss their impending marriage: "Listen, Susie, when I'm upset I know I talk in my sleep. But it's all total gobbledygook, honest! So if you do happen to hear me talking, don't for God's sake believe anything I say, okay?"

Dr. Horace Percy, psychiatrist, to his own analyst, in his analyst's office, at the beginning of a hastily convened session: "Gruesome, Martin! The hollow man from Holloman, codpiece stuffed with straw. Did you hear The Man tonight? A creed for the third millennium, yet! A new opiate for the masses, more like!"

Dr. Barney Williams, anaesthetist, to his wife, over the dinner table: "The poor, poor bastard! All alone in that awful place, and with the guts to die like that. It must have taken an hour after he managed to hang himself up there. Oh, and his face . . . !"

Miss Emilia Massimo, general nurse and captain in the U.S. Air Force, to her male lover, defending her inability to get in the mood: "I will never be able to forget it as long as I live, Charlie. You know how those pictures of Jesus always have eyes that follow you around the room? Well, that's what his eyes did. I laid him out when we got back here, so I moved all around him. And wherever I went, his eyes just followed me. Followed me . . ."

Mrs. Lurline Brown, nurse specialist intensive care and major in the U.S. Army, to her minister: "Oh, Reverend Jones, it was meant that I be there! I come from that country, and every time I go back, I have a mystical experience. Now I know why! So I just told my brothers and my husband, you go on over there to that old island and you get his cross. He is the new Redeemer! Hallelujah! *Hallelujah!*"

Two days later a hard-pressed and grieving Tibor Reece remembered something he had neglected to do, and issued orders. As a result of those orders, three dour middle-aged professional Marines in a Marine helicopter were dispatched the same day to Pocahontas Island, in Pamlico Sound, North Carolina. Their orders were to go into the courtyard of the only house on the island, there locate a stone shed, enter it, remove any large wooden beams of any kind it might happen to be sheltering, take them outside the environs of the house into a no-risk, no-defacement area, pour gasoline on the beams, and wait until they were burned to ashes.

Theirs not to reason why. They landed, they entered the courtyard and then the shed, and out of the latter they carried five dismally ordinary, ancient wooden railroad ties. They bore them to the middle of the grassy clearing in front of the courtyard wall, and as ordered, they saturated the beams with gasoline before setting fire to them. The ties burned well, for they were old and dry and very tired of living. In half an hour a black patch on the swampy grass was all that remained of them.

The Marines boarded their chopper and took off. Back at Quantico they reported to their commanding officer that the mission was accomplished. Their commanding officer reported to his general, and his general reported to the White House. Mission accomplished, *sir!* Since no one, least of all Tibor Reece, had asked for a count of the number of beams, nor mentioned that one of them should be a T-shaped affair made out of two beams, no one realized that the T-shaped affair made out of two beams was not burned. It was not burned because it was not there.

The following week, a rather red-faced scion of an old North Carolina tobacco-growing family telephoned the Department of the Environment, and regretfully informed his friend in Parks and Wildlife that his family had decided to withdraw their offer to donate dear old Pocahontas Island to the nation, thereby also withdrawing their hope that the President might consider it suitable for a nearby yet isolated retreat.

"We've had an offer for it we just can't refuse, a *cash* offer *half as big again* as our original asking price!" the North Carolinan voice explained. "To make things even more complicated, the offer comes from a very big and very powerful black religious organization. Seems they want to turn the place into a center of worship. And since they're more than willing to keep it designated as a bird and wildlife preserve, we honestly feel we just should not refuse. I'll be real honest with you, George. We need the money! We need the money bad."

The Parks man on the Environment end of the telephone conversation sighed, but he was not unduly upset. He had thought the possibility of its being picked up as an Executive retreat was nebulous, and there was nothing in any way unique about it from the Parks and Wildlife point of view.

However, when next he went upstairs to report, he did not

mention the fact that Environment had lost out on Pocahontas Island to Mr. Harold Magnus, because Mr. Harold Magnus had very suddenly and very unexpectedly been removed from office. The official reason given out was ill health, but the whole of Environment was buzzing with a mysterious rumor that somehow or other, Harold Magnus had been involved to his discredit in the death of Dr. Joshua Christian, of all people! The newly appointed Secretary for the Environment was an Environment professional, a Presidential decision which delighted the whole Department. Dr. Judith Carriol.

So when George in Parks and Wildlife went upstairs to report the sad news about Pocahontas Island as part of his routine accounting, he reported it to Dr. Judith Carriol.

She went very still, and her eyes, which he always found unsettling anyway, her eyes just leaped into life. Then she threw back her head and she laughed, laughed, laughed until she literally cried and gasped for breath.

"We can of course insist," he said, at a loss. "The offer to us was verbal, but we also have a letter of intent."

The paroxysm ended; Dr. Carriol pulled a tissue from her personal drawer and wiped her eyes and blew her nose.

"I wouldn't dream of insisting," she said, gulped, had to suppress another spasm of laughter. "Oh, dear me, no! Our interest in that area primarily is in preserving bird and wildlife, and that's not a problem in this case, is it? In fact, I think this comes as a blessing in disguise. I can assure you there is no way the President would ever contemplate asking the nation to acquire the property as a retreat! I happen to know it isn't a part of this great country he admires or enjoys. Besides, it is a black religious body which has asked for Pocahontas Island, and I do not think it would be good Environment policy to wield a big stick, do you? Tell your friend to go ahead and firm up his sale. You can also tell him not to sweat it out until closing day. I would bet my life this is one sale that won't fall through at the last minute!"

And she began laughing again, harder than ever.

"What I can't understand, Judith," said Dr. Moshe Chasen to his new Secretary several days later over lunch in the new Secretary's office, "is why you ever accepted this position. You can't serve two masters! You are now a political appointee tied to Tibor Reece forever and a day. When he leaves the White House, as leave he must sooner or later, even if he does shoot for a fourth term, you will probably be asked to leave your political chair, and you won't be asked to resume your permanent position in Environment. The Secretaryship is not an elected office, but it's sure as hell political. You can't come back on the permanent staff. They're very sticky about public servants having political affiliations, and rightly so, in my opinion." He shrugged. "Public servants ought to be above politics. Their elected masters come and go, so they've got to be prepared to throw their weight behind whatever masters are in power."

"I didn't know you felt so strongly about this," said Dr. Carriol, eyes dancing with some secret amusement.

Whatever Dr. Chasen might have answered under the provocation of that amusement was never offered, for Mrs. Taverner buzzed.

"Dr. Carriol?"

"Yes, Helena?"

"The President is calling."

"Oh. Would you explain to him that I'm in conference at the moment, but that I'll call him back later?"

"Certainly, Dr. Carriol."

Dr. Chasen's eyebrows climbed nearly to his hairline. "I don't believe it! Judith, Judith, you don't relay messages like that to the President of the United States! It's tantamount to kiss my ass!"

"Nonsense," she said composedly. "He wasn't calling on official business. I'm having dinner with him tonight."

"I don't believe it!"

"Why not? He's a free man these days, and I'm a free woman, as ever. You've just finished telling me that my career as a public servant is over, that I'm just a political appointee tied to the White House. So who can object if we have dinner together, appointer and appointee?"

Dr. Chasen decided discretion might be the better part of valor, so he changed the subject. "Judith, I want to ask you something, because I think I should have a yea or nay from you in your official capacity. I would very much like to go up to Holloman to visit the Christians. But if you don't think it's a good idea, I won't go."

She frowned, thought the request over. "Well, I can't say the idea turns me on, but I've no real grounds for objection. I take it it's just a personal call?"

"Yes. I'd never met any of Joshua's family until the funeral, and I can't think of a worse occasion to strike up a friendship. But

343

I really did like Josh's mother. Such a gallant soul! And I just feel I'd like to see for myself that she's okay."

"Conscience bothering you, Moshe?"

"Yes—and no."

"Don't ever blame yourself. It was him. It was always, always him. Some people can't be moderate. You knew him! He was the most immoderate man in the world. A superlative brain, yet he always ended up thinking with his guts. I never understood that! A waste, Moshe."

"Whatever he was, was what made him right for your purpose, Judith. Can't you see that? Don't you sorrow for him at all?"

She smiled, shook her head, but neither unkindly. "To grieve for Joshua Christian is an impossibility. He'll never die, you know. He will outlive your remotest posterity." She smiled again, a secret, triumphant smile. "I have ensured it."

He slapped his hands on his thighs. "Ach! Sometimes I think the world is too much for me." He rose to his feet, looking at his watch. "Back to Section Four. I've got two conferences this afternoon. But I'd much rather be making love to my computer!"

"Oh, come on, Moshe, be fair! I didn't browbeat you into taking the job as head of Section Four."

"I know, I know!" He drew himself up with beautiful and endearing dignity; only then did his recent marked loss of weight show properly. "I am a Jew," he said. "I like to kvetch, it makes me feel better. You dealt with Section Four with all your usual genius, Judith. Me on the think tank end, and John Wayne on the administrative end. It works."

"Moshe," Dr. Carriol said as he headed for the door, "are you well? Have you had a checkup?"

"With *my* wife I haven't had a checkup?"

"Everything okay?"

"Everything is fine," he said, and went out.

Dr. Carriol sat for a moment before she picked up the telephone. Perhaps Tibor's call had been fortunate; it had enabled her to avoid telling Moshe why she had abandoned public for political service. The answer had been on the tip of her tongue, and would have come out. Which might have been a big mistake. Moshe was changed since the death of Joshua Christian. And he didn't even know how Joshua Christian had died!

It was going to be *gorgeous* to be First Lady!

Eat your heart out, Joshua Christian, wherever you are. No dogwood noose for me. Not that I hate you any more. I did for a

344

while, I admit it. I even let you harness me to serve you, instead of keeping it the other way around. But if you had grown up in Pittsburgh the way I did, nothing would ever burrow deep enough to undermine your underpinnings, either. If I was not everything I am, I'd still be sitting there in Pittsburgh, and I'd be drinking myself to death. Or shooting up if I could turn enough tricks to support the habit.

He is a beautiful man, Tibor Reece. I will make him exactly the right kind of wife. I will love him. I will make him happy. I will care for his child. I will endow him with enough enthusiasm to run for a fourth term. I will ensure that he is accounted an even greater President than Augustus Rome. After all, I can't rest on my laurels! And where can I go from Operation Messiah except to Operation Emperor?

Dr. Chasen ended in staying overnight at 1047 Oak Street, Holloman. The Christians made him so welcome, and they spoke so freely of Joshua with him, their eyes less teary and their throats less lumpy than Moshe Chasen's. And they talked of what they intended to do with all the years they would have to live remembering Joshua.

"Miriam and I are off to Asia shortly," said James. "I feel we have a lot of work to do there before Joshua's creed assumes its proper importance in Asia."

"And I'm off to South America again," said Andrew. He did not indicate that his wife would be accompanying him.

She, poor soul, didn't seem to Dr. Chasen to be quite right in the head. She wandered so aimlessly; she sang quietly to herself; she leaned heavily on Mary, who cared for her with enormous patience and tenderness.

They, said Mary, meaning Martha and herself, would keep Mama company in Holloman while the other three traveled in their dead brother's cause.

"I used to think I would shrivel and die if I didn't get the opportunity to travel," Mary went on, and shivered, and paled. "But do you know, Moshe, Washington was too far?"

And after the excellent dinner Mama cooked, they sat in the exquisite living room among the plants that kept on growing and flowering in mindless luxuriance. The talk still revolved around the family's intentions.

"Mind you," said Mama, pouring coffee, "James and Miriam

and Andrew can't leave Holloman quite yet. It isn't forty days since Joshua died."

"Forty days?" asked Dr. Chasen stupidly, because he was not stupid.

"That's right. Joshua hasn't appeared to us yet. But he will! To us. Forty days after his death. At least that's what we think, though we can't be sure. It might be three times forty. Or two times forty. It's two thousand years, but this is the third millennium, so we don't quite know. If it should turn out to be longer than forty days, then of course James and Miriam and Andrew won't wait, because they won't be intended to be here when Joshua comes. I imagine he will only show himself to the women, the two Marys and Martha, but I might be wrong."

She sounded so happy, so sure. And she was calm. She was sane. He looked around at the others, trying vainly to learn what they thought of Mama's theory, but he couldn't even begin to plumb what lay behind their fair placid faces.

"Will you let me know when he appears?" Dr. Chasen asked respectfully.

"Of course I will!" cried Mama warmly.

The others said neither yea nor nay.

Mary leaned forward abruptly, lips parted.

"Yes?" prompted Dr. Chasen eagerly.

She smiled at him; she looked a great deal more like her mother these days. "Drink your coffee, Moshe," she said gently. "It's getting cold."

Additional Praise for *THE DIFFERENCE*

"A disarmingly powerful, fresh-news slant on *why and how* people (you and I and everyone we work for, or with, or work for us), are the most important factor in every facet of business success, and why so many miss the mark. If you're looking to create breakthroughs in your business and in your life, this book is for you."

—TONY ROBBINS

"Subir Chowdhury nailed it with this book. *The Difference* has what you need to succeed in business and life that they don't teach you in school."

—MARK A. WAGNER, PRESIDENT OF BUSINESS OPERATIONS AT WALGREENS

"Subir has simplified the true meaning of business life with his gripping, haunting—yet disarmingly liberating—book. Readers completing the last page of *The Difference* will entirely be transformed—you will be quite different from the person you were when you began the journey!"

—JAY ABRAHAM, WORLDWIDE BUSINESS GROWTH STRATEGIST

"*The Difference* is superb. Subir Chowdhury has again eloquently and insightfully captured why some organizations win and others don't. The STAR framework leads to marvelous cases, tools, and actions that can be quickly adapted to improve organizational success. The applications to professional and personal settings are captivating and useful."

—DAVE ULRICH, RENSIS LIKERT PROFESSOR AT THE ROSS SCHOOL OF BUSINESS, UNIVERSITY OF MICHIGAN, AND PARTNER AT THE RBL GROUP

"When 'good enough isn't enough' is a profound distinction that will make a significant difference in your business and your life. The fact that Subir's extraordinary reputation was informed by his grandfather's wisdom of the ages advice from Bangladesh is a testament that true principles transcend geography, not just time. We are all blessed that Subir chose to pick up the pen as his grandfather intended. The secret of teaching his grandson to write to the authors of the books he was reading is worth the price of this book alone. It reveals the principle used to fuel Facebook and LinkedIn. Read this book twice."

"Drawing on the real-world situations he deals with in his professional life, Subir Chowdhury reveals why certain organizations succeed while others don't. Thoughtfully written, and a compelling read."

"Insightful! *The Difference* shows managers and leaders at every level how to better engage and develop a company's most fundamental resource: its people. It is the difference between good enough and being truly great."

"Myths about how we should live our lives abound. But they are just that, myths. And too often they lead us to lesser and poorer lives. In this straightforward and inspiring book, Subir Chowdhury distills a lifetime of experience, rising from impoverished beginnings in Bangladesh, to his decades of consulting work with CEOs of many of the top Fortune 500 companies, to becoming one of our leading thinkers on workplace culture and organizational values. His STAR model for making a difference at work and in our personal lives is seemingly simple, but surprisingly nuanced and profound. This short but powerful book could change your life."

"We'd all like to make a difference in our lives and make the world a better place; the wisdom and insights that Subir Chowdhury imparts in this short but remarkable book will help to show you how."

The DIFFERENCE

ALSO BY SUBIR CHOWDHURY

The Ice Cream Maker

The Power of Six Sigma

Design for Six Sigma

The
DIFFERENCE

When Good Enough Isn't Enough

SUBIR CHOWDHURY

CROWN
BUSINESS
NEW YORK

Published in the United States by Crown Business, an imprint of the
Crown Publishing Group, a division of Penguin Random House LLC,
New York.
crownbusiness.com

CROWN BUSINESS is a trademark and CROWN and the Rising Sun
colophon are registered trademarks of Penguin Random House LLC.

Crown Business books are available at special discounts for bulk
purchases for sales promotions or corporate use. Special editions,
including personalized covers, excerpts of existing books, or
books with corporate logos, can be created in large quantities for
special needs. For more information, contact Premium Sales at
(212) 572-2232 or e-mail specialmarkets@penguinrandomhouse.com.

Library of Congress Cataloging-in-Publication Data is available upon
request.

ISBN 978-0-451-49621-8
Ebook ISBN 978-0-451-49622-5

Printed in the United States of America

Book design by Anna Thompson
Jacket design by Tal Goretsky

10 9 8 7 6 5 4 3 2 1

First Edition

For Malini

Contents

Introduction

WHEN GOOD ENOUGH
ISN'T ENOUGH

As I was writing this book, the tragic story about contaminated water in Flint, Michigan, was making national news. The city, in a cost-cutting maneuver, changed the source of its water supply. Repeated mistakes were made by local, state, and federal officials, which led to the presence of lead in the water delivered to Flint homes. The lead showed up in the blood of Flint's children, but it affected everyone who used the Flint municipal water supply.

The story grabbed my attention for two reasons. First, I was a longtime resident of Michigan. And second, it is the kind of tragedy that I hope *The Difference* will help people avoid. The story of the contaminated Flint water supply involves failures on the part of local and state regulators to anticipate the problem, or respond to complaints. Community members persisted in efforts to call attention to the contaminated water, despite having their complaints be summarily dismissed. The difference between how those two groups of people responded to the crisis is the very issue that I address in *The Difference*—a difference that ultimately lies in the mindsets of the people involved.

My previous books, several of which have been international bestsellers, contributed to the field of quality improvement. I wrote them primarily for executives, managers, companies, and organizations who want to learn how to go about improving the quality of their products and services. This book is aimed at overcoming a fallacy that too many of us, in today's hectic, demanding times, have succumbed to—that good enough is good enough. What I have found, in my decades of work with many of the top leaders in business, is that we have to do better than good enough. We have to strive for excellence. And that process and way of thinking all begins with developing a caring mindset. While the ideas in this book emerged from my personal experience, and my experiences in the field of quality improvement, its lessons are universal. I believe they apply to everyone, both in their business careers and in their lives outside of work. I believe this book has the potential to resonate with students, stay-at-home parents, shopkeepers, public servants, teachers—anyone who wants to make a difference in their organization and in their lives.

I introduce the challenge of *the difference* in chapter 1, as I grappled with a question that had haunted me my entire career. It ultimately inspired me to look for answers. In chapters 2 through 5, I talk about the four critical attributes or factors that underlie *The Difference*, which I have brought together in the acronym STAR. In those chapters, I discuss a number of stories that show how these attributes impact our thinking and behavior, both at work and outside of the workplace. And I discuss the negative consequences that occur when they are absent from our lives. In chapter 6, I show how so many of the principles behind developing a caring mindset, and for not settling for good enough, were taught to me by my family, so many years ago, growing up in a land halfway around the world.

The stories that I share in *The Difference* are drawn from both my personal life and my work career, consulting with many of America's Fortune 100 companies and senior executives. I have changed many of the names of people involved, but the stories are genuine and true.

It is my hope that the STAR principles will help you to develop a caring mindset, one that will enable you to overcome "good enough" thinking, make a difference in your interactions with others, and allow you to enjoy a more successful, happier, and more fulfilled life and career.

Making a genuine difference in the world is the responsibility of each one of us. We cannot sit back and rely on the good intentions of others. We must commit to act. If we do that, and practice the four attributes of a caring mindset, I believe we can transform our workplaces, strengthen our family ties, reinvigorate America, and transform the world. We can make sure that what happened in Flint, Michigan—or any other preventable catastrophe—does not happen again. We deserve nothing less.

Chapter 1

WHAT A TOOTHPICK CAN TEACH US ABOUT CARING

You can change your mindset.

—CAROL S. DWECK, AUTHOR OF *MINDSET*

"Subir," a senior executive in the manufacturing industry asked me, "What do you do with a toothpick when you are done with it?" I looked back at him with puzzlement on my face. Was this a serious question?

I've overcome plenty of tough challenges in my life—as a child growing up in Bangladesh, I never dreamed that I would enjoy the life I've lived. After moving thousands of miles away to start a new life in the United States, I faced one obstacle after another—a foreign culture, a new social life, a demanding job—but I embraced my new home and became a citizen. Today, as one of the world's most recognized experts on organizational strategy and corporate quality, I've helped some of the world's best-known brands improve their processes, save billions of dollars, and increase their profits and revenues. I've worked with all kinds of organizations:

profit, nonprofit, healthcare, government, manufacturing—large and small. You would think after doing what I've been doing for more than twenty years, I could figure out the answer to a perplexing problem that I noticed in my consulting work: why two companies of roughly the same size from the same industry—both of which have implemented exactly the same processes with the help of my team—have met with drastically different results. It didn't make sense to me: one company achieved a return of 5 times their investment—adequate, to me, but hardly spectacular—while the other saw a return of 100 times their investment. I was determined to figure out the difference.

It was a nightmare morning. I was up at five thirty to make my appointment. It was snowing the kind of heavy, wet Michigan snow that piles up quickly. Traffic was painfully slow. Several drivers had slid off the road. I feared I would be late for the first of three meetings I had scheduled that day. But I kept inching forward and arrived, just in time, for my first meeting with Mark, an executive vice president in a major Fortune 500 manufacturing company.

I want to share several remarkable events that occurred on that day, events that helped me discover why one company achieved incremental improvement while the other was radically transformed. But first I would like to make two important points. One, while the events that I describe in this chapter happened in a manufacturing company, they could have happened in almost any organization.

Second, the company had hired me to help them with problems with quality. But it might just as easily have involved any attempt at changing the status quo: improving customer service, fostering diversity, retaining talents, improving revenues, cutting operating expenses, increasing profits. And although the other people I met that day were mostly senior executives, and people who report to them, they might just as well have been line managers, supervisors, or workers on the manufacturing floor. The lessons are universal.

I had experienced an anxious two and a half hours on the road, the kind of thing that can knock anyone a bit off center. I knew I needed to focus on the task in front of me—on the person who hired me to help solve critical problems at their company—rather than on my own lingering anxiety. When Mark and I met in his office that morning, he lowered his head, as if he were in pain. I knew something was bothering him deeply. It seemed pretty obvious to me that he was having a worse day than I was.

"Is everything okay?" I asked. "I know I got off to a bad start this morning. I was worried I might be late, and you know how I hate being late. But you look particularly concerned. What's going on?"

He replied, "I am worried. Very worried."

A J.D. Power Quality Report had been released the day before. The company had been rated "poor" for initial quality. It doesn't take a rocket scientist—or quality consultant—to know that this is not good news for a company. When disheartening results like that are received, sometimes the first thing the CEO does is fire whoever is in charge of quality. In this case, that was Mark.

"Is your boss upset with you?" I asked. "Do you want me to talk with him? Those results have nothing to do with you. The issues you are dealing with are everyone's responsibility—not yours alone."

It was at that moment that he looked at me and asked, "Subir, what do you do with a toothpick when you are done with it?"

"What do you mean? What kind of question is that?" I asked, confused and a little alarmed. It was not a question I had ever been asked before. Mark was normally a straight shooter. I was so surprised by the question that I did not immediately grasp the significance of the toothpick.

Finally I told him, "I throw it in the trash."

"Exactly. I do the same thing. I asked my assistant what she would do, and she said the same thing. I asked five of my colleagues, and they responded the same way. That's what they would do. But I was here this morning, meeting my boss at six thirty despite the winter storm. I knew he was upset because of yesterday's J.D. Power results. And as I was walking to his office, I noticed a used toothpick on the floor. Someone had tossed it on the floor instead of in a wastebasket! And it bothered me so much because I felt . . ." At this point his voice broke a little. "I felt I had done everything I could to communicate the need for quality in everything we do here. I've been championing quality throughout the company— and then I find a used toothpick discarded thoughtlessly on the floor. Subir, it is indicative of a much larger issue. If an employee doesn't care enough to throw a used toothpick in the trash, but instead drops it mindlessly on the floor the way a selfish motorist tosses litter out the window on the highway . . ."

His voice trailed off. The look on his face was hard to read. "This is where we work. Normally the only people going into the executive suite are executives. But it doesn't matter whether the person who did this is an executive or not. The point is that someone in our company did this. Now I know why our quality sucks. It is because some of the people here just don't care. If they don't care enough about something as basic as throwing away their trash properly, it's clear why there is so little accountability in our operations or production or sales."

"What did you do when you found it?" I asked.

Incredulous that I would even ask, he said, "I picked it up and threw it away." And that was part of his point. No one was above such basic responsibility, even the senior management and the CEO.

I agreed of course that the toothpick was emblematic of a much deeper problem within the company. As is often the case with management issues, the smallest signs can be indicative of more systemic issues. The toothpick episode reminded me of what Jan Carlzon, the CEO of SAS Airline Group at the time, is rumored to have said about passengers who find their seat trays dirty. They wonder if the airline is ignoring other parts of the business, including pilot training and engine maintenance. Dirty trays, he said, meant the airline was settling for good enough.

After our talk, Mark and I went to a group meeting to discuss the J.D. Power quality rating results and other issues. Because of my long-standing relationship with the organization, they included me in the meeting. The CEO had made it clear that he wanted all functional departments and levels of the organization to share their ideas openly. The meeting included both engineers and senior management, including the COO. The COO asked Mark to talk about why they did so poorly on the J.D. Power Quality Report.

You could hear a pin drop in the room. Several people, especially the engineers, knew what the real issues were—machinery that needed upgrades, a workforce that hadn't been trained to make quality their top priority, buggy software, unreliable suppliers—but no one spoke.

The COO, remaining composed, listened intently. He encouraged the people around the table to speak up. The problems Mark raised, he said, belonged to every member in the room—they were everyone's business. He told them they must help one another, even if a problem affected someone else's group or department.

The COO's words were inspiring, yet somehow the tension in the room didn't lessen, but actually continued to grow. It was one of those meetings you couldn't wait to get out of. A few engineers began to open up, trying to describe the issues. However, when they did, several of the managers in the room responded in ways that were clearly intended to shut them up. Their comments were defensive, and dismissive of the engineers' contributions, but they did it subtly enough that the COO did not recognize what was taking place—even though the rest of us did. I remember thinking, How could this guy be so clueless? In any event, the engineers got the message: shut up—we'll deal with this outside of the meeting. Perhaps the managers did not want to be embarrassed in front of the COO. Or maybe this was a facet of the culture the CEO and COO were attempting to change. To me, it was a little of both.

After the meeting, Mark and I went to the cafeteria to grab some lunch; he asked for my observations about the meeting.

I told him, "This company has a culture where people sweep problems under the rug, even in front of their bosses."

Mark gave me a hard look, seemingly offended by my observation. He said, "Subir, you know our CEO's commitment to quality. He has spent millions of dollars to change the culture. And it has become a very different company than it used to be. People speak freely now."

Despite the millions of dollars spent, clearly the message had not reached the managers in the meeting we had just left. I told Mark, "You sound defensive. What are you trying to defend against?" Several moments of awkward silence passed between us. Then I noticed that the group of engineers who were at the meeting had sat at another table nearby. I asked Mark if I could go speak with them. He nodded his agreement.

I asked one of the engineers I had spoken with in the past why he had stopped talking in the middle of what he was trying to say during the meeting. I knew he had participated in a training program that taught employees to talk openly and fearlessly about their concerns and observations.

He replied, "Subir, you are not an employee here. You've been hired to help us change. You can say whatever you like—people expect that from you. But the company culture here is such that if you are that straightforward, if you speak the unvarnished truth, your days are numbered. I have a young family to feed."

His response reminded me of several people at other companies I had spoken with in the past. One was a product line manager for a major food company, who once confided in me, "This stuff [referring to a specific line of products] has no nutritional value whatsoever. I won't let my kids eat it. But I have to produce it to earn my keep around here." It was another example of an employee who was afraid to speak the truth. Like the engineer, he kept his mouth shut in order to keep his job.

The second man was a manager in a financial services firm, someone who demanded honesty and candor from the people reporting to him. He told his team that he had one ironclad rule: "Don't lie to me." He explained, "If you tell me the truth when things go wrong, we can work together to fix it. But if you lie to me, we are both screwed."

The first of those two men was going along to get along. The second was making sure everyone knew that the organization's success—or failure—depended on its integrity and honesty.

I thanked the engineer for his candor in talking with me. I told him I wished that there were more people in the company who insisted on telling the truth. When I rejoined Mark, he asked what we had discussed. I told him, "Mark, you were right in your reaction to the toothpick you found on the floor. This company has a long way to go to become world-class. I will not be surprised if, metaphorically, you find more used toothpicks on the floor in the coming days."

I went on: "Improving quality is not a slogan or a process unto itself. Without a truly fearless culture, it is impossible to implement quality programs with any success, because employees—whether they're on the assembly line, in sales or accounting or inventory, or in the executive suite—lack the needed mindset. From what I've seen so far, fear is part of the company's DNA. It's all about 'good enough.' And it is a formula for disaster."

Those who know me know I love to challenge people— and to be challenged as well. So I decided to challenge Mark: "Can you speak up honestly in front of your boss?"

After a moment of reflection, he replied, somewhat abashed, "No." He was silent for a moment before continuing. "On paper we work in a 'fearless' culture; but in reality it's all a façade. We talk about how we have overcome our past practices that have held us back, that swept problems under the rug, and claim we now embrace a bold and open culture. But, in reality, it's the same old stuff."

I replied, "Look, Mark, until you talk openly about this in front of the group, and as a leader admit to perpetuating what you call a fake culture, you are not being true to yourself. And you are not being a good manager or leader. Face it: If you can't be true to yourself, you will never develop a caring mindset. Good enough isn't good enough. To excel, quality needs to be everyone's business."

Mark told me I wasn't being practical.

So I decided to switch gears. I asked him, "Are you true to yourself at home and at your church?"

He asked, "What does that have to do with our work here?"

"Believe me, it does relate," I said emphatically. "When you are at home or at church, I'll bet that you treat other people as, well, people—with respect, consideration. You value them for who they are. You recognize that they are people with families, with homes, with dreams, and with problems they're trying to resolve. You treat them with respect because you care about them. But when you are at work, you treat other people as if they are just 'employees' rather than people. It's as if their families, homes, dreams, and troubles do not exist. As if they are none of your business, or do not matter in this building. You treat them as if you do not care about them as individuals."

At that point, Mark seemed to have something of an epiphany: "Sometimes, when I get out of my car in the parking lot in the morning," he admitted, "I feel as though I am taking my briefcase and laptop out of the car but leaving myself behind. I think I need to stop doing that. I need to stop pretending that that sense of indifference is okay with me. I need to stop pushing aside my feelings about the people at work and stop accepting good-enough solutions."

"A fake culture is the result of fake people," I told him. "Don't let yourself be a fake person by treating those around you as if they do not matter. I promise, if you treat the people around you as human beings you genuinely care about, and if enough other people do the same, quality will improve dramatically. And not just at work. The quality of their lives will improve as well."

I felt better after my conversation with Mark—at least, he didn't seem to feel so beaten down and he had a better sense of direction. My next appointment was with Lloyd, another vice president. Lloyd is a nice enough guy, but for some reason his assistant is not. In my experience with her, she is someone who never smiles and is frequently rude. Does she have a difficult personality? Is she unhappy with her job? I tell clients who don't know how to smile, "It does not cost a penny to give a smile. And your smile will make my day better." The comment shocked one person so much that she began smiling every time I saw her. I hope she felt a lot better herself as well.

When Lloyd emerged from his office he appeared tense. I greeted him with a big grin, telling him, "Lloyd, you folks have a smile shortage in this organization. Can I buy you some? No charge!"

He laughed. "I will take you up on that one."

"I'm serious," I said. "I will pay ten dollars to your favorite charity each time your assistant smiles. And I'll bet you will smile more if she does."

"Is that what you are consulting about these days?"

"Believe it or not," I replied, "the answer is yes. Look, Lloyd, success—including quality—is all about the mindset of each and every employee. Trust me, your product and service quality will improve dramatically when the mindset of those in this company improves."

I had been suggesting to Lloyd for weeks that he get out of his office more and meet with his engineers and managers on their own turf instead of looking at their performance through spreadsheets and reports, or calling them to his office. Each time I suggested it, Lloyd promised he would act on my suggestion, but he never did. So I decided to force the issue.

"Let's take a walk," I said. "Let's go and talk to your team."

Lloyd made the usual halfhearted excuses—meetings, reports, no time—before he asked, "What would I talk to them about?"

I said, "Lloyd, you run a multibillion-dollar piece of the company's business. I do not have to teach you what to say or what to ask. Simply be yourself. Relax, smile, ask questions, and refrain from giving them your tough-guy look."

"Subir," he said, "as you are aware, our J.D. Power report was disappointing, and we have been using Lean Six Sigma quality processes for quite a while."

"Believe me, I feel a great deal of pain about your poor performance. But here's where I think the problem lies: you have all become too *process* focused, at the expense of your *people*. Achieving exceptional quality requires commitment to both processes and people. That's why I want you to spend time with your engineers and managers on their turf—so you can experience what is truly going on with your own eyes and ears, without any filter or censor. What they say in your office doesn't reflect what's really happening on the ground floor. Not all the news is good—but your people are afraid to speak up. There is a big difference between the action on the battlefield and the action in headquarters, miles behind the lines. I want you to connect with your people."

At last, he got my point. He said, "Okay. Let's go for a walk."

Lloyd seemed uncomfortable walking through the sectors of the company he managed. When we arrived at the location of a large product development team, most of the cubicles were empty; there weren't many people around. He approached an engineer who was in his cubicle, asked where the others were, and was told that they were in meetings of one kind or another.

The meeting rooms were along one wall of the floor. Lloyd looked through the glass partitions that separated the meeting rooms from the open cubicles and saw that the meeting rooms were packed with staff members. He went to one room, opened the door, and we both walked in. The man who was giving a presentation stopped in midsentence. The few senior managers present rose from their chairs as if paying homage to royalty. I got the sense that Lloyd felt very uncomfortable—along with everyone else in the room.

Lloyd said to the presenter and the room at large, "Please, continue the meeting. We are just here as observers."

The people in the room were in shock; they had not seen Lloyd here in months. We spent perhaps ten minutes in the meeting. Lloyd asked a few questions; then we left and went to another meeting room.

The group in the next room was talking about a product failure. The discussion was heated, and there seemed to be a lot of blame being passed—always a bad sign.

Lloyd said to the chief engineer, "We can't change the past. But we can do better in the future. Tell me about the new design."

The chief engineer replied, "We have no budget to make a radical change to optimize the future design. Unfortunately, future products will have the same shortcoming unless we spend the money to redesign the product."

Lloyd, unhappy with the answer, said, "Harold, you know the current financial condition of the company. There is no way we can get additional dollars beyond what has been allocated. Period."

The chief engineer was a straight shooter and refreshingly straightforward. For some reason, he didn't seem concerned about what his response might mean to his career. Instead, he stuck to his guns. He looked at Lloyd and said plainly, "Sir, as I said, unless we invest in new development costs, future generations of this product will continue to have problems, and things may get worse. I need to be honest with you today so that two or three years from now we are not in the same situation. If we can't invest more resources, the product will not improve."

It took guts for Harold to tell Lloyd the truth. In my experience, it was a rare behavior in this company. I noticed several nervous glances around the room.

One of the chief engineer's direct reports tried to tone down the bluntness of the message. But Lloyd realized the chief engineer was right. He was convinced. "Harold is the chief engineer on this product. I appreciate his telling me the truth—clearly, we need to take a different tack if we want this product to succeed."

Then he turned to the chief engineer and said, "Let's talk later about how to solve the design—as well as the budget problem."

The room fell silent; the other engineers were clearly surprised by this turn of events. Lloyd admitted, "If I had not shown up today, I might not have heard this. I am grateful that you stood up to do the right thing for the product and the company. I hope that you will always speak with such candor." With that, Lloyd and I left the room.

"Subir, what are your thoughts about what just happened?" Lloyd asked as we continued down the corridor.

"I felt you did the right thing. And you made your message about the need for honesty and open communication very clear."

"I understand better now why you have been pushing me on this," he said. "Quality really is everyone's business. And if people can't tell the truth without worrying about the repercussions, we'll never get to the heart of our problems and fix them."

Lloyd and I entered another meeting room. He gently interrupted the presenter and told those in the room, "I have been visiting a number of the meetings this afternoon. I just want to make sure that each one of you knows you have the right, and the obligation, to stand up for doing the right thing for the company. You must find out when there is a problem, and speak up about it, even when it's painful to do so. Without knowing the truth about our businesses and projects, we cannot improve the company. I give you my word that no one will be punished for speaking up honestly. Each of us must identify and point out things that will improve our customers' experiences, make our products better, and ultimately make the company more successful."

Then he repeated what was soon to become a kind of mantra with him: "Good enough isn't enough."

After spending almost two hours interacting with members of his team on their turf, Lloyd left the department feeling both exhilarated and frustrated.

As we walked back to his office, he said, "I finally have a better sense of what is really going on in my areas of report. I wish I had done this sooner. But you can bet I'll be doing this every week from now on."

My next meeting was with Brad, the CEO of the company. On my walk to his office, I wondered if the attitudes I had seen so far—attitudes of carelessness, unfriendliness, and reluctance to speak up—extended to the uppermost ranks of the company. I guessed that they did. Such attitudes tend to be embedded throughout an organization's culture. And it usually starts at the top.

Although I had been working at the company for months, this was my first meeting with Brad, and I was a bit apprehensive. When I sat down in his office, I noticed pictures of his children behind his desk. "How many children do you have?" I asked him.

He replied, "I have two girls. One is studying psychology at UCLA and the other is working in New York. Why do you ask? We aren't paying you to do family counseling now, are we?" he said, somewhat coldly.

"When did you last talk to them?" I persisted.

Annoyed with me, he replied, "I don't recall. I have been very busy."

"Okay," I said. "This session is over. You are paying me for an hour's meeting. I am not going to charge you for the hour. Instead, you have fifty minutes of free time. Call your daughters."

Stunned at my request, he somewhat abashedly asked, "What should I say?"

"Tell them you miss them. Tell them you love them. Will you promise me you'll make the calls?"

Obviously shocked by this turn of events, Brad promised to make the calls. I left him to do that.

A week later, to my alarm, Brad abruptly canceled my next meeting with him.

Two weeks later, upon my return to the company, I had a follow-up meeting with Brad. When I walked into his office, he greeted me with a hug! He was a much bigger man than I, and I had a firsthand introduction to what the term "bear hug" means.

"Thank you, Subir," he said. "Thank you so much. After you left our last meeting, I called both of my daughters and told them I loved them. There was a lot of crying on all our parts over the phone. As it turned out, we decided we could all take some time off from our lives to get together. I rented a lakeside cabin and we spent a week together. That is why I had to cancel our meeting last week."

With a chuckle he continued: "I canceled a lot of other meetings and things as well. Things I thought were important. But it turned out that the week with my daughters was far more important."

And then he said simply, "I got my daughters back."

I was pleased by what he had done and told him so. "Look, Brad. There is a lot of burnout in your company. You were burned out, your direct reports are burned out, and their teams are burned out. They are afraid of you, and tell you what they think you want to hear, instead of telling you the truth. If you really want to improve things at this company, including improving your company's quality, you need to be more thoughtful as a leader of this organization. Ask your executives and employees about their children, ask them about their lives. Let them know you care about them."

During the time I spent at the company in the months ahead, I emphasized mindset as a major contributor to the company's malaise. Poor quality was but a symptom of that malaise. The company's people were well versed in the practices and processes of quality. The company had spent a great deal of money learning about and teaching quality processes. But they lacked a genuine interest and concern about what quality means. Even the best processes lose their power and their efficiency if the people enacting them don't genuinely care about what they are meant to produce. The caring comes first; only after that does the process take hold. Good is never good enough.

Mark told me, "Now I know why our quality sucks. It is because too many people here just don't care." In other words, they didn't have the right mindset.

Our mindset predisposes us to think about things in a certain way. Some call it awareness, or consciousness, or mindfulness. It's the voice inside your head that guides everything you do and say. Having an open mindset is an important facet of what makes us human. Carol S. Dweck, professor of psychology at Stanford University, wrote in her bestselling book, *Mindset: The New Psychology of Success:*

> Whether they're aware of it or not, all people keep a running account of what's happening to them, what it means, and what they should do. In other words, our minds are constantly monitoring and interpreting. That's just how we stay on track. . . . Mindsets frame the running account that's taking place in people's heads. They guide the whole interpretation process.

Think of your own mindset as the interpreter of your experience. People can be aware, or unaware, of their mindset, but one's mindset has profound effects on so many aspects and dimensions of life. Whether completely rational or not, Mark's reaction to the discarded toothpick was on target—it was an affront to quality, because it didn't reflect a "caring mindset."

One way to better understand a caring mindset is to look at its opposite, an "indifferent mindset." My day at the company offered lots of evidence of that kind of dysfunctional behavior, from the carelessly discarded toothpick, to the senior managers who shut down discussion during the executive meeting, to the engineer in the cafeteria who admitted his reluctance to speak the truth. The evidence of a "fake" culture was everywhere: the unfriendly attitude of Lloyd's assistant; Lloyd's reluctance to meet his people on their own turf.

Where an indifferent mindset prevails, truth is elusive. People no longer strive to understand one another's point of view. Concessions are accepted because they are easier to deal with than seeking the best possible result. Blaming others is the norm, and people are satisfied with a good-enough result rather than exceptional results. By contrast, where a caring mindset prevails, truth is valued, people strive to understand one another, concessions are resisted in favor of seeking the best possible result or outcome, and people recognize that quality is everybody's business. Good enough is not good enough.

Had a caring mindset been pervasive in Brad's company, there would have been no toothpicks on the floor; employees—executives, managers, engineers, line workers, and everyone else—would have engaged in a lively dialogue intended to raise and resolve issues honestly. Collaboration and teamwork would have replaced finger-pointing and grandstanding. Lloyd would have had no reluctance to interact with his team, and his assistant would have offered me a smile, and maybe even an expression of concern: "Did you have any trouble getting here this morning? The highways are a mess."

Fortunately, the chief engineer cared more about his company's future and the quality of its products than about his own career advancement. But wouldn't it be better if employees did not have to make that choice?

Perhaps the most important lesson in all of this was expressed by the CEO of a service company that I know of. He told an audience of his executives and managers, "Surely we must care about our customers. But first we must care about one another."

There must be caring, and then process.

Some may roll their eyes at this, but trust me—process alone won't get you where you need to go.

The danger of an indifferent mindset is not just that it is a problem for large businesses. I believe it is endemic in our country. According to the J.D. Power 2015 North America Airline Satisfaction Study, passenger satisfaction with the airline industry scored a mere 717 on a 1,000-point scale. That is unacceptable. Nearly 64 million cars were recalled in the United States in 2014. Also unacceptable. Of forty-three industries on which the American Customer Satisfaction

Index gathers opinions, cable TV and Internet companies tied for last place in customer satisfaction. Those companies touch most of our homes. That same organization found that the healthcare industry scored 75.1 out of a possible 100 in the first half of 2015.

And I'm not just talking about businesses. In a Gallup poll published in the summer of 2016, only 56 percent of Americans reported a great deal or quite a lot of confidence in the police. Only 39 percent reported a great deal or quite a lot of confidence in the medical system. Confidence in our public schools came in at 30 percent; television news, at 21 percent. And Congress came in at an absolutely abysmal all-time low of 6 percent.[1] To top it off, the American Society of Civil Engineers' Report Card for America's Infrastructure, last published in 2013, rates both our country's roads and its aviation infrastructure as D, rail and bridges as C-plus, and hazardous waste and drinking water as D.[2] What would you do if your child came home with a report card like that?

We are suffering an epidemic of dissatisfaction with our organizations and the institutions that we rely on. This epidemic is driven by a nationwide mindset of indifference.

Over the next four chapters, I will explore in depth the four facets of a caring mindset—what I sum up as *the difference*:

- Being *Straightforward*
- Being *Thoughtful*
- Being *Accountable*
- Having *Resolve*

It is a list that gives us a useful and memorable acronym: STAR. For this star to shine, you need all four facets to be in place. A mindset cannot be characterized as "caring" if even one of these facets is missing. I saw glimmers of a caring mindset that day at Brad's organization. The chief engineer was straightforward with Lloyd, and the engineer in the cafeteria was straightforward with me. Brad learned to become thoughtful about his relationships with his daughters. Mark certainly felt accountable for the organization's quality. And Lloyd resolved to work on the budget problem with his chief engineer. But these were mere glimmers; what the company needed to do was to create a caring mindset that shone brightly throughout the company.

Think about the last time you picked up trash at a movie theater or on the sidewalk, helped a friend through a difficult time, or thanked someone for a critical but well-intended comment. These are small actions, but the little things add up. They matter. And each of those little things can lead to a much bigger—and better—result. That result is caring, and it is created by every action we take every day of our lives.

How many "toothpicks" do you see in a day? How many things do you see that are not the way they ought to be? And what have you done recently about those things? I challenge each of us to develop a caring mindset, because caring is everyone's business, everywhere and all of the time.

That, in the end, is the difference.

Chapter 2

THE IMPORTANCE OF BEING STRAIGHTFORWARD

It's interesting, the secrets you decide
to reveal at the end of your life.

—RANDY PAUSCH, AUTHOR OF *THE LAST LECTURE*

A few years ago, I received a call from Nick, a senior executive in a Fortune 500 company, who had been a client of mine for nearly ten years.

"I need to see you right away," he told me.

I was not used to hearing such urgency in Nick's voice. "Right now?" I asked.

"Yes. Right now."

Fortunately, his office was only a half-hour drive from me. So I got in the car and went to see him.

The first of the characteristics of a person who has a caring mindset is being straightforward. This does not mean that it is more important than the other three characteristics—I believe they are all equally important. All four have to be present to truly foster the mindset I'm referring to. But I feel one needs the quality of being straightforward in order to embrace the remaining characteristics. By *straightforward* I mean someone who is honest, direct, open, candid, transparent, and fair.

When I arrived at Nick's office that morning, he stood up to greet me. We sat facing each other at the small round table near the window in his office. Nick was a hard-driving, no-nonsense, and ambitious "win at any cost" executive. He was known for being cutthroat in his dealings with others when necessary. He was not afraid to use other people's talents and skills to get what he wanted. But he rarely, if ever, acknowledged his subordinates' efforts and contributions. Instead, he tended to take the credit for their work. When he felt threatened by someone, or whenever subordinates objected to his actions or managerial style, or to his taking the credit for their work, he demoted or fired them. Some very talented people left the company or were given the boot because of his actions. Politically savvy, he made sure that he kept his boss happy—he managed up—while ensuring that other talented people in his organization had little to no access to his boss.

Not surprisingly, few liked working for him. His direct reports were afraid of him and referred to him behind his back as "the snake."

I tried to coach him, pointing out his weaknesses many times. He respected me and my suggestions, because I had been instrumental in several of his promotions. So he would hear me out. But I knew in his heart he pushed me away whenever I pointed out his flaws—his arrogance or his un-willingness to give other people the credit they deserved—and the negative impact it had on employee and executive retention.

That morning Nick sat, seemingly shrunk within himself, his hands folded in front of him on the table. He looked grimly serious. I couldn't imagine what was wrong.

"Subir," he said softly, "I have been diagnosed with liver cancer. It is inoperable. The doctors are doing what they can for me, but I don't have long to live. Maybe a month or two."

I was shocked—devastated. I had known Nick since he was a junior executive struggling to climb the corporate ranks. The news hit me like a ton of bricks. Nick might have been a difficult boss to those under him, but he was also a brilliant executive with real vision who had had a major impact on his industry. My voice was barely audible when I replied, "I am so very sorry, Nick."

"I've told my wife and my children. I haven't told anyone at the company yet. But now you know," he said. "And I need your help."

I was surprised that Nick would confide in me with such a personal and painful revelation. I wondered what I could possibly do to help.

"Help with what?" I asked, unsure of what he needed from me.

"I have been thinking about how I treated Audrey," he said.

When Nick had taken his current position, he had a woman

reporting to him whom he did not like—Audrey. She knew his piece of the business better than he did when he arrived, knew its ins and outs, its strengths and weaknesses. She was very outspoken and straightforward, and never hesitated to challenge Nick and his ideas when she thought it necessary to do so—even in the presence of others.

So Nick removed her from his management team. It was a very public and humiliating demotion. And it was clear that Audrey's career at that company was effectively over. Soon after, she left the company and went to work for a competitor. After she left, the product for which she had held primary responsibility won national awards. Nick had taken credit for her work. He did not acknowledge her contribution.

Nick had not been honest about who was responsible for his group's achievements, and he had not been fair to Audrey.

"What about Audrey?" I asked, unsure of what he was getting at.

"The way I treated Audrey is one of the great regrets I have about my time here. I'm wondering what I can do about it. Should I offer an apology? If so, how? Will you help me think through what, if anything, I should do? Should I reach out to her and ask for forgiveness?"

"Nick, it is not my place to tell you what to do," I said. "I cannot even be a hundred percent certain what *I* would do. I've never been in that situation. All I can say is what I hope I would do. I hope that I would call Audrey and thank her for her work. A straightforward and simple 'Thanks,' I believe, will mean a great deal to her."

He asked, rather meekly, "Do you think she will take my call? She was very angry when she left the company. I did not handle it well."

I was surprised at how aware Nick was of the situation at the time. My impression of him was that too often he was oblivious to the effects of his behavior.

I said, "I am sure she will take your call."

Nick followed my suggestion and did call Audrey. Later, Audrey called me. We had worked closely together before she left the company. She asked if I had put him up to calling her. I assured her that I had not—I had merely made a suggestion in response to Nick's concerns about his behavior toward her. The decision to call was his. She did not relay the details of their conversation, but she did tell me that it lasted about a half hour and that they were both in tears by the end of it.

Nick's belated realization and regret that he often did not act out of a caring mindset only came to him in his final days, and that is unfortunate. But his outreach to Audrey and his simple "Thank you" is an example of one kind of straight-forwardness—an act that communicates appreciation. I can only imagine how much richer Nick's life would have been, as well as the lives of everyone around him, had he worked to be more straightforward during his lifetime.

Most attempts to be straightforward do not involve such dramatic circumstances. For example, a friend told me about something that then-CEO Alan Mulally did to bring his se-nior executives together to fix what was wrong at Ford Motor

Company when he took over in 2006. It is a terrific example of being straightforward.

On his arrival at Ford, Mulally began holding Thursday morning "Business Plan Review" meetings with his leadership team. He introduced the team to a "traffic light" system. He wanted their reports about important initiatives in their areas of responsibility to be color-coded green, yellow, or red to indicate that the report was either positive, cautionary, or negative. At the first meeting, the executives all showed up with reports coded green, and full of nothing but good news. Mark Fields, a member of Mulally's team, told *Fortune* magazine that, prior to Mulally's arrival, "we had a culture where, if you reported bad news, you were done."[1] No wonder there was no yellow or red in sight.

Mulally reminded his executives that the company had lost billions of dollars the previous year. And he asked pointedly, "Is there anything that's not going well?" His first goal in changing the culture at Ford was to get his executive team to be straightforward about the problems they were having. The same thing happened the following week, and the week after. The reports remained uniformly green. That was how entrenched the habit of burying the bad news at Ford was. Finally, Mark Fields broke a dead silence one week and reported to the group that there was a technical delay with a new car model they were launching. When Fields finished his report, the room fell silent. Everyone was waiting to see what the new CEO would do. In the past, the executive would have been fired. After a brief pause, Mulally began to clap, applauding the report; he said to the other executives in the room that he appreciated the straightforwardness. By the next week, several other reports were coded yellow or red, and before long, there was more red than green.[2]

Only when Mulally insisted that his team be straightforward were they able to acknowledge their problems and begin to move ahead. Once they recognized that good enough wasn't enough, they were finally able to begin fixing what was broken. If they hadn't felt they could be honest, open, and transparent about what was working and what wasn't working, the company would have continued to sweep its problems under the rug.

Ford struggled during the recession that struck the United States, beginning in December of 2007, and came close to bankruptcy. But in the end, Ford was the only American auto manufacturer to escape having to accept a government bailout. By fixing its lineup, manufacturing, and quality, the company eventually saw its profits soar. Mulally is credited for implementing one of the most dramatic turnarounds in history.

The direct opposite of being open and straightforward, of course, is being dishonest and deceitful—lying. And our internal antenna recognizes it when we encounter it. It happened to me not long ago at a five-star hotel. The hotel had fabulous views of a pristine lake surrounded by mountain peaks. I had booked a vacation suite for myself, my wife, and our two children. The suite we reserved was stunning in the photographs we looked at on the hotel's website, a two-level affair with windows along one wall overlooking the lake, and along another wall a view of the mountains. In order to secure the room, I had booked months in advance. The hotel confirmed our reservation two days before our arrival—I was told that everything was in order.

When we arrived in the sumptuous lobby of the hotel on the first day of our stay, I was told that our suite was not available. The manager at the front desk explained that the hotel had had a plumbing problem, and nothing was available on the floor that held the suites. With profuse apologies we were given two rooms on a lower floor, with a much less commanding view.

I found that I could not let my irritation go. I made my living helping organizations solve problems and improve their quality, and I had a nagging feeling that the story I had been given about the hotel's plumbing wasn't true. So I went to the floor where the suites were located and knocked on several doors, asking the guests there if their plumbing was okay in their suites. They were confused by my questions until I explained that I had been told there was a plumbing problem and had been given rooms several floors below. None of them, they told me, had had any problems.

"Thank you," I told them.

Now angry, I returned to the lobby and asked the clerk for the manager. I told the man, "I make my living lecturing and training executives around the world about quality. And I am now going to talk about my experience here at this hotel. I am going to talk about this hotel chain in my work and in the media. You charge thousands of dollars a night for your suites and then lie to your customers."

Then I told the manager I had gone to the floor in question and asked other guests about the alleged plumbing problems. And I discovered he had lied to me.

"You knocked on the doors of the other guests?" he said, astonished.

I said, "Yes, I knocked on their doors. Why did you intentionally lie to me?"

The manager, embarrassed, offered to give a discount for our rooms.

I said to him, "Look, this has nothing to do with the cost of the rooms. I can afford it. But that lie I'll remember for the rest of my life. If this were to happen to you on your family's vacation, how would you feel? What would you do if you discovered your room had been given to someone else—and then were told a lie to cover up the fact?" He said nothing.

Had the hotel staff been honest and straightforward with me, I might have still been annoyed and disappointed, but at least I would have felt that they cared enough about me to tell me the truth and apologize for their mistake.

We develop an inclination to lie at an early age. Various studies have found that 61 percent of teens admitted to lying to a teacher, 76 percent admitted to lying to their parents, and 84 percent admitted to plagiarizing material from the Internet.[3] As adults, adopting a caring mindset is a life choice that we make. It requires honesty, openness, candor, and straightforwardness, in every conversation and interaction that we have—with colleagues, bosses, and customers, with friends and family. Without the ability and intent to be straightforward, we cannot create and sustain a caring mindset, or achieve a healthy organization, family, or community.

If Nick had been honest and fair in his dealings with those under him, he would have given his subordinates the credit they deserved rather than taking it for himself. Alan Mulally's executives had to learn that it was safe to be honest and straightforward at Ford. The reason Ford was in such dire straits in the first place was that the company operated as fiefdoms that tried to bury any bad news. If the staff of the hotel I stayed at had been straightforward and honest with their guests, they never would have made up a lie about the plumbing to explain why my room was no longer available.

It is impossible to pin down the economic cost that results from employees who hide the truth or, worse, purposefully lie about the facts. Most research on such corporate behavior focuses on criminal acts, such as embezzlement, bribery, fraud, and tax evasion. A Cornell University study reported that white-collar crime is estimated to cost the United States more than $300 billion annually.[4] But I would add to that the cost of such minor theft as taking home office supplies or using company equipment for personal projects.

Yet apart from the dollar cost, the human cost is considerable. For example, what was the price of Nick's refusal to acknowledge his subordinates' efforts and achievements? I suspect that cost is significant. Did his people give their all to their work? At the very least, it costs the company the loss of valuable employees such as Audrey, in whom it had invested time and training. And what was the cost of Ford's executives burying the failures over the years before Mulally came on board? As someone who works with corporations of this size every day, I would say hundreds of millions of dollars, if not billions, had been lost. It's also not unlikely that workers at a manufacturing company like this may have been injured as a result of lax safety standards, or customers may have been injured as a result of defective products. All because people were not encouraged to be straightforward.

Years ago, Robert Cialdini, Regents' Professor Emeritus of Psychology and Marketing at Arizona State University, and two associates wrote an article, published in *MIT Sloan Management Review,* titled "The Hidden Costs of Organizational Dishonesty." In the article, they describe the results of dishonesty as "malignancies" and claim that dishonesty in an organization tends to grow, like a tumor, and is often difficult to identify as the root cause of poor performance.

One malignancy occurs when organizations develop a poor reputation. The damage can be considerable: lost opportunities, lost customers, lost revenue and growth, degradation of the company's stock, and more. As I write this, automaker Volkswagen has been denounced in the press for installing software in 11 million diesel cars that *deliberately* misrepresented the amount of pollutants they emitted when they were tested. Executives and managers have been fired. The company is facing serious financial penalties. Lawsuits have been filed, and criminal charges may follow. And Volkswagen stock has plummeted. To make matters worse, before the scandal the company had launched a "Think Blue" marketing initiative in which it stated, "Ecological sustainability at Volkswagen is a major corporate objective."

Bottom line, Volkswagen lied. Moreover, the company made *cars* that lied. Volkswagen's executives only came clean after they were caught—and by then, it was too late.

Whether Volkswagen's executives will be honest and candid and forthcoming about what they did remains to be seen. I hope that they will be as frank as Mary Barra was when, as CEO of General Motors, she faced relentless challenges from the government, the media, and its customers in the wake of the organization's ignition switch recalls. In an address to employees, amid the intense scrutiny of the media, she stated, "People were hurt and people died in our cars."[5]

Cialdini and his associates stated in their article, "Past research has found that, by nature, people react more adversely to deceitfulness than to any other attribute."

That same kind of adverse reaction applies to deceitful people as well. That is why those who reported to Nick referred to him as "the snake."

A second malignancy identified by Cialdini and his associates is a poor match between an organization's values and those of its employees. Anyone in a deceitful organization who attempts to create or nurture a caring mindset is in for a rough time. I can only imagine what engineers and others who work for Volkswagen and possess such a mindset are going through right now. My guess is they are angry, resentful, frightened, and disappointed—and perhaps more.

People tend to act less than straightforward out of either greed, fear, or pride. Volkswagen's dishonesty is a clear example of how greed can drive out integrity. There are countless stories like it: stories of companies, politicians, CEOs, Wall Street financiers, and others. Some wind up in jail. New Orleans mayor Ray Nagin was found guilty on twenty counts of bribery and was sentenced to ten years in federal prison. A justice of the Michigan Supreme Court was sentenced to 366 days in prison for criminal mortgage fraud. The speaker of the Rhode Island House of Representatives pleaded guilty to wire fraud, bribery, and filing a false tax return.[6] Stewart Parnell, an executive of a peanut company, conspired to hide the fact that some of the company's products were contaminated with salmonella. He was sentenced to twenty-eight years in prison on dozens of felony counts. The list goes on and on.

I understand the dynamic of such greed. Running a highly regarded consulting practice, I am constantly bombarded with opportunities to cut corners or to outright lie and fudge the facts. Every day could ensnare me in that trap if I let it. I am given access to confidential information about my clients—and as a result, I bend over backward to ensure that this information is never revealed to anyone, even my close family members. It is simply the right thing to do. Clients put their trust in me. How could I sell them my services if I do not believe in them myself? I would never do so. And they know that. To do so would be the antithesis of being straightforward. It would be dishonest, illegal, and unfair. I might make more money in the short term, but I would undermine my integrity and everything I stand for. Personal fulfillment and success is not about achieving financial wealth alone; it is about self-respect and personal integrity.

Our ability to be straightforward suffers when we are afraid. This is true not only in business but in our communities and within our families. When we are afraid, openness and transparency decrease exponentially. We hide the truth, or fake our emotions. We strive to give a false impression to cover up the truth—about how good-looking we are, about how clever or competent we believe ourselves to be, about how much money we make. The result is that we live in a world of deceit and lose sight of the importance of being straightforward and honest.

Nick's cutthroat style created fear in his team, compromising their ability to be straightforward in speaking their mind. Under previous CEOs, Ford's executives were afraid to tell the truth about their products, systems, and operations. I suspect that the manager at the hotel desk was afraid of the hotel chain executives' displeasure.

Fear can undermine openness and honesty in our personal lives as well. When I am angry, I create fear in my own children. I am an efficiency advocate. That is what I do for a living. As a result, I have a tendency to think my daughter should be perfect. I forget she is a teenager. I forget that she is a far better person than I was at her age. I expect her to do certain things my way. I was raised in a lower-middle-class family in Bangladesh. I had to work very hard to become what I am today. She, on the other hand, has lived a very comfortable life. But it is not her fault that she has grown up with more privileges than I. When I decided that she was not working as hard as she could, or should, I expressed annoyance with her. And as a result, she withdrew from me.

When I realized how negative I was being, I had to remind myself to come back to a caring mindset. I invited my daughter out for a walk; we had fun together. And I realized what a fantastic young lady she is and how much there is for me to learn from her. When she understood that my shortness with her was due to the fact that I wanted so much for her to succeed in life, she opened up, and talked about her dreams and her mistakes, telling me that she wants to cut back on the time she spends on social media. This was a huge learning experience for me. Creating fear and apprehension drives people away: they become less straightforward as a result.

I see this same dynamic of fear and withdrawal in many of the companies I work with—but too often without the happy ending that I experienced with my daughter.

Some people are able to break through an environment where openness and a caring mindset are in short supply. Mother Teresa never bowed to others, or wore makeup, but people were mesmerized in her presence. Gandhi wore the simplest clothing and went barefoot much of the time, but people embraced him. Steve Jobs wore a basic uniform of Levi's jeans and black turtlenecks, even after he became a billionaire. None of them were afraid to be themselves. When *Vanity Fair* magazine published photographs of Julia Roberts, Brad Pitt, Oprah Winfrey, and other celebrities without makeup or fancy clothing, Roberts posted a makeup-free photograph of herself on her Instagram account that went viral. She wrote, "Perfection is a disease of a nation. I know I have wrinkles on my skin but today I want you to see beyond that. I want to embrace the real me and I want you to embrace who you are, the way you are, and love yourself just the way you are."[7] I have rarely read words that have made a bigger impression on me.

The third dynamic that causes people to be less straight-forward is pride. Ego. It is a serious problem in a lot of organizations. Too often, senior leaders don't acknowledge their problems. And when they do, they hide them. "How can I tell others that I have a problem with that? They won't respect me. They will think I'm weak."

I once was credited in a magazine article with saving a manufacturing company $500 million. I sent a copy of the article to the head of product development in another company, asking to meet with him. When we got together, I told him that I was certain I could save $500 million for his organization as well.

"Subir," he said, "I don't think so. We are doing pretty well. Plus, I know that other company. I wouldn't be surprised if the data was faked."

I was astonished at his reaction. "What do you mean the data is fake? Do you think that I would condone such behavior?"

He quickly apologized. "No, I'm sorry. So they're really achieving those numbers?"

I assured him that was the case.

He then fell back on his claim that "we are doing well."

I wondered if that was true. Was all going well in his organization? Or was his pride getting in the way of admitting that he and his team needed help?

So I asked him, "Are you telling me that you don't have processes that can't be improved? Processes that aren't wasting money? Is that what you are telling me?"

"No, I'm not," he admitted.

"If that is the case, then why won't you accept my help? You are the head of product development. And yet you have trouble admitting to a problem. Are you afraid to admit you need help?"

He lowered his gaze, and finally nodded his head. "Yes."

When we do not acknowledge our problems, we live in a fictitious world. It is a form of dishonesty, and it is rooted in pride. I find this at the most senior levels of organizations, as well as through the ranks.

So often it is pride that discourages us from saying, "I don't know." When I am asked a difficult question about quality, and I don't have an answer, it is incumbent on me to admit, "I don't know." I can imagine people thinking, What the heck? You are supposed to be the quality expert. And I am. But I am not omniscient. I am not a genius with all the answers. I'm confident enough to admit when I don't know something. When that is the case, I work three times as hard to get the answer.

In my experience, the most successful people are not afraid to say, "I don't know." They are not trapped in dishonesty by their pride.

————

The thing is, when you are authentic, candid, and straight-forward, not only will you be more successful, but you will have more fun. When you are afraid to admit to your failings, you live in fear. The counter to living in fear is to boldly and honestly say what you think. And the feeling of freedom that comes with that is liberating—it is fun. Fear lives at one end of the spectrum of human emotions, and happiness and fun at the opposite end. When I reconnected with my daughter, I was having fun. On the other hand, I would bet that Nick did not have much fun throughout his career. Nor did Ford's executives have fun hiding their company's flaws. And I doubt that the manager at the hotel desk thought it was much fun lying to me about the hotel's plumbing.

Wherever I go, I try to have as much fun in my job and profession as I can. I'm very candid and straightforward, whatever the situation, and I find people appreciate my straightforwardness. I don't try to show people how smart I am. I just enjoy being myself.

Along with ten other well-known executives and consultants, I was recently asked to meet with the senior leadership team of an organization that provides financial support to low-income countries. The meeting was a two-day event focused on world hunger. I was delighted to discover that all of us were being very straightforward. On the first evening the president of the organization spoke about the definition of extreme poverty—living on an income of less than $1.25 a day. He told us that almost one and a half billion people worldwide earn less than that amount.

On the second day we talked about what the organization

was doing to tackle elimination of extreme poverty. It was, I felt, a worthy use of our time. On the morning of the last day everyone was given a large folder containing about seventy pages of material. Twenty of those pages contained printouts of the slides from different presentations. The remaining fifty pages featured the bios of all the people attending the event. One person's bio ran on for nineteen pages.

I was taken aback to see the waste of paper, given the purpose of our meeting. So, in front of the entire group, I asked, "Why do our folders contain fifty pages devoted to our bios? That information was already emailed to us before the event. We already know all this. Add up the cost of the fifty pages and the use of people's time in preparing the material, and I bet we could have fed twenty people."

The other attendees quickly agreed, which led to a healthy discussion of the organization's inefficiencies.

I returned home on Saturday night. Over the next two days I received requests from many of the people at the event who wanted to meet with me and spend some time with me privately. Why? As one of the participants I met told me while sharing a ride to the airport, "Subir, you are authentically straightforward—meeting you was refreshing and a great deal of fun." His comment made my day.

Nick's mindset and behavior changed dramatically after he was diagnosed with cancer. When he knew that death was imminent, many of the things we had talked about over the years finally started to sink in. I met with him each week; he often asked me if I believed that people he had wronged would forgive him. I asked him why he wanted forgiveness and gave him the space to talk about what he had done. I believe it was a form of catharsis; he would become very quiet. He did not tell me if he had reached out to anyone beyond Audrey. Perhaps that was enough for him. I do know that he went out of his way to repair relationships with colleagues, subordinates, and suppliers with whom he had been very tough. He began treating the suppliers he had long-term relationships with as business partners rather than as mere vendors.

At Nick's funeral, Audrey cried. People from organizations that worked with Nick's company attended the service; some stated that he was one of the best executives they had ever dealt with.

I couldn't help but wonder, however, if Nick had led a straightforward life before his diagnosis, would he have lived a much happier life? Would he have been even more successful? Would he have had more fun? I do know that at the end of his life, he was not proud of some things he had done.

Nick's wife introduced me to her grown children as their dad's mentor. I never felt that Nick regarded me as a mentor during our meetings and conversations. But I do feel Nick's story is a tale of transformation. In the end, he was able to continue working for another six months, far longer than his original prognosis. And according to many, he did the best work of his career. He had a positive impact on countless people in his organization, as well as on the company's suppliers. And I know that he was far prouder of his actions and behavior during the last months of his life than he was in the previous decades of his career. I only wish he had not waited so long.

The cost of dishonesty—personally and corporately—is considerable. According to surveys, approximately 25 percent of American adults approve of overstating the value of claims to insurance companies. Fraud in the property and casualty industry is estimated at $24 billion annually. "Wardrobing"—paying for an item, using it, then returning it—was once estimated to cost retailers about $16 billion. The Internal Revenue Service estimates that the difference between what taxpayers pay and what they should pay is nearly $353 billion per year. Another telling statistic—88 percent of children between the ages of eight and eighteen know that sharing downloaded music is illegal, but 56 percent of them do it anyway.[8]

Each of us has a choice to make each and every day about whether to lead a straightforward life, a life of integrity, or a life that is filled with dishonesty and lies. The choice is ours. So let me end this chapter on the importance of being straightforward in developing a caring mindset with these questions:

1. What do you lose when you or the people around you seek the easy way out because you are afraid to be straightforward?
2. Are you being straightforward in speaking up now? Why wait until it is too late?

Chapter 3

THE POWER OF A
GLASS OF WATER

If a man speaks or acts with a pure thought,
happiness follows him.

—GAUTAMA BUDDHA

A t the beginning of a busy week, I boarded my flight
from Los Angeles to Detroit and settled into an aisle
seat, grateful that the client I was going to visit had
agreed to pay for first-class travel. A young man in a charcoal-
gray suit, with a neatly trimmed beard, hoisted his luggage
into an overhead bin, folded his jacket neatly on top of his
roll-on bag, and took the seat across the aisle from me. A
female flight attendant took orders for drinks; I asked for
water. The young man wanted nothing.

The second characteristic of a person with a caring mindset
is being thoughtful. By *thoughtful* I mean that the person
is attentive to others, considerate, unselfish, and helpful.
When we place ourselves in another person's shoes, or see
things from another's point of view, and then act for their

benefit—when we are being empathetic—we are practicing what it means to be thoughtful.

As the flight attendant was serving drinks to the passengers in first class, the people flying coach began to board. Among them was an elderly, frail-looking man with wispy white hair. He took the aisle seat in the first row behind the bulkhead separating the first-class and coach sections of the plane. When the attendant was finished taking care of those of us in first class, she paused near the man. Looking up, he asked her for a glass of water. The attendant explained that drinks were not served in the coach section until after takeoff.

He persisted, repeating his request again, saying, "I'm very thirsty. Can't you please get me a glass of water?" The attendant again refused to accommodate his request, using the same dismissive, rather official tone she had used in response to his first request. Her voice had a robotic quality to it—it was clear she did not care whether or not this older gentleman was thirsty—only that it was "against the rules" to provide a simple glass of water. I understood that she was following the airline's policy, but was nonetheless surprised and somewhat put off that she denied the elderly man's request. Others in the first-class section seemed perturbed and concerned as well; we looked at one another anxiously, searching for an ally, but no one got up or said anything to the attendant. Suddenly the young man across the aisle from me left his seat, went to the attendant's galley, and returned with a glass of water. He handed the glass of water to the man and returned to his seat, ignoring the glare of the attendant, who seemed dumbfounded and annoyed by his actions. The rest of us near the old man who witnessed the incident gave the young man a round of applause. Feeling relieved for the old man, but a bit ashamed that I didn't get him a glass of water myself, I vowed to myself that going forward, I would be as thoughtful and action-oriented as the young man was.

During a trip to India, I was in a taxi in Calcutta, the capital of the Indian state of West Bengal, stuck in traffic. Once India's leading city, Calcutta has been in steady economic decline for many years. It is perhaps best known for its crowded, fetid slums, rickshaws—and Mother Teresa, who lived there. It is a chaotic, crazy place: the traffic, the noise, the colors, the jarring juxtaposition of the richest of the rich rubbing shoulders with the poorest of the poor. The city is a storm of sounds, smells, colors that assault your senses.

My taxi was inching along a street teeming with people. There was a Mercedes in front of us, a rickshaw behind us, a cow, an overcrowded bus, shouting vendors, and men on mopeds whizzing by on either side. A man clad in rags slept on a filthy blanket on the sidewalk. Through the window of the car I saw a naked child, seven or eight years old, reaching his hand in a street drain.

I asked my cabdriver what the child was doing.

The driver told me, "Sir, don't look at it. Just ignore it." I was flabbergasted that he referred to the young boy as "it."

I said, "No, no. I want to understand. What is he doing?"

Once again he told me to ignore the child.

Frustrated, I said, "Just stop here."

I got out of the car and, using the local language, I asked the child what he was doing.

He said, "Sir, I'm just seeing if any food is passing through this drain."

"What do you do with the food?" I asked.

He said, "I dig it out, wash it, and eat it."

I was speechless. I did not know what to say. I was completely frozen for several seconds that seemed a lot longer.

When I regained my wits, I took the boy to a sweet shop nearby and told the man behind the counter, "Whatever this child wants, give it to him." He chose a few things, I paid for them, and then we parted. My taxi had not advanced very far and I got in again.

I did not think ahead before taking the child to the shop. It was an instantaneous reaction, much like the actions of the young man on the plane. Having witnessed extreme poverty during my childhood in Bangladesh, I knew that any human being, if they were hungry enough, might be forced to gather food from the gutter. If someone is starving and cannot afford anything to eat, and I can afford it, should I not help? Of course, I realize I cannot help to feed all of the hungry people in the world. But in that moment, it was my responsibility to help that child. Nothing more, nothing less. For that one moment I was able to have a small positive impact on the world around me, just as the young man on the plane that day made a difference to the elderly man.

I believe there are moments like that in everyone's day, although perhaps not so extreme or dramatic. Metaphorically, these are moments when a colleague, a friend, or a family member has a hand in a drain, searching for something they need in a difficult time, or who simply needs a "glass of water." Those moments are opportunities to act in a thoughtful way: to be attentive to others, considerate, unselfish, and provide comfort or aid.

Barbara, the wife of Kent, a good friend of mine, hurt her back, and given the pain, went to see a top back doctor. The doctor recommended surgery for a disk problem. She postponed the procedure for eight months, until the pain became so severe that she could not stand up straight. At that point her doctor, alarmed, told her, "Tomorrow morning, six a.m., you show up for surgery." The next morning he did the procedure.

Kent was in the waiting room while Barbara was in surgery. After forty-five minutes, the surgeon sent a nurse to tell him, "The operation will take another forty-five minutes, but the doctor will see to it that your wife's pain is gone."

After the surgery was completed, the surgeon came to the waiting room to tell Kent that all had gone well and that Barbara was in the recovery area. Kent and the doctor knew each other; they had friends in common and sometimes showed up at the same social events.

Kent told the doctor, "Thank you for letting me know that Barbara will be okay. Thank you for also sending the nurse to reassure me."

The doctor said, "Normally the kind of surgery I do can take four or five hours, sometimes more. So I try to keep the patient's family in mind. I know that they are concerned and that they worry. So I do my best to keep them informed."

Then Kent asked him the question that was on his mind. "Did you have the nurse come out especially for me, or is that something you always do?" And was the practice part of the doctor's training or a policy of the hospital? In other words, was this common among doctors?

With a smile, the doctor said, "No, it is not a policy of the hospital. Nor was it part of my training. I just feel it is the thoughtful thing to do—for *all* my patients, not just the ones I know personally."

Being thoughtful is a two-step process. The first step involves listening: at work, to your customers and your employees; at home, to your spouse and to your children; in your personal life, to your doctor, elders, trusted friends, or experts. A typical study on our ability to listen (there are many out there) suggests that we listen about 45 percent of the time we spend communicating with others. But results of such studies vary widely and depend on the group of people in the study. For example, a 1980 study of United States college students reported that they listen 53 percent of the time spent in communication with others, while a study conducted in 2006 reported the time spent listening was as little as 24 percent.[1]

Despite the wide variations in results, it is clear to me that we can draw two conclusions. First, listening is the communication skill we use most often.[2] Second, we are generally not very good at it. One study reports that the average person listens at only about 25 percent efficiency.[3] A study of more than eight thousand people found that almost all of them believed they communicate as effectively as, or more effectively than, their co-workers. But of course that is not possible; everybody cannot be average or above average.[4]

Whatever the amount of time we spend listening, I think we can all agree that listening is a critically important skill, and that we can do better. If you don't listen to others, you cannot possibly be thoughtful. Yet most of us do not believe that we need to improve our listening skills; we overestimate our ability to listen purposefully and thoughtfully. We often mistake listening casually to someone speak as understanding what they're saying. Yet too often we're thinking about what *we're* going to say in reply when it's our turn to talk.

At the end of the day, our ability to truly listen to others is in our hands. We can all improve our ability to listen.

Listening to others purposefully involves not just hearing what they have to say, but trying to put yourself in their shoes. It involves empathy and understanding. Simply imagining that you understand what the other person is trying to say, without attempting to fully grasp why the other person is telling you what they are saying, does not demonstrate good listening skills. Yet I see this all the time in my consulting work. It is especially true of managers who are in other ways very smart people. They are so busy that they often don't fully hear what the other person is trying to communicate; as a result, they jump to conclusions about what is being said, when they really only have half the picture. Why? They didn't listen carefully enough, with purpose.

Julian Treasure, a management consultant and author of the book *Sound Business,* says that our unconscious filters inhibit our ability to listen. Those filters include our cultural values, attitudes, and expectations. These filters don't limit our ability to take in the words the other person is conveying, but they do limit our ability to understand the other person. Treasure lists seven filters that inhibit real listening: culture, language, values, beliefs, attitudes, expectations, and intentions.[5] He urges us to engage in *conscious listening:* to be aware of how our own filters influence our ability to listen fully.[6]

Imagine, for example, that a co-worker comes to work late in the morning and leaves early. Let's say that his performance is also not up to par when he is at work, placing a burden on your ability to get the work done in your group or area or department. So he is not meeting your expectations, one of Treasure's filters. Let's also imagine that he is from a different ethnic and cultural background, another filter. With your filters in place, you might jump to the conclusion that he is doing it deliberately, and find yourself angry and resentful, because your expectations and those in the company are high, and because you personally value diligence so much. Perhaps he is one of "those people" about whom you are suspicious, because of your different backgrounds and heritages, whether or not he has done something amiss.

If you are aware of your filters and are determined to not allow them to get in the way of your attempt to understand why his behavior has changed, you might learn, for example, that he is dealing with a difficult but temporary family crisis at home. Knowing that, you might give him a pass for a while, or even ask him how you might help, by offering, for example, flexible hours while he works through the crisis.

Genuine "listening" involves more than just hearing the words that others say: it requires that you pay attention to the meaning behind the words and be observant. My noticing the child in the streets of Calcutta was such an act of "listening"—of observation and understanding. That is why I got out of the taxi to ask after the young boy. Genuine "listening" involves hearing, observing, and empathy and understanding.

My work with large and small organizations, in both the private and public sectors, has convinced me that most people do not practice genuine listening in organizational life. This is a major workforce issue, especially at the senior management levels, where managers and executives mishear one another and those under them, and then come away from meetings and discussions in a state of confusion. Let me give you an example.

I attended a meeting some time ago with a senior executive who was a client of mine. I was there as an observer rather than as a participant. After the meeting, I told him that I did not understand what one of the speakers at the meeting had been talking about.

I asked him, "Did you understand it?"

"No," he admitted to me. He had only pretended to understand to save face.

I told him, "If you didn't understand, why didn't you ask questions? Why did you pretend to understand?"

He fell silent and did not reply.

"I think your ego got in the way. You wanted to appear smart enough to understand, even when you didn't."

The funny thing is that *truly* smart and accomplished people aren't afraid to admit when they don't understand something. They know how to listen and try to make sense of what they are hearing. The senior executive wasn't truly listening. Perhaps he was daydreaming about a vacation or the weekend. But worse, he didn't have the courage to admit out loud, "I don't get it." My guess is that several of the others in the room didn't "get it," either.

I noticed several of the people at the meeting were attending to their smartphones or tablets while the speaker was at the dais. How could they possibly listen carefully and with purpose when their attention was distracted?

There are three important questions I think every person, and certainly every manager, should ask himself or herself about how well they listen:

The first: Do you get out from behind your desk and walk the corridors and floors?

To know what is going on, you have to be where the action is. You have to go to your customers. You have to go to the factory, or to the sales floor, or to where the problems are.

I was at lunch with a group of executives a while back. The executives were from a variety of industries. I asked one of them, the CEO of a food company, "Which age group eats the most cereal?"

"That's a very good question," he replied, and posed the question to the other executives at the table.

One of them said confidently that the end user was mostly children, and the others nodded in agreement. The company's packaging seemed to reflect that belief; it was clearly aimed at attracting children.

But the CEO, to my surprise, disagreed. "No, you are wrong. The answer is baby boomers. Baby boomers eat more cereal than children."

So I asked him, "Okay. How many baby boomers have you sat down with?" The executive himself was in his early fifties.

He immediately became defensive. He pointed out that he was the CEO of the company and it was not his job to meet with the individuals who purchased their products. I asked him again, "How many customers did you meet with last week, last month, last year?"

Reluctantly, he told me the answer was "zero"; he relied on his direct reports to gather such data. I challenged him to ask the members of his management team if any of them had spoken directly with individual customers. None of them had.

He was running a multibillion-dollar food company based on untested assumptions. As a result of my challenge, the CEO and his team started to visit stores where their products were sold so they could speak directly to consumers. Only when they started listening did they learn who their real customers were and what they wanted. You have to go where the action is if you want to learn the truth. Genuine learning starts with listening.

Another time I asked a group of auto executives if they had recently purchased a car, and if so, what the experience was like. I already knew the answer. They had not, of course, purchased a car recently because their cars were provided by the company.

"Go to one of your car dealers," I told them. "Pretend that you are a buyer. See how you are treated. Are you treated the way you expect or want to be treated? Then go to one of your competitors' dealers and see how they treat you. Again, if you want real answers, go where the action is." It's pretty straight-forward advice. Yet I am constantly amazed by the number of people who do not do this basic homework—they refuse to leave the comfort and security of their desks.

To me, Bill and Melinda Gates offer one of the best examples of senior executives going where the action is. Many nonprofit organizations with budgetary concerns do not deliver a high percentage of their income directly to the cause they serve. Thirty percent or more of the money they raise goes to operating costs. In other words, for every dollar you donate to such organizations, the intended audience gets at best 70 cents. The Gates Foundation, on the other hand, does devote a high percentage of its income to helping those in need. One reason is that both Bill and his wife, Melinda, are frequent visitors to the countries in which their foundation is active.

Here is how Bill Gates described their first trip to Africa:

"It was a phenomenal trip. Not long after we returned from this trip, Melinda and I read that millions of poor children in Africa were dying every year from diseases that nobody dies from in the United States: measles, hepatitis B, yellow fever. Rotavirus, a disease I had never even heard of, was killing half a million kids each year. We thought if millions of children were dying, there would be a massive worldwide effort to save them. But we were wrong."

The Gates Foundation then set up a system to guarantee purchases from drug companies to combat the diseases.

Bill Gates concluded, "There's actually no substitute for going and seeing what is happening."[7]

The second question to ask yourself about how well you listen: Am I doing most or all of the talking in my interactions with others?

If you are doing the talking, you cannot be listening. A colleague of mine—brilliant and a technical whiz—did nothing but talk when he met with clients. He didn't learn anything and wasn't able to address the problems he was brought in to resolve. Anyone who knows me knows that I love to talk. But listening is an essential skill for a consultant. If I don't listen to my clients, I won't educate myself about them. When I meet with executives for the first time, they usually expect me to do all the talking. Instead, I let them do all the talking while I just listen. Only then am I able to determine what needs to happen, and add value.

Listening is an educational process. When you don't listen, you don't learn. Marshall Goldsmith, a well-known executive coach and a good friend, advises people who have a hard time listening to do the following: stop, take a deep breath—and let the other person speak up.

The third question to ask yourself about your ability to listen: Do I try to empathize with other people?

Being empathetic is the second step in being thoughtful, and that is the focus of the remainder of the chapter.

Empathy requires that you attempt to identify with the feelings, thoughts, or attitudes of another person. The young man on the plane empathized with the older passenger who asked for a glass of water. He understood what it was like to be thirsty and helpless. I could identify with the child on the streets of Calcutta. The back doctor I mentioned could empathize with the patient's husband.

There are four aspects to empathy. The first is understanding that one person cannot do everything. None of us can. I cannot feed all the homeless children in India, or in the world. But I could feed one child in Calcutta for one day. We all need the help of other people.

Our housekeeper told us she and her family had decided to move away from the town where we lived. As a result, she would be leaving us. She cried when she gave us the news: my wife and I were upset as well. She was like a member of our family, and influenced our lives in such a positive way. I wished her well and told her she was always welcome back if things didn't work out. After she left, I did my part around the house to make up for our losing her—and, trust me, that wasn't easy!

When I came to America, I arrived with a college education and the clothes on my back. I was not better off financially than our housekeeper. With hard work, perseverance, good fortune, and help from other people, I have been successful enough that I now have more than I'll ever need in my lifetime. But because of my struggles to get ahead, I have enormous respect for people like our housekeeper, the work that she does, and her determination to get ahead in life. I am able to empathize with her because I was in her shoes at one point in my life.

I was sorry to see her leave, because she had done such a wonderful job, and because I knew she enjoyed working for us. And we enjoyed having her as part of our household as well. But I could understand her family wanting to improve their lives by moving to the city. I, too, had to change locations and cities several times, so I understood her decision. That is the nature of genuine empathy. When you empathize with someone it doesn't matter who the other person is or what he or she does. I know that every person I interact with is valuable and is deserving of empathy. Our housekeeper. My barber. Our mailman. The person who drives the truck that cleans the street in front of my house. My clients. I need every one of them. As a society, we need them all. No one person's contribution is less important than another's. Empathy requires only that we value another person as a human being who, like all of us, provides worth to the community, to our society, to our country, and to everyone else. We are all connected; we all impact one another.

The second aspect of empathy that I see around us too much is *me, me, and me.* We must transform *me, me, and me* to *you, you, and you.* We must make sure that everything in our lives is not about *me;* it must be about someone else. Nick, whose story I told in the previous chapter, was a perfect example of someone with a *me, me, and me* mindset for so much of his life; he went so far as to take credit for the accomplishments of others.

Americans gave nearly $36 billion to charity in 2015.[8] This is one of the great things about my adopted country. It is part of our culture, our DNA. And I hope we continue to do that. But day in and day out, we live in a world that is still too self-centered.

In the film *Time Out of Mind,* which starred Richard Gere, Gere portrays a homeless man on the streets of New York City. He has a bad haircut, a few days' growth of beard, and disheveled clothes. He begs for money, eats food rescued from trash cans, and sleeps in doorways. Gere said of his experience in the film:

> So I came out there with a certain anxiety, but I quickly realized that no one was paying any attention to me—nobody. I could see from two to three blocks away that people were making a certainly unconscious, sometimes conscious, decision that, "There is a panhandler, he's going to be bothering me, he's going to want money, I don't want to give him any money, I feel guilty for not giving him any money, why's he making me feel guilty that I'm not giving him any money, I don't like this guy." I could feel all this anger, this

swirling of emotions. And, I think on a deeper unconscious level, I could see people react to me like I was
a black hole that they would be sucked into, that there
was a black hole of failure.[9]

Making the film was a profound experience for Gere, and
for the film's director, Oren Moverman. Moverman said, "I
learned about the value of just recognizing someone's humanity." Richard Gere said, "Yeah, you give the dollar, but
it's not like you give the dollar because you're guilty. It's that
genuine sense that you're my brother, you're my sister, and I
wish you well."[10]

You're my brother, you're my sister, and I wish you well.
Think about those words. Carry them with you as you go to
work, and as you interact with your family and with friends
in your community. At work, how thoughtful are you toward
the people in your organization at the bottom of the organizational chart? How thoughtful are you to the cabdrivers you
flag down, or the men and women who collect the trash from
your wastebaskets at night? Only by transforming ourselves
to think of others, to think of *you,* instead of *me,* will empathy and thoughtfulness begin to take root in our lives. It's a
daily challenge, I assure you—but it's essential to developing
a caring mindset.

One of the top performers in my organization left to fulfill his dream of working for one of my competitors. I was
upset when he resigned, but I tried to accept his resignation graciously. I told him that I hoped he would be even
more successful and happy. Six months later, a few of my

colleagues mentioned to me that he wanted to come back. At first I declined to even consider taking him back—my ego got in the way. But eventually I realized that I had to at least *listen* to his reasoning.

I met with him on a fall evening after business hours. I asked why he wanted to leave what he had described as his "dream company." He looked me straight in the eyes and said: "Subir, your firm treated me as a human being. My current employer treats me like a machine."

When I asked what he meant by that, he said: "If I died today, you and the whole organization would attend my funeral; not one person from my current employer would show up. I do not need money as much as I need the empathy of a caring community."

I was humbled that he would think of our organization that way, and I welcomed him back. It was another reminder to me of the power of empathy.

The third aspect of empathy that deserves attention is our acceptance that each of us is but a very tiny speck in the universe. I am very fortunate that the back of my house overlooks the Pacific Ocean. When I do nothing but look out at the ocean, I sense how small I am. I am known in my field and to my friends and associates as an energetic person. But when I stare out at the Pacific, I am humbled. However, I am also inspired. That sense of my smallness in the world is what gives me energy. It causes me to question myself, and accept that I am not good enough, that I am not contributing enough. I am not making enough impact. I'm not adding enough value to the world around me. My sense of humility does not come from thinking about how important I am, but from how small and insignificant I am compared to the endless expanse of the universe. And ultimately, I believe, our humility is what defines us and makes us selfless.

Former NFL wide receiver Brent Celek knows about selflessness. In December 2013, the Philadelphia Eagles played the Detroit Lions in an NFL football game punctuated by heavy snow; eight inches fell during the game. With two minutes left, and the players ankle-deep in snow, Philadelphia held a fourteen-point lead—and had the ball thirty-seven yards away from another score. The game was, for all practical purposes, over. Eagles quarterback Nick Foles connected with Celek for what would surely have been a touchdown. Celek, who enjoys a well-deserved reputation for being a selfless team player, could have walked the final ten yards for the score. Instead, he slid to the ground in the snow and waited for a Detroit player to touch him and stop the play. The Eagles then ran out the clock.

After the game, Celek said that he planned his slide before the play unfolded. If he scored and then the Eagles kicked off, someone could have gotten hurt on a meaningless play in the snowy, slippery field. It was a selfless act—Celek declined to pad his résumé with another touchdown. "Besides," he said, "who could resist sliding through the snow?"

I find that I often learn some of my most important lessons from children. So I asked a schoolchild what empathy meant to him. I knew that he had just completed a school project about it.

Here is what he said. "If somebody fell at our school while we are playing together, even if we are all enjoying the game, if someone goes to try to help out, to take care of the kid, or maybe go get the nurse, I think that is empathy." To me, that is a perfect description of a caring mindset.

He thought of empathy as "kindness." And that is the fourth aspect of empathy that I want to focus on. Kindness is an *action*. It is the *doing* part of empathy. I try to practice it in my work every day.

The CEO of one of my client companies called me to say that I had to wrap up my contract. His company was behind in paying my firm for six months of work. He told me that his firm might soon declare bankruptcy.

I told him not to worry about me, that I was more concerned about him and his company. I told him that my father taught me that we are obliged to help a fellow human being who needs help at a difficult time. I offered to continue my service to his company, even though I knew I might lose all my fees if his company declared bankruptcy.

My stance did not make sense to him, but he reluctantly agreed. Despite my help, the company did in the end have to declare bankruptcy. However, to my surprise, twenty-four hours before declaring bankruptcy, he made sure that our fees were paid. Later I heard that he also took care of other suppliers who had cared for his company. It was an incredibly kind and thoughtful thing to do. Perhaps my empathy toward him helped teach him to be empathetic toward his suppliers.

There is one more story about thoughtfulness that I would like to share. My first job was as a senior software engineer for a company in which my team and I worked many hours beyond the standard nine-to-five. I was assigned to lead the company to the first Southeast Asian Apple World Conference, in which many other companies also showcased their works. I was not only in charge of the software demonstration, but also responsible for the design of our booth, and the creation of our presentation. During that time, many of my friends were studying at a medical school close by. One of my friends happened to also be an artist. He and a few of his friends offered to help make our display really stand out. I was grateful and excited—I was eager to win the coveted prize for the best presentation.

I had been working on our presentation eighteen or twenty hours a day for several weeks straight. One night, around eleven o'clock, the organization's office caretaker came to my office while a few friends and I were deep into a brainstorming session about the project. He had already been by four times before. Very politely he told me, "Sir, you forgot to have your dinner. Do you want me to bring something for you and your friends? If you do not eat, you may not be at your best."

Once again I told him to not worry about us and suggested that he go home and go to bed. Instead of doing what I suggested, he called the company CEO and told him of his concern for us. At midnight, the company's owner and CEO showed up at my office with a feast for all of us! He told us that his mother had cooked the food after the caretaker called to express his concern about our well-being. We were speechless.

To me, the caretaker and CEO both illustrate what it means to be more thoughtful: they were not only empathetic, but took action—and took the time to listen to what we needed (food) even though I kept insisting we were fine. Both treated us as though we were special, and expressed their compassion and concern. Both expected nothing in return for what they did.

I still get a little emotional when I think about this experience. Genuine thoughtfulness and a caring mindset aren't defined by someone's position in an organization. Together, a caretaker and a CEO showed me what it means to be truly thoughtful.

And in the end, we did win the prize for the best presentation.

I will conclude my discussion of thoughtfulness with several questions:

- Is there anyone in your life today, at home or at work, who needs a "glass of water" right now, or who is desperate enough to "plunge his or her hand in a drain" searching for emotional sustenance? How might you express your own empathy and thoughtfulness?
- Is there anyone at home, at work, or in your community with whom you cannot empathize? If so, are you truly listening to that person?
- Are you willing to look at the world through someone else's eyes?

Chapter 4

TAKING RESPONSIBILITY

Do not wait for leaders, do it alone.

—MOTHER TERESA

A teacher at a school my children once attended wrote a harsh email to my daughter. My daughter, eleven at the time, was offended and I was completely shocked. I could not comprehend that a teacher would write such an email to a sixth grader. I decided two things that day. First, I was going to hold myself accountable for doing something about the teacher's affront to my daughter. Second, I was going to hold the school accountable for the affront.

I use the term *being accountable* to mean accepting responsibility for one's actions or inaction, in matters for which you are obligated or answerable. Being accountable is the third element of a caring mindset, and the third letter in the acronym STAR. When you take responsibility for your actions, good or bad, you are being accountable.

———

I have no issue with my daughter being criticized when it is warranted. As you have already surmised from stories I told previously, I can be a pretty demanding parent. But the teacher's email was so disturbing that my first impulse was to do what most parents would do: go to the school and complain to the teacher. However, I decided not to do that. Instead, I made an appointment with the school's development officer. I read the email to him without identifying the teacher.

I asked, "Do you think the teacher was justified in sending this email to a student?"

There was no hesitation in his voice. He said, "Absolutely not."

I knew that this school, like many others, had a set of core values that it endeavored to live up to: respect, caring, achievement, citizenship, and learning. Parents had been told over and over again how important these values were to the school—as well as to its students, teachers, and parents.

"When is the last time you held training for your teachers about your core values?" I asked.

A bit defensively, he asked what I meant by my question.

I explained: "Your school has a set of principles. I know that as human beings we cannot always live up to our values; none of us is perfect. We benefit from frequent reminders about how we are supposed to act according to what we say we value. So my question is, when is the last time your teachers were reminded of those values and what they mean? When was the last time they got training about them?"

Agitated, but doing his best to maintain his composure, he said, "I don't remember."

I told him that, since he could not remember the last time his teachers examined the school's core values or received formal training in what they meant, it was likely that the email sent to my daughter was a sign of a systemic issue. And as such he was responsible for fixing the problem.

Then I told him, "Ask your teachers who America's leading instructor is. Why not ask this person to teach them about the school's core values? Once the teachers select someone, I will cover the cost of inviting that person to come to the school to conduct an all-day event for the teachers, focused on the school's core values." The development officer decided to take me up on my offer. He then discussed what had happened—as well as my offer—with the school's headmaster. A few weeks later, an instructor was selected, and I made arrangements to bring him to the school to address the teachers and staffs. The training took place and, I'm happy to report, was well received. I was in the audience as the event's sponsor. Moreover, I could see that the teachers were excited about the event, and many expressed their appreciation to me for arranging it. And I could tell their enthusiasm was genuine—they appreciated that I took personal responsibility and acted on it.

There are five factors involved in being accountable: (1) being aware that something needs to be done, (2) taking personal responsibility for it, (3) making a choice or decision to act, (4) thinking deeply about the potential consequences of that choice, and (5) setting high expectations.

The first factor is being aware that something needs to be done. In the previous chapter, I wrote of becoming aware of a child with his hand in a drain on the streets of Calcutta and of believing that something ought to be done about it. I relayed the story of the executive who was out of touch with the rest of his team but made the decision to do something about it when he realized he needed to be accountable. And when my daughter was offended by an abusive email, I believed something ought to be done about it.

Being aware of a problem doesn't always result in a person believing that something ought to be done about it. Let me give you an example. The IT department of a large and well-known financial services organization made some tweaks to its intranet site. Shortly afterward, an employee called to report that he was unable to log in. An IT technician responded to help the person. Then another person called with the same problem, and another, and another. Each time, a technician responded. But no one in the organization spoke up to say, "I think we have a systemic issue. We need to address it." This is a telling example of an indifferent mindset. Those who were charged with helping others log in to the intranet provided a Band-Aid instead of a solution.

The department's delay in solving the problem ended up costing the company $5 million, when it could have easily been solved at little or no cost if someone had taken responsibility for the problem early on. Technicians were aware of the problem; but awareness alone is not enough.

———

The second factor is taking personal responsibility.

We are often very good at pointing a finger at someone else, often without thinking about our own part in a situation or problem. I knew that the teacher who sent the ill-considered email to my daughter was a very good teacher, even a brilliant one. Maybe he was just having a very bad day. I could empathize; I have had my share of bad days. I should probably have followed my own advice and just asked him about the email and why he sent it. But I was upset and concerned that I might say something I would regret. Still, as a member of the school community, I had a responsibility to do something.

It is not enough to merely believe that something ought to be done. That is why the second facet of being accountable involves asking, What can I do to improve the situation? When it comes to being thoughtful, we change the focus from me, me, and me to you, you, and you. We think about the other person. But when it comes to accountability, we need to put the emphasis on ourselves—what can I do?

One of the things I like about living in California is how aware and personally responsible so many of the people I meet are. For example, according to polls, the majority of California's citizens believe that taking care of the environment is their personal responsibility. No matter what the law states, or what the governor or the legislature says or does, if the majority of the citizens don't feel that caring for the environment is up to them, it will not happen. But in this case, Californians do. I see the evidence of it everywhere around me, even in the actions and thinking of my own children. In school, our children have become much more environmentally conscious about water conservation, air pollution, and land use than they had been before we moved to California. And I find that I am far more environmentally conscious than I was previously.

Sadly, I do not see that kind of personal responsibility often enough in large corporations. Too often there is finger-pointing, people seeking to blame someone else. The mindset too often tends to be, "It's not my job."

I went with a vice president of a major manufacturing company to visit one of their plants, where we saw a burned-out lightbulb in front of the facility. The vice president mentioned it to the plant manager. I was back at the plant two weeks later and the bulb had still not been replaced. The plant manager had mentioned the burned-out bulb to someone who mentioned it to someone else who mentioned it to the maintenance people, who only changed lightbulbs once a month. No one said, "Let's change it now." It's a small thing, but indicative of systemic issues. Here is an example of the opposite mindset. My editor met with the person responsible for running the Magic Kingdom theme park at Disney World. As the two of them were walking, the head of Magic Kingdom, Dan Cockerell, noticed some litter on the ground. Without skipping a beat, he stopped and picked it up to put it in the trash. That is taking responsibility for caring for your workplace.

One place I often see a high level of personal responsibility is in well-run hospitals, where doctors and nurses do everything in their power to help their patients. Once when I was a patient in a hospital, a nurse came into the room as I was sleeping. I woke up, but she did not notice that I was awake. She took a half-empty glass of water from my tray table, went to the bathroom, washed the glass, and then refilled it from a pitcher.

I asked why she had done that; the glass was not empty.

She said, "Honey, we have to be very careful here about the possible spread of infection. Every time I see a used glass, empty or not, I have to wash it."

I would not have noticed if she had not washed the glass. She did not do it to score points with me. She did not leave the small task for the next nurse on duty. She did it because she took personal responsibility for my welfare.

That same nurse did many other seemingly small things to ensure my comfort. When I was leaving the hospital, I gave her a big hug to show my appreciation.

"I have been in a lot of hospitals," I told her. "In fact, I used to consult for several hospitals. But I have never come across a more caring person than you. Why do you do all that you do?"

She told me, "The hug you just gave me means so much to me. As a nurse, I don't make a whole lot of money. That hug means more to me than the money. I put in a lot of overtime hours. My colleagues think that I'm doing it to earn more money. But that isn't the reason. I want to make sure that you have a good experience; that you feel some comfort from my service."

She had taken personal responsibility for my well-being and the quality of my experience in "her" hospital.

When I become aware of a problem in my company, or in any organization I am working with, or at home, or within my community, I feel it's my responsibility to address it. If I see trash on my neighbor's property, and I know he is not there, I consider it my responsibility to pick it up, because I am part of the community. It is my job. It is not just his problem—it is my problem, too.

You may be aware of these things, and dismiss them; life moves on and nobody seems to notice. But inside, you know. How much better would you feel if you responded to a situation by saying, "No, I'm aware of it and therefore it is my responsibility"? This is one hallmark of a caring mindset.

How many people at General Motors knew that the widely publicized faulty ignition switches posed a hazard and yet dismissed that concern? How many people at Volkswagen knew that eventually they would get caught cheating on those infamous emissions tests and yet denied or dismissed their inner fears or apprehension?

A friend told me about the first black senior executive in a large financial services corporation. The executive had started his career in the company as a teenager working in the mailroom. When asked how he managed his rise through the corporate ranks, the executive said, "I based my entire career on looking around to see what needed to be done that no one else wanted to do, and took on the task." In other words, he took responsibility for problems that he became aware of.

Here is another example of someone becoming aware

of a problem and taking responsibility for it. Lynne lived in Minneapolis. Her best friend had recently moved across the Mississippi River to St. Paul. Lynne went for a visit on a cold Sunday afternoon. On her way home, she had a flat tire in an unfamiliar and run-down neighborhood. It was getting dark. She was able to maneuver her car into the parking lot of a convenience store, where she opened the trunk to get out the spare tire, only to find that her spare was also flat. She tried to call her home phone number and then her husband's cellphone, but there was no answer on either phone.

As she surveyed her surroundings, she noticed a tire shop on the other side of the busy street. The place was dark and looked closed, but she crossed the street and peered in the door. She didn't see anyone there. Her heart sank, and she started to panic. Then she noticed a handwritten sign on the door with an emergency phone number. So she called it. The man who answered, after hearing her problem, assured her that he would come to the convenience store and get her back on her way.

As the sun set, it was becoming colder, so Lynne waited inside the convenience store, warming herself with a cup of stale coffee. Ten minutes later a white pickup truck arrived and parked next to her car. A guy with shoulder-length hair, dressed in jeans, a denim jacket, and a Minnesota Twins baseball cap, emerged. When she went outside to greet him, he introduced himself as Josh, the owner of the tire shop.

Lynne watched as Josh jacked up her car and removed the flat tire. He removed the flat spare from the trunk as well, and placed both tires in the bed of the pickup.

He turned to her and said, "It's probably best if you stay with your car while I work on these tires." She did as he suggested as he drove across the street. She saw lights go on in the tire shop. She hoped he would not be too long. It was getting colder, but she didn't want to leave the car and go back inside the store.

Lynne cannot remember how long it took, but it didn't seem long at all when the shop went dark again, the white pickup returned, and Josh hopped out. He had patched both tires. He first replaced the tire on the wheel, then fastened the spare in the trunk.

"You are good to go," he said, smiling broadly.

Lynne reached into her purse for her wallet.

"How much do I owe you?" she asked.

He replied, "Nothing. Don't worry about it."

She protested: "I must pay you for coming out here on this cold Sunday night and rescuing me."

"No," he said. "I normally never work on Sundays anyways."

He got back in his truck and left. Lynne's flat tire had become his problem, and he had taken responsibility for it.

Lynne drove home in a state of wonder, and couldn't stop smiling. She thought of the television hero she had grown up with, the Lone Ranger: "Who was that masked man?" Her husband was home when she arrived. He had been at a church function and his cell had died. She told him her story and how Josh had refused her offer to pay.

His response? He said, "I need new tires on my car. I think I'll go visit Josh." And he did.

The third facet of being accountable is making a choice or decision to act. In 2013, Trisha Prabhu, a thirteen-year-old girl from Illinois, was shocked and angered by the story of an eleven-year-old Florida girl who had been bullied by classmates and committed suicide. That was the step in Prabhu's journey of becoming accountable; she became aware that something needed to be done about cyberbullying.

Prabhu had been studying the role of the brain in distracted driving, and she sensed that what she was learning might also apply to the act of bullying on social media. She decided to take responsibility for doing something about that kind of bullying, even though she had never experienced it personally. She then took the second step, asking, What can I do about it?

Here is Prabhu in her own words:

After careful background study, I believed that a system may be considered effective in preventing cyber-bullying in adolescents if that system results in reduced numbers of mean/hurtful messages that the bully or potential bully will be willing to post on social media sites. With this understanding of effectiveness, the primary question that I investigated was, "How could I create a more effective system to reduce cyber-bullying in adolescents on social media sites?" After much research, I realized that a system where adolescents (ages 12–18) would pause, review and rethink the decision of posting a mean/hurtful message before they post that message would be more effective in reducing cyber-bullying than if they are not given that chance to rethink.[1]

The result was an app known as Rethink. It provides an alert that suggests to someone writing a message that the words in the message might be hurtful. It then urges the writer to either delete, edit, or post the message. Parents can request that a message be sent to them if their child consistently overrides the alert. Prabhu's research about the app's effectiveness showed that 93 percent of adolescents who used the app decided not to post hurtful messages after they had the opportunity to rethink what they were writing.[2] They started to take responsibility for their actions, because Prabhu took responsibility. It caused a national chain reaction.

Trisha Prabhu might have easily said to herself, It's not my brothers and sisters who committed suicide. Not my friends. Not my problem. But she didn't. She made a choice to act on a problem that disturbed her.

Make your choices positive choices. When I was attending an event in London, a friend and I—along with her son—wanted to grab some dinner. My friend's son had a craving for Italian, so we asked the hotel's concierge for the name of a good Italian restaurant. After arriving at the restaurant and ordering drinks, we picked up our menus and started to scan our choices. To our surprise all the menu options were

Asian, not Italian! The concierge had sent us to a very fine restaurant, but there wasn't a pasta dish in sight! Apparently, there were two restaurants with the same name, owned by the same company, each with a different cuisine and menu— the concierge had sent us to the wrong one! We could have left, but we had already ordered drinks. We could have stayed and complained later about the mix-up and the food. Instead, we decided to stay and focus on enjoying a great evening together. And you know what? The food was outstanding!

My home stands on an earthquake fault in California. Every day I could wake up thinking, If we have a major earthquake, I'm dead, my family is dead. I could allow fear to get the best of me. On the other hand, every day I could wake up thinking, I'm so blessed. I always dreamed of a home with an ocean view, and I have a view of the Pacific Ocean. The choice is mine. I never think about the earthquake fault. I think about the positive choice I made to live here.

In the first chapter, I pointed out that only 7 percent of Americans expressed approval of and confidence in the US Congress. I wonder how many members of Congress make the positive choice every day to do what is best for our country rather than what is best for their party or their reelection campaign or their career. Are they really thinking of all the people who make up this vast, amazing country, or are they thinking of themselves and their own special interests? It seems that most of us believe those who make positive choices are few and far between.

Having and exercising choice are the most important freedoms we have. And nobody can make those key choices for you. So make positive choices. I might have made a negative choice by complaining about the teacher who sent the rude email to my daughter, without offering a positive step or any assistance to the school. The nurse who replenished my water glass might have decided to ignore it that night, because she had too much to do. Trisha Prabhu might have gone to a social media site, posted a negative rant about bullying, and have done nothing to tackle the larger issue.

Researchers involved in studying consumer choices can shed some light on the choices we make when it comes to accountability. Often the choice involves a decision between what will give us pleasure in the short term, and what will bring lasting happiness and well-being.[3] Do we choose the tempting sugary treat or the healthy salad? The latter choice, while not as immediately satisfying, is often associated with a higher purpose. "It's not my problem" provides short-term relief from accepting responsibility; it is like the sugary treat. You might get a temporary "high" from avoiding getting involved, but nothing will have been resolved. "What can I do about it?" suggests that whatever problem is in front of us calls on us to achieve a meaningful goal; it is like the healthy salad. But the results will make a lasting difference.

Consumer research also suggests that, when considering what to do about a problem, it may be best to consider more than one option. In one experiment, people were shown two DVD players. Roughly a third of the people said that they would buy one of the players, while another third said they would purchase the other player. So two-thirds said they would buy one of the two players. But when shown only one player, only about 10 percent said they would buy it.[4] Reducing the options forces you into a yes-or-no choice.

When deciding on an action to take about a problem that is in your field of vision and for which you have taken responsibility, consider more than one option. Having only one option may be paralyzing, and do more harm than good.

Making positive choices is difficult if you tend to surround yourself with too much negativity. Many people endlessly reflect on negative things, and actually seem to get pleasure from that behavior. Moreover, negative speech and actions tend to attract more negative speech and behavior. There's some truth to the expression "Misery loves company."

In an article for the *Harvard Business Review,* Marshall Goldsmith cites research showing that one-third of employees spend twenty hours a month complaining or listening to others complain about their bosses or upper management. He offers four questions designed to help reduce what he calls "whining time."

1. Will this comment help our company?
2. Will this comment help our customers?
3. Will this comment help the person that I am talking to?
4. Will this comment help the person that I am talking about?

"If the answers are 'no,' 'no,' 'no,' and 'no,'" Goldsmith writes, "I have a suggestion that doesn't require a PhD to implement. Don't say it."[5]

With only slight alterations, Marshall Goldsmith's questions can apply anywhere. I might have gone to my daughter's school to "whine" about the teacher who sent the offensive email. Would my whining have helped the school? No. Would it have helped the students? No. Would it have helped the headmaster? No. Would it have helped the teacher? No.

Once you make a decision to take positive action about a problem, rather than merely whine about it, you gain access to an internal source of power. Instead of making excuses or complaints, make things right. Make a positive change. Each of us has that kind of choice every day of our lives in our community, in our workplaces, in our families. I have always felt that if I make a positive choice, positive things result. Pay it forward.

The fourth facet of accountability has to do with thinking deeply about the potential consequences of your choices and actions. It is easy to make a poor choice if you are not thinking about the consequences of that choice. Thinking deeply requires that you ask profound questions of yourself. Are you working toward a short-term goal or a long-term solution? Will you embarrass someone? Are you only serving your ego? Is what you are about to do right or merely expedient? These are the kinds of questions you want to ask yourself.

A study of six thousand people conducted by the Neuro-Leadership Group, a global human performance consultancy, asked questions about where, when, and how people did their best thinking. Only 10 percent said it took place at work.[6] James L. Heskett, professor of business logistics at Harvard Business School, tells this story:

> A since deceased, highly-regarded fellow faculty member, Anthony (Tony) Athos, occasionally sat on a bench on a nice day at the Harvard Business School, apparently staring off into space. When asked what he was doing, ever the iconoclast, he would say, "Nothing." His colleagues, trained to admire and teach action, would walk away shaking their heads and asking each other, "Is he alright?" It is perhaps no coincidence that Tony often came up with some of the most profound insights at faculty meetings and informal gatherings.[7]

You don't need to sit motionless on a bench or at a desk to think deeply. Go for a walk. I like to think as I walk by myself, with no cellphone and no music device. Deep thinking comes from quiet and solitude, from sensing how small I am in the universe—a speck compared to the enormity of the Pacific Ocean. You cannot be thinking deeply while constantly checking your email, fiddling with your iPad, looking for external gratifying information. Our smartphones, used without restraint, can become an endless source of distraction.

A friend once told me about a plumber who was doing some work at his house. It was tricky work, and, when it was done, my friend complimented the plumber on the creative way he had solved a difficult problem.

"You are an artist," my friend told the plumber.

The plumber replied, "I am here on the planet, so I think someone is supposed to be me. I guess I better do it the best I can."

The plumber's reply suggests that he had asked himself and answered one of life's most profound questions: "Why am I alive on the planet?" My own answer to that question explains why I am so client-centric, why I am so adamant about my clients' success and so emotionally committed to them. I could easily say, "I just want to make some money and wash my hands of this." Many people do say that. I won't. I can't.

I am alive today to contribute in my own way to my family, my community, and my clients, just like that artful plumber. If a client's product is subjected to a recall, it is my responsibility to take action. I accept the blame, even if the client does not feel I was responsible. If a colleague makes a mistake or creates a problem, it is my responsibility to help. I hold myself accountable.

The world of business has its share of deep thinkers, of course. One such person was Steve Jobs; another is Jeff Bezos, who capitalized on the Internet business boom with Amazon.com. I think of Jack Dorsey, who gave us Twitter, or Bill Gates, who founded Microsoft and created the Gates Foundation. Most of these people and others are successful today because they thought deeply. Most were not well-known when they began the work that made them famous. Do you think deeply about what you do? If not, ask yourself what is preventing that.

―――――

The fifth aspect of accountability has to do with setting high expectations. When you set your sights high, you cannot help but inspire others. When you inspire others, you know what it means to feel accountable.

I went into a men's washroom in Detroit Metro Airport recently and found it in impeccable condition—absolutely spotless. It was like walking into the lobby of a five-star hotel. It surprised me because I had been in other men's rooms in that airport and found them, frankly, pretty disgusting. I spied the janitor there, cleaning a sink, so I complimented him on the condition of the room.

He said, "Hey, man, this is my restroom. Thank you so much for telling me you like it, because I want to make sure that anybody who comes to my restroom has a good experience."

I asked him why his restroom was so much cleaner and tidier than the others.

He said, "My mama taught me well."

"Do you like your job?" I asked.

He said, "Oh, I love my job. I love my job."

I told him that I used that airport often and vowed to continue using "his" restroom.

He said, "I may not be in this one. Next week I might be in another one. But you'll know the difference."

Later, on the plane, the man sitting next to me began complaining about the airline. Everything out of his mouth seemed to be negative.

So I said, "Let me tell you about something positive." And I told him the story of the janitor. I am still inspired by how high he sets his expectations. The passenger smiled, relaxed, and enjoyed the rest of his flight.

I am inspired by the words of Mother Teresa, who accepted the Nobel Peace Prize "in the name of the hungry, of the naked, of the homeless, of the blind, of the lepers, of all those who feel unwanted, unloved, uncared for throughout society."[8] Her charitable works are well chronicled. But what inspires me most is that when confronted with suffering she did not wait for someone else to act. She acted. She held herself accountable.

Genuine leaders like Mother Teresa know that they need to hold themselves accountable if they hope to hold anyone else accountable. When those under a leader see their leader being accountable, they tend to act similarly. An associate of Mother Teresa described accompanying her to an affair at which she was to be the guest of honor. As they left their residence in Calcutta, they spied a man in a bad way lying in a little alley. Mother Teresa knelt beside him, picked him up, and said, "We need to look after him. He needs help."

Each of us has a God-given capacity to inspire others. It is expressed in our hearts, in our words, in our actions, and in our emotions. It does not matter if we are sitting in a corner office or cleaning washrooms at the airport. The important question is, "Are you ready to take that step up?" Do you try to inspire others? Do you work to inspire your customers? Do you strive to inspire your colleagues? Do you endeavor to inspire your children? Do you reach out to inspire your community? Why is it so important to inspire others? Because, when you do, you will become accountable.

And accountability, in all of its facets—being aware that something needs to be done, taking personal responsibility, making a choice, thinking deeply, and setting high expectations—is a key component of a caring mindset.

Being accountable doesn't mean you shouldn't ask for help. It means you know enough to ask for help when it's needed. It means resisting the urge to fall back on the same solutions that you tried in the past. It means stretching a little, and engaging your intellectual and creative abilities.

As I close this chapter, let me pose four questions to you:

- In what part of your life is it most important for you to take accountability right now?
- Are you making the right choices today in everything you do?
- Are you thinking deeply enough to make a difference at work, at home, or in your community?
- Do you set your sights high enough, taking responsibility for inspiring your customers, your children, your family, and your friends?

Chapter 5

NEVER GIVE UP

*Resolve to perform what you ought; perform
without fail what you resolve.*

—BENJAMIN FRANKLIN

I n August 1991, I arrived in the United States to attend
graduate school. In order to save money, I took the cheapest
route possible from Dhaka, Bangladesh—a fifty-six-hour
journey. My adviser had promised me a graduate assistantship that would take care of my tuition fees, as well as room
and board if I could come two weeks before the academic
session that started in the fall. So I arrived at the university
two weeks early. I dropped my luggage in my dorm and went
straight to my adviser's office, where I received some devas-
tating news: the assistantship had been given to another student and was no longer available.

Resolve is the fourth characteristic of a caring mindset; it is
also the last letter in the acronym STAR. Resolve means having the passion, determination, and perseverance to find a

solution to a problem or improve a situation. To me, resolve requires humility and a willingness to change.

A few students that I met from Bangladesh and India tried to console me, but the problem was I no longer had enough money to register for classes. The other Bangladeshi and Indian students advised me to drop out and work illegally. But I refused. I had come to the United States to continue my studies. That was my path to getting ahead.

Then I had an epiphany: I had to adopt a positive attitude. After all, this is America, I told myself, the land of opportunity. Anything is possible. So I visited every department in the university and went to the offices of every department chair—economics, business management, literature, journalism, science—to convince them to give me a graduate assistantship or a fellowship, promising to make a positive impact on the students in their departments. For the most part they listened politely to my pleas; most of them understood my desperation. But they had no fellowships to offer. A few were rude, telling me I was wasting their time.

After two days of making the rounds, I was near the end of my rope. At the very end of the second day, the mathematics department chair, listening to my plea, introduced me to another faculty member, who was very excited to find out that I had graduated from one of the top universities in Asia: Indian Institute of Technology, Kharagpur, India. She asked me if I would be interested in doing research on polymers. When I replied yes, of course, she advised me to apply for a research fellowship provided by Dow Chemical. She cautioned me that the application process was very competitive, but if my interviews went well, I might have a chance.

After a number of interviews, I was selected to receive the research fellowship; in fact, my entire graduate education was paid for by Dow. Two years later, my research was given the university's annual best graduate thesis award. But I never would have won either the fellowship or the award if I had not maintained a positive attitude and a clear sense of resolve.

I've found that in most organizational settings, innovation and change are met with a great deal of resistance: our colleagues disagree with us or our bosses are on the fence about a new idea. And when we encounter resistance, most of us have a tendency to give up. That is why having a firm sense of resolve—an unflagging determination—is so critical in getting things done.

A major manufacturing company that I know dismantled its research and development department, deciding to rely on outside suppliers instead. Many years later, one newly appointed executive was appalled to discover that the company had stopped innovating from within. He made the gutsy move to advocate for reestablishing an R&D department in the company. Other executives told him that R&D just isn't sexy, and that it costs lots of money with no guaranteed return on investments.

But he was determined. He found the necessary funds, created the department, and hired the best talent he could attract. Today the department is thriving—and contributing significantly to the organization's bottom line.

Jim Collins, author of the bestselling classic *Good to Great,* in which he researched what makes great companies great, identified the resolve of an organization's leader as one of the key factors behind a company's long-term success. According to Collins, companies that achieve greatness are driven by what he termed a *Level 5 leader,* an executive who blends genuine personal *humility* with intense professional will, a mixture he described as *fierce resolve.*

Collins points to people like Darwin E. Smith, CEO of Kimberly-Clark for twenty years, who grew the company into a leading paper products company, and Colman M. Mockler, the CEO of Gillette in the 1980s and '90s, who faced down numerous takeover attempts that he felt would have damaged the company, as examples. Smith demonstrated his fierce resolve throughout his life, and not just as a CEO. Collins wrote of him:

> His lack of pretense was coupled with a fierce, even stoic, resolve toward life. Smith grew up on an Indiana farm and put himself through night school at Indiana University by working the day shift at International Harvester. One day, he lost a finger on the job. The story goes that he went to class that evening and returned to work the very next day. Eventually this poor but determined Indiana farm boy earned admission to Harvard Law School.[1]

These executives, Collins maintains, demonstrate "an unwavering resolve to do whatever must be done to produce the best long-term results, no matter how difficult."[2]

Note Collins's use of the words *long-term*. In general, people are very good at applying a "quick fix." There is nothing inherently wrong with that, and applying quick fixes certainly has its place. But we often do not consider the consequences of our quick fixes. I met a Fortune 100 executive who happily explained to me how a problem he solved saved his company millions of dollars. His bonus, as it turns out, was tied to the savings, so he benefited handsomely as well. When I asked him if he could guarantee he did not create another problem by solving the problem the way he did, he simply smiled and told me that if he did, he would tackle the second problem in the future. So I asked him if he would again claim to have generated millions of dollars of savings, and be granted another bonus, if the second problem was created by solving the first problem. He didn't respond.

It can be fun to successfully put out a raging fire and become a corporate hero. But an organizational culture that encourages firefighting as a standard approach does not promote fierce resolve—and it does not encourage a caring mindset. Resolve is about fire *prevention,* not heroic efforts to ward off a catastrophe that might have been avoided.

Collins's research, although driven by a great deal of data, was necessarily anecdotal in nature. How does one measure resolve? How does it produce positive outcomes? No one has definitively answered those questions. My own conclusion, based on my experience and observations working with many of the top manufacturing companies in the world, is that resolve is a characteristic of a caring mindset.

Clues about the importance of resolve in companies can be found in data about the success and failure rates of specific projects. If an organization commits resources to a project, one can assume there is, at the beginning, some measure of resolve to complete it successfully.

But the research around project success is not encouraging. McKinsey & Company, in conjunction with the University of Oxford, studied 5,400 large IT projects. They found that 45 percent of them ran over budget, 7 percent ran over the schedule committed to, and they delivered only 56 percent of the value that was predicted. An IBM survey of change management executives found that only 40 percent of projects met schedule, budget, and quality goals. And a study of government projects in the United Kingdom by the *Guardian* newspaper found $4 billion in wasted effort as a result of failed projects.[3] The success rate of large projects in organizations is abysmal.

The International Project Leadership Academy, a school that provides training in project management and leadership, lists more than one hundred common mistakes that contribute to the failure of projects. Among them are sponsors who fail to take ownership of the project seriously (in other words, they show little resolve), insufficient project team participation, avoidance of difficult decisions, and failure to provide sufficient training.

Given that the factors that contribute to project failures

have been so well studied and documented, and are not particularly difficult to overcome, it seems reasonable to assume that most project failures are due to a lack of resolve at the top to commit to an effective process. The bottom line: there is far too little of it.

A key part of resolve is a *willingness to change and adapt.* In too many organizations, middle managers and senior leaders resist anything new. But if they are not open to change, they will not be able to solve the inevitable problems that crop up. In a meeting I had with senior executives of a Fortune 100 company, they tried to convince me that their 3 percent scrap rate in their manufacturing process was acceptable, even though the waste was costing the company millions of dollars.

I asked an executive vice president, "Why is three percent scrap acceptable?"

He replied, "Subir, this has been going on for the last ten or twenty years. It's okay."

I replied, "No, it's not okay. That waste is costing you millions of dollars. Why not try to improve on that rate?"

Over time, and with a great deal of prodding from me, I was able to convince them that improvements in their business and manufacturing process could significantly reduce the percentage of waste. In the end, we were able to reduce their waste from 3 percent to 0.25 percent, contributing an enormous amount of money to the company's bottom line. That is the power of exercising resolve in tackling a problem.

Here is a second example of combining resolve with a

willingness to change—in this case, my own willingness to change. When corporate America embraced Six Sigma, I became a Six Sigma leader in American industry as a result of the success of my book *The Power of Six Sigma*. A few years later, I was invited to consult with a healthcare organization that had been attempting to apply Six Sigma training over the past year, assisted by another consulting firm.

"Six Sigma is failing in my company. Why is that?" the CEO asked me when I met with his leadership team. So I asked them how many had gotten Six Sigma training. They told me that they all had received four weeks of training. But they admitted to finding it boring. In other words, they were hardly the most inspiring group of evangelists for Six Sigma. When I asked how many applied Six Sigma tools at their jobs, the executives said that they used a handful of tools—perhaps 10 or 20 percent of the total. They decided that the rest of the tools did not apply to their industry or the organization.

Hearing their response was like having a light switch turned on for me. It convinced me that we *all* had to change our approach to Six Sigma training. I called my consulting staff and told them that I felt our offerings to clients were flawed. Although we were a well-known and respected consulting firm on Six Sigma methodology, I felt there was a better way to train executives and managers in using Six Sigma. I challenged my team to develop a methodology that could be customized to each client's needs, rather than relying on the one-size-fits-all approach that was popular at the time.

My willingness to change how we trained people in Six Sigma had many happy consequences. We developed a methodology I call LEO (listen, enrich, and optimize). Since then, we have used LEO to help our clients to lead thousands of Six Sigma–inspired projects—with exceptional results.

Had I not listened to our healthcare client, and genuinely taken their input and feedback into account, LEO would never have come into being. I had resolved to improve how we worked—and we did.

Here is another example of the power of combining resolve with a willingness to change. It involves a neurosurgeon who was deeply concerned about the amount of time a diagnostic process took after a patient first came through a physician's door. In the case of brain tumors, often four to six months transpired between the first office visit—with the patient complaining, say, of a headache—and the diagnosis. And sometimes the diagnosis came too late for a neurosurgeon to successfully intervene.

The neurosurgeon was determined to shorten the time between the first visit and the time a diagnosis was made. So he commissioned a study to examine the entire diagnostic process. In most cases the process began with a patient's visit to a doctor to complain of a symptom—often a headache. The doctor would ask the patient, "What kind of headache are you experiencing?" and prescribe medication as a first line of defense. If the headache persisted, the patient would return to the doctor after a period of time, and a stronger or different type of medication would be prescribed.

If there was still no change, the doctor might suggest an eye examination. So the patient would make an appointment with an ophthalmologist. If the eye doctor found nothing wrong, and the headache persisted, the patient would go back to his doctor for a further consultation.

By the time the patient landed in front of a neurosurgeon, who would prescribe an MRI, months had gone by.

At the neurosurgeon's urging, those conducting the study interviewed physicians, and patients who had tumors, in order to identify the earliest symptoms that led to a first office visit. The result of that inquiry led to a set of questions to be asked of a patient complaining of certain symptoms. The answers to those questions would indicate whether an immediate referral to a neurosurgeon was recommended.

The next issue was one of scheduling referred patients so that they were seen by a neurosurgeon quickly. The neurosurgeon who was guiding the study convinced his associates and others to set aside a certain time each week to see only those patients who were referred.

As a result, the amount of time between an initial visit and a complete diagnosis was reduced from several months to two weeks. The neurosurgeon's resolve to tackle a problem that had vexed him for years, and his willingness to change and improve the process, saved lives.

Sometimes exercising resolve means saying no. Susan Bishop is the founder and head of Bishop Partners, an executive search firm. The firm was only two years old in 1992, when she was approached by a large cable TV network that needed help in filling a vacant executive position. Bishop was eager for the visibility that work with that client would provide, not to mention the hefty placement fee. However, the client was known to be difficult, even, according to the rumor mills, abusive. Nonetheless, she took the job. The client did indeed prove to be difficult and abusive. He would not share critical information, insisted on offering candidates a salary well below market rate, and delayed paying the full fee.

Seven years later, a similar situation arose. A firm was looking for a high-level executive in the lucrative e-commerce business; it was another arena in which Bishop Partners could have used greater visibility. An even heftier fee was offered. But again the client was known to be difficult, even wildly unrealistic in its demands. This time, Bishop declined.

In a *Harvard Business Review* article, Bishop described what had changed for her during those seven years. She began the business by heeding the advice of professors in her MBA program to make customers "deliriously happy." To her, that meant every customer. So she kept saying yes whenever a company asked for her firm's help. But her company wasn't thriving as much as she had hoped. Searching for answers to why her firm was struggling, she attended Harvard Business School's Owner/President Manager program. There she was presented with a fresh set of questions she hadn't thought about before: "What business are you in, and what business are you *not* in? Who is your customer?"[4]

Armed with those questions, she challenged her employees to describe what business they were in. And everybody had a different answer. After much intense debate and discussion, they decided that, instead of making customers *happy*, the firm's top priority would be to focus on working with the *right* customers. That decision, along with creating a set of criteria for customers they would accept (and not accept), led to better use of the firm's time and staff. As a result, the firm developed a better reputation with its clients, which ultimately led to more business.

Managing the transition to the new business focus required a great deal of resolve on Bishop's part. Work practices were changed, employees were let go, and her own role changed dramatically—she became "the boss" rather than a colleague. She had to hire employees with more experience and initiative—and offer more competitive salaries. It was a stressful time, but her resolve to improve her business sustained her.

Bishop's firm is now twenty years old, with an impressive client list. And she continues to describe saying no to potential clients as an essential discipline.

One of the greatest frustrations I face in my business is the lack of resolve on the part of some of the executives we work with. Let me give you two stories to illustrate the difference between those who don't exhibit resolve and those who do, and the potential consequences down the line. The first firm called me out of the blue and said, "We have a critical problem. We need to save $200 million. Can you help us?" I responded, without hesitation, "Yes, I can if I find projects worth that much." And my team and I did just that—we saved the client more than $350 million in the first eighteen months. Despite the fact that we had a five-year contract, and there were many additional savings that we could foresee on the horizon, the client then told us, "You know what, now we know how to figure this out for ourselves." Their sense of resolve extended only to solving their immediate problem; they were only interested in a quick fix.

The other client called me and wanted help with saving $100 million. We ended up saving them $250 million. Afterward, they told us what a fantastic job we had done for them. Again, we had an understanding for a longer-term agreement, but the company, satisfied with how much they had saved, wanted to pull the plug. In this instance, however, we were dealing with a thoughtful, experienced, and straightforward executive team. My firm showed them how we might save them considerably more money going forward, and they agreed to continue our partnership together. We did business with them for almost eight years and saved them close to $1.5 billion. This client did not settle for the temptation of the quick fix, but resolved to let us help them find a great many more savings, and become an even better company.

The first of those clients was bankrupt five years after they ended our relationship together. Their quick-fix mentality and lack of long-term resolve ultimately caught up to them. The second client, after we helped them reach their intended target savings, resolved to set their goals even higher, and we then helped them meet that new target.

In 1993, after completing my graduate degree, I landed my first job in the United States as an industrial engineer. I dreamed of making a difference in terms of improving the quality of American automobiles. After I had published my first book in 1996, I was selected to receive the Automotive Hall of Fame's Young Leadership and Excellence Award, given to up-and-coming movers and shakers in the automotive industry under the age of thirty-five. I was extraordinarily proud of the recognition I had received. I was twenty-nine, and unmarried, so I invited my parents to attend the black-tie award ceremony with me in Detroit, which I knew would be attended by a who's who of the global automotive industry. However, both my parents' US visas were denied. The US Embassy gave no reason. I was very upset when they were turned down. My dad was also very upset and wanted me to return to Bangladesh. The day after learning my parents had been denied visas, I complained angrily to my colleagues about the government's move even as I was being recognized for my contribution to the American auto industry.

Within a few hours of telling my colleagues what had happened, I got a call from Jim Barcia, who at the time was a US congressman from Michigan. A colleague who knew the congressman had told him about my plight. Barcia told me that he was grateful for my contributions to the auto industry, and he was sorry to hear my parents' visas were being denied. He asked my permission to assist in obtaining them. Of course, I said yes. He promised that he would not quit until the visas were issued.

Barcia drafted a letter that he faxed to the US Embassy, and told me to ask my parents to apply again. But when they went to the embassy, they were insulted by an embassy official there, who said, "Tell your famous son not to mess around with United States Immigration."

My countrymen and friends recommended that I not fight the issue. They were afraid it might jeopardize my green card application to become a permanent resident. But I knew I had to do something. So I called Congressman Barcia back to tell him what had happened. He was dismayed—shocked, in fact—at my parents' treatment. He seemed to take it personally, and vowed to make things right.

I am not sure what exactly Congressman Barcia did, but sometime later the embassy called my parents, asked them to come in, and issued them their visas. So they were able to attend the award ceremony after all, and I was incredibly proud to have them there. Congressman Barcia's *determination*—his resolve—to obtain the visa for my parents still amazes me. But what is even more amazing is that he did not stop there. Despite having been in an accident during a hunting trip that caused him difficulty in walking, he came to my apartment to personally apologize to my parents on behalf of the United States government! He also organized a tour of Capitol Hill for my parents and arranged for my work to be recognized on the floor of the United States Congress.

I am still in awe of all that he did. His kindness and determination inspired me to contribute even more to my adopted homeland. In 2004, when I received the US Department of Homeland Security's Outstanding American by Choice Award for my contributions to the United States, my thoughts went back to Jim Barcia, and his resolve to help obtain my parents' visas. He deeply cared about me as a person and was determined to help me before we even met, and long before I became a citizen.

To me, Maggie Doyne, named the CNN Hero of the Year in 2015 for her social service work in Nepal, is the epitome of resolve: she acts persistently on a problem, is willing to change course where needed, and maintains a positive attitude.

After graduating from high school, Doyne, all of nineteen, traveled to India, where she worked at a children's home. While there she befriended a refugee from Nepal's civil war, and went with her to visit her village. There she found children living in deplorable conditions. One of the children, Hema, touched her deeply. She found Hema breaking stones and selling them to help feed her family.[5]

Doyne had saved $5,000 working as a babysitter during high school. She called her parents in New Jersey, asking them to send the money to her. Using that money, and other funds donated by supporters, she bought a plot of land and opened a home for children who had no family to care for them. Doyle had intended to spend a year traveling and living in India; instead, she committed herself to helping the children of Nepal. At the time she received her CNN award, fifty-one children were housed in her home. She was the legal guardian for each of them.

In 2010, dissatisfied with her children's education, she opened a primary school—the Kopila Valley School—using the $100,000 grant money from the CNN award. Here is the description the school proudly boasts:

Most of our 350 students come from poor socioeconomic backgrounds. Living in mud huts, abandoned or lacking access to education. So as much as our school serves as a place to learn, it is much more than that. It is also a day program where students enjoy a nutritious meal, basic medical and dental care and after-school activities like sports, music, crafts and cooking classes. The campus includes a Mental Health and Counseling Center, the Kopila Valley Health Clinic, tutoring room, computer lab, stage, and small library. We provide school uniforms and books for each student.[6]

Pictures of Maggie Doyne show her smiling broadly, surrounded by laughing and smiling children. Her positive attitude and resolve have helped to change the lives of countless Nepalese children.

What does resolve mean to you? Ask yourself these questions:

- The last time you were faced with a quandary, did you do everything possible to solve it? Is there anything else you might have done? Is there anything more you can still do?
- Do you communicate clearly and often with your colleagues that "good enough is not enough"? Is it a message that you convey in your daily life?
- Do you ever settle for less than your best? Or are you determined to excel at whatever you put your mind to?

Chapter 6

THE COIN OR THE PEN: CHOOSING TO BE THE DIFFERENCE

You have to trust in something—your gut, destiny, life, karma, whatever.

—STEVE JOBS

When I was four or five years old, growing up in Bangladesh, my grandfather offered me a coin and a pen and said, "Choose one." Without giving it much thought, I picked the coin. Perhaps most of us at that age would have done the same thing. My grandfather tried to convince me that I had made the wrong choice.

In the previous chapters, I gave you a roadmap for how to create a caring mindset: the STAR principles. I believe it is essential that each of us adopt the STAR mindset if we want to truly make a difference at work, in our families, or as a part of our communities. There is no question in my mind that practicing the principles of being straightforward, being thoughtful, being accountable, and having resolve will surely enrich your life. I speak from my own experience and the experiences of so many others I have encountered and worked with.

But I had an advantage, a jump-start on learning the principles of a caring mindset. I was taught them at an early age by the significant adults in my life: my grandfather and my parents.

In a commencement address Steve Jobs gave at Stanford University in 2005, he said,

> You can't connect the dots looking forward; you can only connect them looking backward. So you have to trust that the dots will somehow connect in your future. You have to trust in something—your gut, destiny, life, karma, whatever. This approach has never let me down, and it has made all the difference in my life.[1]

I have found that has been true in my life as well. At the beginning of *The Difference,* I wrote that the concept of a caring mindset and the STAR principles arose in response to the question of why some organizations succeed while others fail, or succeed less well, at making needed changes. But looking backward and connecting the dots, I can see that a caring mindset and the STAR principles have been a fundamental part of my own DNA since I was a young boy in Bangladesh.

It was my grandfather who taught me one of the most powerful lessons about exhibiting resolve. A humble man, a poor elementary-school teacher with seven children, he nonetheless had an extraordinary value system, and profound inner wisdom.

When he asked me to choose between the coin and the pen, I argued with him that, with the coin, I could buy chocolate, and with enough coins I could buy toys. So he offered me the coin and pen again, and again I chose the coin.

Finally, he hugged me, kissed my forehead, and told me, "If you pick the pen, you will reach so high in your life that many coins will follow." It was a lesson I never forgot. In his straightforward way, he told me that, with a pen, I could create something; that all books began with someone choosing to pick up a pen.

When I was seven or eight years old, he encouraged me to write to the authors of the books I was reading, offering my opinions about what they wrote.

"Do you think they will reply?" I asked.

He said, "If they don't, then write to them again."

"Suppose I write a hundred letters and still get no reply?" I said.

"If that is the case," he told me, "write another letter. Let me tell you something," he said. "The pen creates a powerful magic. If necessary, write a hundred and one letters, or two hundred letters. Eventually, they will reply. Never give up." So I resolved to do just that.

By the time I was twelve I had friendships carried on by correspondence with countless well-known authors, poets, and film stars. How did they come about? I simply wrote to them. These new friends and mentors taught me a great deal about life, success, the importance of failure, and many other things. At a very young age I learned about leadership and communication skills, skills that shaped my life. Because of my grandfather's teaching, I have never felt the need to take formal classes in leadership, and yet today I advise leaders all over the world. Because he convinced me to pick up a pen rather than a coin, I am now an author of many books.

My grandfather also taught me that you can learn from anybody, and that learning is a lifelong journey. And so, at the beginning of my career, I spent lots of time on the assembly-line floor. Most of my colleagues—other industrial engineers—thought I was crazy. But I learned so much from the people who worked on the manufacturing line building and assembling cars; they helped me develop a genuine passion for the automotive industry.

Just as important, my grandfather taught me to be thoughtful in my interactions with others. When I came in first in my class in fifth grade, the father of one of my classmates made a comment during a school function questioning how, in an independent Bangladesh, a Hindu boy (I was a minority in my birthplace) could be first in his class. The father was a college professor who later became one of the most celebrated intellects in the country.

My grandfather, deeply insulted by the comment, told me not to be upset by it. He explained that one day I, too, would be an influential person, and he urged me to never treat others in the way I had been treated.

"Always remember, forgive. Let go of any negative feelings. To change the world, think big. When you are in power, try to help others when you can."

Twelve years later, when I was working in a software company, I was assigned a project that was led by the same man who had insulted me so many years before. He was very pleased with my work and thanked me. Since he did not recognize me, I reminded him of his comment during the school function so many years before. He was shocked, dismayed, and finally in tears. And then he apologized. One aspect of being thoughtful, my grandfather had taught me, is refraining from judging others because of their ethnicity, age, or financial position.

I share these stories about my grandfather, and my parents, later in this chapter, to make a point. Anyone—even a person of the most modest means—can make a difference and inspire others, if they adopt a caring mindset. Having a caring mindset has nothing to do with where you were born or how much money you make. You do not need to be anything other than who you are.

Earlier, I mentioned that I won the Automotive Hall of Fame's Young Leadership and Excellence Award following the publication of my first book. Writing it and getting published was a Herculean exercise in resolve. And it is a vivid illustration of the power of the pen.

How did I come to write it? The major automotive

companies had agreed to adopt common quality standards for their suppliers, who could then be certified, and would undergo periodic reviews to verify that they were in compliance.

The companies mandated that all suppliers had to be successfully certified by a certain date. However, suppliers had very little in the way of guidance about how to apply. Teaming up with a coauthor, I published a book that contained case studies describing the efforts of suppliers to attain certification, as well as lessons drawn from those studies, and a simple process that any supplier could use to become certified.

I faced a lot of resistance from the management of my employer during the time that I was writing the book. I was working for one of the automotive suppliers, and my bosses did not understand why I was trying to help other automotive suppliers achieve certification. They accused me of working on the book during business hours, when I wasn't.

Nonetheless I was determined. Ultimately, I didn't care who said what about me. When I finished the book, I insisted that it could not be published until every single living quality guru had endorsed it. I didn't know any of them at the time, having just finished my master's degree. But I reached out to them in the same way my grandfather had taught me. I wrote to J. D. Power III, to Dr. Genichi Taguchi, and to Philip Crosby, hoping for the best. None of them replied. I wrote to them again. Still no reply. So I wrote to them a third time. Eventually, every one of them replied and agreed to endorse the book. J. D. Power III referred to the book as an "automotive industry primer for quality."

Many of these gurus came to Chicago to attend the book's publication launch, paying their own way.

The book turned out to help thousands of automotive suppliers, and I became something of an industry hero, profiled in magazines and newspapers, recognized as one of the top quality experts in the automotive industry. J. D. Power III, Dr. Taguchi, and others privately advised me. Suddenly I, too, was perceived as a quality guru, at the age of twenty-nine. But it wasn't because I had become an overnight genius; it was all due, in fact, to my exercising resolve.

During that period of my life, I spent most of my time with veterans in manufacturing and management who had decades of experience. I gravitated to them for their wisdom. I was hungry for their knowledge, and they gave it to me freely. As a society, we seem to have lost some of our respect for the wisdom of those who have a lifetime of experience. In our era of social media, too many of us see older people as out of touch, not technologically savvy, or uncool. We overlook the experience and insight and wisdom they have acquired in their years of working, collaborating, and competing. I would say the vast majority of those who have influenced me the most were senior managers and employees, people who ended up being great teachers with compelling ideas who practiced a caring mindset in everything they did.

Perhaps the most important lesson my grandfather taught me is that the greatest strategy for developing a caring mindset is to hang out with people who already have one.

———

Three years after the publication of my first book, I read a book called *The Leader of the Future,* a collection of essays on leadership edited by Frances Hesselbein, Marshall Goldsmith, and Richard Beckhard. I loved the book, but I felt that there was also a need for a book about *management* of the future: a book that not only addressed leadership but also addressed organizations and processes of the future. So I wrote to the authors (and wrote to them) until they replied.

Their basic response? "Why don't you write a book about it?"

So I did.

I didn't have any formal academic management training. But I did have resolve. So one day, a month after getting married, I woke up at three in the morning. My wife made coffee as I went to a big easel and wrote down a list of the world's top management thinkers. Then I put my name on top. I told my wife I wanted to make that dream, that list, come true. Would she support me in my efforts?

She said, "Subir, this is crazy. You don't have a PhD in management, nor do you have an MBA. This is impossible."

I responded gently, "I didn't ask you if it was possible. I asked you if you will support me until I achieve it."

"Of course," she said.

Two years later, my second book, *Management 21C,* came out; I had become not only an acclaimed quality guru, but a management guru as well. My grandfather was right—by choosing the pen, I could achieve anything.

———

My parents also taught me a great deal about the importance of a caring mindset, and in particular, they taught me to be thoughtful, to be accountable, and to develop a steady resolve. When I was attending what in America would be called elementary school, my father, who had a small pharmacy, would wake me at five o'clock in the morning. Together we would go outside and run for forty-five minutes. I would shower when we returned home, and immediately afterward, my yoga teacher would arrive for a half hour of yoga instruction. After yoga, a music teacher would arrive and I would practice playing the tabla—Indian drums—which I continue to play today. After my music lessons, I was expected to study for my classes, eat breakfast, and then leave for school, which started at ten. I attended the public school in Chittagong rather than a private school, as we did not have the money for a private education. But my father was determined that I be educated.

My father also taught me about the importance of being thoughtful toward others, and being aware of the effect I had on others. Most people could not afford a car, or even a bicycle, so they traveled from one place to another by rickshaw. When encountering a hilly area, my father used to get down from the rickshaw and walk.

"Why do you walk?" I asked. "You hired the rickshaw." We lived in a neighborhood that was extremely hilly. "It's very difficult for the rickshaw puller to climb the hills," he replied.

I did not always appreciate the lessons he taught me about

empathy at the time and sometimes fought with him. But eventually the lessons sank in. And when I graduated from college I did the same thing as my father. When I hired a rickshaw and the terrain was hilly, I would get out and walk with the rickshaw puller. They would protest, of course, but I was adamant. I refused to ride in the rickshaw when they had to go up a steep hill.

Moreover, I began talking with the pullers—usually the poorest of the poor—about their lives and their families as I walked with them. I would try to encourage them to get their children an education, citing my father's example. I visited their homes and they would talk to me about their lives. I wrote an article about what I learned from them that was published in a national newspaper.

But to be honest, I did not fully understand the importance of empathy at that period of my life. I was just doing what seemed like the right thing to do.

After the Bangladesh Liberation War in 1971—more than three million people were killed—Bangladesh was in dire economic straits. There were beggars and poor people everywhere roaming the countryside. A constant stream of beggars knocked at our front door. My mother would give them a small amount of money or a handful of food. Their knocking at the door interrupted my morning studies, and I fought with her about their interruptions.

"Don't open the door. They will go away. If you give food to them they will come again tomorrow."

"They are hungry," she would reply.

And sure enough, they would be back again the next day.

I was resentful of her handouts at the time. But she taught me an invaluable lesson about caring for others. She taught me about the importance of taking responsibility, in however small a way, for alleviating the hunger and poverty of our fellow citizens.

Thirty years later she visited me in Detroit. I had helped establish a foundation that focuses on educating those less fortunate in the world. The foundation partnered with Volunteers of America. So I asked the foundation to find ten families in Detroit who had so little money that the children had to skip meals.

I invited the ten families, and many of my friends and customers, to lunch. My mother attended as well. During the lunch, the foundation announced that it was donating money to each of the families. In addressing the audience, I told the story of the beggars at our front door. I went on to say that it was my mother who taught me about caring for others, and the need to give back.

Afterward, she came up to me with tears in her eyes. "That is the best gift you could have ever given to me. You were so frustrated with me at the time that I thought you hadn't learned anything." It meant so much to her that I had shared our story with my friends, my customers, and the other families.

Today, my wife and I continue to try to pass along the lessons that I learned as a child to our own children. We try to hold ourselves accountable for their education, just as my grandfather, and my parents, held themselves accountable for mine. Our family recently visited Calcutta, and arranged a visit to a nonprofit organization—Ramakrishna Sarada Mission[2]—that sponsors a free primary school for underprivileged children. It was a profoundly moving experience for both my wife and me, as well as for our daughter, Anandi, who was fourteen at the time, and Anish, our son, who was nine.

Roughly four hundred children come to the school each day, where they are provided with books, uniforms, medical attention when needed, and warm clothing during cold winter months. They are children who would otherwise be wandering the streets. Along with their studies, they are given a nourishing lunch. For most of them it is their only meal of the day.

We had the privilege to sponsor lunch for these children one day during our visit. At the end of the lunch period, Anandi and Anish helped to distribute oranges to the children, a rare treat.

I asked one of the teachers, "How long have you been doing this work?" She explained to us that she began her teaching career in her early twenties; she was sixty when we visited. Clearly, she held herself accountable for the well-being of the children.

"Every single child matters," she told me, "and I am responsible for this. God put me on earth to do this."

The STAR system is not a step-by-step process. You don't need to embrace, practice, and develop the four aspects of a caring mindset in any particular order. But you do need to practice and incorporate them all to create a caring mindset. Each of us already has a measure of these principles within us, some more strongly or fully than others. I would suggest that you focus first on those areas in which you are the weakest. If you do not excel at being thoughtful, look for opportunities to strengthen that part of your thinking and awareness, and improve on that. Keep in mind that the four aspects are intertwined. What I refer to as "being accountable" you might think of as acting responsibly. The words do not matter, as long as you are focused on the goal of making a difference for others.

Practicing a caring mindset is first and foremost about selflessness, about making a difference for others. Ask yourself at the end of each day, Did I do something today selflessly for another human being, or to better the world I live in? If you can answer yes, acknowledge that accomplishment. Commit to encouraging others to make a difference. If your answer is no, devise a game plan to make a difference tomorrow.

To be more straightforward in your actions, thinking, and behavior, practice developing the habit of being honest, direct, fair, and candid with those you interact with, both at work and in your personal life. To do that you must be honest with yourself, and that takes courage. I'm convinced the more truthful you are with yourself, the more successful you will be at whatever you do.

To practice being *thoughtful,* work to develop your ability to listen, empathize with others, be attentive, act with consideration, and avoid selfishness. Try to avoid or put aside jealousy and self-interest. Being jealous of another's success is a cancer in anyone's life. If you cannot genuinely celebrate the achievements of others, you will never achieve great success on your own.

To be more *accountable,* be aware of circumstances in which something needs to be done, and take personal responsibility to do it. Decide to act; think deeply about the potential consequences of your action; and set high expectations. Never allow yourself to wallow in self-pity or despair, or permit yourself to feel that you or your actions don't matter.

To strengthen your *resolve,* act consistently to support what you are passionate about. Do so with humility, but be willing to embrace change when necessary to accomplish your goals.

I hope *The Difference* will help jump-start a caring mindset in you *and* make a difference in your life, and in the lives of those around you.

I believe that when you practice the four aspects of a caring mindset, you will inspire others to do so as well, and ultimately help to create a STAR culture throughout your organization and community. Practice them until your caring mindset has no Off switch. Own them—make them yours. When you do, you will inspire everyone around you to do the same. The principles, after all, are contagious. *You* can be the difference.

Notes

Chapter 1

1. http://www.gallup.com/poll/1597/confidence-institutions
.aspx.

2. http://infrastructurereportcard.org/a/documents/2013
-Report-Card.pdf.

Chapter 2

1. P. Sellers, "The Tipping Point in Ford's Turnaround," *Fortune*, December 20, 2010, http://fortune.com/2010/12/20/the
-tipping-point-in-fords-turnaround/.

2. S. M. Caldicott, "Why Ford's Alan Mulally Is an Innovation CEO for the Record Books," *Forbes*, June 25, 2014, http://www
.forbes.com/sites/sarahcaldicott/2014/06/25/why-fords-alan
-mulally-is-an-innovation-ceo-for-the-record-books.

3. T. Koehrlen, "The Hidden Dishonesty with Youth—6 Things Every Parent Should Know," http://www.ontheroadtohonesty

.com/3-the-hidden-truth-behind-dishonesty-with-youth-6
-things-every-parent-should-know/.

4. "White Collar Crime," Cornell University Legal Information Institute, https://www.law.cornell.edu/wex/white-collar_crime.

5. C. Isadore and E. Perez, "GM CEO: People Died in Our Cars," *Money,* September 17, 2015, http://money.cnn.com/2015/09/17/news/companies/gm-recall-ignition-switch/.

6. "List of American State and Local Politicians Convicted of Crimes," *Wikipedia,* November 22, 2015, https://en.wikipedia.org/wiki/List_of_American_state_and_local_politicians_convicted_of_crimes.

7. Julia Roberts, Instagram, https://instagram.com/juliaroberts original/.

8. N. Mazar and D. Ariely, "Dishonesty in Everyday Life and Its Policy Implications," *Journal of Public Policy & Marketing* (Spring 2016), http://people.duke.edu/~dandan/Papers/PI/dishonesty.pdf.

Chapter 3

1. L. Janusik, "Listening Facts," http://d1025403.site.myhosting.com/files.listen.org/Facts.htm#Time.

2. D. Lee and D. Hatesohl, "Listening: Our Most Used Communication Skill," University of Missouri Extension, October 1993, http://extension.missouri.edu/p/CM150.

3. Scott Williams, "Listening Effectively," Raj Soin College of Business, Wright State University, http://www.wright.edu/~scott.williams/skills/listening.htm.

4. W. V. Haney, "Communication and Interpersonal Relations," McGraw-Hill, October 1991, cited at http://www.wright.edu/~scott.williams/skills/listening.htm.

5. https://inaspaciousplace.wordpress.com/2014/07/02/listening-filters/.

6. J. Treasure, "5 Ways to Listen Better," TEDGlobal, July 2011, transcript of TED Talk, https://www.ted.com/talks/julian _treasure_5_ways_to_listen_better/transcript?language=en.

7. B. Gates, "The Turning Point: Our First Trip to Africa," *Gatesnotes,* September 2012, http://www.gatesnotes.com/About-Bill -Gates/The-Turning-Point-Our-First-Trip-to-Africa.

8. A. Smith, "Americans' Generosity Has Never Been like This," *CNN Money,* June 16, 2015, http://money.cnn.com/2015/06/16 /news/giving-usa-charity-donations/.

9. R. Young and J. Hobson, "Richard Gere Brings Homelessness to the Big Screen," *Here and Now,* September 10, 2015, http:// hereandnow.wbur.org/2015/09/10/richard-gere-time-out-of -mind.

10. P. Larsen, "Richard Gere Hits the Streets as a Homeless Man in 'Time Out of Mind,'" *Orange County Register,* September 24, 2015, http://www.ocregister.com/articles/says-684489-gere -movie.html.

Chapter 4

1. *Rethink* website accessed at http://www.rethinkwords.com/.

2. Ibid.

3. J. Aaker (curator), "Meaningful Choice," JCR Research Curations, http://www.ejcr.org/Curations/curations-11.html.

4. *Harvard Business Review* staff, "The Value of Choice," *Harvard Business Review,* October 2013, https://hbr.org/2013/10 /the-value-of-choice.

5. M. Goldsmith, "Reducing Negativity in the Workplace," *Harvard Business Review,* October 8, 2007, https://hbr.org/2007/10 /reducing-negativity-in-the-wor.

6. D. Rock, "Three Ways to Think Deeply at Work," *Harvard Business Review,* September 28, 2012, https://hbr.org/2012/09 /three-ways-to-think-deeply-at-work.

7. J. Heskett, "Why Don't Managers Think Deeply," *Working Knowledge*, June 6, 2008, http://hbswk.hbs.edu/item/why -dont-managers-think-deeply.

8. H. Heyman, "Teresa of the Slums," *Life*, July 1980, http://www .maryellenmark.com/text/magazines/life/905W-000-014 .html.

Chapter 5

1. J. Collins, "Level 5 Leadership: The Triumph of Humility and Fierce Resolve," *Harvard Business Review*, July 2005, p. 7, PDF accessed at https://hbr.org/product/level-5-leadership -the-triumph-of-humility-and-fierce-resolve-hbr-bestseller /R0507M-PDF-ENG.

2. Ibid., p. 2.

3. Calleam Consulting Ltd., "Why Do Projects Fail? Facts and Fig- ures," http://calleam.com/WTPF/?page_id=1445.

4. S. Bishop, "The Strategic Power of Saying No," *Harvard Business Review*, November–December 1999, https://hbr.org/1999/11 /the-strategic-power-of-saying-no.

5. A Mighty Girl Facebook page, https://m.facebook.com/amighty girl/photos/a.360833590619627.72897.316489315054055 /929603487075965/?type=3&source=48.

6. Web page of Kopila Valley School, http://www.blinknow.org /pages/kopila-valley-school.

Chapter 6

1. Steve Jobs, commencement address, Stanford University, June 2005, http://news.stanford.edu/news/2005/june15/jobs -061505.html.

2. http://www.srisaradamath.org/gangarampore.php.

Acknowledgments

As any author knows, writing a book involves many people, and *The Difference* is certainly no exception:

- Roger Scholl is an editor's editor—the absolute best. He provided guidance, continuous inspiration, and unwavering support. This is the second book I've published with Penguin Random House under Roger's tutelage—he is an enthusiastic advocate. Thank you, Roger.
- Cynthia Zigmund has provided encouragement, support, and coaching, beginning with my very first book more than twenty years ago. A great friend and publishing professional, she has worked with me behind the scenes to challenge my ideas before they become books. I feel lucky to know Cindy.
- Dick Richards has an unassuming way of coaxing stories out of me that I didn't realize were even there. He was

integral in helping me translate my message into the book you are holding in your hands. I am enormously proud of this book and feel a deep sense of gratitude to Dick for his immense support and incredibly hard work.

- The entire Crown Business publishing team: Tina Constable, publisher; Campbell Wharton, associate publisher; Ayelet Gruenspecht, assistant marketing director; Owen Haney, publicist; and Megan Perritt, assistant publishing manager, who have all done an outstanding job.

- My colleagues at ASI Consulting Group, LLC (www .asiusa.com), have always been unwavering in their continuous support—all of you truly know what it means to practice a "caring mindset" each day.

- More than a hundred people, including Fortune 100 CEOs, professors, high-school teachers, executives, middle managers, physicians, engineers, college students, attorneys, assembly-line workers, politicians, nonprofit volunteers, and well-known leadership experts, agreed to review the manuscript and provide feedback. Each of you made a difference.

- Clients have made a difference in my career every day; I have learned so much from each of them. I hope *The Difference* will make a difference in each of their organizations.

- Readers of my books from around the world have provided me with feedback, encouragement, and support— thank you.

- Chittaranjan Biswas, my maternal grandfather, introduced me to the principles of having a caring mindset when I was still a child. His lessons have had a profound impact on my life and inspired me to write *The Difference*.

- Sushil and Krishna Chowdhury, my parents, showed me the power of making a difference through their often generous and self-sacrificing actions.
- Ashim and Krishna Guha, my in-laws, made a difference to our family through their love and deep *caring*.

This book would never have become reality without the selfless support of my wife, Malini. She has been making a *difference* in our family from the first day I met her. I am so fortunate to have her in my life.

My son, Anish, and daughter, Anandi, provide joy to me every single day of my life—being a parent has shown me why it is so important for each of us to make a difference. My wish is that they will make a *difference* in the world in the same way they have made a difference in my life.

About the Author

S ubir Chowdhury is chairman and CEO of ASI Consulting Group, LLC, a global leader on strategic initiatives, quality consulting, and training. Under Subir's leadership, ASI Consulting Group has helped hundreds of clients around the world save billions of dollars and increase revenues. Subir has worked with many organizations, large and small, across diverse industries, including manufacturing, healthcare, food, government, and nonprofit organizations. His client list includes global Fortune 100 corporations and industrial leaders such as American Axle, Berger Health Systems, Bosch, Caterpillar, Daewoo, Delphi, Fiat-Chrysler, Ford, General Motors, Hyundai Motor Company, ITT Industries, Johns Manville, Kaplan Professional, Kia Motors, Leader Dogs for the Blind, Loral Space Systems, Make It Right Foundation, Mark IV Automotive, Procter & Gamble, the State of Michigan, Thomson Multimedia, TRW, Xerox, and more.

Subir is recognized as one of the "50 Most Influential Management Thinkers in the World" by *Thinkers 50* of London, UK. Hailed by the *New York Times* as a "leading quality expert" and by *BusinessWeek* as "The Quality Prophet," Subir is the author of fifteen books, including several international bestsellers, *The Ice Cream Maker* (Doubleday Random House, 2005), *The Power of Six Sigma* (Dearborn Trade, 2001), and *Management 21C (Financial Times,* 1999). His books have sold more than a million copies and have been translated into more than twenty languages.

Subir is an honorary member of the World Innovation Foundation (WIF) and has been inducted into the Engineering, Science and Technology Hall of Fame and honored by the Automotive Hall of Fame. He is a recipient of the Society of Manufacturing Engineers' Gold Medal, the Society of Automotive Engineers' (SAE) Henry Ford II Distinguished Award for Excellence in Automotive Engineering, and the American Society of Quality's first Philip Crosby Medal for authoring the most influential book on quality. The Society of Automotive Engineers established the Subir Chowdhury Medal of Quality Leadership, an annual award that recognizes those individuals who promote innovation and expand the impact of quality in mobility engineering, design, and manufacturing. The United States Department of Homeland Security presented the "Outstanding American by Choice Award" to Subir for his contributions to the field of quality and management.

In 2014, the University of California at Berkeley established the Subir & Malini Chowdhury Center for Bangladesh Studies—the first of its kind in any academic institution in the United States. The center awards graduate fellowships, scholarships, and research grants that focus on ways to improve the quality of life for the people of Bangladesh. Each year, the Subir Chowdhury Fellowship on Quality and Economics is awarded by both Harvard University and the London School of Economics and Political Science to a doctoral and postdoctoral student, respectively, to research and study the impact of quality in the economic advancement of a nation. The Subir & Malini Chowdhury Foundation focuses on the education of those less fortunate in the world.

Born in Chittagong, Bangladesh, Subir received his undergraduate degree in aeronautical engineering from the Indian Institute of Technology (IIT), in Kharagpur, India, and his graduate degree in industrial management from Central Michigan University, in Mt. Pleasant, Michigan. He has received distinguished alumnus awards from both institutions, as well as an honorary doctorate of engineering from the Michigan Technological University. He lives with his family in Los Angeles, California.

INSTILL QUALITY
INTO YOUR CULTURE—
AND INTO EVERY PRODUCT
YOU DESIGN, BUILD,
AND MARKET

"In 115 jargon-free pages, [Chowdhury] boils down most of the wisdom of modern management theory and practice that is equally relevant to chief executive and frontline clerk."
—*Washington Post*

The CE CREAM MAKER

AN INSPIRING TALE ABOUT MAKING
QUALITY THE KEY INGREDIENT IN
EVERYTHING YOU DO

Subir Chowdhury